HAVE YOUR HEART
Again

DEDICATION

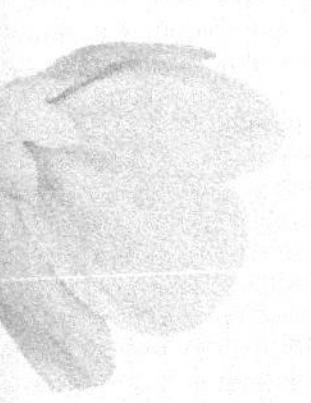

To bad ideas, tequila courage, and saying yes
when you should run.

ASHA

PROLOGUE

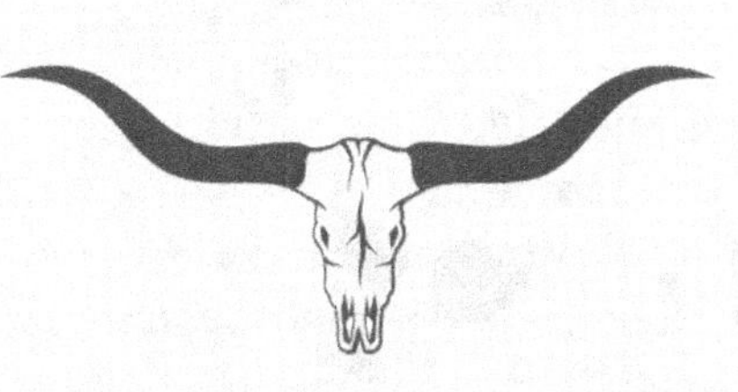

AGE SIX

"That kid is so weird. Look at him. He's skinny and pale, and those eyes... He looks like a zombie," Preacher says to Remy.

"What's wrong, kid? You look like you're going to be sick or something," Remy chimes in.

I look over my shoulder from my spot on the swings to see him for myself. There, sitting atop the monkey bars, is the new kid, hunched over slightly, legs swinging, eyes on the dirt. They're not wrong; he does look sick. It's the end of summer in Kentucky, and we're a bunch of country kids with endless creeks, farm ponds, and pastures to run through, yet he looks like today is his first day seeing the sun. His hair is almost as black as the coffee my father drinks every morning, and his dark eyes match the color of the chocolate chips Mom puts in my pancakes. His words might be mean, but what Preacher says is kinda true. *The kid does look sick.*

His pale skin does nothing for the circles under his eyes. He looks tired, like he hasn't slept in days. He looks the way I look when I stay up too late on Christmas Eve. I quickly look back at the ground in front of me and shuffle my feet in the dirt so he doesn't catch me staring.

"He's probably stuck up there. If he jumped down, those twigs he has for arms might snap," Preacher taunts some more, trying to get a rise out of the boy, but he keeps his eyes pinned down on the ground.

"If I looked like that, I wouldn't be at school. My mom would take me to the doctor," Remy says, not so much as a joke but a fact. However, it only eggs Preacher on.

"Yeah, well, your mom isn't embarrassed by you. Could you imagine having a zombie for a son?" Preacher chuckles.

I flick my head over my shoulder once more, waiting to see if Preacher's and Remy's comments will earn them any type of response, but this time, when I look at the kid on top of the monkey bars, I see something different. He doesn't look sick; he looks sad.

I hop off the swings and turn around.

"Leave him alone," I say with my hands firmly planted on my hips.

"Asha, what are you doing?" my friend Gabby asks, bringing her swing to a stop. "Do you know him?"

I peer up at the monkey bars, and for the first time, the boy looks up, and his dark eyes lock on mine. My hands get clammy, and I clench my fists. When I hopped off this swing, it was to get the boys to back off, but I can't be sure if the eyes staring back at me are grateful or annoyed. I suppose it doesn't matter. My momma always taught me to be kind and to stick up for what's right, even if it's hard, and Preacher is being a jerk.

"No, but neither does Preacher," I say.

"Go away, Asha," Preacher dismisses me like he's not scared of me, but he should be.

"Okay." I shrug my shoulders and crack my knuckles. I didn't think I needed to remind him about our little incident in pre-k, but I guess I do. "But you know I don't like it when you pick on me."

On my first day of pre-school, I sat in my chair and cried for the first hour of the day because I missed my mom. I hated being separated from her. Until that day, I'd been her mini-me, her shadow, and then she left me all alone with a bunch of snot-nosed kids. Preacher was one of the first kids to talk to me, except he wasn't trying to make a friend. He asked me if I was crying because I missed my mom in the most whiny, irritating voice imaginable. To this day, I remember it so clearly. Bright-red hair and a face full of freckles, going out of his way to poke fun at someone who was sad. What I did next came without thought. I punched him square in the nose, and then I was no longer the only kid in class crying.

His face turns into a scowl. "Whatever, if you want to catch cooties..." He waves his hand toward the monkey bars. "Be my guest. It's your funeral, Fairfield."

I roll my eyes and put one foot in front of the other, stomping past him. He's not going to turn this around on me with cooties.

"Asha, don't do it," Gabby pleads.

With one foot on the bottom rung of the bars, I grab the sides and turn to my friend. "I'm not going to catch cooties. We already got our shots...remember?" I say, eyes wide. Gabby puts her finger to her lips and looks at the ground like she has to think about it, but I don't give her time to think it through before I reach the top and crawl the three bars it takes to reach him. "I'll give him the shot, and then no one has to worry about him being sick."

When I turn to the boy right in front of me, his forehead is all crunched, and his eyes look worried, like he's trying to figure out if I'm really gonna help him or if I'm gonna be scared and jump down now that I'm actually up here with him.

"Hi," I say hurriedly, my nerves getting the best of me. "I'm Asha...Asha Fairfield." I carefully settle into my spot beside him before asking, "What's your name?"

For long seconds, he's quiet, and for a moment I wonder if I made the wrong choice sticking my neck out to save a boy that didn't want to be saved. But then he says, "Trigg." My eyebrows rise slightly, surprised he gave me a response, and my journey up these bars wasn't for nothing. He thins his lips, like he messed up and gave me the wrong answer, and then adds, "Trigger. My name is Trigger Hale."

"Hale?" I ask, unable to keep my nose from crinkling. "As in Hale Ranch?"

"Yeah, you've heard of it?" he says somewhat timidly.

I look over toward Gabby. Of course I came up here and risked my own hide for the enemy.

Preacher's amused glare catches my eyes as he moves to cross his arms. "Well, get on with it, then—unless you're afraid to touch him."

"I wasn't afraid to touch your nose," I snap back, my eyes still glued on the boy in front of me.

"What's she talking about?" Remy asks, unaware of what happened in pre-k since he wasn't in our class back then.

"Nothing." Preacher rolls his shoulders. "Ten seconds, or I'm telling the whole class you caught cooties from zombie boy."

I shoot him a glare before turning to Trigg. "Give me your arm." He slowly extends his arm. "Who wears long sleeves in the summer?" I ask as I push up his sleeve. His brows tug together before I look down, and my mouth parts as a little whoosh leaves my lungs. The underside of his arm has bruises running from his wrist to his elbow.

"It's okay," he says, his other hand reaching for the hem of his sleeve.

"No." I stop his hand. My eyes dart up to his. "I'll be quick." I lick my lips and clear my throat as I hold up my index finger. "Circle, circle, dot, dot," I say, my finger tracing the design over what looks like an old scar. "Now you have your cootie shot," I finish, and our eyes stay focused on the spot where my finger touched his skin. It's pebbled now, and when his eyes finally trace up to mine, my stomach does something funny.

"Whatever," Preacher says with a huff, drawing our gazes to him. "Recess is almost over. Let's go play kickball."

We watch as he turns on his heel before running toward the kickball field with Remy.

"Thanks," Trigg says, tugging his sleeve down.

"Yeah, well, don't make me regret it." I swing my legs back and forth.

"How would I do that?" He tilts his head to the side.

"You're a Hale. It's in your blood." I point at him like I'm solving a mystery.

"What does that mean?" He scoots a little closer, making the whole monkey bar wobble.

"Your ranch is right next to mine." I wave my hand toward the direction of our houses.

"So?" He shrugs his shoulders and kicks at the air like he doesn't care at all.

"So...your ranch is the competition! Your family and mine both breed horses. You're the enemy." I cross my arms and almost lose my balance.

"Oh," he says, blinking real slow, like I just told him the sky is blue, and he never noticed before.

Now I'm the one with my eyebrows tugged together. Maybe his parents don't speak freely around him about the business. I've never known anything but horses. It's in my genes. I know one day Fairfield will be mine. My mother has told me this as far back as I can remember. I don't know much about his family. The little I know comes from my father's rants. Trigg is my enemy because the last name attached to his is one my father despises, but that doesn't mean he has to be mine. Does it?

"What did you mean before when you said you weren't afraid to touch his nose?"

"I punched him in the nose on my first day in pre-k. He was making fun of me for missing my mom."

He laughs. "So, it's not your dad I need to worry about; it's you. Are you sure your name is Asha and not Trouble?"

I smile and bite the inside of my lip so it doesn't take over my whole face. "Hey, I didn't go looking for trouble. He poked the bear. What about you? How did you get those bruises on your arm?"

"I just got out of the hospital a few weeks ago," he says, shifting his weight.

"Are you sick?" Maybe after all that, Preacher was right.

"I was. I'm not anymore. I had a kidney transplant."

My eyes go wide. "That sounds serious."

"It is. I could have died if they didn't find a match."

"I'm going to punch him. I'm going to punch him square in the nose just like I did the first time," I spit, and my cheeks flame as I look across the playground at Preacher kicking around a ball without a care in the world about the hurtful words he said to a boy he never took a second to know.

"You'd do that for me?" he asks, his dark chocolate chip eyes finding mine.

"Yeah, that's what friends do." The words are out of my mouth before I can think them through. He's supposed to be the enemy, or at least that's what my dad says, but he looks like he could use a friend, and since that's the word I used, it's the word I must have meant. My mother always says there are no such things as accidents, only things that were always going to happen.

"Friends? But you just said I was the enemy." His hands tighten around the bars.

"I know what I said. Take the title or don't."

"I'll take it," he says quickly.

"Good. Now just promise you'll never tell my dad," I say as I extend my hand and pop out my pinky.

His pinky wraps around mine. "Promise." My finger tingles, and my eyes snap to his to see if he feels it too, but before I can figure it out, he's letting it go and asking, "Why can't I tell your father we're friends?"

One of the teachers blows a whistle, and we both turn toward the sound. However, I must whip my head around too fast, because everything spins. Before I know it, my hands are slipping, and I'm falling. I crash to the ground hard, and it feels like all the air is sucked from my lungs as sharp rocks dig into my back. I can feel that my arm is twisted funny underneath me, but when I try to move it, my head explodes with the worst pain I've ever felt. I blink, and a hand is on my arm, a shadow at my side, and I hear Trigger calling for me, but he sounds so far away. Another sharp pain rips through my head, and then everything goes dark.

Part One

ASHA

CHAPTER 1
FRESHMAN YEAR

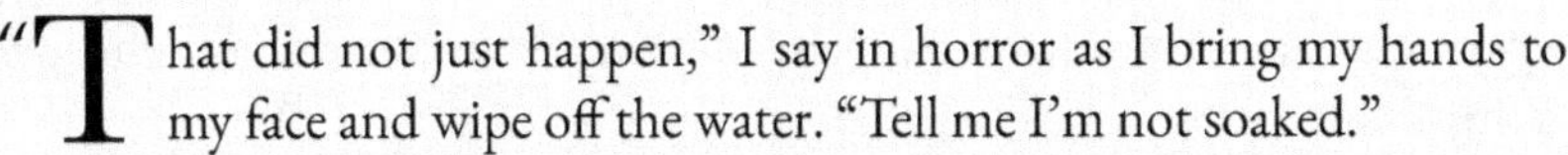

"That did not just happen," I say in horror as I bring my hands to my face and wipe off the water. "Tell me I'm not soaked."

"Oh, my god." My friend Emma moves to my front, her eyes scanning my body. "You're drenched." Blue eyes drift up to mine. "Completely wet." She holds my gaze, her eyes empathetic for all of two seconds before her lips start to curl into the start of a smile.

"You are not about to laugh," I say, wholeheartedly upset. "This is so not funny. You know how important today is to me."

"You're right. I'm sorry. It's not funny." She pulls her backpack off and unzips it. "You can wear my sweater." She offers me her Ridgewood embroidered pullover. I stare at the sweater, shocked that I'm standing on the side of the road for my first day of freshman year with my outfit completely ruined. "We can run back to the dorms and change. We'll only miss the first period."

"No." I take the sweater defeatedly. "I can't skip first period. I have Mr. Greco, and he's one of the teachers who oversees the council."

She blows out a breath. "Okay, well, let's hurry up, and you can freshen up in the bathroom..." she trails off, pinching the top of the sodden papers I'm still clutching against my chest. "We can make you a new banner during homeroom."

This is what I get for stopping at the stables instead of walking straight to campus. I needed to see Buttercup before my first day; she's my reminder of home. Dad sent me to Ridgewood when I was six, and Buttercup has been my comfort since. Pressing my face into her neck almost brings back my mom's laugh in the stables back home.

She's my good luck charm, and God knows I needed it today for my first day of freshman year. Apparently, the universe had other plans. My uniform now clings to me like a second skin. My once-pristine white knee socks are splattered with mud. Fantastic. I look ahead. What once seemed picturesque and magical now feels like a postcard gone wrong.

The white-trimmed dormers and tall chimneys that have always felt so stately and welcoming now feel like they're watching me trudge up the hill like a soggy disgrace. Ridgewood is surrounded by the rolling Adirondack foothills, maples and birches pressing in on all sides. In autumn, the trees are gorgeous, all gold and crimson like a painting. But now, in the gray August morning, their branches look skeletal against the low clouds.

"Whose car was that anyway?" I say as I clomp toward the entrance where clusters of students in perfectly pressed uniforms are already gathered.

"I don't know. It must be someone new. No one drives to school."

No one drives to school because Ridgewood isn't your typical private school. It's a boarding school, and we're all trapped here behind ivy-covered walls. Our student body is a catalog of wealthy dysfunction, split into three types: the misfits, the afterthoughts, and the silver spoons.

The misfits were shipped off by parents who had given up. They hoped boarding school could fix what years of therapy couldn't. The afterthoughts come from families too busy with mergers and galas to raise their own kids. They learned early that nannies make better listeners than mothers.

Then there are the silver spoons, the legacy kids. They see this place not as exile but as birthright. They walk these halls like they own them. In many ways, they do.

Three types of wealth, three types of damage, all in matching navy blazers. Except for me. Mine is now splattered with mud, but I suppose it's only fitting. I've never been able to fit myself into one of those boxes. My reason for being shipped off to boarding school isn't black and white. As messed up as it sounds, I wish it were.

❦

"Asha, I know today started off shit, but you have this in the bag. You've been at the top of our class since third grade. Everyone is scared of you," Emma says as she finishes coloring in the last bubble letter on my new banner.

"What?" I question, confused, looking up from the printer.

"You know what I mean. Everyone knows you're smart, and this is your thing. No one would dare try to take this from you. You're focused on more than changing the snacks in the vending machines." She snaps the lid on a marker. "And I can promise no one wants to go head-to-head with you in a debate." Standing up, she smooths her skirt. "So, it's like I said, you've got this in the bag."

"I wouldn't be so sure." Eldridge pops his head up from the back row, startling us both.

"How long have you been sitting there, you little twerp?" Emma asks, her hand over her heart as she glares at her twin brother. They're twins, but technically she's three minutes older and never fails to remind him of that tiny detail.

"I suppose as long as you." He smiles. "Did I scare you? I didn't mean to," he says sincerely as his eyes roam down my body, taking in my disheveled appearance, only fueling the self-consciousness that's already plagued me for the first half of the day.

I don't have any romantic feelings for Eldridge Morrison, but he's also not hard to look at. He's your typical pretty boy and mirror image of his sister with blond hair and blue eyes, the only difference being his tall stature, angular face, and muscles that refuse to stay hidden beneath a polo and vest.

"I had my earbuds in. I didn't know the two of you were in here until I pulled them out," he adds tossing his bag over his shoulder and crossing the room to where we have our things scattered across one of the tables. "This year, Headmaster Trejo is making sure athletes participate, male athletes specifically."

"I'm not following," I say as I tap my marker against my lips.

"To boost involvement and give the school board what they want. More well-rounded portfolios for Ivy League colleges to scout." He leans against one of the desks.

I pace in front of the printer and search for a solution.

"What if you volunteer?" I whip around, excited that I may have just found a solution. He's on the lacrosse team.

Eldridge and I aren't close, per se, but I'm friends with Emma, and while the two of them throw jabs at each other regularly, they're actually really close. The three of us have hung out together more than once. I can't say that he likes me, but I also don't think he hates me.

"Can't. The polo team drew the short end of the stick. From what I heard, when the coaches got word of Trejo's plan, they all got together with a plan of their own. None of them want their teams focused on anything outside of winning a game. This student council election would do that." My face visibly deflates as I try to think through another plan, and he adds, "If you want, I'll run for treasurer." His tone peaks with playfulness as he tries to lighten the mood. That's the one thing I've always liked about Emma's brother. When the people around him are down, he tries to pull them back up.

"Let me guess," Emma says flatly. "Because you're a treasure?" Her eyes narrow, and her voice drips with unimpressed sarcasm.

"You're finally catching on," he mocks before heading toward the door. "It only took you, what, fifteen years?" His hand slaps the door-frame, garnering my attention. "If you're there, I'm there, Fairfield. See ya around."

"Sorry about that," Emma sighs when he's out of earshot.

"You have nothing to be sorry for," I say as I start packing up my supplies. "Eldridge is always trying to make light of the heavy stuff. He's harmless."

"I'm not so sure that's all that was." She grabs her bag off the floor.

"Are you implying your brother likes me?"

"The better question would be, *who doesn't?*"

"That's your op—" I start before slapping both hands on the table. "I got it. I'll just make Hollis run against me. He doesn't care about winning, but running will satisfy Headmaster Trejo's participation requirement. He might want them to run, but he can't make them win. Class presidents are elected, not appointed."

"See, in the bag." Emma pops her hip out. "Now help me roll this up. Lunch is almost over, and I need to eat something, even if it is just a piece of fruit. My stomach feels like it's going to eat me from the inside out."

I consider going back to her comment, the one where I was about to tell her that the way she perceives everyone liking me is her perception, not reality. Instead, I leave it. Emma has made those comments offhandedly since we became friends, and I've never liked them. They make me feel like she puts me on a pedestal—one I never asked for. While they still bother me, I don't see them the way I once did. It's not a *me* problem. It's a *her* problem. She had a falling out with her friends—one she never talks about—so I can't be sure what exactly went down. But I think her comments about how everyone likes me stem from her own insecurities about herself.

I glance at the Cartier watch my father got me for my birthday over the summer. "If we hurry, we'll make it to the lunch hall before the lines close."

"Mrs. Jean, did you make me one of your veggie packs?" I raise up on my tippy toes and lean over the glass a little to ask my favorite lunch lady for the special snack she makes me when she's chopping up vegetables for the salad and soups.

"I'm sorry, Asha," she says regretfully. "Lunch was almost over, and I thought maybe I'd missed you coming through the line. I just gave your snack to another student."

"You gave my snack bag away?" I say, a little upset because I'm missing out on my snack, but more so surprised. No one knows about her veggie snacks. That's our thing.

"Yes, there was a boy asking a lot of questions about ingredients and holding up the line, so I sent him on his way with the veggie sticks, quinoa, and hummus."

"It's okay. I understand," I offer. "Just don't let it happen again," I say teasingly.

I grab a wrap, an apple, and water before joining Emma at the cashier.

"What's with the face?" she says, doing a double take.

"I didn't get my veggie sticks," I say, thoroughly irritated.

"Veggie sticks? Since when have those ever been an option?" She glances over her shoulder.

"They aren't," I rush out, internally scolding myself for slipping up and almost giving someone else the ability to steal my snacks. "Hence why I'm upset."

"Okay..." she draws out, my bizarre behavior clearly too much for her to process. "Where do you want to sit today?"

The second my eyes scan the commons, they fall on the boy who Mrs. Jean gave my veggie sticks to. Even leaning against a pole, he's tall. His dark hair is longer on top, long enough that a stray lock is dusting his forehead. He reaches for his water bottle on the table, and the fabric of his polo stretches tightly around his bicep. My eyes drag down his body, cataloging every detail as my mind races to put a name with his face, only to come up blank.

I'm not the best with names. I can meet someone ten times and still not remember their name; however, I'll remember details like where they went on vacation, how many pets they have—heck, I might even remember their pets' names. But their name...forget it. And right now, that particular fail is driving me absolutely insane.

He laughs at something Hollis says, and my eyes snap back up to his face. The sound is warm and genuine, and I hate how my pulse quickens in response. There's something so achingly familiar about the way his eyes crinkle at the corners, the tilt of his head, but I can't place it. It's like having a word on the tip of your tongue that refuses to surface, except a thousand times worse because now I'm staring like some kind of creeper while simultaneously wanting to march over there and demand he explain why he needed *those specific* veggie sticks when there were other snacks available.

"Earth to Asha." Emma waves her hand in front of my face. "Are we going to sit or what?"

"Yeah, sorry," I say. "Wherever you want to sit is fine," I add, my frustration building at the stranger across the room for being annoyingly attractive, and at myself for caring about stupid vegetable sticks, but mostly at my brain for failing me. Because something tells me that remembering where I know him from is important.

Emma glances toward the corner where the dance team sits and then rolls her eyes before choosing a table right beside the exit. She falls squarely into the "silver spoons." Her parents shipped her and Eldridge off to Ridgewood, not because they needed the education, but because it was where *they* had attended school. For years, Emma had been the perfect little legacy student, following in her mother's footsteps by joining the dance team, and debate club because that's what her father had done. A carefully curated path, but last year she torched it all, quit dance, and joined Key Club instead. That act of rebellion was where our friendship started.

I had seen her around school before the great Emma Morrison reinvention. We'd shared classes, but she was always surrounded by her dance team satellites, all blonde highlights and matching everything. I've never had any interest in breaking into those social circles, especially not that one. Socializing with kids my own age isn't my thing anyway. I'm not shy; I just refuse to wade into the exhausting politics that come with belonging to any group. I'm too busy grinding through advanced classes, padding my volunteer hours, and building the kind of college resume that might actually get me somewhere. But post-rebellion, Emma made herself impossible to ignore.

"Are you ever going to tell me what happened between you and your team?"

We are walking contradictions as friends. She is the quintessential Malibu Barbie brought to life, blonde hair, blue eyes, flawless cream complexion that has never known a blemish, and a bubbly personality. I, on the other hand, am all dark angles: long black hair that refuses to hold a curl, dark eyes, and toffee-colored skin that doesn't fade with the seasons. Most people mistake my seriousness for being cold, maybe even cruel. I know exactly what they call me behind my back, and I've made peace with not caring. The only thing Emma and I have in common when it comes to looks is our chests. We both bloomed early.

"I already told you," she mumbles, tearing off a giant piece of bread and shoving it in her mouth like she's trying to physically block the conversation. "Nothing. I quit. End of story."

I nod, letting the silence stretch between us. The way she won't meet my eyes tells me everything I need to know about that particular lie. People don't usually quit a team and lose all their friends as well. You don't just choose a table next to the exit because you lost interest in herkies and competition.

We've gotten pretty close over the past year and a half, spending most of our free time volunteering together, hunched over textbooks in the library until they kick us out, and planning our once-a-month escapes into the city. I've let those countless hours of shared secrets and inside jokes fool me into thinking there were no walls left between us. But her casual brush-off is a sobering slap of reality, reminding me of the truth I keep forgetting: everyone has a vault where they lock away the pieces of themselves too sharp or too damaged to share. Even Emma, with her sunshine personality and apparent openness, keeps her darkest corners carefully guarded.

I take a bite of my sandwich, chewing slowly as my armor slides back into place, because this is the lesson I should have learned by now. Trust is just another word for the moment before inevitable disappointment.

∾

I CAN'T GET MY STUPID LOCKER OPEN. THE COMBINATION dial keeps slipping in my damp hands from the milkshake I had to grab after last period, a free "welcome back to school" treat from the faculty. As the hallway starts to clear out, I'm starting to regret taking it. I just want to grab my chemistry book and get out of here so I can change. Finally, it clicks open, and I grab my stuff.

"Practice is behind Hill House across from the library today, right?"

That voice. I freeze with my hand still on my textbook. It's loud and deep, and something in its tone is familiar. I peer over my shoulder, and sure enough, it belongs to the same guy who scored my veggie sticks, the boy with the eerily familiar face that I haven't quite been able to place, a detail that's infested my mind since lunch. I haven't been able to focus on a single word spoken in any of my classes since.

"Yeah, it's the same field we practiced on during summer warm-ups," one of the guys from the polo team says as he squeezes his shoulder. "I'll walk with you."

He's talking with the guys, not being obnoxious, cocky, or arrogant like most jocks. In fact, he's not doing a damn thing to provoke me, but something about him makes my chest feel tight. Why does he seem so familiar?

I chew on the inside of my lip as he keeps walking with the team.

"I just have to grab my duffel bag out of my car," he says as Hollis finishes packing up his bag at his locker a few doors down from mine. I watch them, trying to figure out why this rando is making me feel so weird. I know I haven't seen him around here. I'd remember that; I'd be able to place it. It's as if my body remembers him, even though my brain doesn't.

They head toward the exit, and I stare momentarily, transfixed by the light on the other side of the doors. I could attempt to let it go, but unfortunately, my brain doesn't work that way. If it did, I would forget about this creepy feeling and go home. But something won't let me.

I grab my strawberry milkshake, close my locker, and follow them. Maybe something will click into place.

I try to keep a non-stalkerish distance behind them as I follow them through the parking lot, even though stalking is exactly what I'm doing. They're droning on about polo and the first match this weekend, and my heart starts racing when I hear him say, "Yeah, I grew up on a ranch. Just because I haven't been playing polo since I was old enough to ride a bike doesn't mean I don't know my way around a horse."

My heart starts beating faster, and I don't even know why. He grew up on a ranch. There's a pinch of pain in my temple, and I squeeze my eyes closed, a flicker of familiarity flashing across my mind, but it's gone too soon, and when I open my eyes, an unmistakable dark-green Bronco is trumping every care I had about placing him. That Bronco is the exact reason my flyers were destroyed. It's the truck responsible for the stains on my clothes, and now my mystery man is tossing his backpack into the passenger seat.

I'm closer now, closer than I was this afternoon when I saw him across the commons at lunch. At this distance, I can see everything. The way he moves. The angle of his jaw. But it's his arm as he shoves his hand in his back pocket to grab his phone that recognition doesn't just return, it plows into me, stealing my breath.

I don't just know him. I hate him. He ruined my life.

TRIGGER

CHAPTER 2
FRESHMAN YEAR

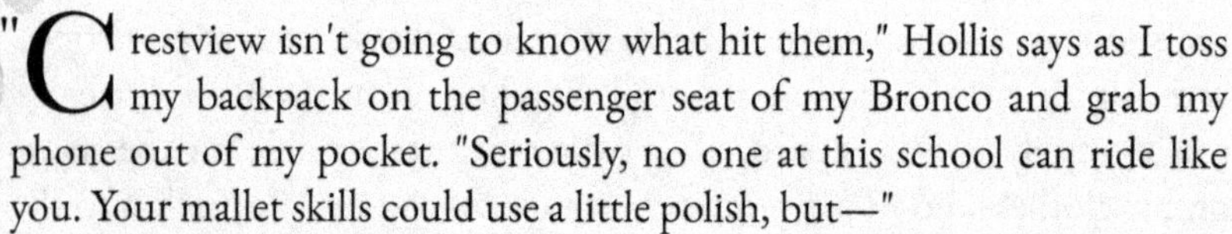

"Crestview isn't going to know what hit them," Hollis says as I toss my backpack on the passenger seat of my Bronco and grab my phone out of my pocket. "Seriously, no one at this school can ride like you. Your mallet skills could use a little polish, but—"

"Polish? What's wrong with the way I hold a mallet?"

I'm not trying to sound like a pompous ass, but I seriously have the biggest arms on the team, and that includes the upperclassmen. Most of these guys look like they haven't done a day of manual labor in their lives. Sure, they're in shape, but they're gym strong, not bred strong, and there's a difference.

"You're new, and you still swing with your arm—" Hollis attempts to explain.

"How the hell else am I supposed to swing?" I cut him off and give him an incredulous look before he can finish.

"Polo players who have been doing this for longer than a few weeks"—he flaps his hands toward his torso, reminding me he's the expert in this conversation—"pull the strength from our bodies. Our swing isn't just in our arm—"

A finger tapping on my shoulder from behind steals his words.

"Is this your car?" a female voice questions, and from the way Hollis is pressing his tongue into his cheek, she must be hot.

"Yes, it is," I say as I turn around, expecting to find one of his admirers. Today was literally my first day in the building, and the only female I spoke to was the lunch lady, but that's not who I find.

Dark-brown eyes stare back at me. Eyes I've memorized during countless summer afternoons. They were kind to me when the world around me sucked. My heart instantly starts hammering against my ribs as recognition sinks in, and I search her expression for any sign she remembers me. She's older now. Her baby cheeks are gone, and she's got this whole sophisticated thing going on. Her hair used to be short, but now it flows down her back. But those eyes... Damn, those eyes are exactly the same.

A slight gap forms between my lips, ready to say her name, because I can't be sure she's real until I do. It's possible I'm just imagining this, like all the other times where I pretend to thank the girl who actually gave a shit about me when I was a mess. The girl who saved my ass when everything was falling apart. My tongue darts out because my mouth is suddenly dry as hell, and she raises a brow, her gaze drifting over the stubble on my jaw that wasn't there all those years ago. Her lips press together before her eyes drop lower, roaming over the exposed skin on my arms, no doubt searching for the bruises that once marred my pale flesh.

The second her eyes find that familiar spot, her lips part, and I stop breathing. I'm terrified I'll somehow screw this up. The air between us feels electric, loaded with all the stuff I never got to say. God, I've thought about this moment so many times, but what about her? Has she thought about me at all?

Her proximity is intoxicating. She smells like warm vanilla, and I can see her pulse beating fast at her throat. For a second, it's like we're the only two people here, and the polo team might as well not exist. I want to touch her face so bad, just to make sure she's real. But before my heart can resume beating at its normal pace enough for me to plot my next move, something shifts in her expression. She recognizes me, alright, but not in a good way. Her jaw clenches, and I can literally see the moment she puts her walls back up.

"Good," she says, her voice sharp enough to cut glass. "I hope you hate strawberries."

Before I can even process what she said, I'm getting hit with what feels like a frozen bomb. The milkshake slams into my chest, strawberry and vanilla exploding everywhere. The shit is so cold it actually burns, seeping through my polo and hitting my skin like ice water.

"What the actual fuck just happened?" I rasp out, my voice strangled with shock and something dangerously close to betrayal.

The polo team is losing their minds, laughing and cheering like my spectacular downfall is the best thing they've ever seen. But I can't focus on them because I'm watching her walk away, and it's like getting punched in the gut.

She doesn't run. Instead, she simply walks away, but there's something about each step that has me thinking she planned it. The girl who once stuck up for me just became the girl who humiliated me in front of everyone. As I stand here, watching her put space between us, I memorize the absolute dismissal in the sway of her hips. She doesn't look back, not even once, and somehow that hurts worse than the ice cream still sliding down my torso in cold, sticky streams. She's walking away from me again, but this time I don't know why.

~

"WHICH ONE OF YOU PRETTY BOYS SMELLS LIKE strawberries?" Coach grumbles as we all huddle around him after practice.

A few of the guys snicker, and I roll my eyes. "That would be me, Coach." I raise my hand.

"He got iced by the ice queen," someone teases in a hushed tone to my right.

"That's enough," Coach says firmly. "I'm not asking to poke fun at your choices, but don't come smelling like a strawberry to practice tomorrow, son." He waves his clipboard in my direction to fan my stench away. "You're making me hungry."

"Won't happen again, Coach." I cross my arms, and Hollis elbows me with a shit-eating smirk. He knows damn well I can't control whether Asha Fairfield chooses to dump another milkshake down my shirt.

"Now, some of you may have already heard the rumors going around school that athletes are being forced to run for student council this year..." Groans amongst the team drown him out before he can continue. He raises a single hand in the air, motioning for us to quiet down. "From the sound of it, I'm going to go out on a limb here and say all that moaning and groaning means we have no volunteers." He takes a second to look around the circle, and when no one speaks up, he says, "I thought so." Then, reaching into his back pocket, he pulls out a handful of popsicle sticks. "We do have to nominate someone to run for the seat. Grade level is insignificant. You will be required to run against the incumbent in your year. To make this fair, everyone will draw a stick. Whoever ends up with the short one is our nominee."

There are a few more groans before he starts making his way around the circle, letting everyone draw. I'm not the last to get a stick, Hollis is, but looking at his stick, I already know I'm the unlucky son-of-a-bitch who got the short one.

"Everyone, hold up your stick," Coach says, his eyes quickly falling upon my stick and then announcing, "Hale, you're the polo team's nomination for student council."

"Coach, I'm new here. Literally no one knows me," I try to argue.

"Everyone's about to know exactly who you are," Brenner, who's one of the seniors on the team, tosses out, though I can't tell if his tone is mocking or friendly banter.

We have our first game this weekend, and I'm starting, and while polo is the equivalent of Friday night football at these hoity-toity prep schools, I can't help but think his offhanded comment has nothing to do with the game and everything to do with the stick I'm holding in my hand.

"Look, son." Coach Sullivan shifts to face me, running a callused hand through his gray beard as he squints against the setting sun. "I never said you had to win." His voice carries an authority that can only be earned through decades of coaching blue-blood kids whose trust funds could buy small countries. "But you don't strike me as someone who's comfortable with losing."

His pale-blue eyes lock onto mine, and I see something there—not pity, but recognition. The crow's feet etched deep around his eyes speak to years of reading players, of knowing who has the fire in their belly and who's just playing because it looks good on their boarding school transcript. He's right. Whatever I do, I do it all the way. Half-ass isn't my style. "Alright, that's enough for today." He checks his watch before his eyes sweep over every player. "Same time tomorrow," he says, dismissing the team.

The guys start to walk away, and I bump Hollis. "I thought Brenner liked me."

In all honesty, I don't give a shit who does and doesn't like me. I'm not here to win popularity contests, but it's smart to know your enemies. The team has felt like a brotherhood in many ways, everyone dishing out as much trash talk as they take, and while tonight will be my first night staying on campus in one of the dorms, from what I gather, all the guys hang out off the field too, but I'm not naïve enough to think I don't have to earn my stripes.

"He likes you as much as his DNA allows," he says as we head toward the locker room. "If you're talking about his comment...that had nothing to do with the game on Saturday and everything to do with the reason you smell like strawberries."

"I'm not following."

He stops dead in his tracks, his mouth quirking up to one corner. "You're running against the ice queen for president."

"Fuck me." I let out an exhausted sigh as I tip my head back to the sky.

Just when I thought the day couldn't get any worse, he drops this bomb on me. I knew what I was doing back home when I started messing around and competing in local rodeos behind my dad's back. I knew he'd be furious if he found out I was riding bulls. I've grown up riding horses. Horses are in my blood, but bull riding is a taboo sport in my house. My father doesn't have many hard limits, except that one, and I crossed it multiple times. Disobeying him got me exactly what I'd been hoping for: exile. But this complication I hadn't planned on.

"How ugly it gets depends on you," he says, squeezing my shoulder. "Victory always has a price, but few are willing to sacrifice. Asha won't go down without a fight."

That makes the corners of my lips turn up stupidly. Of course she won't. I wouldn't expect anything less.

My cleats squelch against the damp earth with each step as I pull off my gloves and stuff them into my helmet and ask, "Why do people call her the ice queen? Is she a mean girl?"

Hollis wipes sweat from his forehead, leaving a streak of dirt across his temple. "No, she's not mean...per se. Asha Fairfield is a one-woman show." He shrugs. "Well, I guess she has Emma now. Asha let her stick around for some reason. But mean, nah. She's not mean; she's a force.

The girl is smart as hell—maybe too smart for her own good, if you ask me."

We pause as two of the guys jog past us toward the stables, and Hollis shifts his weight, favoring his left leg. He probably pulled something during the last chukker.

"Most of her classes are advanced," he adds, his tone fairer. "If she's not in the library, working on assignments, or jumping her Thorough-bred, she's volunteering. It's nothing bad. She just keeps to herself."

"So, you call her the ice queen because she's a smart snob who doesn't bother to pencil in making friends into her schedule." I adjust the mallet slung over my shoulder.

"You left out hot in your list of adjectives." He holds his hands in front of him, palms up. "Look, I know it sounds mean and maybe even a little discriminatory, but it is what it is. If she has a friend list, I probably fall on that list. She knows what people say about her, and she's fine wearing the crown." He shrugs. "The girl likes to be alone."

The sound of our footsteps on the gravel path fills the silence as we start walking again.

"You said she probably considers you a friend. Why?"

Hollis stops dead in his tracks, and a slow grin spreads across his face.

"Well, for starters, she's my cousin."

How did I not know this? I'm a details guy, always have been. I pride myself on picking up on connections, on reading between the lines. I feel like I would have caught this earlier. Then again, they don't share the same last name, and I haven't had a reason to bring her up until today.

"She's going to be pissed when she finds out I'm not the nominee," Hollis says as he starts walking again, his stride a little more confident after successfully blindsiding me.

"Why is that?" I ask, jogging slightly to catch up.

"Today, after algebra, she cornered me in the hallway and asked me to run against her for student council."

"Why would she do that?"

"She heard the rumors like everyone else. If they were going to make jocks run, she wanted the candidate to be someone she knew wouldn't want it."

Great. I've just earned another reason for her to hate me.

"Any idea why she blasted me with a milkshake?" I ask, leaving out the part about how, in that moment, she could have recognized me.

I should tell him that I know Asha, but that wouldn't be the whole truth, because I don't. Not really. We met once, when we were six. I could tell him that my family's property neighbors hers, and that according to six-year-old Asha, we're sworn enemies due to some decades-old family feud. But I don't, because none of those things justifies what she did today, and when the time comes that I tell Hollis how I know Asha and why I went out of my way to get sent to this school, it won't be like this, clueless of his connection with her and smelling of pungent strawberries.

"You don't have any classes with her?" he asks, rubbing the back of his neck.

"No, at least not today. That could change tomorrow with block scheduling."

"Then I'm going to say it probably has something to do with the mud stains on her uniform. You're the only student who drove to campus today."

I furrow my brow until the pieces click into place. I'm the only one who didn't have a dorm ready before school started. I had to drive. The mud stains splattered across her pristine uniform were there because of me. Because I'd been careless, probably speeding through puddles in the parking lot like some kind of entitled asshole.

Shit.

We reach the locker room doors, the familiar scent of teenage desperation wafting out as Hollis pulls them open. But I barely notice. My mind is spinning as I try to process everything that has just been laid out for me.

Asha Fairfield wasn't just some ice queen who threw milkshakes for sport. She was Hollis's cousin, and just because their relation is news to me, doesn't mean my name hasn't come up in one of their conversations. It's possible my attendance isn't news to her. Asha is smart enough to manipulate student council elections before they even happened, resourceful enough to track down the source of her ruined uniform, and apparently vindictive enough to exact immediate revenge. And I have managed to piss her off before we've even officially met—well, at least for the second time.

The worst part about all of this is I'm actually impressed, even if it's at the expense of my own discomfort. It took balls to corner someone in broad daylight and nail them with a milkshake in front of an audience. It took a complete disregard for social consequences that I can't help but admire, even with the scent of strawberry still clinging to my skin.

Hollis was right about one thing: she isn't mean. Mean implies petty cruelty without purpose. What Asha did was calculated justice, swift and public, and probably exactly proportional to the offense in her mind. She'd made me look like an idiot because I'd made her look like one first, even if it had been an accident.

Ice queen. The nickname doesn't sound fitting to me. Ice is predictable. It freezes and then it melts, following the laws of physics. What I'm dealing with is something far more dangerous and infinitely less predictable. Asha Fairfield isn't ice. She is pure, undiluted trouble wrapped in a pristine uniform and armed with a smile that could probably convince teachers to give her extra credit while she plotted their downfall.

And I'm starting to suspect that getting on her bad side is going to be the most interesting mistake I'll make in a very long time. Because I'd rather be on her bad side than no side at all. At least this way, she knows I exist.

~

"Is this AP Biology?" I ask one of the students in the first row as I check the slip of paper in my hand one more time.

She peers up at me, annoyance plastered across her face for having to look up from her phone. "Yes," she clips out, only to do a double take and put on a smile. "I'm Emma. Are you new here?" She leans forward, flipping her phone over. "I don't think I've seen you around campus before."

"Yeah," I answer plainly before making my way to the back of the class and putting as much distance between me and her as possible.

She was rude and then tried to fake charm after noting that I was new on campus. I could tell by the way she batted her eyelashes and changed her tone that she was interested. That's not me being vain; that's just me being able to spot a wolf in sheep's clothing. A genuinely kind person isn't only nice when it's convenient.

As I take my seat and watch the class fill up, I note who's not here.

It's my second day and last class of block scheduling, which also means it's my last shot at having a class with Asha. Hollis said she takes all AP classes, and this is the only advanced course I'm taking this semester. I tap my pen against the desk, my eyes now zeroed in on the motion, perturbed that we're not sharing any classes together, when suddenly a flyer is slammed down on my desk.

The bright-yellow paper reads: *Your Freshman Student Body Elects Trigger Hale and Asha Fairfield. Who will have your vote, New Energy or Experience that Works?*

Damn! That was fast. I was literally selected less than twenty-four hours ago.

"Do you want to win?" she asks, her words pulling my eyes away from the flyer to hers.

Do I want to win? Not necessarily. I know exactly why she haunts every corner of my mind. It's the same reason I'm sitting in this chair and now running against her. Because any attention from Asha Fairfield is better than being invisible to her, even if it means she hates me.

Before I can even process what my answer would be, the classroom door swings open, and Mrs. Chen walks in, her heels clicking against the linoleum.

"Seats, everyone! Quickly now!" She claps her hands twice, and Asha shoots me one last dark glare before retreating to her own chair.

Mrs. Chen waits at the front, arms crossed, until the noise settles and everyone has taken a seat. "Good afternoon," she begins, adjusting her glasses. "I know you're all eager to dig into the class curriculum, but before we do, the administration has a special project to introduce. One that will span your entire high school career. And if you're wondering... yes, it's mandatory, and yes, it counts toward your graduation requirements."

A collective groan ripples through the classroom.

Mrs. Chen holds up a hand. "This project is called Pen Pals, but we won't be assigning the pen pals in the traditional sense, i.e, writing letters —we are in the twenty-first century after all. Instead of pens and paper, we will use cell phones. This project, at its core, is designed to foster genuine communication and understanding between students who might never otherwise interact. In a moment, our student aid will be distributing phones, basic models with limited functionality. Each phone has been assigned exactly one other number. That person will be your secret pen pal for the next four years."

Four years. The words echo in my head, and I want to laugh at how ridiculous that is. Four *years* of texting some random person. Four years of playing this stupid guessing game. I'm not the only one who thinks this is bullshit. The entire room erupts in groans and complaints, and someone yells, "Are you kidding me right now?" The girl to my right drops her head on her desk with a dramatic thud.

Mrs. Chen doesn't even blink. She just walks around to the front of her desk and crosses her ankles like she's got all day. Like she's *enjoying* this. The room slowly goes quiet, and I swear she's trying not to smirk.

"If everyone is finished..." She raises an eyebrow before continuing. "The rules are non-negotiable," she continues, her voice taking on a stern edge. "No exchanging names. No physical descriptions. No clues about your identity whatsoever. The person on the other end must remain completely anonymous until graduation. Any violation of these rules will result in a failing grade for this project, and you'll be assigned fifty hours of community service to make up for it."

Four years. Through all of high school. I glance around the room, suddenly aware of how many people this could be when the door opens again, and a student aid pushes in a cart stacked with small boxes. Each one has a name label on top.

"When you receive your phone," Mrs. Chen says, "it will already be charged and activated. You may text your pen pal whenever you wish. The only rule besides anonymity: be authentic. This project is about genuine human connection, not performance. Now, when I call your name, come collect your phone."

She starts reading from her roster, and one by one, students shuffle to the front. My heart's beating faster than it should. Somewhere in this room or maybe in another class, there's someone who's going to be assigned to me. Someone I'll talk to for the next four years without knowing who they are.

The yellow flyer still sits on my desk, Asha's name printed next to mine.

"Trigger Hale," Mrs. Chen calls.

I stand, weaving through the desks. As I return to my seat, the bright-yellow flyer staring back at me, I can't help but wonder: *What are the chances?*

The bell rings, and the class is over in what feels like seconds after my mind was left reeling over unlikely probabilities.

I'm out of my chair quick, so I reach her before she gets a chance to stand. Returning the flyer, I slide it across her desk. "I don't like to lose," I say in answer to the question she asked before class started. It's not the answer she wants to hear, and that's why I gave it. A *no* would have earned me a *'Good,' most likely followed with a hair flip as she sauntered off with dramatic flair,* but an open-ended response keeps those stormy eyes on me a little bit longer.

Her eyes narrow on mine, my response clearly grating on her nerves but earning me the response I'd hoped for all the same as she stands, uncaring of the little amount of space I've given her to do so. Toe to toe, I can smell the mint of her gum when she says, "Look, this is what's going to happen. You're not going to run against me. You're not so much as going to come up with one single idea for a campaign strategy. Instead, you're going to act as the place holder you are. Smile for the faculty, attend the meetings, but offer zero suggestions, and when you must campaign—because the staff will be watching—it's my name you tell students to cast their votes for."

I bite my lip to refrain from smiling, fighting the urge to lean closer, to close the dangerous distance between us. I liked it when Asha Fairfield was nice to me, but I think I like it more when she's mean. There's fire in her when she's angry, and it's intoxicating.

"And why would I do that?"

"Because you owe me," she states without reservation.

I pause, our gaze imperceptibly locked as I consider her response. What is she insinuating I owe her for? If anything, she evened the score when she dumped a milkshake down my chest, which has me questioning if she's not referring to something else, an admission that would give me a firm answer to the question that's been driving me crazy. Does she remember?

I cross my arms and allow a deceiving grin to pull at my mouth, giving her the impression I'm unbothered when that couldn't be further from the truth. She's all I've thought about since the second I laid eyes on her yesterday, but even before then, she was every other thought. The way she moves, the tilt of her head when she's thinking, the dangerous curve of her smile...it's all burned into my memory.

"I don't know, after the strawberry milkshake, I'd say we're pretty even," I tactfully challenge, noting how her lips press together and her fists clench at her sides. "Unless there's something else?" I say, unable to hold back my probe.

"Why are you here, Hale?"

And there it is. The confirmation I was looking for. She remembers. She could have used any other combination of words, but she chose those specific ones.

"Ridgewood has an excellent reputation," I say, curiously watching her wheels spin in hopes of figuring out what's changed.

"So do fifty other schools that aren't mine. Try again."

"And if I said you?" She hears a taunt. I can see it in the way she rolls her lips, but it's a question all the same. One I want a real answer for.

"Don't you think you've ruined my life enough?"

Ruined her life? I try hard to keep my face impassive, even though inside I'm scrambling to put the pieces together. I feel like I'm missing something big. How did I ruin her life?

"Whatever." She slaps her desk, frustrated with my delayed response. "Have it your way. You can play games all you want, but you better believe I don't lose. You'll regret—"

My hand covers hers and steals her words. The moment our skin touches, it's like getting shocked, but in a good way. Her breath catches, confirming she feels it too. Her head might make me the enemy, but the rest of her isn't sold on that label. Her hand is smaller than I expected, softer, but she doesn't pull away immediately. Her words might sound like pure hate, but the way she's staying...that says something totally different. For a second, we're just frozen, just like we were in the parking lot, and I can't tell if I want to fight her or kiss her.

"Regret implies a mistake. This wasn't a mistake," I finally say, knowing any second this moment will disappear, and I'm not ready to show my cards—not now that I have to figure out how I ruined her life. For now, I have to let her hate me a little longer. She tries to pull her hand away, but I'm faster, grasping it tightly and holding her in place. Her pulse hammers against my thumb, betraying the effect I have on her despite the ice in her glare. "If I ruined your life, you corrupted mine. Make no mistake, you're no ice queen. You're trouble, sweetheart."

This time, when she tries to yank her hand away, I let her, but not before running my thumb across her knuckles. Her breath catches subtly. She rolls her glossy pink lips before saying, "You know what they say about trouble...it never sleeps."

"Oh, I'm counting on it." Her practiced, icy glare stays fixed on mine. "I like trouble. It follows me like a shadow."

I doubt she caught the double meaning in my words, but I felt her pulse racing. Her mind is swimming, too busy plotting her revenge and all the ways she'd kill me if she could to notice the way she unconsciously leans toward me even as she tries to pull away. But I've waited this long to see her again. I can wait a little longer to see what happens next.

ASHA

CHAPTER 3
SOPHOMORE YEAR

I set down the gel filters in my hand as I crouch beside one of the spotlights in the dance hall, my lips rolling of their own accord when I see the message. I have no idea who the person on the other side of this message is, but I'm certain I like them even though I vowed I wouldn't. I roll my eyes and quickly reply.

I slip my phone into my back pocket and get back to work. There's less than a day left to get the dance hall ready for homecoming, and my to-do list feels endless. Still, I don't mind the distraction. Every time my mystery friend texts, I can't help but wonder who they are.

In years past, classes buried time capsules, produced documentaries, and spearheaded community projects that actually led to the construction of parks. But our class...we got assigned secret pen pals like we're a bunch of summer campers homesick for our parents.

I was beyond livid. That night, I stormed back to my room, opened my laptop, and drafted what I was convinced would be a protest speech that would go down in the history books. This wasn't just about a disappointing senior project; this was about my future. I wanted these years to count. Needed them to count after being sent away, after missing everything I could never get back. I couldn't stomach the thought of not building something substantial.

For three hours, I sat there, fuming, making endless pro and con lists and looking up ways to fight faculty decisions. Then my school phone buzzed with a text from an unknown number.

> Pen Pal: So...on a scale of 1 to planning a coup, how much do you hate this assignment?

My finger hovered over the keypad for long seconds. If I started typing, I would have lost the battle. It hadn't even been a whole day since the project was announced. There was a chance I still could have made my case and swayed the board. However, that's not what happened. Instead, I caved, too eager to voice my annoyance. I quickly updated my contact info, assigning myself a name that echoed my protest.

> Academic Hostage: I'm the program's number one adversary. I've already drafted my PowerPoint.

> Pen Pal: A PowerPoint? That's impressive but also mildly concerning.

> Academic Hostage: Why not both?

I still recall biting the side of my thumb as nerves riddled my body. It was in that moment that I realized I was slightly unhinged, so I tapped out another reply.

> Academic Hostage: I also have a backup plan involving interpretive dance, in case the presentation doesn't work.

I shouldn't have cared what the person behind the proverbial veil thought of me, but I did. That was why I'd spent years suffocating the messy, imperfect parts of myself. At school, my reputation preceded me, but responding to that first text cracked something open. I didn't have to be the ice queen anymore, at least not with my pen pal. For the first time in years, I could choose who to be. Everyone saw the polished surface, perfect grades, and perfect behavior, the perfect daughter who never colored outside the lines, but this stranger knew nothing of my carefully constructed façade. I could unearth the version of myself I'd buried beneath all those expectations. I could remember what it felt like to breathe.

Pen Pal: Skip the PowerPoint and go straight for the dance. A dance protest would be legendary.

I found myself actually smiling at my phone, which on some levels felt like a personal betrayal, but it also felt good.

Academic Hostage: I think I'll save it. A legendary dance protest deserves a worthy opponent. When they announce our next project is friendship bracelets, I'll bust out my dhol and lehenga.

That was my first slip. I was the only student at the school with Indian heritage, and that detail could have spelled game over if my pen pal had connected the dots. Most people at school saw only the surface: dark eyes, black hair, golden skin that marked me as vaguely "other" without caring enough to dig deeper. I held my breath, waiting for a reply, but they either completely missed my careless mention or they were decent enough to ignore it. Instead, they did something unexpected and changed their name.

Captive Audience: Careful, you're dangerously close to making this assignment seem less terrible.

Once again, my fingers hovered over the keypad, a smile tugging at my lips. I had no clues about who my new pen pal was. All I knew as I flopped back onto my pillows was that I didn't hate the assignment as much anymore.

"Asha, come on. Let's get out of here. We can finish this up after the game," Emma says, pulling me away from my new favorite thoughts: him.

And yes, I do officially know it's a him. He slipped up, mentioning where he was one day. He might have ignored my slip, but I called him out on his, quickly letting him know I wasn't aware the men's locker room had poor ventilation and reeked of sweat and overpowering cologne that burned your nose.

"I know to you this is just another dance, but for me, my name is tied to it, and I need this to go perfectly." I stand, backing away from the spotlight, settling on an amber hue that will drench the walls and stage.

"Correction, Hale's name is tied to it. He won the election, remember?" she snaps, and I roll my eyes.

The defeat still irks me. I was so sure I was going to beat him for student body president last year. Trigger claimed he transferred to Ridgewood for me, and I promised him he'd regret it. So far, I feel like I've failed at keeping my word.

I campaigned hard, and everyone was congratulating me before I'd even won. To my surprise, Trigger did exactly what I asked of him, and then he won. When I asked for a recount, Mr. Greco made me his VP. My blood boiled so hot I had to walk out of the room before I said something I'd regret. I wanted to set his office on fire and all the ballots, demand another election where the counting of the votes could be observed, but I didn't. I learned a long time ago that not everything in life will go your way, but Emma isn't entirely correct.

"True, but winning and losing are fundamental outcomes in life, and I'm playing the long game," I tell her as I retreat to my supply table.

"So, you're fine getting your hands dirty to make him look good?" She hops off her step stool with a roll of crepe paper that hasn't been used. Emma has been doing more texting than helping me tonight.

"Three faculty members, including Mr. Greco, have strolled through while I've been in here decorating solo."

"But they know he's warming up with the team for the game. I don't see how that helps you," she says, popping her gum and tossing the unused roll on the table.

"It proves he can't fulfill his duties as president." I begin opening the battery-operated tea lights that I plan to place in vases. "I'm building my case to have him removed."

"Or..." She takes the bag out of my hands and sets it on the table. "For just this once, you can be busy too. Look around. You more than pulled your weight. Make him finish tonight after the game or tomorrow morning—his choice—but you..."—her voice elevates with excitement as she takes a tape gun out of my hand—"need to get your fine ass to the game. Come on, you have to admit you're at least a little excited to meet Penn in person."

Last month, I missed our only off-campus day, which happened to be the day Emma met her new boyfriend and his best friend, Penn. Rather than exploring the city, I was stuck re-strategizing homecoming themes because Trigger didn't like any of the ones presented in the meeting. Naturally, I spent the meeting texting my pen pal, venting about the entire situation.

Academic Hostage: Meetings suck. That's all.

Captive Audience: The WORST, especially when you must repeat yourself for those who aren't paying attention.

Academic Hostage: Or dictators who shoot down all your ideas. Probably going to create a focus group after this one to determine why buffoon's hate masquerade balls. Is it the masks, balls, or just the concept of joy itself?

I watched bubbles appear on my screen only to disappear in time for me to look up and catch Trigger smirking at me from across the table and say, *"Meeting adjourned. Go enjoy your day off. My VP is about to blow my mind with her ideas, to ensure we create the most legendary home-coming this school has ever seen."*

Trigger knew exactly what he was doing with those words, the manipulative ass. He was getting me back for texting during his precious meeting while simultaneously throwing me under the bus by announcing the theme would be MY idea. If this homecoming sucks, everyone will know exactly who to blame.

"He's literally the captain of the other team. I doubt he'll have time to meet me," I argue, suddenly nervous.

I like Penn. He's nice, easy to talk to, and attractive, and his title doesn't hurt. I'm not looking for a boyfriend, but dating the captain of our biggest rival's team? That kind of positioning is too good to pass up. *So why am I nervous? Why does meeting face-to-face feel like it changes everything?* Suddenly, it's real, not just a safe distance. And if texting every day means something serious, what does that say about my pen pal?

"Oh, I have it on good authority he has every intention of making time." She smiles and bites the corner of her lip.

My face instantly reddens. "What does that mean?"

I missed one trip into the city for that damn homecoming meeting, and Emma ran into three guys needing a jump. She had no clue how to jump a dead battery, but she had the cables. The guys bought her dinner, and by the end of the night, she had a boyfriend, and I had an admirer: Penn.

She decided to show him my private social media pages. I told her I wasn't interested, but she begged me to at least try a phone call so we could all hang out next time. Obviously, I agreed, and now I'm here with sweaty palms.

"I don't know the details. All I know is Philip told me Penn had two goals tonight: win the game and meet you."

My stomach knots, just as my phone pings with another text.

> Captive Audience: Tell me what you're wearing.

He knows that's against the rules, but I also like knowing he wants to break them. It tells me I'm not the only one feeling some type of way about our exchanges.

"Isn't that your school phone?"

"Yep," I say, noting the tendril of judgment in her tone.

"I can't believe you carry it around. I keep mine in my desk in my room. There is no way the school is going to have me carrying around an outdated phone twenty-four seven so they can track me."

"Well, you know me," I say, trailing off as I read the text. "Always following the rules." I pause to check another message.

> Captive Audience: Give me something.

> Academic Hostage: Navy.

"Well, not tonight. You're coming with me. If someone says anything, I'll tell them you were kidnapped," she says, looping her arm through mine and dragging me toward the doors. "Trust me, after you meet Penn, you'll be thanking me for dragging you out of here."

I set my phone to vibrate, knowing I won't hear it once we're at the game, and another text comes in.

> Captive Audience: The whole school will be wearing navy.

> Academic Hostage: I know.

> Captive Audience: Give me something else. Pleassseee.

> Academic Hostage: My hair is pulled up.

It's another vague detail, but it still makes me smile.

"See, I knew if I could get you out of that hall, you'd finally get excited. You're allowed to have fun sometimes, Asha," she says as we cross the courtyard and make our way down Bald Hill toward the polo field.

I don't correct her. Technically, she's not wrong, but I don't tell her my smile has nothing to do with Penn and everything to do with knowing that, somewhere out there, someone knows the real me. I still can't identify who they are, but I'm already in rule-breaking territory, abandoning the dance to sit in these stands, dropping hints in texts that dance dangerously close to revealing too much.

What's another violation if it's worth it?

I glance around, wondering what's taking Emma so long to get back. We've been neck and neck all night, and I know she'd be pissed if she misses her boyfriend score a goal. The horn sounds, signaling the last thirty seconds, and my eyes snap back to the field.

I spotted Penn immediately when we arrived. Sandy-blond hair, tall in his saddle, that genuine smile that you can't help but mirror when it's pinned on you. Our eyes met across the field, and just like on our Face-Time calls, my face flushed. Except, this time, our exchange wasn't private; it was public. And his gaze didn't go unnoticed.

It took Trigger Hale exactly one second to track the source of Penn's smile. When his eyes found me on the benches, clearly not in the hall decorating for the dance, something unrecognizable flickered across his face. Our eyes locked for a moment longer than comfortable.

Then his eyes swept over me, slowly, deliberately, and I could practically *feel* the path they traced. Heat instantly started blooming across my skin as his attention lingered on the deep V of my navy cap-sleeve body suit. My pulse kicked up even more as his gaze dropped lower, taking note of the light-washed bell-bottoms that hugged every one of my curves in a way the school-issued plaid skirt never could. I watched his jaw tighten almost imperceptibly. He knew. Without a word being spoken, Trigger knew I wasn't here to watch Ridgewood, but instead to watch someone else.

Satisfaction burned through me. I got in his head, but the win was short lived because something else twisted there too. Something I couldn't name because it felt wrong. His jaw tightened as he turned away, shoulders set in a way that looked suspiciously like jealousy. Which was impossible. Trigger Hale didn't get jealous over me.

That thought has had me wound tight the entire game. Trigger Hale can't be jealous. What I saw was anger, pure shock that I ditched my duties for Penn Hadley. I wanted that reaction, planned for it. But anger alone wouldn't keep pulling his eyes back to me, wouldn't have us locked in this silent game of watching and being watched. And the worst part? The idea that he might actually be jealous shouldn't send heat through my chest. But it does.

"Hey, what did I miss?" Emma says, stepping in front of me as she reclaims her seat on my right.

"You mean besides the entire last chukker?" She looks at the score-board and then back to me.

"So, nothing. We're still tied."

"What took you so long?"

"There was a line." I furrow my brow, looking past her to the bathroom. There's only one chukker left, and we're tied. A bathroom line seems odd. "Only one toilet was working. So, seven more minutes..." She anxiously drums on her thighs. "And then you get to meet Penn."

"Yeah," I say with a fake smile. I'm not *not excited*, but damn it, tonight is not at all going as I thought it would.

Penn is everything I thought he'd be, and I haven't even met him yet. We have the same ambitions, same drive, same ridiculous GPA, and finding that relentless dedication in a guy feels rare. At our age, most guys are chasing other forms of validation.

Then there's Trigger. Every stolen glance burns, every *accidental* touch when we're in student council meetings sends electricity straight through me. He's chaos with a heartbeat, turning every shared space into a war zone where I'm my own worst enemy. It's because of him I'm even at Ridgewood. He's always been the opposition. But my traitorous body doesn't seem to care that I hate him. Just because he's the enemy doesn't mean I'm blind to the way he fills out his letterman's jacket, all dark eyes and dangerous edges. Trigger Hale is trouble in human form, and I'm apparently a masochist.

And then there's my pen pal, who's gone radio silent. Zero texts since the game, which makes no sense, considering the exchange we shared right before the game. I sent him a picture during the divot stomping at halftime, and he didn't respond. The sudden silence has been gnawing at me the entire game, only serving as a reminder of why I've chosen to keep to myself all these years at school. My head is a literal mess, and I'm supposed to be having fun. Instead, I'm sitting in the center of three storms, wondering which one will hit me first.

Emma smacks my thigh and murmurs, "Look," through clenched teeth.

My eyes snap to the field where I catch Penn looking directly at me. He touches the brim of his helmet in the smallest of gestures and flashes me a big smile that has my cheeks instantly warming from the attention.

However, his isn't the only gaze trained on me. I feel it before my eyes slide over to his. From across the field, Trigger is watching too. His horse stands as still as stone beneath him, but his eyes are fixed on me with an intensity that makes my entire body hum. When he realizes I am looking back, something raw and unguarded passes across his face. He knows I want nothing to do with him, but ever since he's arrived at Ridgewood, he's made it his mission to torment me and drive me crazy. That's when it occurs to me...I'm playing right into his hand.

The goody-goody who doesn't color outside the lines, always following the rules. It never occurs to people that maybe I *choose* structure. It isn't my prison. It's my power. Every assignment completed, every commitment honored, every goal achieved is something I can stand on later. It won't fade away.

I tear my gaze away from his with a renewed vengeance igniting in my veins. I've taken the backseat and dutifully played the VP role, building my case against him, but I'm done waiting patiently. I'm taking what's mine. Whatever moments I thought existed between us were never really real; they were manufactured to keep me in line.

Penn intercepts a pass at midfield, and I find myself leaning forward as he drives his horse toward the goal. Trigger is thundering alongside him in pursuit. The two of them are perfectly matched, their horses neck and neck, and for a moment, it feels like the entire match has narrowed down to this, Penn and Trigger, racing not just for the goal but for something else entirely.

Then at the last second, Trigger hooks Penn's mallet with his own, stealing the ball. In one fluid motion, he sends it sailing between the goalposts just as the final horn sounds.

"Holy shit!" Emma jumps out of her seat with the rest of the crowd as everyone celebrates our homecoming victory.

I watch as our team heads toward the pony lines, and then I see Penn sitting motionless on his horse, disappointment clear in his posture. No one likes to lose, but when he finally looks up, his eyes once again find me in the stands, and his expression shifts. The loss hitting differently because while he may not have won, at least he gets to see me. He trots over to the pony line and hands his horse off to one of his teammates before crossing the field. They all watch, and the anger I had felt seconds ago fades quickly, replaced with giddy excitement at his grand gesture of running off the field, his destination clear: me.

"I'll meet up with you in a bit. I'm going to go meet up with Philip," Emma says, tucking a strand of hair behind her ear and ducking off into the crowd before I can respond. She's been acting sketchy all day. After she told me about tonight and Penn's plan, I thought things would level out, but if anything, she's only been acting more strange.

Big arms wrap around me, lifting me off the ground before I can give it any more thought. "How is it possible you're even prettier in person?" Penn says as he spins me in a circle.

"If you set me down so I can get a good look at you, I might say the same thing," I tease, breathless from the spinning or maybe from the way his arms feel wrapped around me.

"Sorry, I couldn't help myself." He sets me on my feet, steadying me with one hand on my waist while quickly taking a sign from a guy nearby who's gone in a blur. His hair is damp with sweat, curling slightly at his temples, and there's a flush across his cheekbones from the match. "Plus, I needed to give my friend a chance to give me this." He turns the sign around, and I catch the nervous flicker in his eyes before he masks it with that confident smile. "You're my main goal. Homecoming?"

My eyes go wide. "You don't like dances."

"I only said that to throw you off my trail." His tongue darts out and sweeps over his bottom lip. "Say yes."

A big goofy smile takes over my face as warmth floods through me. I nod my head and manage, "Yes," my voice barely carrying over the small crowd around us clapping in celebration. I'm once again swooped up in his arms, and this time, I notice how his heart pounds against my palm where it rests on his chest. "What if I had said no?" I ask on a laugh.

"Honestly, I hadn't thought that far ahead. When I put my mind to something, I'm all in." This time, when he sets me down, it's on the bench, and we're almost eye level now. This close, I can see the green flecks in his hazel eyes, and there's a slight scrape on his jaw from the match. "The second I found out you were planning the dance, I started thinking up ways to ask." His gaze briefly flicks over the people leaving. "But I'm glad you didn't say no." He grimaces. "That would have been embarrassing. Want to go somewhere?"

"I can't leave campus."

"We don't have to leave to be alone." His fingers intertwine with mine before he gives my hand a gentle tug.

"Sure," I say, hopping off the bench.

We've only managed to take two steps when I freeze, my eyes closing in automatic annoyance as I hear my name called, "Asha," his voice like nails on a chalkboard. I consider ignoring it, taking another step, and then another, like I never heard him at all, but ignoring him would be a kinder fate, and I'm not in the giving mood. "Is the decorating done?" he asks as I spin around to face him.

"Almost," I say with a sweet mocking smile. "You can finish."

"That's not how this works," he says, closing some of the distance between us.

"That's exactly how this works." I step toward him, unafraid. "You ditched all day for polo." I put my hands on my hips. "Now it's my turn."

"Greco gave me a pass. Polo is an extracurricular. So, unless you have a late-night competition tonight, we need to get to the hall," he challenges with a smug 'gotcha' look written all over his face.

"We..."—I gesture between us—"aren't going anywhere." I step dangerously closer and stab my finger into his chest, feeling the heat radiating through his shirt. "I'm leaving with Penn, and you're not going to stop me," I state firmly, hating how my voice wavers just slightly. "I've been playing nice. I know why you are here. Why you were sent to Ridgewood. And I'm not the one trying to correct an unfavorable track record, so I suggest from now on you stay out of my way."

His file spelled it out: *flight risk, pattern of reckless behavior, refusal to prioritize academics.* His father sent him here to get serious about school, to prove he could focus on something other than rodeos and ranch work. His family breeds Thoroughbreds. Horses are in his blood, but that wasn't enough. Mr. Hale wanted his son to get an education, not just callused hands and belt buckles.

And I've done my homework. I know Trigger is failing calculus—or close enough to it that one bad test could tip him over the edge. I wonder how Daddy Hale would feel knowing his son was spending more time at the stables than in the library.

If my words touched a nerve, I wouldn't know it. If anything, the arrogant ass looks amused. His dark eyes practically sparkle as he crosses his arms, and I swear I see his jaw tick, just once, before that infuriating smirk returns. "I'm flattered you called home to talk to your daddy about me." He leans in, close enough that I can smell his sweat mixed with his cologne. "I didn't realize you thought about me outside of the classroom."

My heart hammers against my ribs. "In your dreams. I saw your file."

"Call it what you want, sweetheart." The nickname rolls off his tongue like a caress, and I hate it. "It doesn't change the fact that you were in a room without me, and Penn Hadley wasn't the guy on your mind. It was me." His eyes trail the side of my face, lingering at my temple, then my jaw, and I stand statue still, my nails digging crescents into my palms, determined not to let him see how he gets under my skin. How every nerve ending feels electrified standing this close to him.

"Whatever, Hale." I force steel into my voice even as my pulse races. "I'm not doing this with you, and I won't be at the hall tonight. I'll see you at the dance tomorrow night, or I won't. I really hope the latter is true." I turn on my heel before I do something monumentally stupid, like hauling off and punching him in the nose. If I want to beat him at his own game, I have to be a thorn in his side the way he is mine.

I wrap my arm through Penn's, and he asks, "Everything okay? Do you want me to handle him?"

Penn's arm feels wrong somehow. Too loose. Too comfortable. Not like the electric charge that shot through me when I pressed my finger against Trigger's chest. I shove the thought away viciously.

He's heard me complain about Trigger Hale on more than one occasion, and after Trigger's comments just now about thinking about him outside the classroom, I feel foolish more than anything. I want to deny it. I should be able to deny it, but the truth sits heavy in my chest. He does take up space in my mind when he's not around. Not because I want him to, but because he's an obstacle, a problem I need to solve. That's all it is. It has to be. He took something from me. Something that can never be replaced. And I'll never forgive him for that.

"No, I can handle him."

"Oh, and Asha..." Trigger calls after me again, his voice carrying that rough edge that scrapes down my spine, causing both Penn and me to look back. "Nice ponytail."

The words hit like a punch. My hand flies instinctively to my hair, the high ponytail I'd pulled it into this morning without thinking. The same way I wore it that day. The day my mother styled it for school. The day we don't talk about.

I furrow my brow as his hard glare holds my eyes for what feels like an eternity, and there's something molten beneath that stare, something entirely too knowing. Of all the comments he could have made, that one hits close to home. Too close. As if he's been cataloging details about me that I didn't realize anyone could see.

He pulls his gloves off slowly, his eyes never leaving mine, before giving me his back and walking away. Even his retreat feels like a challenge. I pull out my phone with shaking hands I refuse to acknowledge. Still no reply from my mystery friend.

    Academic Hostage: I really wish you had texted me
    back.

As soon as it's sent, it's read. When dots appear, I glance up in the direction I saw Trigger walking, but he's gone. My chest tightens with something I refuse to name.

> Captive Audience: I didn't have my phone. I thought I lost it. I just found It between the seats in my car.

My blood runs cold. Normally, that would be a likely excuse, but we don't drive on campus.

> Academic Hostage: Why would you lie?

The dots appear and disappear three times before his response comes through.

> Captive Audience: Do you want the truth?

My finger hovers over the screen as my mind races to Trigger's knowing look, to the ponytail comment, to the way he called me "sweetheart" like he's said it a thousand times before in the privacy of his own thoughts. To the timing of every message I've ever received.

> Academic Hostage: No.

I shove my phone into my pocket and let Penn guide me toward the dorms, but my mind is spiraling. It can't be Trigger. It can't be. Because if the boy who infuriates me and the boy who understands me are the same person, then I've been lying to myself about more than just how much space he takes up in my thoughts. I've been lying about the real reason my heart races when he's near, the real reason I can't stop myself from rising to every challenge he throws at me, the real reason that, even now, walking away from him, all I want to do is turn around and demand the truth I just told him I don't want. God help me, I think I already know it. And if I'm right, then everything, absolutely everything, is about to get infinitely more complicated.

TRIGGER

CHAPTER 4

SOPHOMORE YEAR

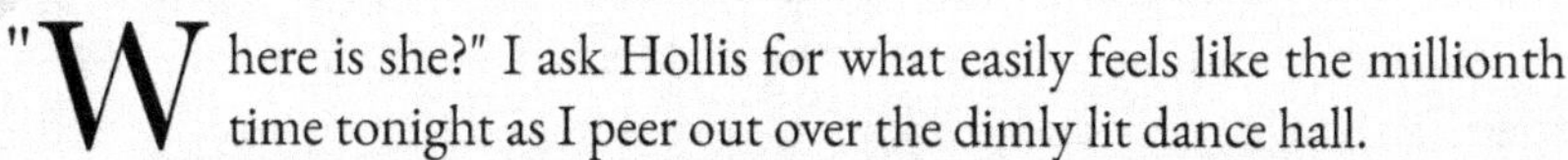

"Where is she?" I ask Hollis for what easily feels like the millionth time tonight as I peer out over the dimly lit dance hall.

The homecoming dance has been going on for almost two hours. After last night's fight at the polo match, I thought Asha would show up just to make my life difficult. Being late could be another way she's choosing to stick it to me. There's no doubt in my mind she knows her tardiness is getting under my skin. She's smart, but she still hasn't realized I actually enjoy getting a reaction out of her. I like a challenge, but I also need her to be present to accept one.

"Dude, you need to chill," Hollis says, adjusting his tie as his date spins away from him to grab a punch. "You're acting like a stalker."

"I'm not—" I start, but he cuts me off with a knowing look.

"You've checked your phone, like, fifty times. You're wearing a path into the floor. And you keep whipping your head around like you're following a play every time the door opens."

I force myself to lean back against the wall, trying for casual. He's right. I look like a crazy stalker or, worse, like I'm planning for my own counterattack. While both of those things are true, I don't need the world to know—at least not before she knows it. "I just want to know if she's coming. She said she'd be here."

"She said, and I quote, 'I'll see you at the dance tomorrow night or I won't. I really hope the latter is true.'" Hollis grins. "Let's be honest, she has you permanently benched."

"Who said I was trying to play her games?"

My phone buzzes. I have it out before Hollis can even smirk at me. *Not her.*

I shove it back in my pocket and scan the entrance again. The thing is, she's never late. Ever. She always shows up early to every meeting we have, just so she can make some comment about my time management.

"Look, I get some guys are into that whole girls-playing-hard-to-get thing, and you can lie to me all you want, pretend you aren't interested in her, that this obsession stems from her throwing a milkshake on you and your bruised ego needing payback. But she's not just some girl; she's my *cousin*. And I can promise you that's not what's happening with Asha. She genuinely hates you. There's no game. No secret interest. She looks at you the way most people look at gum on their shoe."

I tap my thumb against my thigh. Hollis has become my closest friend at Ridgewood, and I still haven't told him about my history with his cousin. I haven't told him about the one time we met when we were six, or how our families are enemies, or that the fascination I have with Asha Fairfield doesn't border on obsession—it is obsession. I could tell him now; this could be a segue, but I don't because my reasons for keeping it to myself center around her doing the same. Hollis hasn't ever mentioned that she's talked about me, which means Asha must have her reasons for not bringing me up too.

Asha and Hollis might be family, but he doesn't know her the way I do. He's not in our AP class. He doesn't see the way she steals glances when she thinks I'm not looking, or how, in our student council meetings, the hairs on her arms stand at attention when I'm near. He doesn't see the way her pulse quickens or how her eyes dilate the second all my attention is pinned directly on her. Hollis doesn't know what it's like to hate the fact that you *more than like* someone. But I don't need him to.

"If I were to make a bet, I bet she decided you weren't worth the effort tonight," Hollis offers unhelpfully.

"Nah, that's the thing about girls who play hard to get..." I say, my tone laced with more confidence than I feel. "They don't back down from confrontation."

He shakes his head with a smirk, and the double doors behind him swing open. My pulse kicks up before I even register why. Then I see her.

"Never gamble, Hollis. You're shit at it," I say as my eyes trace over every inch of her.

She's wearing a dark-green satin dress that catches the light as she moves, and her hair is down, flowing in thick, wavy locks. She looks...different. Still her, but softer somehow, as she pauses in the doorway, scanning the crowd.

Our eyes meet across the room, and hers narrow immediately, that familiar fire sparking to life. She squares her shoulders and starts walking, her steps quickly turning to a march as she makes a beeline straight toward me, and despite the murderous look on her face, I can't help the stupid grin spreading across mine.

"Here we go," Hollis mutters, melting away into the crowd.

She stops in front of me, close enough that I catch a hint of something floral in her perfume. Close enough to see the slight flush in her cheeks that might be from rushing, or anger, but confident there's a good chance it's from something else.

"You're late," I say, because apparently, I have a death wish.

"I wasn't aware I owed you a timely arrival." Her tone could cut glass, but she's here. She came.

"You don't owe me anything. I just noticed, that's all."

"Noticed?" She crosses her arms. "Or were you obsessively watching the door like some kind of creep?"

"Can't it be both?"

The corner of her mouth twitches, almost imperceptibly, but I catch it. I always catch it.

"You're insufferable," she says.

"And yet, here you are." I hold out my hand, nodding toward the dance floor. "Dance with me?"

"Absolutely not."

"Afraid you'll enjoy it?"

Her eyes flash, and for a split second, I believe my words are spot on, but then her mask is firmly slipped back into place, and the murderous look she had stomping across the room is replaced with a devilish one that promises calculated revenge.

"Dancing requires touching, and the thought repulses me."

The words sting more than they should, but before I can respond, her smile sharpens into something truly dangerous.

"Besides, while you were busy *not finishing* the dance hall last night..." She pauses, letting that particular failure sink in while I internally scold myself. She came after she said she wouldn't, and I was too damn tired. "I put together a surprise fundraising auction to help raise more money for the charity this year's dance is sponsoring."

"What kind of auction?"

"Oh, you know. The usual. Donated items, experiences, that sort of thing." Her voice is pure innocence, but her eyes are gleaming with malicious delight. "I may have included a few special lots. Very exclusive. Very...personal."

The way she says "personal" makes my blood run cold.

"Asha, what did you do?"

"You'll see." She pats my chest with false sympathy. "Don't worry. It's all for charity. You're not the type to back out of helping a good cause, are you?" she says before waltzing up to the stage and heading straight to the DJ. Leaning in close, she says something in his ear, and he hands her the microphone, looking all too amused.

The music fades, and conversations die down as people start to notice the change in volume and look toward the stage where Asha stands in that dark-green dress, poised and confident, every inch the girl who's spent her life commanding rooms full of people twice her age, at her dad's galas or at show-jumping competitions. She's in her element.

"Good evening, everyone!" Her voice rings out across the dance hall. "I hope you're all having the best time at homecoming."

There's applause and a few whistles, and her smile never wavers as she waits for them to simmer.

"As you all know, Homecoming at Ridgewood has a long-standing tradition of raising money for the local shelters as we head into the winter months." She pauses, letting the weight of that settle. "This year, instead of betting on *stuff*, we're betting on *time*. It's our most valuable resource and the gift that keeps on giving."

What in the actual hell is she talking about? It was her idea to pull the auction this year, instead choosing to raise the price of a ticket, arguing that attending homecoming in general was the money grab. None of these trust-fund babies cared to bid on things their parents could buy them with one call home, so why waste time on silent auction tables? However, they would willingly pay whatever price we put on a ticket just to ensure they attended.

In her words, *the higher the price tag, the more exclusive the dance becomes.* The cost itself transformed homecoming from just another school event into something elite, a velvet rope only the wealthy could cross. She'd actually said it made them *want it more*, that charging five hundred dollars per ticket did more for the dance's prestige than any decorations or DJ ever could. The price wasn't just admission. It was a status symbol, proof you belonged to the inner circle that could afford not to flinch at the cost. I couldn't disagree, and though you'd never catch me paying that ticket price to attend a dance, I didn't object because, as class president, I don't have to pay admission.

Hollis appears at my elbow. "Why does it look like you didn't know about this?"

"Because I didn't," I mutter, unable to look away from her.

Suddenly, there are cards in her hand. I'm not sure if they were there before she took the stage, all I know is they are there now, and my heart is pounding as I wait with bated breath for her words.

"Our opening bid is for something money usually can't buy: total control over the winter formal. Pick any theme you want, any venue the budget allows, curate the playlist, and design the whole experience. This is a once-in-a-lifetime chance to throw the party everyone will remember. Bidding starts at one hundred dollars."

My eyes narrow as my knuckles rub against my jaw. *What is she doing?* Of all the words I expected to hear leaving her lips, those weren't them. Multiple hands shoot up, and I listen as the bidding quickly ticks up from interest.

"One thousand. Do I hear eleven hundred?" Her eyes scan the room, looking for more takers, until she says, "One thousand...and sold to Emma Morrison."

I cross my arms, believing I know exactly where this is going, until she announces the next item.

"Second item up for bid this evening is the chance to coordinate Legacy Trivia Night. This isn't just some school dance; this is *the* fundraiser that keeps Ridgewood competitive. Alumni fly in from across the country for this. Win this bid, and you're planning an event that raises six figures, impressing people who actually have the power to change your future. This would be incredible for your college application and even better for bragging rights. Trust me, this one's worth fighting for. Bidding starts at five hundred dollars."

My feet are moving the second the words "Legacy Trivia Night" leave her mouth. That's all it takes to figure out what she's doing. The winter formal alone is one thing, but now this? One of the most time-consuming but biggest honors at Ridgewood. She's not just auctioning off time. She's auctioning off *her* time. Time that would be spent with me.

I'm up the stage steps before I can think better of it, before Hollis can grab my arm, before anyone can stop me.

My hand reaches for the mic, covering the top. "What the hell are you doing?"

"Raising money," she says with a fake smile that doesn't reach her eyes.

"I didn't approve this," I say through clenched teeth.

"Maybe if you'd shown up yesterday—"

"What has gotten into you? Are you seriously that mad I asked you to help finish decorating?"

"We both know it's more than that," she says, as if her defiance should be obvious, as if I'm supposed to read her mind.

"Do we?"

Her jaw tightens. "I'm not doing this with you anymore. I should be president, not you."

The words hang between us for a moment. The crowd is starting to notice something's wrong, and whispers begin rippling through the room.

"Bidding starts at $500," she announces to the audience.

I lean into her ear. "You're right," I say.

"Excuse me?" She blinks, like I've just confessed to murder. "Twelve hundred. Do I hear thirteen?" She carries on like we aren't holding a very important conversation.

"I said you're right," I confirm it, watching her face.

She covers the mic. "So, you're admitting you cheated?" Then she removes her hand. "Do I hear fourteen hundred?"

"I didn't cheat."

"And now I'm bored. Get off the stage, Hale. We're done here."

I take the mic, ensuring I have her full attention. I cover it before saying, "You've been intent on making me the enemy since I arrived. Perhaps you should focus more on the company you keep. I'm a man of my word. If I say I didn't cheat, I didn't cheat."

Sure, I don't hate being stuck with her, but I didn't sabotage her. I did the opposite. When I was campaigning on her behalf, as she requested, I stumbled upon a conversation outside the library. Her so-called best friend and running mate was whispering with someone I couldn't see. Their voices were low, but I knew what I heard. '*We have to make sure Asha doesn't win this*,' followed by, '*The plan is already in motion*.' That's part of why I went to Headmaster Trejo with a proposal to reseat the VPs running our tickets and automatically give the position to the losing candidate. I could have told her, but I knew she wouldn't believe me, so I made my own moves and waited for her to discover what I already knew. However, she's been too busy painting me as the villain to see the knife aimed at her back from someone she actually trusts.

"And it wasn't you who put sugar in Penn's tank either."

The accusation hits like a slap, and my eyes widen in surprise as a glaring fact I didn't notice until just now makes itself seen. She's here alone. That fucker went through all that trouble last night to make a scene in front of the entire school to ask her to homecoming, and now he's a no-show. Dick.

"That's what this is about? You think I fucked with your little boy toy?"

"I don't think. I know."

Her eyes hold mine, and someone in the crowd yells out, "Two thousand," reminding me we are in the middle of an auction.

"Two thousand, one hundred," I raise the bet into the mic before once again covering it to ask, "And how do you know that?"

"Someone saw you."

"Who?" My head tilts to one side, genuinely curious since I know exactly where I was last night.

I was tired and had amends to make with my feisty pen pal, so after the game, I went straight back to my room, flopped on the bed, and hit send.

Captive Audience: I'm sorry about tonight. You have
no idea how much I want to be the hero in your story.

My pen pal and I talk more than our assignment requires, and I've admittedly become a fiend. This girl has me wrapped around her finger.

Academic Hostage: I'm not into heroes.

Captive Audience: Villains then?

Academic Hostage: Always the villain. What they say,
they do.

Captive Audience: Is that an invitation?

Academic Hostage: I want it to be.

I pushed my head into my pillow with a groan as I bit my bottom lip hard and then poked my bare foot out from beneath the sheet, took a picture, and sent another text.

Captive Audience: Should I get dressed then?

Academic Hostage: It's only 10 pm! I thought I was
the goody two-shoes in this relationship.

Academic Hostage: Will you be at the dance
tomorrow?

Captive Audience: Yes.

Academic Hostage: Don't Lose Your Phone.

There was no way I was coming to this dance without it. One, because she asked me to come, and two, because I'm ninety-five percent sure the dark, stormy eyes glaring back at me belong to my pen pal. Early on, she slipped in one of our very first text exchanges, mentioning an Indian dhol. I never said anything because I was new at school. It was possible that another student had the same ethnic background, but I did my research and read between the lines of every conversation since. It has to be her, which is another reason it's been too damn easy to fall. She may not want to break the rules, but I've never been a rule follower. I'd shatter every last one to have her. Consequences be damned.

"Emma."

I let out a sharp laugh, tongue in cheek. "Funny how the girl managing your campaign is the same eyewitness to my alleged vandalism. Maybe you should be asking yourself why the person you trust always seems to have her hands dirty when it comes to you. I have no motive to mess with Penn's car. I beat him fair and square, and his girl spends her free time thinking about me."

Her hand cracks across my face before I see it coming. The sound echoes across the now-silent dance hall.

"You're an ass," she breathes.

My cheek stings, but I don't touch it. Don't give her the satisfaction. "Sold to Preston Hughes." I hand her back the microphone and rub the stubble lining my jaw. "Always the villain," I quote the text I'm sure she sent to a nameless man I know she has feelings for. Technically, I'm not breaking any rules. I'm not giving anything away; I shouldn't. But if she is indeed the person I think she is, she'll hear my words for what they are. Her glossy lips roll, a small crease forming between her brows when I lean an inch closer and add, "I'm not the one who let you wear that dress alone tonight."

Her eyes flash with hurt, then fury, then something I can't quite read.

"For the record," I add, my voice dropping lower, "a little sugar wouldn't stop me."

She stares at me for a long moment, her chest rising and falling with barely controlled rage. As I turn to leave the stage, the entire hall is still quiet. My shoes echo against the stage floor, each step measured and controlled, even though my pulse is racing.

Always the villain. The moment those words left my mouth, I saw it, that split second where her eyes widened, where the possibility crashed into her. She'll spend tonight dissecting every word, every conversation, wondering if I'm him. If the person she's been texting, the one she actually opens up to, has been standing in front of her this whole time.

I reach the stairs, my jaw still tight.

Let her wonder how I know about that text. Let her replay this moment over and over, questioning everything. She wore that dress for someone she thought cared enough to show up, but he didn't. And now she's realizing maybe, just maybe, the person who actually noticed, who actually said something, was the last person she expected.

She'll lie awake tonight thinking about me. About us. About what's real and what's pretend in this war we've been waging. We're enemies. We have to be. Because admitting anything else would change everything. She'd have to admit she not only remembers me, but we'd have to talk about the day I'll never forget—one I'm still uncertain if she remembers or is determined to erase.

In the silence at my back, I can't help but wonder if it's all clicking into place. She won't take it all back, but maybe she'll extend an olive branch and end this nonsense auction. The girl I once knew would have.

"The last lot of time up for auction tonight is a week of private polo lessons from the star of last night's polo match, Trigger Hale. Bidding starts at five hundred dollars."

I shake my head. I should have known. Not an olive branch. No one wants my time.

Hollis is at my side before I make it to the exit. "The dance sucked anyway," he tries to make light of what just happened.

"You're not leaving with me. Stay." I hear someone actually bet on me, and I add, "Win that lot, and when you go to pay, put Asha's name on the ticket."

He runs a hand through his hair. "Trigg, she's my cousin. I can't hurt her like that." My eyes hold his in silent challenge. We've been close since I arrived at Ridgewood. Out of people who truly know me, not just here but in life, he's one. I shouldn't need to defend my character to him. He should know without words that I wouldn't hurt someone he cares about, so I wait.

He concedes with an exasperated sigh before turning on his heel, and I exit the hall. Tonight, I gave her enough pieces to start seeing the truth. Tonight, I changed the game.

ASHA

CHAPTER 5

JUNIOR YEAR

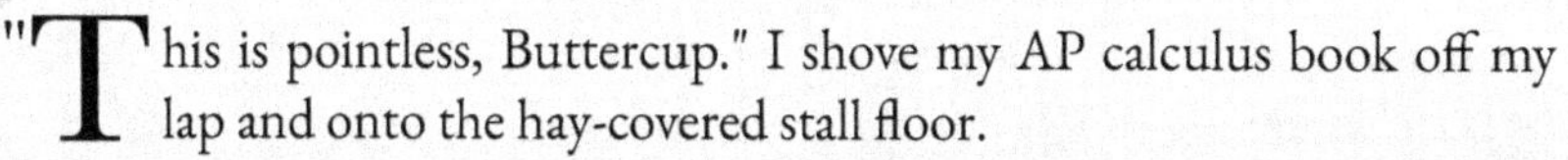

"This is pointless, Buttercup." I shove my AP calculus book off my lap and onto the hay-covered stall floor.

The past few months have been a mess. After homecoming, I was convinced my pen pal was the one person I couldn't stand, someone wrapped in memories I didn't want to touch. I stopped responding and considered failing the project rather than knowing I'd been confiding in him.

However, when I cut contact, I started noticing things about Eldridge, small habits, phrases, references to things I'd never shared with him. He appeared right when the texts dried up. It seemed pretty clear: Eldridge was the guy on the other end of my texts. Or at least that was what I thought until a few days ago, when I discovered what was really going on. It's why I'm hiding at the stables instead of my dorm. I can't face Emma.

I was cutting through the courtyard behind Hill House when I heard voices drifting from the shadowed alcove near the service entrance. I almost kept walking, but then I recognized Emma's laugh—not just any laugh, the one she makes when she's nervous. I slowed, ready to rescue her from an uncomfortable situation. Instead, I caught her in a lie.

"I can't believe I let you talk me into this, Eldridge." Emma's voice was *strained.*

"You love me. Stop acting like this is so terrible. It's a white lie. Harm-

less. You know I'm not going to hurt her, otherwise you wouldn't be helping me," Eldridge answered confidently.

"We both know that's not why I'm helping you," she hissed back.

I should have kept walking. Emma and Eldridge got into arguments all the time, and this sounded like another one of their endless sibling fights, but just as I was about to continue walking, Eldridge's response stopped me cold in my tracks.

"Make sure when you put this back on her nightstand, you check the picture. If the cord isn't exactly as she left it, she'll know."

I could feel the heat in my cheeks as my anger instantly skyrocketed. Sure, I was betrayed, but even worse than that, I was made a fool. Emma had gone behind my back again, and I still couldn't figure out why. I kept playing the friend, kept showing up, and kept pretending I didn't know because her betrayals didn't add up. They were scattered, inconsistent, like pieces from different puzzles forced together, and you couldn't fight what you didn't understand. It was why I stayed.

"What are you going to do senior year when the other person on the end of that phone is revealed and it isn't you?"

"It won't get that far. I just need to get close. I need her to see me, and since we both know she wouldn't risk asking me directly because doing so would mean failing the assignment, we won't get caught," he argued.

"I don't know, Eldridge. She really likes the person on the other end of those texts, and if she decides to start texting him again—"

I never told her I had feelings for my pen pal, but it was yet another detail that proved I was even failing at maintaining a fake friendship. Just being in my orbit, she was privy to every flicker of emotion that crossed my face when I'd respond to messages.

"She'll be in love with me by then."

"And how do you plan on getting her actual boyfriend out of the way?"

"Who, Penn?" he chuckled. "She's not into him. He's a beard."

That was it. The last straw, not because I was offended for Penn, but because I was tired of being made a fool. I stepped around the corner, closed the distance, and held out my hand.

"I think you have something that belongs to me," I said, my tone void of any emotion.

Eldridge looked defeated and held onto to a sliver of dignity by not offering me fake apologies. Emma, however, has been blowing up my phone and waiting by my door all week. That's why I've stayed away.

Being around Buttercup always soothes me, so after our show this evening, instead of heading back to my dorm room to study, I stayed with her in the stables. Taking my time, I brushed her coat, cleaned her hooves, gave her fresh water and a banana for getting us in first place at tonight's competition. You'd think that would be enough to clear my head, but it isn't. The minutes I'm not unraveling Emma's deception, I'm thinking about Penn Hadley.

After Penn ditched me at homecoming, I wrote him off. As much as I hate admitting it, Trigger was right—someone truly interested would've shown up. And truth be told, in hindsight, a big reason I said yes to Penn that night was because I knew it would get under Trigger's skin. There were too many stolen glances during that game for it not to. Plus, dating someone from another school had its perks: it kept the guys at my school at a distance, which was exactly what I wanted.

The problem was, the following weekend on our off-campus day, Penn showed up with purple flowers he thought were my favorite, but he got the species wrong. Purple wisteria is my favorite. My mother loved them so much that she planted them all over the property. They were her favorite, and for that reason, they are mine too. Then he took me to a five-star Indian restaurant he'd rented out for two hours. We cooked alongside their master chef, and I learned to make my father's favorite dish: chicken tikka masala. My mother's recipe. One of the last dishes we made together before she died.

Penn didn't know how important that day would become. He only knew what I'd told him once: I'd like to learn to cook authentic Indian cuisine for my dad. Working with the chef, I discovered what I'd been missing—the pizza oven. My mother always cooked it that way. Traditional tikka needs a scorching-hot clay oven for that charred flavor.

That day, Penn notched himself into my heart. He gave me back a piece of my mom I thought I'd lost forever.

"That's it. It has to be," I say to Buttercup. "I don't have deep feelings for Penn. I love what he was able to give me." I grab my book from the floor and set it on the ledge of the door before getting the broom.

I've spent too much time cataloging what he makes me feel and what's conspicuously missing. I've been obsessing over all the things I want to feel and don't because I wanted him to be the one making me feel them. But when I close my eyes at night, it's not him I'm kissing, and when I dream, it's not his eyes staring back at me. His touch isn't the one setting my soul on fire.

A branch breaking followed by the faint sound of a hushed whisper outside the barn steals my attention. It's 10:30 p.m., and the stables are located at the back of the property. There is no reason students should be back here unless they are coming to the barn. I slowly set the broom against the stall, my heart now racing as I realize that I'm utterly alone, at night, too far away from any other building for anyone to hear me scream.

The whisper comes again, low and definitely human. My mouth goes dry. Behind me, Buttercup shifts in her stall, and the creak of wood sounds deafening in the sudden silence I'm straining against. Every horror story I've ever heard about girls being alone at night flashes through my mind. *Stop it. Stop.*

But my hands are shaking as I inch toward Buttercup's window, careful to keep my body pressed against the wall and out of sight. The old floorboards protest under my feet, and I freeze, certain whoever's out there must have heard. My pulse pounds so hard I can feel it in my fingertips as I hold my breath and peer through the window.

Nothing. Just the dark paddock stretching toward the tree line. Then, a glint of light in the moonlight catches my eye. Reflective tape. The kind Headmaster Trejo made mandatory after a student nearly got hit by the groundskeeper's truck. Relief crashes over me. Just a student sneaking around after curfew.

But then the figure moves, and my relief crystallizes into something else. I know that walk, the slight hitch in the left stride, the hunched shoulders. I've seen it a thousand times across the dining hall, on the way to polo practice.

"Hollis?" I whisper.

My cousin. Why is he sneaking through the woods at 10:30 at night, wearing that stupid reflective jacket?

The relief I feel spirals into confusion then curiosity. Hollis doesn't sneak. He doesn't break rules, which is probably why he didn't think to change jackets. He doesn't skulk through the woods in the dark, until now.

I watch him pause near a twisted oak, looking left then right before continuing deeper. He's heading toward the old access road, the one that leads to the maintenance buildings and the back gate.

He's moving faster now, with purpose. In seconds, he'll be out of sight. Every rational instinct tells me to let it go, finish my work, head back to the dorm, and pretend I saw nothing. But he's my cousin. We've been at this boarding school together since we were kids. What could be so important that Hollis would risk breaking curfew?

"This is stupid. Mind your own business, Asha," I scold, but I'm already reaching for my jacket. I grab my phone and slip out the barn door.

At the fence, I pause. The woods are a solid wall of black, and those stupid horror movies scream at me once more, *Turn around!* But then I see another flash up ahead, and I duck through the fence rails.

The darkness swallows me. I can't see him, but I hear him crunching leaves and snapping twigs. He's not trying to be quiet anymore; he's rushing. My eyes adjust, and I can make out his silhouette on a narrow path ahead. I'm a few yards behind him when he stops. I freeze, pressing myself against the nearest tree, sure he must have heard me, but he doesn't turn around. Instead, he's looking at something ahead.

A light flickers between the trees, and this time, it's not reflective tape. It's real lights—headlights. My breath catches when I see the vehicle crawling down the old access road, moving slowly with its lights on low, navigating the old path. It rolls to a stop in front of Hollis, and I recognize it immediately: a Bronco. Trigger Hale.

My fear is quickly replaced with anger. Of all the people Hollis could be sneaking out to meet, it has to be him. *What the hell is Hollis doing meeting up with him?*

Hollis is a good kid. He doesn't get into trouble, but here he is, standing in the woods at almost eleven at night, waiting for Trigger Hale like they've done this before.

I watch as the driver's side door opens, and Trigger's unmistakable frame emerges, all lean muscle and cocky confidence, even in the dark. He says something to Hollis; I can't hear the words, but I can hear the casual tone, as if this is completely normal.

Hollis moves toward the passenger side, his hand reaching for the door handle. And that's when I make a snap decision. *No. Absolutely not.*

I don't know what they're planning, but I'm not letting Hollis get pulled into whatever scheme Trigger has going. Hollis could get expelled. He could get hurt, and I'm not standing here watching it happen.

Before I can second-guess myself, I'm out of the woods, my hand pulling open the back door, before I slide across the backseat and ask, "Where are we going?"

Hollis whips around, his face draining of color even in the dim glow of the headlights. "What the hell?"

Trigger turns too, but his face isn't marred with shock. Instead, there's nothing but annoyance. "WE..." he emphasizes the word, "aren't going anywhere. Get out, Fairfield."

"If Hollis is going, so am I. I'm not going to let you take him off grounds and get him in trouble," I say plainly.

"You realize we've been going off grounds together once a month on our free days since freshman year," he points out smugly.

My eyes narrow on his, hating that he makes a valid point, but this is different. "You just made a case against yourself. This isn't a free day; this is the middle of the night. And the fact that the two of you are sneaking around proves you're up to no good."

"Fine." Trigger turns to Hollis. "Get out."

"What? No, I'm going. He's my—"

"She can't go," he cuts him off, his glare piercing through Hollis as they share something unspoken that I don't like.

This thing between me and Trigger doesn't need to involve my cousin. "Even if you kick him out, I'm still going. I'm not getting out."

"Oh, I can get you out." Trigger's eyes catch mine in the review mirror.

"And when you do, I'll head straight to Headmaster Trejo and fill him in on your little night ride," I say with my own sweet arrogance.

He's quiet, clearly weighing my words with his options. I don't know what they are up to, but it's possible they scratch it altogether. Hollis runs a hand through his hair and presses his head against the seat rest. I can tell whatever this is, it's important to him, and my curiosity is thoroughly piqued.

"You know what your problem is?" Trigger's eyes lock onto mine in the mirror, dark and cutting. "You think being a pain in everyone's ass makes you useful. Like, if you're annoying enough, people will mistake it for actually giving a shit. But it doesn't make you useful; it just makes you someone we have to deal with."

His words are unexpected. They're sharper than he probably realizes, and they cut deep. I've been left to make numerous assumptions over the years. Assumptions about why I'm here and not at home. I mean, technically, I know why I was sent here, but right now, it feels like he knows too. But then the static ringing in my ears as my panic starts to rise reminds me that no one knows, and I'm letting my insecurity show.

I fake bravado before leaning one elbow onto each captain's seat with a confidence I certainly don't feel. "That was a low blow. Didn't your mother ever teach you any manners?"

"Nah, she didn't want me," he says, one hand tightening around the steering wheel as the other shifts the car into drive with a force that almost drowns out Hollis's groan, but the look of disappointment he shoots me tells me I unknowingly hit back with equal measure. But how?

"Asha," Hollis says my name, his voice heavy with annoyance, regret, and apology that I can tell isn't for me. "Please, just for tonight, let it go." Then, turning, he adds, "This is important."

I hear his words, but it's the plea in his eyes that has me folding. I give him a subtle nod and sink back into the seat, swallowing my protest. Hollis is family, and he's never asked for anything. Until now. So, I'll bend. Besides, my problem isn't with him. It's with the man gripping the steering wheel.

Since homecoming last year, there has been a noticeable shift between me and Trigger. I hit a nerve with my move that night, auctioning off all my time so he no longer had control of it. The move was one I think he had to applaud. He knows me more than I'd like to admit, so I don't think it surprised him. Instead, it was my words that drove the stake between us. His taunting, playful smirk was gone, replaced with a scowl reserved only for me. I get it. I accused him of something I know he didn't do. But to be fair, when I said it, I didn't know I was wrong. However, I also never apologized.

"How did you get your Bronco past the campus security guard anyway?" I ask as we start down the dark rocky path, trying to climb out of whatever icy tomb I stepped into with my last comment.

"We parked it on the old path on the last free day and told them it broke down and was in the shop."

"Why would you tell her that? The more you say, the more she has against us when this all blows up in our faces."

"Wrong. I wouldn't rat out my cousin—just you," I answer, my tone dripping with fake honey.

I watch in the rearview mirror as Trigger keeps his eyes focused on the dark road ahead, but I don't miss the way he runs his tongue over his teeth, like he has something more he wants to say but is choosing not to. The victory feels hollow before it even settles. I've made a career out of needling him, finding the exact words that'll burrow under his skin. But this time, I went too far, and I know it. His comment hurt, but what I said back...that wasn't just a jab. That was a knife, and I twisted it.

"Keep an eye on her. She's your responsibility tonight," Trigger says, not even acknowledging my presence with a glance, which is new. Even when he's mad, his gaze lingers, but not tonight. Not after what I said.

"I can take care of myself," I call out to his back as he disappears into the crowd.

"Where are we?" I ask Hollis as I try to figure out why all these people have gathered at what appears to be an old abandoned farm. There's an almost dilapidated barn about one hundred feet away, a few bonfires, and people gathered around a paddock.

"You'll see," he says as he pulls his wallet out and thumbs his finger over a wad of cash.

"Hollis," I hiss. "What are you doing with all that cash? Are you trying to get jumped?"

"No." He pulls out the wad and taps a guy wearing a black suede vest on the shoulder. "Five hundred on Hale."

The man takes his money and gives him a slip before tipping his hat.

"Explain," I demand.

"You'll see soon enough. Come on." He grabs my elbow. "Let's get a good spot."

People wandered through the night around us, barely visible until they passed close enough to catch the moonlight. We pushed through to the front, and I blinked as floodlights snapped on, bathing everything in white light. An old paddock stretched before us, weathered wood and rusted metal, and at the far end, guys were dressed in riding gear and protective vests. I watched one adjust a rope around his gloved hand, and my stomach dropped. Bull riders.

"We shouldn't be here," I said, taking a step back. "This is illegal."

"No, it's not." Hollis dismisses my comment with a tsk, as though it's completely baseless, and leans against the cool bars of the arena, utterly relaxed. "Bull riding isn't illegal."

"Then why does this place feel so sketchy?" I look around at the crumbling structures surrounding the arena. "And why is it so late at night?"

"It's the only time we could make it work, so the organizers worked around our schedule."

My eyes scan the far side of the arena, and my breath hitches. There, across the paddock, adjusting his vest and rolling his shoulders is Trigger. The one person I've spent months trying not to think about, trying not to notice in the hallways, trying to convince myself I don't feel anything for. And he's suited up to ride.

"You know he's at Ridgewood because his dad sent him away for this, right?" I turned to Hollis. "He could get in so much trouble if he gets caught."

"Then I guess you better not tell." Hollis faces me, something knowing in his eyes. "I think we both know something more than bull riding landed him at that school."

I stare blankly back at him. Hearing it said out loud makes it real in a way my private suspicions never did. Of all the schools in the country that would've taken a Hale, his father chose Ridgewood. Mine. Two kids from the same small town in Kentucky, two feuding ranches. In the eight years I'd been gone, surely Mr. Hale got wind of where I was sent and why. So, why would he send his son, the boy responsible for my departure, to the school I was exiled to? You don't put your enemy's daughter and your own son under the same roof by accident. Someone wanted us here, and I've often wondered if that someone is the person here with me.

"It won't matter if he gets hurt." The words came out sharper than I intended, panic laced with something else creeping into my voice. "How are you guys going to explain that to the headmaster?"

"Now you sound like you care." Hollis quirks a suspicious brow.

"I don't—"

"You know Headmaster Trejo put him on the polo team specifically because of the bull riding that landed him at Ridgewood." He turns back to the paddock. "His dad doesn't want him bull riding, but the kid is good. That's why Trejo put him on the team. He knew he'd be a natural."

"I wonder if he'll still appreciate his bull riding skills if he can't play in the match this weekend," I say, not to be snarky but to point out a very real fact. This is serious. They can't sneak their way out of this if it all goes sideways.

My eyes drift back to Trigger, the way he moves confidently, controlled, like he belongs in that gear more than he ever did in a pressed Ridgewood uniform. I imagine him on the back of a bull, imagine the raw power beneath him, the way his body would move with it. And then I imagine him thrown, trampled, and my chest tightens. I don't want to care. Don't want to feel this pull toward someone who infuriates me, who challenges me, who looks at me like he can see right through every wall I've built. However, watching him now, knowing what he is about to do, I can't push the feelings down.

"What did he mean earlier on the ride over about his mom?" The question tumbles out, a desperate attempt to distract myself, to replace the fear with something else. "When he said 'she didn't want me'?"

Hollis hangs his head. "That was a shit comment you made, Asha."

"It was not. That's a common phrase. Lots of people say, 'Didn't your momma teach you manners?'"

He shakes his head slowly. "Maybe so, but he doesn't have a mom."

I swallow hard, my throat suddenly tight. "I didn't know."

I'm starting to realize there's a lot I don't know about Trigger Hale. In the beginning, I didn't care. I didn't want to know. Knowing left room for understanding. My dad told me he was the enemy, and he needed to stay that way, especially after all that he took from me.

"Tonight is important. It's worth the risk. Hopefully, he doesn't get hurt. There's a lot of money on him tonight."

"So, are you going to explain it to me now?"

"Remember, Jermey Cantu?" My brow furrows as I try to place a face with the name. "The kid who climbed to the top of that oak tree in sixth grade, and the fire department had to come and get him down."

"Oh yeah... He was always in the computer lab. I'm terrible with names."

"This ride is for him. His mom had a heart attack at the beginning of summer and lost most of her cognitive and physical abilities. She has had to relearn how to talk, move her body, and think rationally. The medical bills are now drowning the family. If Hale wins, he's donating the pot to the Cantu family."

"Why don't we set up a fundraiser at school?"

"That was the first thing Trigger tried to do, but not only was Jermey attending Ridgewood as a scholarship recipient, he's not enrolled this semester at the school, so he's technically not even a student. He's home-schooling this year so he can stay home and help with his mother's reha-bilitation."

"We raise money for charities all the time. There's no reason we can't raise money for one of our own," I say, my tone piqued with irritation.

"I don't know all the details. All I know is we are here tonight because other shit fell through."

I look around the crowd with a little more care this time, and I see a few students from Ridgewood. Trigger is one of the riders and probably one of the organizers, which is why this event had to be held so late. They had to sneak out.

This time, when I look across the arena, my eyes connect with his. His face is impassive. Gone is the cocky smirk and the challenging glare we've perfected over the past two years. It almost feels like a distant memory, because in his eyes is something else. Something that reminds me of summer all those years ago, before everything fell apart, before I learned to hate him to keep from feeling anything else.

Now, instead of feeling nothing, I find myself looking into the eyes of the boy I once saved and offered friendship, the boy I once cared about before I knew caring could hurt. A whole new feeling starts to surface. Regret. He didn't take from me; my grudge is doing that all on its own.

His lips part, like he might say something, and I find myself pulling in a stuttered breath, but then the crowd erupts, and my attention is jerked toward the arena as the first rider bursts from the chute.

The bull barrels into the center of the paddock, a mass of twisting muscle and rage. The rider's arm whips above his head, his other hand locked in the rope. The bull spins hard to the left, then kicks its back legs up with brutal force. The rider's body snaps forward, his chest nearly hitting the animal's shoulders, but somehow, he pulls himself back, his core fighting to keep him centered.

The bull spins in a tight circle, faster than something that size should be able to move, and the rider's body swings wide. His grip is slipping, and I can see it in the desperate way his fingers claw at the rope, the way his whole body has shifted too far to one side.

Three seconds. Four.

This time, when the bull kicks, the rider can't recover. His hand rips free of the rope, and he flies sideways through the air, hitting the ground hard on his shoulder. The bull spins toward him immediately, and my heart stops, but the bullfighters are already there, waving and shouting, drawing the animal away.

The crowd roars, and the rider rolls to his feet, clutching his shoulder as he limps toward the gate. Shit. That's going to be Trigger.

The arena falls silent as they prepare the next chute. Trigger climbs onto the rails with an ease that makes my stomach flip. From here, I can see the definition in his arms as he grips the metal, the way his shoulders roll when he settles himself. He's strong—stronger than I realized. Not bulky, but solid muscle, lean and powerful. He's not that much bigger than the rider who went before him, but there's something different in the way he moves. Something deliberate. He's not up there for the sport of it.

Sure, the charity money is on the line—Hollis said as much. But watching him now, the way he tests the rope, the way his jaw sets as he slides down onto the bull's back, I understand. Bull riding isn't something he does. It's in him. Part of him. Like breathing.

The announcer's voice crackles over the speaker, but I don't hear the words. My eyes are locked on him as he nods once, sharp and certain, and the gate explodes open.

The bull launches into the arena, and my breath catches. It's massive, bigger than the first one. It twists hard right out of the chute, but Trigger moves with it, his body anticipating the shift. His free arm stays high and controlled, not windmilling like the first rider. His hips stay centered even as the bull bucks and spins. He's locked in.

The animal drops its head and kicks viciously, but he doesn't snap forward. He leans back into it, using the momentum, and somehow manages to stay on. The bull spins left, then right, trying to throw him off balance, but he reads every movement like he's inside the animal's head.

Three seconds. Four.

He's making it almost look easy, and I know it's not. I just watched another rider get rag-dolled by a smaller bull. But he's still up there, so focused, like nothing exists except him and the animal beneath him.

Five seconds. Six. Seven.

The crowd is screaming now, on their feet. Even Hollis is yelling beside me, but I can't make a sound. My heart is in my throat, pounding so hard it hurts.

Eight seconds.

The buzzer blares, and the crowd goes wild. He's done it, set the record to beat for the night, but he doesn't let go yet. The bull is still bucking, still furious, and he waits for the right moment, the safe moment. Then he releases the rope and pushes off. When he hits the ground, he takes off running, already moving toward the rails, but the bull is faster. It pivots, rear legs kicking out, and catches Trigger square in the chest. The impact sends him sprawling backward into the dirt.

"No!" The word rips out of me before I can stop it.

The bullfighters are there instantly, bodies between him and the bull, drawing it away with shouts and waves. He's on his hands and knees in the dirt, head down, and he's not moving.

My hands grip the cool metal of the arena bars so tight they ache. Hollis is yelling something, but I can't hear him over the roaring in my ears. *Get up*, I think desperately. *Get up.*

One of the bullfighters crouches beside him, hand on his shoulder. And then, finally, he pushes himself up slowly. His hand goes to his chest, and even from here I can see him wince. But he's standing and walking toward the gate.

The crowd erupts again, louder this time, and he raises one hand to acknowledge he's okay, but I can see the tightness in his jaw, the way he's breathing too carefully.

"He's fine," Hollis says beside me, but his voice sounds uncertain. "He's walked off worse."

I can't look away. Can't stop my hands from shaking where they grip the bars. Can't stop the flood of relief and terror and...something else—

something I've been trying so hard not to feel—from crashing over me all at once.

The crowd starts to disperse as the next rider gets ready, but I can't move. My eyes track him as he disappears through a gate on the far side of the arena, one hand still pressed to his chest.

"I need to use the bathroom," I say suddenly.

Hollis glances at me. "Now?"

"Yeah, now. Unless you want me to go in the dirt like everyone else here seems comfortable with."

He snorts. "There's a building behind the main barn. Can't promise it's clean."

I'm already walking, weaving through clusters of people, my heart still hammering. I don't know what I'm doing. Don't know why my feet are carrying me toward the back of the arena instead of toward any bathroom.

The area behind the chutes is darker, less crowded. A few riders mill around, and I spot him immediately, leaning against a post, his vest hanging open, breathing shallow. There's dirt streaked across his cheek, his hair a mess from the helmet. I've always known Trigger was attractive in that infuriating way that made hating him more complicated than it should be. But this is different. Maybe it's the adrenaline still coursing through me or the panic that gripped me when I thought he might not get up. Whatever it is, I can't stop staring at the way his chest rises and falls, the exposed skin at his throat where his shirt collar's torn, or the flex of his forearm as he grips the post for support. He looks wrecked and alive and utterly unaware of what watching him almost break did to me. My pulse hasn't settled when he sees me coming.

"Come to tell me how stupid that was?" he says, wincing as he attempts to stand straighter.

"Yeah, actually." I stop a few feet away, crossing my arms. "That was incredibly stupid."

"Noted." His jaw tightens as he shifts his weight. "You can go now."

"Are you hurt?"

"I'm fine."

"You don't look fine. You look like you got kicked by a two-thousand-pound animal."

"Seventeen hundred, actually." The corner of his mouth twitches, that insufferable almost-smirk. "And I said I'm fine."

I take a step closer, and his expression shifts as he starts to place his guard up. "What are you doing, Asha?"

"Making sure you're not about to collapse and make this my problem." I move closer still, until I'm right in front of him. Close enough to see the tightness around his eyes and the way his breathing falters as I close in. "Let me see."

"It's just a bruise," he attempts one last time to stop my advances.

"Then you won't mind showing me."

I want to be a vet. I've known since I was a little girl that's how I wanted to contribute to the family business. I also know animals and humans are two completely different species, but I'm certain I can diagnose a broken rib or, God forbid, an internal injury that needs immediate attention. He stares at me for a long moment then sighs and lifts the edge of his shirt. Even in the dim light, I can see the angry red mark spreading across his ribs, already darkening.

"You're an idiot," I whisper. And then, before I can think better of it, before I can remember all the reasons I'm supposed to hate him, I step forward and wrap my arms around him. Carefully. So carefully. My arms slide around his waist, avoiding the injured side, and I press my face against his shoulder.

He goes completely still. "Asha—"

"Shut up." My voice comes out muffled against his shirt. "I'm making sure you didn't crack a rib. If you collapse later, Hollis will blame me."

"That's not..." He stops. His hands hover at my sides, not sure what to do with them. "You're checking for broken ribs by hugging me?"

"Do you have a better method? Should I poke at it? Press on it?"

"God, no." His hands finally settle, one at my lower back, one between my shoulder blades. His heart is racing under my ear. "This is... this is fine. Hug me. Hug me until I smell like you."

"Did you hit your head?" I ask, and I feel him huff something between a laugh and a breath. He was wearing his helmet. This is something else.

"Maybe," he answers softly.

We stand there in the shadows, and I can feel him breathing, feel the rise and fall of his chest. He smells like dirt and sweat and something else, something that makes me want to hold on tighter.

"You scared me," I say quietly before I can stop myself.

His hand moves slightly against my back. "Yeah?"

I pull away. His words, his touch, all of it overwhelming me. The cool air rushes between us. "Because if you'd gotten seriously hurt, Hollis could have gotten in trouble for being an accomplice."

He's looking at me with something unreadable in his eyes. "Right. Of course."

"And because Headmaster Trejo would probably expel you, and then I'd be student body president by default, and I don't want a handout. That would be worse."

"Much worse," he agrees softly.

"So don't do it again."

"The bull riding or scaring you?"

"Both." I'm backing away now, putting more distance between us. "Just...be more careful."

His hand is still pressed to his ribs, but he's smiling now. Really smiling. "I'll try."

"Whatever." I turn to go then stop. "Ice it. And don't tell Hollis I came back here."

"Wouldn't dream of it, sweetheart."

I make it three steps before reality hits me. None of those reasons were why I came back here. Not Hollis, not my spot on student council, none of them were even close. I came back because seeing him on the ground scared me in a way I can't afford to examine, which means I'm in serious trouble.

TRIGGER

CHAPTER 6

JUNIOR YEAR

A muted ding has me groaning as I twist, forgetting my ribs, even though I've covered my torso in kinesiology tape, but it can't be helped. It's been almost a year since I last heard that specific tone, and the last time I heard it, the message was clear.

> Academic Hostage: I HATE TRIGGER HALE.

We were done. I received that message after I'd left the dance; the writing was on the wall. If there was any question before, there wasn't then. Asha was, in fact, who I thought she was: my pen pal. While she's never once brought it up or even hinted at the possibility, she didn't need to. Her silence was answer enough. So, why is she breaking it now?

I stare in the direction of my nightstand, where my school-issued phone has been sitting on the charger for months, untouched, and my mind flicks back to the charity ride. She came looking for me, and then she hugged me. Her gentle touch, the hug, her scent. All of it has consumed my every thought since she walked away, because it felt like something had finally flipped. But after the words I gave her in the truck, I couldn't imagine what. I was harsh, but the way she's been riding me since I arrived at school, the weight of that night, and then her comment about my manners, I couldn't help myself. The girl she's been toward me is not the girl I remember. It's not the one I've carelessly let myself fall for before I ever even saw her again.

> Academic Hostage: My mother passed away when I was seven.

I stare at the message. Of all the words I thought I might see, these weren't it. It's no secret that Warrick Fairfield is widowed. Her mother's death made him one of the most eligible bachelors not only back home but in the country. His face has graced more than one headline. I don't know all the details surrounding her mother's death. All I know is she died young.

I could say I'm sorry, but I don't think that's what Asha wants to hear. She's not someone who seeks sympathy. She would never want someone to feel sorry for her.

> Captive Audience: I'm here if you want to talk about it.

> Academic Hostage: I never got to say goodbye.

I exhale a long breath I hadn't realized I was even holding as my chest aches for the little girl who went out of her way to stand up for me all those years ago. We didn't talk about her mother that day, but I'm sure her strength that day came from a strong woman who raised a strong girl.

I have questions I want to ask. Was her death sudden? How did she die? But none of that feels right. My thumbs hover over the keys. I want to support her through this, but I'm unsure how. I don't have a mom either.

> Captive Audience: Why weren't you able to say goodbye?

> Academic Hostage: There was an accident at school when I was younger, and my father sent me away.

"Fuck." I grip my phone so hard the case starts to come undone. The accident was my fault. I'm the reason she fell. The reason her father sent her away. The reason she lost time with her mother. ME.

I push off the mattress and start pacing. There are a million things I want to say to her, starting with I'm so fucking sorry. I never asked her to come to my aid. She was my savior that day, and I became her destroyer. No wonder she fucking hates me. I'd hate me too.

I rake a hand through my hair and stop to stare blankly out my window. Every fight we've had, every cutting remark, every time she's looked at me like I'm something she scraped off her boot...it all makes sense now. She's still the same girl she was back then; the only difference is that it turns out she had a reason for hating me now. A damn good one. What the hell am I supposed to say now?

Captive Audience: Why are you telling me this?

Academic Hostage: I wanted you to know.

I stare at the screen, her words burning into my brain. She wanted me to know. Not to make me feel guilty, but because she needed me to understand. The weight of what she just gave me settles in my chest. She could've kept hating me from a distance and let me stay ignorant, but instead she gave me a hard truth. I'm sure of nothing except that wanting her has just become infinitely more complicated, and walking away has just become impossible. I don't know how to fix what I broke, but I'm sure as hell going to try, starting with figuring out how to turn my enemy into something more, even if she fights me every step of the way.

"WHAT ARE YOU DOING AFTER THE GAME TONIGHT?" LAYONI asks, rushing to my side as I get off the bus.

One of the reasons I agreed to play polo for Ridgewood, aside from the fact that Headmaster Trejo didn't offer me another option, was that sports allowed us to leave campus more frequently than the once-per-month free day non-athletes were afforded. It's been good to get away. The only downside has been Layoni. She's a nice girl, but I seem to be her new obsession, and that's been a thorn in my side, considering she's the coach's niece and I'm not interested. It's her title that affords her the luxury of attending these games.

"I have a lot of studying to catch up on. We put in extra hours this week, knowing we need to win tonight to clinch our seat at regionals."

"Well, maybe I can help you study," she offers in a suggestive tone as she brushes against my arm, and I awkwardly shrug away.

"Sorry, I'm a little sore," I say, not wanting to hurt her feelings.

"I'm sure I can help with that too," she offers as a ping from my duffel bag saves me from another uncomfortable response.

"I have to get this," I say as I fumble through my bag.

> Academic Hostage: Do you ever just want to end it? Be done. Set it all on fire and revel in the burn until all that's left is silence.

My eyes practically bulge out of my head as my heart starts racing.

> Captive Audience: What the hell are you talking about? Where are you? I'm coming now.

"Is everything okay? You look pale," Layoni says as I stop dead in my tracks and look around for Coach. I have to get back to school.

"No, I'm—"

Another text steals my words.

> Academic Hostage: Does that mean you know who I am?

I take a deep breath and attempt to calm my racing heart as I try to keep her talking. If she's talking to me, I can keep her mind busy until I can get to her.

> Captive Audience: Are you saying you don't know who I am?

"I need to find Coach," I say to Layoni as I start walking faster toward the stalls beside the field, hoping to find him.

"He goes to the announcer's box before every game," she says as her fingers wind through mine, and she pulls me toward the stands and tents.

I look down at my phone, waiting for a response. Dots appear, but then they're gone in a blink.

"Shit," I curse.

> Captive Audience: Answer me or I'll break the rules.
> Consequences be damned. I'm way past caring if
> you hate me.

I almost broke them last night. It's killing me not to cross campus and apologize for being the reason she lost any time with her mother. I'm trying so hard to stay in my lane, to let her lead. I stopped trying to insert myself in her life after the dance. I let her date her douchebag boyfriend and keep her shitty best friend because Asha is a smart girl. If I see the bullshit, so does she. I might know things first, but she doesn't leave a stone unturned. If she's allowing it, she's choosing it.

You don't win Asha Fairfield by bending her to your will. She'll fight you tooth and nail, because the thing is, she doesn't need a man. She's a force on her own. You win Asha Fairfield by making her want you.

> Academic Hostage: I'm just mad and over
> pretending.

> Captive Audience: Pretending?

"Hey, there's Asha and Hollis. Maybe they saw Coach walk by."

"Asha's here?" The words burst out before I can stop them, too loud and too eager. Shock and relief flood through me in equal measure, and for a split second, I forget to guard my expression, forget that Layoni is right beside me, watching.

Her head turns toward me, and I catch the curious sidelong glance she gives me.

I clear my throat. "Let's see if they saw Coach," I say, aiming for nonchalance. I start walking in their direction, forcing my pace to stay measured when everything in me wants to sprint. "I need to catch him before he leaves."

It only takes about five more paces before Asha does a double take, her eyes locking onto me headed straight for her with Layoni in step beside me. Even from this distance, I catch the way her expression hardens. She rolls her eyes, a gesture so pointed it feels like a slap to the face, as she turns back to Hollis. It's seconds like this that make me doubt the one percent chance my pen pal is indeed Asha Fairfield, because how do you go from texting me in a time of need, even if it's just to vent, to glaring at me with enough hate that it feels like a physical blow?

I don't even realize my hand is in Layoni's until she squeezes it. Shit. I was too focused on the phone, too focused on finding the girl who's now right in front of me. I extract myself and rake my fingers through my hair when Hollis glances over his shoulder. His gaze is dismissive, already back on Asha, before I can even process what I see in it.

He's talking with his hands, which means he's pissed. It doesn't take much to rile him up, so the fact that he is has my stomach dropping. *What the hell is going on?*

"Oh, that's why she's here," Layoni says beside me, unaware of the knot tightening in my chest. "She's filling in for Milli on the yearbook committee. She's laid up in bed with mono."

I follow Layoni's line of sight and suddenly notice the camera hanging around Asha's neck. There's a strap cutting across her collarbone, and the lens cap is dangling. The distance between us closes, and I step up to them. There's silence, the tension so thick it's almost suffocating. Now that I'm in front of them, I can see Hollis's cheeks are reddened, evidence of his anger.

"Is everything alright?" I ask, my gaze flicking between them.

Asha crosses her arms, and Hollis clenches his fists at his sides, his eyes locked on her as she looks toward the field. "Everything is fine," he grinds out.

"Asha, do you want me to walk around and show you the best spots to shoot from since I've been here a few times?" Layoni throws out, attempting to diffuse whatever this is.

Asha's gaze swings back from the field, stopping on me, her eyes searing into mine with something I can't place before dropping to my hand where my school-issued phone is still clutched tightly in my hand. She knows. *That look has to mean she knows, right?*

She doesn't spare me another look before giving her attention to Layoni. "Sure. That would be great. We can start now," she says, turning on her heel toward the field and walking away without another word.

Hollis starts heading toward the stables before I can wrap my head around what just happened. "What the hell was that about?" I say, following hot on his heels.

"You know who we're playing today, right?"

"Yeah, man, we're at their fucking school."

"I didn't ask if you knew what school we are playing; I asked if you knew *who* we were playing."

I shake my head and release an anxious breath. Of course I know, and I can't wait to kick his ass on the field tonight. "We're playing your cousin's pretentious, silver-spoon boyfriend, Penn Hadley."

I can't help but grind my teeth in annoyance as her willingness to fill in for Milli today sinks in. She came to see him.

"No, we're playing a dead man," he spits.

I grab his arm and bring him to a stop. "What are you talking about? What fucking happened back there?"

"He didn't know Asha would be here." He glares toward their stables across the field. "So, when she walked out to the field to shoot, guess who she caught in her lens kissing another girl beside his horse?"

"She saw him?" My voice comes out raw, barely controlled.

"In high definition." He pinches the bridge of his nose. "I happened to walk up behind her when she lowered the camera and quickly turned around, clearly upset."

Fury ignites in my chest. Penn Hadley, the golden boy with his perfect polo record, his bottomless trust fund, and the girl every guy would trade places for—gorgeous, loyal, and completely wasted on a guy who doesn't deserve her. He just hurt the only girl who's ever made me believe I could be worth something to someone.

"How long until we're up?" I ask, my voice eerily calm.

Hollis studies me for a second, and I see the exact moment he understands. A slow, dark smile spreads across his face. "Twenty minutes. Why?"

"Because I need you to switch positions with me."

"You want me to play number three?" His eyebrows shoot up. Number three is the attacking position, the glory position. The position that goes head-to-head with the other team's best defender. "You're captain this year. That's your seat, and Coach will never—"

"Leave Coach to me. Penn isn't playing number three tonight; he's playing the one seat for some reason." I meet his eyes, letting him see everything burning behind mine. "I need to be on Penn."

Hollis's grin turns feral. "You know he's going to come at you hard. He plays dirty when he's threatened."

"Good." The word comes out like a promise. "I'm counting on it."

Twenty-three minutes later, I'm mounted on Santiago. Across the field, Penn sits on some overpriced mare, stretching in his saddle like he doesn't have a care in the world. Like he didn't just royally fuck up and hurt the girl... I force the thought away and focus on the weight of the mallet in my hand.

The umpire throws in the ball, and the game explodes into motion.

I'm on Penn immediately, riding him so close our stirrups clash. He tries to hook my mallet on the first play, but I'm faster, driving the ball downfield with enough force that it cracks like a gunshot.

"You're playing aggressive today, Hale," Penn calls out, positioning himself between me and the ball. There's a smirk in his voice, that entitled confidence that comes from never having consequences. I don't answer. I don't need to.

On the next play, I cut him off so hard he has to pull up short or risk a collision. His mare sidesteps nervously, and I see the flash of irritation cross his face. *Good.*

"What's your problem?" he snaps, recovering.

I lean in close as we ride parallel, close enough that only he can hear me. "My problem," I say, my voice deadly quiet, "is that you're still breathing."

I accelerate past him, calling for the pass from Hollis. The ball arcs through the air, and I'm there to meet it, my mallet connecting with a satisfying *crack*. The ball rockets toward the goal, and their defender is too far out of position to stop it. Score.

Penn's face darkens. He knows something's wrong now, knows this isn't normal gameplay. This is personal.

The next chukker is even worse for him. Every time he touches the ball, I'm there. Every time he tries to position, I'm blocking. Every time he thinks he has an opening, I shut it down with a precision that borders on violence. I'm not just playing polo anymore—I'm hunting.

"What the fuck is your deal?" he finally explodes after I bump him hard enough that he nearly loses his seat. He's sweating, and his face is red with fury.

I circle back, positioning Santiago nose to nose with his mare. "You," I state simply.

The single word hangs in the air like a threat. I'm not going to give him the luxury of a heads-up, not going to spell out exactly what I know. He didn't give Asha any warning before he shoved his tongue down another girl's throat. Besides, getting in his head is working. I can see it in the way his grip tightens on his mallet, the way his jaw clenches. He's unraveling, playing defense in his own mind. He'll lose tonight. He's already losing. He just doesn't know yet how much more he's about to lose when this is all over.

"Whatever, Hale," he grinds out, but there's something uncertain flickering behind his eyes now. "You want to play dirty? Let's go."

I lean forward slightly, my voice dropping low enough that only he can hear over the thundering hooves around us. "I'm not playing dirty, Hadley." A cold smile touches my lips. "I'm playing *honest*. You should try it sometime."

His face goes momentarily blank as he tries to piece together the true meaning behind my words. "Fuck you," he spits.

"No," I say, backing Santiago up and spinning away. "I think you've already fucked yourself."

In the final thirty seconds of the game, we're up by five. Penn's teammates have stopped passing to him, but he's still trying to salvage something from the wreckage of his performance.

The ball comes loose near midfield, and Penn makes a desperate play for it, overextending, his mare already tired from his erratic riding. I see the opening he's too tired to defend and go in for the kill. I don't even have to do much. Just crowd him as he swings wild for the ball. His mallet catches air instead of leather, and the momentum throws him off-center, causing his mare to sidestep hard to avoid Santiago.

It happens almost in slow motion. Penn's foot slips from the stirrup. His hand grasps for the reins, and for one suspended moment, he's neither on the horse nor off it, just falling with his arms flailing and his eyes wide with the realization that he's lost control. Then he hits the ground. Hard.

The game whistle blows at the exact moment Penn lands in the dirt, flat on his back with the wind knocked out of him.

I slow Santiago to a stop and look down at him from my saddle. He's gasping, stunned, staring up at the sky as players from both teams circle. His perfect white uniform is streaked with mud and grass stains. His hair, which is always so carefully styled, is now a mess.

"You alright, Hadley?" I ask, my voice carrying just enough false concern that he'll know it's deliberate.

He turns his head to glare up at me, still struggling to breathe, humiliation burning in his eyes brighter than any physical pain. I don't gloat. I don't need to. The scoreboard says everything: 12-6. And Penn Hadley is exactly where he belongs, in the dirt while everyone watches.

I turn Santiago toward the stables, and that's when I see her. Asha is standing by the fence with her camera lowered, no longer shooting. Just watching. Our eyes meet across the field, and for a moment, everything else falls away: the crowd, the noise, even Penn groaning behind me. I don't smile, don't nod. I just hold her gaze, letting her see that I know. I know what he did to her and that he paid for it.

I'VE JUST FINISHED UNTACKING SANTIAGO AND PREPARING him for transport back to Ridgewood when I spot Asha sitting on top of the wooden fence that surrounds our team's tent. She has the lens pointed toward the scoreboard, which also happens to be beside Crestview's tent. She slowly lowers it, and my eyes find the source of her distress. Penn Hadley has spotted her. If he didn't know she was here before, he does now. From the way his face drops, I'm certain this is the moment everything is coming together for him.

"You could kiss me," I say, announcing my presence.

Her pretty brown eyes find mine, her eyes dancing with entertainment. "Why would I do that?"

I shrug and take a step closer. "Let him see. Make it hurt."

She lets out an amused huff. "It wouldn't hurt him. Clearly, he wasn't that into me."

Earlier, she was upset. I may not have seen her phone in her hands, but I'm certain those messages are hers, and if that's not enough evidence, the annoyance written all over her face when I walked over was, but now I'm not sure what I see. Her anger seems to have morphed into something else.

"I disagree. If he was stepping out, it's because he needed his ego stroked. It has nothing to do with you. Standing next to a strong woman isn't easy," I say in a rare moment of vulnerability. We don't exchange compliments, only underhanded jabs, but even those are starting to feel like a form of love language. She wants to leave her mark on me.

Her eyes narrow as she tries to determine my intent, waiting for a trick because this isn't us right now. "You really want me to kiss you?"

I pull off my gloves slowly, one finger at a time, and feign nonchalance even as my pulse hammers against my ribs. I can't lay all my cards on the table. Not yet. Not when she could still walk away. "Kiss me or don't..." I say, closing the distance between us and placing a hand on either side of her as she sits atop the fence, caging her in. "I just figured I'd offer, you know, since you hugged me the other night."

Her eyebrows shoot up, and fire returns to her eyes. "See, this is why you are so infuriating. I wasn't hugging you, and you know it. I was checking for broken ribs."

"Semantics," I hiss, my voice dropping lower as my eyes drag lazily from her mouth up to dark eyes. The air between us crackles. "You know you can still hate me and kiss me, right?"

The words hang there, suspended in the inches between us. The rise and fall of her chest quickens with each breath, and my jaw clenches. Neither of us moves, both refusing to be the one who breaks first, but the want is written across every tense line of our bodies, in the way her fingers are curled and white-knuckled against the fence rail, and how I haven't backed away despite every instinct inside of me screaming this is dangerous territory.

The silence stretches between us, heavy and charged, and I sigh, leaning back to give her an out. Hell, to give us both an out before I do something we can't take back. But her hands shoot forward and fist in my shirt, yanking me back with a force that catches me off guard. My palms slam against the fence on either side of her hips to catch myself, caging her in.

Our shared breaths mingle, uneven and desperate. Her lips are mere inches from mine, so close I can feel the warmth radiating off her skin and see the rapid flutter of her pulse at her throat.

"I'm sorry about the other night. What I said about your mom."

My jaw clenches. "What about her? Did Hollis say something?" Annoyance spikes through me, sharp and defensive. The last thing I need is people talking about a woman who doesn't deserve the space she'd take up in any conversation.

"No," she says quickly, nervously wetting her lips, a movement I can't ignore. "You did. And I didn't know. I would never have—"

"I don't want to talk about it." The words come out harsher than I intend. "Don't be sorry. I don't want your pity."

Her eyes search mine, and I can see her recalibrating. "What you did out there tonight? That was for me?"

"Yes." The admission costs me, but I give it anyway.

"Why? You hate me."

"Do I?" I step closer. "You hate me. You decided we were enemies. I just played along."

She goes still and I watch the truth reorder itself behind her eyes. Every cruel word, every cold shoulder, every time she pushed me away suddenly means something different.

"Then you understand why I need to apologize." Her voice is quieter now. "For earlier..."

I subtly shake my head and close my eyes, trying to shut out the image of her face, the genuine regret written there. Of all the directions I imagined this moment going, my mother wasn't one of them. I don't have one. She gave up that right the day she abandoned me, put me up for adoption without even telling my father I existed. She's nothing. Less than nothing.

"What about your girlfriend?" The question comes out barely above a whisper, but I hear the deflection in it. She sees my pain, recognizes it, and she's trying to pull me back from the edge.

"We both know I don't have a girlfriend." My voice comes out rough. "Layoni exists because *you* made it so when you refused to show up to the lessons you put up for bid at that auction."

Hollis won the top bid for the private lessons she auctioned without my consent, and in return, I had him put her name down. However, in true Asha fashion, she flipped the script. I knew she would, I just didn't expect her to give them to Layoni. She knew the girl had a crush on me. Maybe her intentions weren't rooted in revenge; she could have just been trying to play matchmaker. But because this is Asha and she loves to wreak havoc on my life, I doubt the latter is true. She was trying to get me caught up in an affair with the coach's niece. She still hasn't figured out that there's only one girl I'm here for, and I'm looking at her.

"Come on, sweetheart. You enjoy driving me crazy. Do your worst."

"Why do you call me that? The least of things I am to you is sweet."

"I see who you really are," I say gently. Behind the cold exterior, the carefully constructed walls, there's someone who cares so deeply it scares her. I see her heart, even when she won't let herself.

Her forehead settles against mine, her hair cascading around us, and my heart feels like it might literally pound out of my chest as I wait to see if she'll close the distance and put her lips to mine. Her hand glides up the side of my neck, and I know she can feel my pulse racing. But because she doesn't mock me for it, I can't help but believe she likes knowing the effect she has on me. Her touch sends shivers across my skin, and my eyes stay laser-focused on her mouth, watching as she rolls her pretty pink lips and leans in slightly before pulling up short.

"You came this far. Now what?"

"You should probably touch me," she says, her breath slightly labored. I bite my lip, and she clarifies with a subtle smile. "Wrap your arms around my waist like you like me."

"Yes, ma'am," I say slowly, letting my hands glide around her waist. My thumb brushes against the soft skin on her lower back, and I get a reward when I feel her skin pebble beneath my touch. I affect her too. "Now what?" I ask, eager for more instruction.

"Now we wait." She sucks in a stuttered breath that I feel more than hear.

"Wait?" My tone is full of gravel as one hand fully flattens against her bare skin. The night air is thick with the smell of summer grass, but all I can smell is her, something sweet like vanilla and reckless decisions.

"Yes, we wait." Her eyes flick up to mine for the first time since she's pulled me close, and Christ, they're darker than I've ever seen them. "He doesn't know your mouth isn't on mine."

A breeze rolls across the field, carrying the distant sound of heckling and laughter, and that's when her foot slips against the fence rail. She gasps, and her fingers clutch my shoulders as gravity pulls her into my arms. My arms band tight around her waist as I catch her against my chest, her body now flush against mine. I can feel her heart hammering, or hell, maybe that's just mine, but every rapid breath she takes feels like it's stealing mine.

"What if I want it to be?" slips out, uncaring of the pretense that's existed between us for years.

This moment changes things. It has to. There's no way she doesn't feel anything for me, no way the venom she's been so intent on feeding me is anything but affection gone wrong. Every barbed comment, every eye roll, every time she's gone out of her way to push my buttons are feelings she doesn't know what to do with. The more I've learned about her through our texts, the stories Hollis tells me, and the things she says when she thinks I'm not listening, are all cracks in her armor, and I've been cataloging every one of them because the more I know, the more I understand how the girl I once knew grew into the woman now in my arms.

She doesn't know *how* to do this. How to let someone in. Her hands are still tightly clutching my shoulders, and her pretty mouth parts for words or a kiss. I'll never know because before she can make a move, a throat is clearing behind us.

"Am I interrupting something?" Preston, the team's number three, asks.

Asha quickly unwraps her legs. "Not at all." She clears her throat. "Trigg was helping me off the fence." She takes a step back from me, and my whole body physically aches from the loss of her warmth.

"Okay," he says slowly, clearly not buying her story. He points to Asha. "How did you get here?"

"Oh, I drove," she says, her voice tinged with something reminiscent of guilt as she looks away.

My eyebrows tug together in confusion before I say, "You don't have a car."

"I borrowed one." She shrugs as she shoves her hands in the back pockets of her jeans.

She stole my damn Bronco.

I look to Preston. "I'm riding back with Fairfield."

He nods and starts toward the bus, and I hold out my hand. "Hand over my keys."

She has the audacity to look offended. "Technically, it's not stealing if I was planning to give it back."

"That's literally the definition of stealing."

"It's *borrowing* without permission. There's a distinction."

"Yeah, one that holds up real well in court." I step closer, hand still outstretched. "Keys."

She pulls one hand from her pocket, dangling my keys just out of reach. "You're being dramatic. I filled up the tank. Premium, not regular. You should be thanking me."

"Thanking you for committing a felony?"

"It's a misdemeanor at best." Her smile turns sharp. "And you're not going to report me."

"How do you figure?"

"Because then you'd have to admit that you hid her in the woods to sneak off campus."

I step closer, closing the distance that existed once more, catching her off guard and stealing her breath. It takes real strength not to pull her close and try to go back to the moment that was interrupted, but I manage and snatch my keys back in the process. "You're trouble, sweet-heart." I tilt her chin up so her eyes have nowhere to look but into mine. "Don't take what's mine again unless you're ready to pay the price."

Her breath hitches, and I watch her pupils dilate. For a second, I think she might actually back down. Then that defiant spark I've come to know too well flares back to life.

"And what price would that be?" she whispers, not pulling away from my grip.

The kind that involves me finally admitting what we both already know.

But I don't say that. Instead, I let my thumb brush along her jawline, just once, just enough to make my point before I step back and leave her standing there, looking dazed and furious and something else I'm not ready to name yet.

"Guess you'll have to steal from me again to find out," I say over my shoulder as I head toward my truck.

And we both know she will.

ASHA

CHAPTER 7

SENIOR YEAR

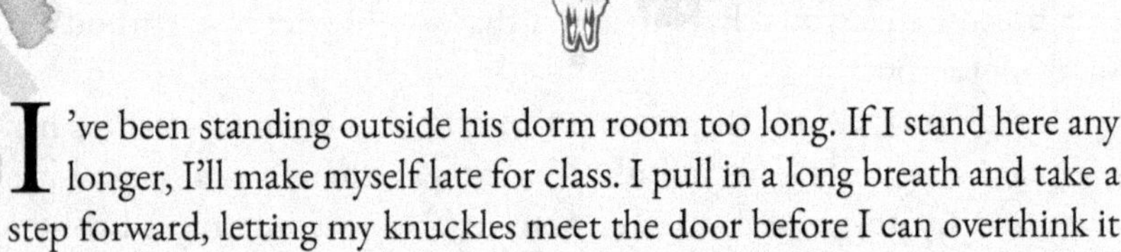

I've been standing outside his dorm room too long. If I stand here any longer, I'll make myself late for class. I pull in a long breath and take a step forward, letting my knuckles meet the door before I can overthink it any more.

The Tupperware container feels ridiculous in my hands. I made protein-packed chocolate chip cookies because, of course, I researched what he actually eats instead of just bringing regular cookies like a normal person. Apparently, I can't do anything halfway when it comes to him.

I hear footsteps grow closer, and then the door swings open, and he's there.

God, it isn't fair. How is it possible that he looks better every time I see him? His dark hair is perfectly messy in that way that suggests he's been running his hands through it, and there's stubble along his jaw that wasn't there in AP biology yesterday. He's wearing a fitted black t-shirt that clings to shoulders that have definitely gotten broader since freshman year, and I can see the definition of his arms, the way his muscles shift as he grips the doorframe.

His eyes widen. "What—"

"Hi." My voice comes out smaller than I intend. I thrust the container toward him. "I made you cookies. They're high-protein, almond flour, Greek yogurt, that kind of thing."

He stares at me like I've sprouted a second head. "You made me cookies?"

"Don't make it weird."

A smile tugs at the corner of his mouth, and I feel that familiar flip in my stomach that I've been trying to ignore for months now. "You're standing outside my door with cookies you specially formulated for my diet. It's already weird."

"Do you want them or not?"

He takes the container slowly, his fingers brushing mine. That brief contact sends electricity up my arm, and from the way his breath hitches slightly, he feels it too. "Why are you really here?"

I wrap my arms around myself, suddenly cold despite the warmth of the hallway. "We're graduating in four days."

"I'm aware."

"And I realized..." I swallow hard, forcing myself to meet his eyes. Those eyes that have looked at me with anger, frustration, and then, over the past year, something softer. Something that terrifies me. "I never apologized."

His expression shifts, becomes more guarded. "For what?"

"For what happened at the homecoming auction. That was... You warned me about Emma." My throat tightens. "You were right, and I knowingly threw it in your face."

He's quiet, watching me with an intensity that makes my skin tingle.

"For the milkshake." I take a shaky breath. "And for what I said about your manners. About your mom. That was—" My eyes burn. "That was unforgivable, and I'm so sorry."

The silence stretches between us, heavy with everything we've been dancing around for months. All those late-night student council meetings that ran long, the accidental coffee runs that became intentional, the way we somehow always end up at the stables at the same time. The way he looks at me sometimes, like I'm something precious instead of the girl who made his life hell for four years.

"Do you want to come in?" His voice is rough, careful.

I look past him into his room. I can see his desk, books stacked neatly, a sweatshirt thrown over his chair. It would be so easy to say yes. To step into his space, to let down the walls I've spent so long building.

But I can see his roommate's empty bed too, and I know what

coming inside means. Not physically—though, God, the way he's looking at me makes heat pool in my stomach—but emotionally. It means opening a door I've been holding shut with both hands. It means trusting someone again.

Everyone I trust leaves. Or uses me. Or proves that my faith in them is just another weakness to exploit.

He shifts, and the movement draws my attention to his chest, the way he's still gripping the doorframe like he needs to hold onto something. Like maybe I'm not the only one affected here. That scares me more than anything.

I take a step back, and his face falls, just slightly, but I see it. That flash of disappointment, like he's been expecting this all along.

"No," I say, and my voice cracks. "I just wanted you to know. I'm sorry. For all of it."

"That's it?" Something sharp enters his tone. "You show up, apologize for years of making me your personal villain, and just leave?"

"I'm not..." I wrap my arms tighter around myself. "I can't."

"Can't or won't?"

"Does it matter?"

"Yeah," he says, stepping into the hallway, close enough that I can smell his cologne, something woodsy and clean that I've started associating with safety and late nights where I forget to be afraid. "It actually really does matter."

I can't breathe. He's too close, and I can see the way his jaw clenches to hide the hurt he's trying to hide behind frustration.

"I have to go," I whisper.

"You don't."

"I do." I take another step back, even though everything in me is screaming to move closer. "Enjoy the cookies."

I turn before I can do something stupid, like confess that I want to step inside his room more than I've wanted anything in years.

"Hey."

I stop but don't turn around.

"Never apologize for who you are." His voice is achingly soft now. "It's what makes you...you, sweetheart."

That damn nickname.

I inhale sharply, and I have to bite my lip to keep from making a sound. He started calling me that years ago. That stupid, infuriating endearment that I claimed to hate, that I rolled my eyes at, that I told him to stop using. But somewhere along the way, it became the thing I waited for with bated breath. The proof that whatever this thing between us is, it's still there. That he still sees me as more than just the girl who made him miserable. That he still cares, deeply, in a way that terrifies and thrills me in equal measure.

I close my eyes and keep walking. Behind me, I hear his door click shut, and I'm not sure if I made a mistake. He heard an apology. I bared my soul. I showed him a part of me I don't give people, that I know when I'm wrong, that I care, that I *feel* something. And that's the part that might be a mistake. Feeling. Caring. Wanting.

Things are going to change tonight for better or worse, I don't know. But I do know this: I'm done collecting regrets, and not giving him those words would have been one I couldn't live with.

"ALL THAT'S LEFT ON THE AGENDA FOR TODAY'S MEETING IS tonight's prom. We have been asked to collect the school-issued phones thirty minutes before the dance is over," Eldrige drones on about the evening as I stare out the window, feeling anxious about this evening.

Sure, my costume is ready; that was the easy part. The moment the faculty announced they'd chosen this year's prom theme, *masquerade ball*, to coincide with our secret pen pal assignment, I knew exactly who I'd be. Rapunzel. This school has been my tower, a gilded prison designed to keep me from the only place I want to be, home. I want to believe my father meant well when he sent me here. I know he loves me. We talk regularly, our bond somehow surviving the distance. But every year when I bring up coming home, he shuts me down. The conversation always ends the same way: "You can come home when you're eighteen, if that's what you *still* want."

Still want.

Those words haunt me. Why would he phrase it like that? As if I'd want to be anywhere else. As if years of begging haven't made my feelings crystal clear. What is he afraid I'll discover? What does he think will change?

However, it's not the costume or my father's cryptic words. None of that is what's keeping me awake this week. Tonight, I finally meet my secret pen pal face to face. Our texts have been my oxygen in this suffocating place, each one a reminder that someone sees me. But words behind a screen are safe. Controllable. Tonight, we step out from behind our careful sentences, and I don't know how I'm going to feel once all our cards are finally on the table.

"Earth to Asha," Eldridge says, waving his hand in front of my face as he stands between me and the view out of the window.

"Hmm," I say, leaning back in my chair. "Tonight, you and me at 11:30. We're collecting phones."

"Oh, I can't. You'll have to find someone else," I say, setting down the pen I'd been anxiously tapping on my notebook.

Things haven't been the same since I caught Eldridge and Emma scheming behind my back. Catching someone in the act, hearing the lies come from their mouth rather than discovering the truth after the fact, is a different experience. I'm cordial in our student council meetings and classes, but outside of that, we don't talk.

"You can't?" Trigger questions from the head of the table.

Just like me, he's been unusually quiet for today's meeting. His eyes tracked my every move when I entered the meeting. I could feel them, though I didn't meet his gaze. I couldn't after giving him the cookies this morning. Of course, I knew I'd have to see him today more than once, but the way I'm feeling is new, and I honestly don't know what to do with it. He let Eldridge run today's meeting, and I assumed it was because he no longer cared to carry out the task. The school year is over. We're all graduating. But if that were true, he wouldn't be questioning me now. Why push me to work with people he knows crossed me? Why give a damn about this last task?

"Yeah, I can't. I have plans."

"Plans?" He folds his hands on the table in front of him. "We all have plans tonight. It's prom."

"Exactly. So you understand why I'm busy," I reply, my voice sugary sweet.

"We're all meeting our pen pals tonight. Phone duty is at 11:30." His tone is flat, almost bored. "Unless you need extra time to get ready."

He asked me to stay this morning, and I didn't. Is he mad?

"What's that supposed to mean?" My eyes finally flick up to his.

"Nothing." He shrugs, the picture of innocence. "Just that some people are treating this pen pal thing like it actually matters."

"It does matter. It's an assignment," I snap, crossing my arms.

"Right. An assignment." He drums his fingers on the table. "That's why you've been staring out the window during the meeting, doodling in your notebook instead of paying attention."

"I'm taking notes." I challenge back with a look that says *why are you doing this?*

"Really? Let me see." He reaches for my notebook. I snatch it away with a scowl before he can grab it. "Defensive." His eyebrow arches, and there's something dangerous in his expression, something pointed and deliberate. "You catching feelings, Fairfield?"

My heart stutters then slams against my ribs. *Ah. There it is.*

He's testing me. Deliberately pushing buttons to see which ones make me flinch, what truths I'll accidentally spill. The realization sends equal parts excitement and terror coursing through my veins. *He's figured it out.* Or he thinks he has. He's fishing for confirmation, trying to catch me in a reveal I'm not ready to make. And God, as certain as I am about who's been receiving my messages, the one person who understands me in ways that terrify me, who responds like he can read between every line I write, I've doubted it just as fiercely. Hope is dangerous. Hope has teeth. And every single time I've let myself believe in something good, it's turned around and gutted me.

His eyes don't leave mine, waiting. Watching.

I stand, my chair screeching across the floor, my face giving away nothing before I turn my gaze back to Eldridge. "I can't do phones."

"You're Student Council VP, and phone duty is on your schedule tonight," Trigg says, his voice tinged with a hint of annoyance at my defiance.

"And I'm delegating. That's what good leaders do." And because Eldridge owes me, I keep my eyes locked on his when I say, "Is this going to be a problem, Eldridge?"

"No." His eyebrows rise, and I know he hears the finality in my question. I'm not asking. I've kept his little ruse to deceive me quiet. Not once have I brought it up, but he's aware I know every sordid detail of how he attempted to portray himself as someone he wasn't. "Emma can help me."

I roll my lips at the mention of his sister's name, who I know is sitting to his left, but I'm currently refusing to acknowledge her existence.

He stutters, "Or Martin. I'll ask Martin."

"Great," I say, grabbing my stuff off the table in one swoop before heading toward the door. "See you guys tonight," I say without glancing back.

"The meeting hasn't been adjourned," Trigger calls out behind me.

I don't validate his comment with a response. I can't. I need air. My heart pounds as I push through the door, and I hate that it's racing. I hate that, even now, walking away from him, all I can think about is the way he looked at me when he asked if I was catching feelings. Like he cared. Like it mattered to him. It's ridiculous. He pushes every button I have, gets under my skin in ways no one else can. But that's the problem, isn't it? No one else can. And as much as I hate the way he makes me feel off-balance and defensive and alive, I like it. God help me, I like it.

I've just stepped outside when I hear the sound of the school door pushing open behind me. "Asha, wait up," Eldridge calls after me.

I tuck a strand of hair behind my ear as I wait at the top of the steps. "What do you want, Eldridge?" I can't help the tinge of annoyance that carries in my tone.

"I know you're mad at me, but don't be mad at Emma. I messed up. She was only trying to help me."

"You guys both lied to me," I state firmly, holding his gaze so there's no mistake, no way for him to twist the meaning.

"I know." He exhales a sigh of regret. "But you have to understand. I didn't know another way. I wanted to get to know you on a deeper level and..." He averts his gaze before adding, "You're not exactly approachable."

"That's a cop-out," I say before turning on my heel and starting down the steps.

"Asha, hear me out." He follows in step beside me.

"I heard all I needed to hear," I say coldly, my arms crossed tight over my chest. "You, of all people, don't get to use that 'not approachable' bullshit. I was friends with your sister, and we serve on the student council together."

"Maybe so, but you never remove the *fuck off* stamp from your fore-head," he counters defensively. "You're smart as hell and..."

He stops as we pause for a student riding their bike across the path, and a warm breeze kicks up the scent of fresh mulch from the newly planted flowerbeds lining the walkway.

"Have you looked in the mirror recently? Look, I knew you wouldn't talk to me otherwise. When I got word that you might have a thing for your pen pal, I saw an opportunity, and I jumped on it," he continues, his words tumbling out in a rush. "It wasn't meant to be a lie forever, just a door opener," he tries to reason as he reaches for my elbow.

I jerk away, picking up my pace down the tree-lined path toward the residential quad. The dormitories loom ahead, their brick facades warm in the late-afternoon sun, window boxes overflowing with bright petunias and trailing ivy.

"I had a boyfriend; there was never an open door," I remind him icily. When he got caught in his lie, I was still dating Penn.

He bites his lip, frustration evident in the hard set of his jaw. "We both know Penn was a D-bag. If he wasn't, you wouldn't have been catching feelings for your pen pal."

I roll my eyes, hating the truth that lingers in his statement, but I had my reasons for keeping Penn around.

"Penn lied to me, just as you did," I say wearily before continuing down the tree-covered path back to my dorm. "So how are you any better?"

"Come on, Asha. I never would have fumbled you. There's no way in hell I'd ever look at anyone else."

"What do you want from me, Eldridge? This can't possibly be your argument to fill the spot," I say, eyes forward.

"Just give Emma another chance. I threatened to tell our parents about her boyfriend if she didn't help me."

I stop short of reaching for the door to enter my building because that comment piques my interest. "Is she not allowed to date?"

"She can date, just not him. He's a Gallagher, and our families have been rivals for years. They would accuse him of using her to get to them, forbid the relationship, and ship her overseas to live with my mother's sister."

I stare blankly at him for a second as his words hit a nerve I wasn't expecting. But only for a moment; I can't leave space to care.

"Fine," I say flatly, swiping my card and pulling open the door.

"Really?" His voice drips with hesitant relief, a hint of hope creeping into his features.

"Yes, but I'm still not doing phone duty tonight," I tell him as I pull open the door. I don't bother explaining. I planned to break my silence tonight anyway, when I asked for answers.

The door clicks shut behind me, sealing him outside. I lean against it for a moment, listening to his footsteps finally retreat down the path. I've been waiting for this. I've kept count of every transgression, filing them away until I was ready to collect. He doesn't realize how easy it was for him to think everything is forgiven, and for that, his guard has been lowered. I know he'll text his sister, and hers will lower too, and that's when accounts will get settled. But tonight, everything gets laid bare, every secret dragged into the light where there's nowhere left to hide.

I exhale an anxious breath because it's not just their secrets that are being put on display tonight. So are mine.

I watch as Emma stands in front of the full-length mirror, adjusting the band of lace woven through her hair. She's wearing a baby-blue dress with delicate fairy lights sewn into the hem of the skirt. She holds up an ornate purple-and-gold mask and studies her appearance for the thousandth time tonight before her gaze catches mine in the mirror.

"You know the whole point of the masks is that you can hide behind them, right? You look like you're about to face a firing squad," she says before turning to face me, where I lie sprawled across my bed. I quirk a brow and take a deep breath before toying with the lavender lace on my bodice. She once again mistakes my silence for nerves over meeting my pen pal.

I should've been more careful. I never admitted out loud that I was falling for my pen pal, but because I let her get close, she saw things. The constant texting throughout the day. The stupid grin I'd get reading certain messages. The way I'd check my phone the second it buzzed. It wasn't exactly subtle, and she's not an idiot. She put it together. What bugs me is that I slipped up in the first place and gave her the chance to use it against me.

"If you're worried he's not going to be interested once the mask comes off, don't be. That boy has been texting you good morning every single day for the past three months. He sends you playlist updates and remembers your aversion to cilantro. You literally have nothing to stress about. I, on the other hand, have no idea who's on the other end of my phone."

Oh, I'm worried, but not for the reasons she thinks. I'm worried because of what I am confident is ninety-nine percent true, and what that means. Going home was already going to be hard, but if what I think is true is real, going home is going to be that much more complicated. But the stress etched across my face right now isn't for the man behind the mask. It's for the conversation I've been saving for her.

She thinks I don't know every way she's crossed me since freshman year. Time's up.

"Why did you throw out my ballots for president freshman year?" I ask, raising my gaze from my dress to her eyes.

Her face pales, confirming my words are true. "How long have you known?" she asks quietly.

Looking back, I should have figured it out sooner. I had suspicions after the election. Too many people mentioned voting for me without being asked, and I even heard two students talking about how Trigger had threatened them if they didn't cast a vote for me and not him. The problem was I couldn't put together where things had gone wrong. It wasn't until I was on that stage with Trigger, watching his anger hit its boiling point, that I not only heard his words but believed them. After homecoming, I stole the security camera footage from voting day. There it was: Emma picking the lock on the ballot boxes, sorting through them, and stuffing her backpack with votes cast for me before continuing onto Headmaster Trejo's office to count the ballots.

"Since sophomore year," I say with indifference. Her betrayal means less to me than the reason why. I've never been able to make sense of her reasons for going behind my back.

Emma nervously runs her hands down the front of her dress. "It's not what you're thinking. I mean, I know this looks shitty, but—"

"Nothing is ever as it seems," I agree. I learned that at a very young age. "But you're wrong. It doesn't look shitty; it is shit. You completely betrayed me."

"I know," she whines. "But it's only because I was trying to get closer to you." I narrow my eyes, not following her train of thought. "I was running for vice president, and when you lost, I was planning to step down and give you my seat, but Trigger ruined my plan by going to Headmaster Trejo and making a case that whoever lost their campaign for president would automatically become VP." She lets out a sigh of annoyance. "You realize his petition fundamentally changed how elections would be handled going forward. He argued that candidates who demonstrate enough dedication to run for presidency should be rewarded for their commitment to the student body." She rolls her eyes as if the whole argument is preposterous, and a small smile tugs at my mouth.

For the first time, I see what I thought was a power play by Trigg in a different light. I think Trigger suspected foul play in the election, but he didn't have proof, which is why he presented his case to Headmaster Trejo.

"Do you really see it that way, or are you just mad your plan failed? The way I see it, his proposal doesn't leave motivated students without any role."

"I ran for VP. It should have been mine." She shakes her head, the loss clearly still leaving a sour taste in her mouth.

After the election, she didn't lose her spot on the council, but Trigger didn't assign her an officer role. Instead, he gave her a representative role as student council historian.

"That's all history now. You asked me why I did it, and that's what matters. My intent was never malicious. I only wanted to get closer to you. I wanted to be someone you could trust, someone you could count on." She shrugs. "We'd only just become friends back then. In hindsight, it was a terrible idea and incredibly selfish. If I could take it back, I would."

While I don't agree with her methods of forming friendships, I've known her long enough to recognize when she's being sincere. Her explanation borders on psychotic, but it's her truth.

"Can you forgive me?" She perches on the corner of my bed, her silver heels dangling just above my cream carpet. She won't look at me.

"Perhaps, if it was the only time you had betrayed me, but I think we both know that was only your first." The words taste bitter on my tongue. Her eyes widen, genuinely surprised, as if she hadn't cataloged every lie herself.

"I thought since I was here, I was forgiven for helping Eldridge convince you he was your pen pal." Her voice shrinks.

I flip over my phone to check the time. Have I forgiven her? Forgiveness is given when someone decides to let go of resentment or a desire for vengeance. I can't say I harbored that. If anything, I was hurt. Through all of this, I kept her close because that's what I've been raised to do. It's smart to know your enemies. But I haven't wanted vengeance. I just wanted answers, and she still owes me a few.

"I'm not talking about Eldridge. I'm asking about Penn Hadley." My reflection stares back at me from the mirror across the room.

She's quick to stand and give me her back. "What did he tell you?" The question comes out defensive, already armored.

That's not the reaction or the response I saw coming. Penn Hadley didn't tell me anything. I never spoke to him after I caught him kissing another girl at the polo match. There wasn't anything to say. There's no coming back from that.

"I know it was you who poured sugar in his gas tank the night he asked me to homecoming," I admit, not wanting to give her too much but starting from the beginning. She was acting strangely that night, and after Penn's grand proposal, I chalked up her weird behavior to keeping his secret, but now I know it was more than that.

She turns around, her fingers twisted up. "That night, when the team arrived, I went to visit Philip, and when I walked up, I heard Penn having a conversation with one of his other teammates. He was telling him about his plan to ask you to homecoming, so I hid in the shadows with a big smile on my face, but then I heard his friend ask about another girl. Penn's response was, 'That's the beauty of dating girls from other schools. You don't run the risk of them finding out about the other.'" Her eyes are full of apology when she looks at me. "I was so mad. That's why I poured the sugar in his gas tank. He lied to me too."

"Why didn't you just tell me?"

She had so many opportunities to come clean, but instead she kept quiet. The silence in my room feels suffocating, broken only by the sound of laughter outside as other girls leave for the dance with friends who haven't lied to them.

"I thought you'd be done with him after he stood you up for home-coming. Asha Fairfield doesn't keep a guy who doesn't find a way. Hell, he could have called an Uber, but he didn't." She shrugs, casual, like my humiliation was just a minor inconvenience in her master plan.

My jaw tightens on instinct, hating how stupid he made me look. But she played a role in that by never telling me the truth.

"Okay, I understand why you did what you did that night, but what's your excuse for letting things play out for the next year? If you were truly my friend and had my best interest at heart, why would you let me date him? I never would have kept something like that from you." I'm off the bed, anger slowly bubbling. "I wouldn't keep that kind of information from my worst enemy."

"After you took him back and things went so well on your first date, I didn't want to ruin things. I didn't want to be the girl who introduced you to the devil. I was the one pushing you to him. It was my idea for the two of you to meet. My boyfriend and your boyfriend were best friends, and we were friends. That was always supposed to be the plan."

"But we weren't, not really, because a friend wouldn't keep something that ugly from me."

"I know that now, but I didn't then. It's partially why I helped Eldrige. I knew you had some kind of special connection with your pen pal. I hoped that the connection might grow stronger than the one that existed with Penn. I knew my brother really cared about you. I tried to make it right. I just did it in all the wrong ways."

"You could say that again." I exhale my annoyance as I start pacing the beside the bed, breaking in the new heels I bought for tonight.

The room feels smaller now, the walls closing in with each revelation. I stop pacing and face her, really look at her. The worst part isn't even the lying; it's the arrogance of it. She genuinely believed she knew better than me what I could handle, what I deserved to know about my own life. She played puppet master with my relationships, my trust, and my heart and convinced herself it was all about friendship.

"At the core of every lie was your unwavering desire to be my friend. Tell me something, Emma. Why do you want to be my friend?"

That's the question. That's the root of all this betrayal. Friendship, but why? What does she believe she'll gain?

Her eyes drop to my dress, the telltale sign of a lie. "I didn't know I needed a reason."

"A normal person wouldn't, but I think we both know that the lengths you went to in the pursuit of gaining my favor meant you wanted more."

"Fine. I really do want to be your friend, but I also hoped you would help me get into the class your father teaches once every two years at the University of Louisville." She forces the confession out, as if it physically pains her.

That's unexpected. My father's class? He's not even a professor. He's a guest lecturer—at best, an adjunct professor. Every two years, he teaches an advanced course in Equine Entrepreneurship.

"Why?" The question comes out flat, disbelieving.

"Everyone who takes his class has gone on to land major jobs in the equine industry. I'm talking top-five breeders in the US and France, as well as management positions at all the major US tracks," she rushes through the explanation.

I nod, staring down at the floor as the information settles. I hadn't done that much research on my father's classes. I had no idea those stats existed, but it doesn't surprise me. My father is a smart businessman. It's the dad part that could use some work.

"I think you should go. I'd like to finish getting ready alone." My voice is ice now, controlled and distant.

"Asha—" She reaches for me, her hand trembling in the space between us.

I hold my hand up to stop her, building a wall with just a gesture. I don't have anything else I care to say. School is over, and while I may have once called her a friend, we were never really friends at all. There's no reason for me to stay in touch. I just want her to be done.

"I won't put in a good word for you. I think we both know you don't deserve it." I let my gaze slowly trail up her gown before finding her face. "But I won't hinder your chances either. My father knew about our friendship. If you get into that class, it will be on your own merit, not because of any words I give him."

She swallows hard, and I can practically see the pieces falling into place. If she'd take a second to think about it from my perspective, she'd realize I actually went easy on her. I don't need to be the one to make her pay for what she did. Karma has a way of handling that stuff on its own.

"Thank you," she whispers, the words barely audible over the sound of my own heartbeat thundering in my ears.

I don't respond. Instead, I turn back to my vanity, picking up my brush with deliberate precision. In the mirror's reflection, I watch her hover uncertainly in the doorway, caught between leaving and staying, between apologizing again and accepting defeat.

Finally, she moves. Her heels click against the hardwood floor until she reaches the door, opening it softly. "Asha?" her voice wavers from the threshold.

I don't turn around. "Close the door on your way out, Emma."

The latch clicks shut with a finality that echoes through my chest.

Silence rushes in to fill the space she left behind, heavy and somehow cleansing. I reach for the silver masquerade mask laying on my vanity, running my fingers along its delicate curves and the small crystals embedded along the edges. Tonight isn't about Emma, or Penn, or any of the lies that have been building around me like walls. Tonight is about something real.

My pen pal.

The one person who's known me without agenda, without pretense, without anything to gain except my thoughts and my words. We've shared secrets Emma never earned, dreams Penn never cared about, and fears I've never spoken aloud to anyone else. And tonight, at midnight, when the masks come off in the center of the ballroom under that ridiculous chandelier the prom committee spent three months installing, I'll finally know who he is.

My heart does this strange flutter-kick thing it's been doing all week whenever I think about it. We agreed, 11:30, the hallway behind the stage, no masks. No more hiding. No more carefully crafted texts or deliberately vague descriptions. Just truth.

One story may have found its close, but I can't help but feel like another one, a real one, is just starting.

TRIGGER

CHAPTER 8

SENIOR YEAR

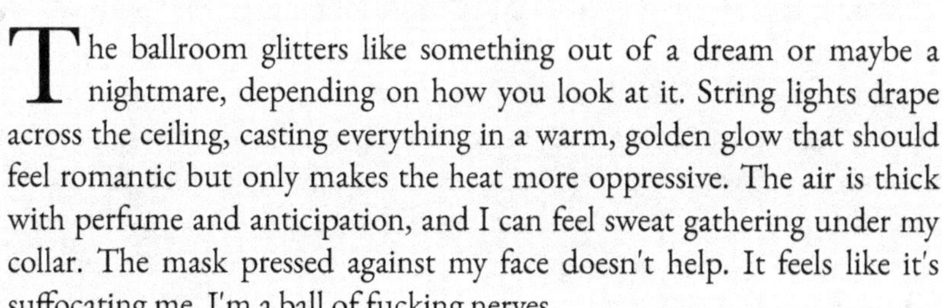

The ballroom glitters like something out of a dream or maybe a nightmare, depending on how you look at it. String lights drape across the ceiling, casting everything in a warm, golden glow that should feel romantic but only makes the heat more oppressive. The air is thick with perfume and anticipation, and I can feel sweat gathering under my collar. The mask pressed against my face doesn't help. It feels like it's suffocating me. I'm a ball of fucking nerves.

I've been watching her for the past hour and seventeen minutes. Her lavender dress and blonde wig, meant to mask her identity, does nothing; I'd know that laugh anywhere. It has an edge to it, like she's in on some joke the rest of us aren't. I've heard it a thousand times, usually right before she takes over a meeting or steals the lunch Mrs. Jean sets aside for me just because she can.

Asha Fairfield. My academic rival. My vice president from hell. The girl who looked at me on the first day of freshman year and decided we were going to be enemies, for reasons I still don't fully understand. Also, if I'm right—and I'm always right—my secret pen pal for the past four years.

My phone buzzes in my pocket, and I anxiously pull it out, believing it might be a text from her, only to remember I set a five-minute timer on my phone to ensure I wouldn't miss the exact time we said we would meet.

"Hey." Hollis lightheartedly punches me in the arm, his own mask now on top of his head, signifying he and his pen pal have already met. "Why haven't you gone to get your girl?"

"I have five minutes," I say as my lungs deflate.

"You're lucky. My partner was Rizz from the math club. He's cool and all, and I never would have talked to him were it not for this assignment, but I'd rather have some hot piece of ass on the end of my text messages to take home tonight."

"It's not like that," I'm quick to add, not just because Asha is his cousin but because it's not. Because every word I wrote, every vulnerability I shared, every late-night conversation was all real. It mattered. Even if Asha doesn't know it yet. Even if she's still wandering around this ballroom with no idea that I'm the one who's been writing to her for four years.

"Sure, it's not. If you think the feelings are mutual, why not make a power play? Girls like it when a man takes control." He bumps my shoulder with his. "Show her who's boss."

My mouth can't help but quirk into the semblance of a smile. I've thought about what he's suggesting countless times. Dreamed about her submission, and while I think a move like that could win over even a strong-willed woman like Asha in the moment, knowing her allowance would ultimately lead to pleasure, I don't think it would win her in the long game. I still think about the night of the charity ride, when she came to see me after I was hurt. She let her guard down. She looked at me with something other than contempt, and I saw the real Asha beneath all the armor. The Asha who might actually feel the same way I do.

I squeeze his shoulder. "Time to go. If I don't see you again tonight, don't come looking." I give him a wink and head toward the stage.

Tonight, I'm playing by her rules. She set the time and place we would meet, and yes, that time was 11:30 p.m. It's why I had to push her today in our last student council meeting. I was further collecting evidence to prove that she is, in fact, who I believe she is, but more than that, I was seeing if she'd crack. I'm tired of pretending, tired of acting like I'm not the one she's been leaning on for years. Sharing the weight of our parents' expectations, fears of disappointment, and dreams she'd never say out loud because they're not the same as her father's.

But I've shoved it all down, every instinct that was screaming for me to snap and lay it all out there, because if she knows the truth, and she's still sharing anyway, then all of the secrecy is worth it. That's why I followed her instructions and agreed to her new flex, buying a Flynn Rider costume to match hers. As if setting the exact time and location to meet weren't enough, she wanted to ensure, without a doubt, I was indeed her guy, and I dutifully followed her instructions to a T. But once our masks come off, I can't guarantee I'll bend to her will if she doesn't want the same things I do. I'd chase her to the grave and haunt her in the afterlife just for a chance to show her how good we can be, to prove to her what I know in the depths of my soul. She is meant to be mine.

The hallway stretches before me like something out of a fever dream, too long and too quiet. My phone screen glows in my hand, the time-stamp mocking me: 11:29 p.m. One minute. I refresh our chat thread for the hundredth time, re-reading her last message even though I've memorized every word, every carefully chosen punctuation mark. *Tower corridor. 11:30 p.m.*

As I wait, my mind can't help but circle back to this morning. To her standing at my door with homemade cookies, protein-packed, specifically formulated for my diet, and an apology she didn't have to give. The more I think about it, the more convinced I am that she knows. She had to have figured out it was me on the other end of those messages, and the cookies were her insurance policy. Her way of making sure that when everything came out tonight, I'd remember she tried to make things right first. I've analyzed it from every angle, replayed her nervous energy, and I keep landing on the same conclusion: those cookies weren't just about guilt. They were about us. They have to be.

I stop at the alcove where the tower stairs meet the main corridor. This is it. The exact spot. I check my phone one last time: 11:30. Then I hear it. The sharp, rhythmic click of heels on tile echoing down the hallway behind me, each step driving a spike of adrenaline straight through my chest. I know that walk. It's confident and purposeful, the kind of stride that parts crowds and makes boys out of men. My throat goes dry, and I turn.

The Rapunzel mask still frames her face, that golden braid draped over one shoulder, but it's the way she moves through a room like she belongs there more than anyone else that I can't get enough of. The dim hallway lighting catches on the shimmer of her dress, and suddenly, I can't remember how to make my lungs work properly. My heart kicks into overdrive, hammering against my ribs so loud I'm sure she can hear it from twenty feet away.

She doesn't slow down. Doesn't hesitate. Just keeps walking toward me with those devastating eyes locked on mine through the mask, and I'm rooted to the spot like she's cast some kind of spell. I lick my lips, trying to summon words—her name, a greeting, anything.

"Don't." Her voice cuts through the space between us, low and urgent and tinged with something that sounds dangerously close to desperation. She's closer now, close enough that I can see her chest rising and falling too quickly, like she's as terrified as I am. "Don't speak."

She stops directly in front of me, so close I can smell her perfume. My palms ache, and I flex my fingers at my sides to fight the urge to reach for her and close this impossible final distance, but I'm paralyzed by the weight of this moment, by the terrifying knowledge that once we cross this line, there's no going back.

"Don't ruin this." Her hand rises, fingertips ghosting along my jaw, her touch searing through me. Her thumb traces my lower lip, and I forget my own name. "Not yet."

Then she kisses me, and the world ends and begins in the same breath. Her mouth is soft and fierce and perfect, and she tastes like mint and something reckless, and I'm drowning in it, in *her*. My hands finally remember how to function, and I'm pulling her closer, one palm sliding to the small of her back while the other tangles in that golden braid, and she makes this small sound against my lips that destroys me completely.

Every argument we've ever had, every sharp word and sharper glance, every moment I've pretended to hate her while wanting exactly this...it all combusts into this kiss, into the way she's gripping my shirt like I might disappear, into the way I can feel her heartbeat racing against my chest, matching the frantic rhythm of my own. The kiss shifts and deepens.

What started as desperate and searching transforms into something raw, something that's been building between us for years of anonymous messages and charged glances across crowded rooms. Her fingers fist in my shirt, nails scraping against my chest through the thin fabric, and a groan tears from my throat before I can stop it.

She responds by pressing closer, eliminating every breath of space between us, and suddenly, gentle isn't enough. Careful isn't enough. The restraint I've been clinging to for years through every argument, every heated debate where I wanted to grab her face and kiss her silent, every night I've lain awake thinking about her...it all snaps like a frayed wire.

I walk her backward. Three steps. Four. Until her back hits the wall with a soft thud that makes her gasp against my mouth, and God, that sound. That perfect, breathless sound that I want to swallow, to taste, to hear again and again until it's branded into my memory. My hands are everywhere. One sliding up her ribcage, my thumb brushing the underside of her breast through her dress, the other gripping her hip hard enough to leave marks. She arches into me, all soft curves and yielding heat, and when she hooks one leg around my waist, I nearly lose my mind entirely.

"Yes," she breathes against my lips, breaking away just enough to gasp for air. "God, yes."

I lift her without thinking, pressing her fully against the wall, her thighs wrapping around my hips as I pin her there with the weight of my body. My mouth finds hers again, and the new angle makes us both moan, a harmony of want that echoes down the empty hallway. My mouth travels from her lips to her jaw, down the column of her throat, where I can feel her pulse hammering wildly beneath my tongue. She tastes like salt and perfume, and I want to devour every inch of her.

"I can't—" she rasps as my hips roll against hers, and I pause, chest heaving. Her head falls against the stone wall as she shakes it from side to side. "I can't think when you're..." She rotates her hips, pressing her hot core against my hardened length. Then her tongue dusts over her lips before adding, "I don't want to think. Please don't stop."

I pull back just enough to look at her, a question in my eyes even though I can't speak, won't speak, because she asked me not to, and there's no way in hell I'm ruining this. Her lips are swollen, and the way she's looking at me through that mask, like I'm everything she's ever wanted and everything she's been afraid to reach for, makes my heart stutter. I want her, but I don't want to be her mistake, a regret.

Her fingers thread through my hair before she yanks my mouth back to hers, kissing me with a ferocity that makes my knees weak. Her tongue slides against mine, demanding and teasing and wrecking any semblance of control I have left. I press harder against the wall, against her, and she whimpers—actually whimpers—into my mouth, her body moving against mine with a rhythm that's threatening to kill me. The golden braid falls over her shoulder, and I wrap it around my fist, tugging gently until her head tilts back, exposing more of her perfect throat.

"More," she pants, her voice breaking. "I need...please, I need more."

My hand abandons her braid and slowly skates down her side as my eyes stay pinned on hers, giving her ample time to tell me to stop, to tell me this isn't what she wants. When I finally reach the soft skin on her upper thigh, her entire body shivers, and she pulls her bottom lip between her teeth as my hand pushes the fabric of her dress higher, and my fingers dig into her soft flesh before reaching the fabric covering the place she wants me. The only place I want to be.

"Don't you dare back out now. Don't tell me you haven't imagined this after every late-night text, every time our eyes met across the hallway, every time you couldn't decide if you wanted to fight me or—" She breaks off with a gasp the second I give her exactly what she asked for, not because she begged but because, without saying so, she's just told me she knows exactly who I am, and she's still asking. She makes a sound of pure satisfaction as my thick digit slides all the way in. "You can't take it back now. Don't hold back," she pleads, her voice raw with need.

And I don't. I couldn't if I wanted to, because she's right. I've imagined this very moment countless nights after every text and even before, but none of those dreams could compare to this. To the way she feels wrapped around me, to the sounds she makes, to the fire burning through my veins with each ragged breath she takes.

I capture her mouth again, and she kisses me back with a ferocity that steals my breath. Her hands roam everywhere, my shoulders, my back, my chest, like she's trying to memorize every inch of me through touch alone. I'm so lost in her, her scent, her noises, her taste that I don't realize her hands have drifted to my belt. To undo it. I want more of her, but not here, not taken quickly in a hallway where anyone could see.

"Not like this," comes out quick, the gravel in my tone so thick I barely recognize my own voice. I'll give her this, but nothing more. If she wants me, she can have me, but it will be without a mask, where we're no longer hiding who we are from each other.

"I know who you are." Her eyes flick between mine as if those are the magic words.

"Good," I answer, laying my forehead to hers. "Say it when I make you come." My voice is coarse and thick with desire as I slip in a second digit and capture her gasp with my mouth, pumping into her in long, hard strokes that make her forget about her other pleas.

Her hands desert my belt and glide around my hips, where her nails sink into my skin, making me harder still as my hard length envies my fingers. I want to throw her over my shoulder and take her back to my dorm, where I can peel off this dress and have her uninterrupted, mapping out every inch of her body, every spot that makes her tick until there isn't an inch my lips haven't touched. With every thought, my pace quickens, and I can feel her reaching her peak.

"I want to hear it," I rasp out against her sweet lips. "I want you to scream my name before you see the stars."

That's all it takes to send her spiraling, but it's not my name that comes tumbling from her sweet mouth. Instead, her words are stolen by a door slamming open at the far end.

"Asha," a familiar voice calls out. My head whips left, finding Hollis squeezing the bridge of his nose before facing away. "Shit. Asha, come on, we have to go."

"Give me a minute. I'm kind of in the middle of something." She tries to force levelness into her voice as her walls spasm around my fingers.

"I'm sorry, but we don't have a minute. It's your dad. There's been an accident. A car is waiting out front to take us to the airport."

Her breath catches as the color drains from her face and her whole body goes rigid against mine as terror floods through her. I slowly remove my hand and put her down, easing her dress back over her hips so no one can see when I feel her tremble so badly the fabric of her dress shivers.

She slides her mask up, and her lips part on a silent gasp she can't quite release before for her wild eyes find mine. "I'm sorry. I have to go." Her voice fractures. "He's all I have left."

And then she's running down the hall. Not my enemy. Not my rival. Asha. The girl I've been messaging for months, the one who has been pouring her heart out to me in the safety of anonymity. The girl whose father I know has been her entire world since her mother passed. The girl who just fell apart in my arms and is now racing toward what might be the worst night of her life.

I stand there, frozen, for a heartbeat, watching her sprint away from me, her heels clicking frantically against the floor. Hollis has already disappeared around the corner, and she's about to do the same without knowing for certain it was me. She said she knows who I am. But does she? Or was that just hope speaking, a desperate need to believe the person behind the mask was the one she wanted it to be? We never got to finish. Never got to that moment where the masks come off and all doubt is erased.

My hand, the one that was just inside her, the one that still trembles with the memory of her coming undone, flies to my mask. I need her to see my face. Need her to *know* with absolute certainty that it was me. That I'm the one she's been falling for. That every message, every confession, every promise was real.

I break into a run.

"Wait!" The word tears from my throat, breaking my silence, but she's too far ahead, too focused on getting to the car, on getting to her father.

I round the corner and see the main entrance ahead, the doors already swinging shut behind her. Through the glass, I can make out her silhouette descending the front steps, Hollis's hand on her back, guiding her toward the waiting car. When I finally burst through the doors and the cool night air hits my face, I stumble onto the top step, my hand reaching up to rip off my mask, but I'm too late.

The car door is already slamming shut, and through the tinted window, I can barely make out her profile. I have no idea if she's even looking back for me. The vehicle pulls away from the curb, red taillights growing smaller as it speeds down the tree-lined drive, and I'm left standing there on the steps, mask clutched in my hand, chest heaving, watching the car disappear into the darkness. My skin still burns where she touched me. I can still taste her on my lips, still feel the phantom sensation of her wrapped around me, still hear the way she gasped my name, or tried to, before Hollis interrupted.

Students mill around me, laughing and talking as they come and go from the masquerade, completely oblivious to the fact that my entire world just drove away without knowing for certain who I am. She said she knew. But what if she was wrong? What if she goes to the hospital, sits by her father's bedside, and convinces herself it couldn't have been me? What if the doubt creeps in during those long, terrible hours of waiting, and she decides it was someone else entirely?

I sink down onto the stone steps, the mask dangling from my fingers.

Music and laughter drift from the ballroom behind me, but all I can hear is her voice.

"Don't you dare back out now."

"I know who you are."

"I'm sorry. I have to go."

Three sentences that changed everything and resolved nothing. Three sentences that felt like a door slamming in slow motion, and I just stood there, frozen, watching her slip away.

The taillights disappear through the gate far in the distance, and something in my chest tears. I should've run faster. Should've grabbed her hand before she got in the car. Should've ripped this whole charade apart the second she stepped foot in the hallway. But I didn't. And now she's gone, and I don't know what she knows.

Maybe she's already connected the dots: the sickly boy next door who she defended on the monkey bars, and the stranger she held tightly to moments ago, her pen pal, and the boy she's been determined to forget, the one that's part of a past she tried to bury, are one and the same. Or she hasn't.

Either way, the truth won't stay buried long. Not after tonight. Not after she looked at me like I was both the answer she'd been searching for and the question that terrified her. I won't allow it. I *can't*. Not when I finally saw the recognition flickering in her eyes, even if she drove away before it could catch fire. Tomorrow, she'll wake up and replay every word, every touch, every breath between us tonight. She'll remember things she tried to forget. And when she does, when the pieces finally lock into place, everything will either fall apart or fall together. I just don't know which will destroy me more.

The mask slips from my fingers and hits the stone with a crack that sounds too much like a starting gun.

Whatever comes next, there's no more hiding.

TRIGGER

CHAPTER 9

ONE MONTH LATER

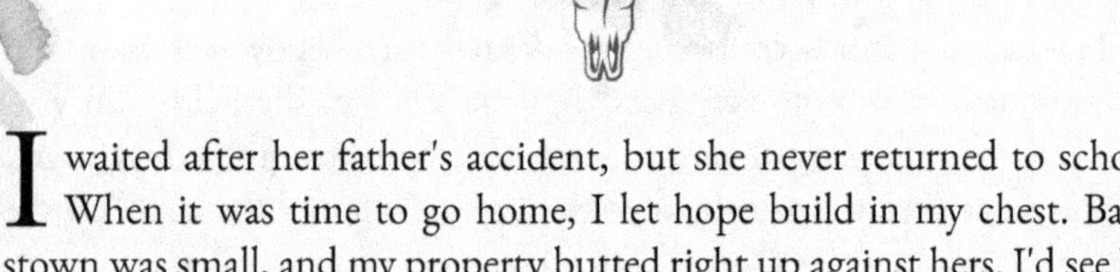

I waited after her father's accident, but she never returned to school. When it was time to go home, I let hope build in my chest. Bardstown was small, and my property butted right up against hers. I'd see her again.

I should have known better.

Walking into my house for the first time in four years, I found a kid my age standing in the living room. Same eyes. Same dark hair. My father wasted no time: "This is your brother."

The words seemed as much news to the kid as they were to me. The grandfather clock ticked five full seconds before I broke the silence. "Where are you from?"

"Texas."

"Welcome to the family, Dallas." I instantly gave him a nickname like we were old friends. We weren't, but it didn't change the fact that I wanted him to be.

I'd always wanted a brother. Only, when I thought of having one, the schematics worked out differently. My mother hid her pregnancy from my father, then she put me up for adoption without his knowledge and ran off to marry his brother only to turn around and leave them too.

I never knew my father had a brother. But that day, years of silence ended with a police escort and a broken boy in my living room. My uncle's son. My blood. My brother.

He needed me, so I stayed. Weeks passed, and I kept hoping I'd run into Asha in town, but it never happened. Which is why I'm now standing on her porch, staring at the door knocker, trying to recall the words I'd planned on giving her. I've thought about what I would say countless times, but now that I'm standing here, I can't remember any of them.

"Fuck it," I say as I ring the doorbell.

Heels click across the foyer, filling the silence. But they're all wrong, and then the door opens.

"Deliveries go around back," a maid says, mistaking me for someone I'm not.

"Oh, I'm not here to deliver anything. I'm here to see Asha."

Her brows tug together before she says, "Miss Asha is staying in Louisville with her father. Do you want me to give her a message for you?"

"No, that's alright. I'll give it to her myself. Thank you."

The door closes with a soft click that sounds like finality.

I stand there for a moment, staring at the brass knocker again. Four weeks. Four weeks of waiting for her to appear, only to find out she's not even here. Of course she's not. Nothing about coming home has gone the way I thought it would. I have a brother I never knew existed. A mother who's worse than I imagined. A father who won't speak about what happened. And now this.

I turn and walk down the porch steps, my boots heavy against the stone. She's in Louisville with her father. Part of me wants to get in my truck and drive there right now, but I know that's desperation talking. I've already waited one month. I can wait a little longer. As I reach my truck, I glance back at the house one more time. The maid has probably already forgotten about me, the nobody who came to the front door asking for Asha.

I'll give it to her myself, I'd said like a promise.

I climb into the truck and slam the door harder than I need to. The engine roars to life, and I pull away from the circular driveway and watch as the house shrinks in my rearview mirror.

Four weeks down and who knows how many more to go. But I'll wait. I've gotten good at waiting.

TRIGGER

CHAPTER 10

SIX MONTHS LATER

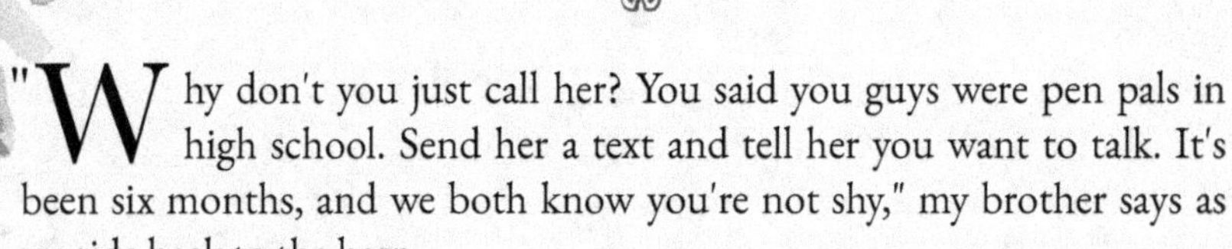

"Why don't you just call her? You said you guys were pen pals in high school. Send her a text and tell her you want to talk. It's been six months, and we both know you're not shy," my brother says as we ride back to the barn.

I've been showing him the ropes since he arrived, teaching him the basics of breaking and training a horse. Though, I haven't had to teach much. He may not have grown up on the land like me, but you can tell horses are in our blood.

"We had school-issued phones. I never had her personal number."

"What about her cousin? Ask him," he says as though it's the obvious solution, which it fucking is.

I've been so damn caught up in everything going on here and hyper-focused on just running into her again, I didn't even think to use our shared connection.

"I'm a fucking idiot," I say as I pull out my phone. I hold it up, and it feels like my lucky day because we're still miles from the house and I have a signal.

> Trigger: Can you give me Asha's number?

Hollis and I have texted a few times since school ended. His family lives in Ontario, not too far from New York, so visiting isn't ideal, but we talked about planning an annual ski trip with some of the guys on the team. Perhaps I should have led with that. Asha has been a sore subject between us since school ended, not because he doesn't like the idea of me hooking up with his cousin—I'm pretty sure he saw right through our constant bickering in high school. He knew I liked her, but that's not why he's upset. I left him in the dark too many times when it came to her.

Hollis: I thought you were neighbors. Go knock on her door and ask her yourself.

Yep, still bitter. I can't say I blame him. I should have been up front with him from the start, but I didn't expect him to become my best friend. It's not easy to say, '*Oh, hey, by the way, when I got wind that my father wanted to ship me off to boarding school because I wouldn't stop bull riding, I intentionally kept going out of my way to do it and get caught in hopes he'd send me to the same school your cousin was shipped off to.*'

Trigger: We are. She hasn't been home in over a year.

I watch as bubbles appear and then disappear.

"Well, did he give it to you?" Dallas asks, trotting along beside me on his horse, Titan.

"No." I blow out a frustrated breath.

"Why not?"

"It's a long story."

"Want to talk about it?"

"Want to tell me why you showed up on my front porch in the back of a cop car?"

He stays silent. Dallas and I grow closer every day. Some days, it feels like we've always been together, but then there are times, like now, when it feels like there's an ocean between us. He refuses to talk about what brought him here, and because I know what it's like to live with demons, I don't push.

My phone dings with a text.

Hollis: If she hasn't called, she doesn't want you to have it.

Trigger: She can't call. I never gave her my number.

Hollis: I did.

I stop my horse to make sure I read that right. *What? Does that mean she asked for it?*

Trigger: Why?

I try to play it cool even though my heart is suddenly racing with this revelation. She's had my number all this time. That has to mean she knew it was me at prom.

Hollis: I gave it to her when we were in the hospital. We didn't know when Warrick would wake from his coma, and since the two of you are neighbors, I told her to ask you for help.

Warrick's accident made the local news. It was bad enough that everyone was talking about it, but no one mentioned the coma. I didn't know. If I had, I would have found a way to be there, to do *something*. I pinch the bridge of my nose, hating myself for not realizing how serious it was. But I can't rewrite history. I was drowning in my own family's crisis, and by the time I came up for air, it was too late.

Hollis: You should have told me it was her.

Not the answer I was hoping for, but I get it. Junior year, after the charity ride, I told Hollis about my past with Asha. I told him everything that happened on the monkey bars, her fall, and our family's rivalry. I didn't want to keep him in the dark anymore. During our talk, two different narratives were casually mentioned about why Asha was sent away. Asha's version is that Warrick did it to keep her safe, while Hollis's parents claim it was for her own good.

My mind immediately went down the rabbit hole. Why make that distinction unless he thought there was more to it? I pressed him, but he shrugged it off like it wasn't anything, and hell, maybe it's not. But in my head, his parents' version suggests something more complex. Sending someone away for their own good suggests you might be the harm they need protecting from.

Regardless, I could have divulged my suspicions that she was my secret pen pal, but I didn't. It felt like a lot to pile on in one conversation. Besides, I promised Asha I wouldn't tell him about her visit to check on me after I was kicked by that bull. Telling him any more felt like crossing a line she asked me not to. And at the time, there was still a sliver of doubt, anyway. I still thought I could have been reading into things that weren't there.

Trigger: I know.

Trigger: I'm sorry.

Hollis: If she tells you to fuck off, you listen.

Trigger: I'll fuck off.

Hollis: 364.666.1432

I quickly type out a text before I can think better of it and say too much or too little.

Trigger: We need to talk.

It's straightforward and to the point. It doesn't give anything away. There's nothing to be implied, just facts. But none of that matters because the text never goes through.

The status never updated to Delivered or Read because I was blocked. But why?

Was I blocked simply because I am the enemy, the boy next door she was told to stay away from because of the last name attached to mine, or is there more to it? Has she already written me off because I didn't call sooner?

Regardless, the way I see it, she blocked me before she could tell me to fuck off, which means I'm not breaking my word to Hollis. If anything, this is a loophole. She asked someone for my number, which counts for something. It means she thought about me.

TRIGGER

CHAPTER 11
ONE YEAR LATER

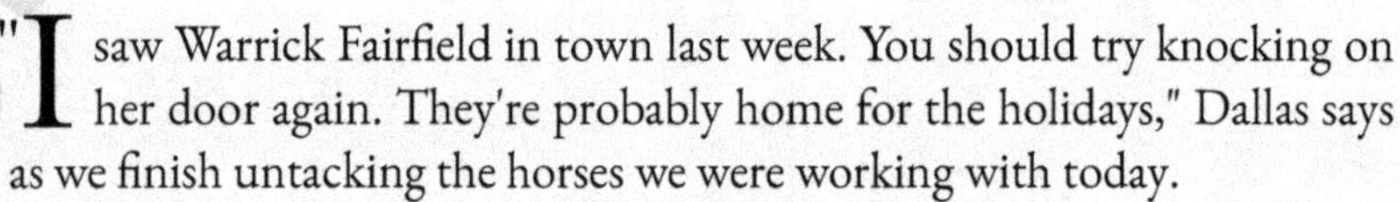

"I saw Warrick Fairfield in town last week. You should try knocking on her door again. They're probably home for the holidays," Dallas says as we finish untacking the horses we were working with today.

He's been working with my dad a lot more, helping him with his bourbon hobby. Though, I'm not sure how much longer we can continue calling it a hobby. With Dallas's help, he's converted fifty acres of land into barley, corn, wheat, and rye, and he converted an old silo into his tasting room. His tinkering has produced enough bottles that we had to start selling them just to get rid of them. It was that or pour damn good bourbon down the drain.

My brother may have horses in his blood, but farming is in his heart. He loves the land.

"Yeah, I saw his town car turning down their road on my way back from the feed store yesterday. She's not there. When I knocked on the door, the maid told me Warrick was spending the holidays with Asha at their Louisville estate."

"That's crazy. You'd think she'd want to be here," he says, leaning against the frame of my stall.

"I mean, it makes sense. She's attending classes at Louisville."

"I guess, but her mother planted all those purple flowers that run along the fences." He shrugs before straightening. "You'd think she'd want to come home after being gone for so long. If nothing more than to surround herself with memories she had with her mom."

I think back to our time at school and the way she tried to push me away, to keep me at arm's length even when I could tell she didn't want to. When I found out I was the reason she got sent away, that all made more sense. I was wrapped in memories she didn't want to remember, but I know she loved her mom dearly. She said as much, daring to touch some of the happier memories she could never forget. When we weren't talking about how we hated our senior class assignment, horses, food, and teachers we couldn't stand, then she would talk about how she couldn't wait to go home and sleep in her old room. Bardstown is home, so why hasn't she been here?

Unless someone's keeping her from here.

"Can you finish up here?" I ask as I hastily brush past him.

"Yeah. What's the rush?"

"I have some business I need to handle," I say, exiting the barn and leaving off the *in Louisville* part.

Here I am again, staring at another one of Asha's doors. I look insane, and showing up here feels reckless, but I'm out of ideas, and I'm done waiting.

I rap my knuckles against the door and wait. There's silence on the other side of the door. When I pulled in, I didn't see a car in the driveway, but there's also a huge attached garage, so no car doesn't mean no one is home. I try to peer through the window and look for a light, but I can't do so without climbing into a bush, which would definitely make this entire encounter teeter on the edge of stalker if I let one toe step off this porch to peek inside a window.

I take my chances and knock once more. This time, the door opens before I can finish, but it's not Asha.

A heap of messy blonde hair piled atop the head of a brown-eyed girl in a sweater and socks, opens the door. Her eyes trail up my body from head to toe before a smile tugs at her mouth.

"Can I help you?"

"This is the Fairfield residence, correct?" My voice comes out more formal than I intended, like I'm delivering a package.

"That depends. Who's asking?" she says coyly, leaning against the doorframe.

"So that's a yes," I say, refusing to be sidetracked. She's pretty, but not who I came here to see. "Is Asha home?"

She purses her lips. "Damn, already taken. No, you just missed her. She left for the Poconos with her father to spend Thanksgiving with family."

Of course she's gone. Of course I'm too late. Again. But just as my stomach feels like it can't sink anymore, I hear a silver lining in her response. *Damn, already taken.* If she thinks I'm someone to Asha, that has to mean Asha isn't seeing anyone.

"Want to come in?" She opens the door wider.

"I'm sorry. I didn't catch your name," I say, trying to put pieces together. She's not a maid, and I don't think she's a relative since she just said they left to spend the holidays with family. So, who is she to Asha?

"I'm Sydney. We're roommates, but there was a water leak on the floor above our place, so we're staying here." She looks behind her, where there's a fire burning in a stone fireplace. "Not too shabby." She raises her shoulder, turning back to me. "Care for a drink?"

"Sure, one drink," I agree. *What else am I going to do? Drive back home and stare at a blocked number?*

She's not the girl I hoped I'd find, but she's close to the one I've been searching for.

Close might be the best I'm going to get. Months of missed chances, blocked numbers, and closed doors. But Sydney is here, and Sydney knows her. What she does on weekends, who she spends time with, if she talks about home, or if she's ever mentioned me at all. It's not the conversation I wanted, but it's the one I'm getting. And right now, that has to be enough.

TRIGGER

CHAPTER 12

TWO YEARS LATER

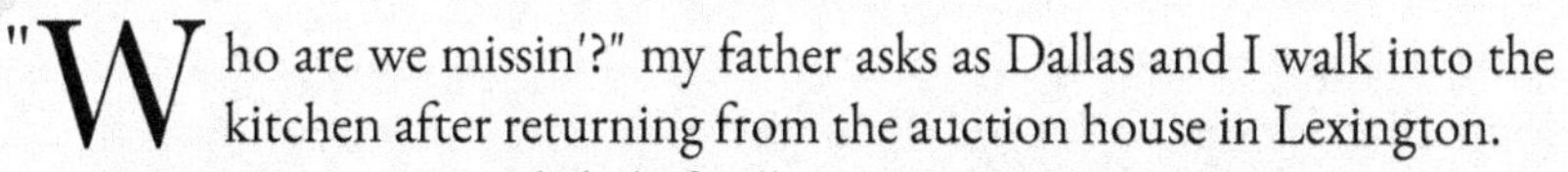

"Who are we missin'?" my father asks as Dallas and I walk into the kitchen after returning from the auction house in Lexington.

"No one," I answer, disbelief still overpowering my annoyance.

"No one?" He sets his coffee cup on the counter and gives me his full attention. "Now, how in the world is that possible?"

This is the first time my father has ever let go of the reins. He let us go alone to the auction house, and we came home without one sale. I've been attending auctions with him since I was seven. Dallas might be new to the game, but I'm not. I know how they work. I knew exactly what to expect because I'd grown up watching the game played, and I still failed today.

"Warrick was there," Dallas answers for me as I lean onto the large granite island to keep myself upright.

"What's that got to do with anythin'? He's the competition. He's always there," he argues pointedly.

"He undersold us on everything," I say defeatedly.

"As you expected he would—" my father starts.

"No, this wasn't normal. There's no way we could have matched him," Dallas interjects.

"Nor would we want to. Dropping your prices that low calls our elite breeder status into question. I'm not even sure how he's making a profit," I point out.

"Hmm," is all my father says before he turns his face toward the barn that can be seen out the floor-to-ceiling windows of the kitchen.

Dallas and I share a questionable glance before I press my father.

"'Hmm.' That's it? I could have made a sale if you'd let me expand our breeding operation. There's money to be made breeding bulls."

He raises his hand. "A well-bred horse gets more."

"Our operating costs are higher. It's cheaper to breed bulls, and the market is bigger—"

"No," he says firmly.

But something's different this time. In all the times I've brought up this conversation—and there have been many—I'd say this response has gone the best. And that's saying something.

I expected anger. Annoyance. A whole lot more berating for coming home with this kind of failure. My father has been a great dad since he found out about me at age five, after my adoptive parents knocked on his door as a last resort, desperate to save my life, asking him for a kidney. From that day on, he stepped up in ways that changed everything.

But here's the thing about him: he's not a coddler. He doesn't blow smoke up your ass or hand out participation trophies. When you succeed, he's proud. When you fail, he'll point out every single mistake without hesitation. He'll tell you exactly where you went wrong and what you need to do better. That's just who he is. It's how he's always been. *So, what the hell is this?*

I study him, trying to understand why. Then it hits me: he's barely listening. His mind is somewhere else. *On someone* else.

"Maybe Warrick wasn't trying to make a profit today," Dallas says, unknowingly bringing the topic full circle, back to the crux or, better yet, the person at the center of my father's distraction.

"What other reason could he possibly have for underselling us like that?" I ask, believing my father suspects something he's not telling us.

"I guess he's lightenin' the barn," he says as he rubs the backs of his fingers against his beard.

There's more. I can tell there's more. There has to be. We just lost roughly a million dollars in revenue, and all he has to say is, '*Hmm,*' and '*I guess he's lightening the barn.*'

"What's your deal with Warrick Fairfield?"

"Deal?" He snaps his head toward me.

"Yes, this generational feud. Why did it start? I've never understood why you hated him so much. He's not the only competition. I've seen you be cordial and even share meals with other sellers, so why not him? Is it just because we're neighbors?"

"Son, when did I ever say I hated Warrick Fairfield?"

My brow furrows as I consider his question and try to recall an instance where he's said as much, but I come up empty, because he hasn't. I cross my arms and look him square in the eye. Regardless of what words he's used, he knows what I'm asking. Maybe he didn't say hate, but there is bad blood.

"The feud was never generational. It started when Maya married Warrick. Before then, there was nothin' but flowers and peace." My mind instantly starts searching for some small piece to latch onto, a clue or hint, anything that could help pinpoint a cause, because surely his answer supplied one. He must see the wheels in my mind spinning. "There's no point in diggin' up history, son." He heads to the back door. "I'll be attendin' the next auction. In case you've forgotten, we're in the business of sellin' horses," he adds, walking out the door without another word.

There it is, the jab I was waiting for—deserved, I suppose—since I didn't make a sale, but he's wrong about digging up history. I have to know what happened so I can get the girl.

"If you ask me, that was progress," Dallas says, blowing out a breath. "Want to come with me to the Holiday Classic tonight?"

"Are you meeting up with the vaulter girl afterward?"

"She's in the show," he neither confirms nor denies his plans.

It's been two years since Dallas moved in, and every girl in town wants to get in his bed, but he has no interest. The only one he's ever talked to is Madison, and I think the draw is that she's not from town. She's here for a few days, and then she's gone, always on the road. I get it. I'm the same way. I don't care to lead someone on, and spending more than one night with someone gets messy.

"A few of the girls want to go out on the Bourbon Trail after the show." His voice trails off with innuendo. Basically, if I go, it's a sure thing my night will have a happy ending.

The problem is, my night is already fucked. There's no way I'll enjoy a second of going out. Not after seeing Warrick Fairfield today, and especially not after my father's cryptic responses. If anything, the girl I try to forget as much as I hold onto is fresh in my mind. Except, this time, I'm not going to sit here and stew on it.

"Nah, I got somewhere I got to be. Maybe next time," I say, swiping my keys off the counter. Time to go dig up another memory.

OF ALL THE CRUEL JOKES THE UNIVERSE COULD PLAY, OURS has to be the worst. Loving someone who hates you. I used to lie awake, trying to figure out when it started. Was it before the fighting or because of it? Did I fall in the middle of one of our wars, or did I love her first and only learned to fight because it was the only way she'd look at me at all?

I know this infatuation I have borders on obsession. I'd provoke her just to see that flash in her eyes, to have her full attention on me, even if it was rage. Better her anger than her indifference. Better to matter as her enemy than not matter at all, because that was always my goal. Ever since the day a fearless little girl stood up to two class clowns on the playground and proved that appearances didn't matter, confidence mattered. I knew I wanted her as a friend, and damn it, she offered me as much. In a way, she started it all. She offered to be my friend even when doing so could get her in trouble. Maybe it's pathetic how much I've held on to that.

The milkshake she threw on me on the first day of freshman year probably should have been my sign to let it go, to let her go, but if anything, it might have been the exact moment I knew I was in trouble. *I hope you hate strawberries.* " I was speechless, and for as much as I didn't understand what had happened, what had changed to make her hate me so much during all those years we spent apart, all I could think was how beautiful she was. How much I wanted to kiss her. How completely screwed I was. What kind of person falls in love with someone in the middle of having a milkshake poured down their chest? What does that say about me? That I'm so desperate, so broken, that I'll take whatever scraps of attention she throws my way and call it love?

How pathetic is it that I became a scholar of someone who couldn't stand me? I memorized her tells, her patterns, the way her jaw clenched before she delivered a killing blow. I knew her through our wars better than most people knew their friends. And I told myself it was a strategy, that I was just trying to win our battles. But I was lying. I was studying her because I was desperate for any way to know her.

That's why I'm sitting outside her place now, still desperate, still waiting, as rain hammers against my windshield in sheets.

"Come on," I mutter to the sky, watching the rain. Just a break, just enough to cross the street without arriving at her door looking like a wet dog. I check my phone: 7:43 p.m. At least she should be home this time when I ring the doorbell.

The building door bursts open, catching my attention, and I sit straight up in my seat. It's her. Reaching for the door handle, I'm out in the rain, ready to get soaked, when a black sedan appears from nowhere, pulling right in front of her. I freeze halfway out of my car, one foot on the wet pavement.

The driver's door opens. A man steps out, tall in a tailored suit under a designer raincoat. He walks around to Asha with the umbrella, holding it over her like she's something precious, as I blink drops of water off my eyelashes. Then, opening the passenger door, he hugs her—and not like a friend, like someone who knows her intimately, like someone who's done it a thousand times before.

Asha laughs at something he says before ducking into the car. The sedan pulls away, and I stand in the street, rain plastering my shirt to my skin, watching until they disappear around the corner.

It's been hours, and the concrete steps are cold and unforgiving beneath me. The rain stopped, but I'm still wet, still waiting, refusing to let another year go by where we don't talk. However, she's not coming back—at least not tonight. I pull myself up from the steps, legs stiff, clothes heavy with rain. The street is empty now, just pools of water reflecting the streetlights. I look one more time toward the corner where the sedan disappeared, and something in my chest finally unclenches. Not relief. Not quite peace. Just...exhaustion. The kind that comes from holding on too long to something that was never mine to hold.

I head toward my truck, each step feeling lighter than the last.

My phone buzzes in my pocket, and I stop walking as my hand

hovers over it, caught between seeing who it is and letting it ring. She doesn't know I'm here. She never asked me to wait, and for the first time in years, the ghost of hope that's had me in a chokehold for more years than I can count is gone. It buzzes again, and I close my eyes, but I keep walking.

For now.

TRIGGER

CHAPTER 13
FOUR YEARS LATER

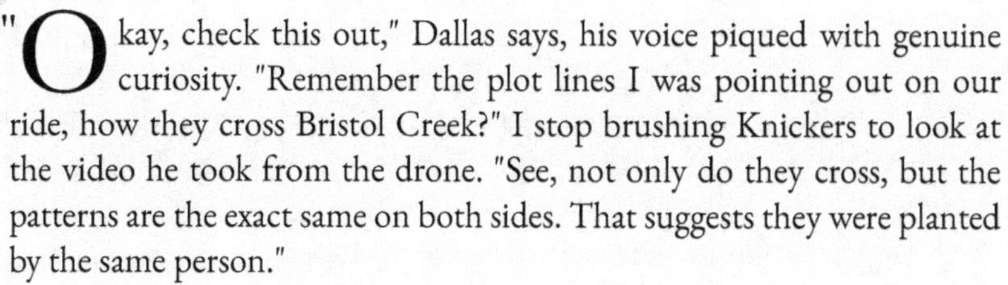

"Okay, check this out," Dallas says, his voice piqued with genuine curiosity. "Remember the plot lines I was pointing out on our ride, how they cross Bristol Creek?" I stop brushing Knickers to look at the video he took from the drone. "See, not only do they cross, but the patterns are the exact same on both sides. That suggests they were planted by the same person."

There's no generational feud. It was all flowers and peace before Maya married Warrick. A conversation I had with my father pushes through as I try to make sense of the aerial view that suggests our land was once shared.

"Can you tell what kind of crop was once planted there? Is it possible there were once flowers here?"

"Flowers?" He furrows his brow, and the sliver of excitement I had fades. "It's possible."

"Can you send me those images?"

He pulls out the SD card. "Here, just give this back to me when you're done. I'm going back over there tomorrow to take soil samples. I need to determine a good place to expand the wheat field."

I thin my lips. My father's small batch bourbon is definitely no longer a hobby. I don't care that the man wants to make bourbon. We only live once, so do what makes you happy. I just wish he'd let me do what I want. I've never understood why he's so opposed to letting me start a herd. Dallas already said he'd help me get it off the ground, plus his friend Fisher is staying with us now. He's our intermediary between tracks and buyers for our horses, but he likes to get his hands dirty too.

"Well"—I squeeze his shoulder—"if the soil is no longer ripe for planting, I guess I'll just have to zone it for grazing."

He laughs before saying, "I can't tell if the idea is growing on him or if he's just flat out ignoring you. Has he ever said why he's so against it?" Dallas asks as we walk down the center of the barn, checking stalls.

"He hasn't told me, but I figured it out," I say, locking one of the stalls.

"Are you planning on sharing that with me or..."

"I know our fathers refuse to discuss each other, but I assumed yours mentioned our grandfather," I say, pausing to give him my full attention. "The reason Grandpa Hale stopped riding horses wasn't by choice. It was because he was injured while bull riding. On his last ride, a bull stepped on him, and he broke six ribs, suffered a punctured lung, and a spinal injury. He was lucky to walk after the spinal injury."

His eyes are wide, and I can tell this is his first time hearing of the story. "When my dad talked about his family, it was never about the family business. I guess that's because he walked away and chose a woman who ultimately didn't choose us back." He shrugs, the memory of our mother clearly no longer a source of pain. "I get why he doesn't like the idea now that I know about the accident. Perhaps you should try explaining that you don't plan on riding them."

"I could, but saying I'll never ride a bull again might be a lie. Plus, I want him to trust me. To trust my decisions. Sure, I could get hurt, but that can be said for any job. We take risks every day. The thing is, they're ours to take."

"I get that," he says, pushing off the wall. "I'm going to head up and get a shower. I'll ride over to the creek and take samples tomorrow. Soil samples won't take that long. If I ship them off tomorrow, we could have answers by next week," he says, his back to me as he disappears onto the gravel path that leads up to the house.

"Dallas," I call out before he gets out of earshot.

He stops and turns. "You ever going to stop calling me that?"

"I didn't know it bothered you." The nickname has always felt like a lifeline to me. Our way of surviving what we were handed all those years ago.

"It doesn't." His voice drops, goes serious. "But you're my brother, and I'm not hiding anymore."

The words hit harder than they should. All this time, I thought the nickname kept us close, but for him it was something else entirely.

"Thanks for helping me with this...London." I test his real name out.

Something passes between us, years of unspoken understanding condensed into a single look. He nods once then turns and walks out.

I stand there a beat longer than necessary before heading toward the tack room to pull up the images.

The room smells like old leather and saddle oil. I drop into my father's desk chair and wake up the computer. The chair creaks as I lean back and click the mouse, simultaneously sending a binder and documents to the floor.

"Shit." I crouch down, gathering them up. Most of it is what I'd expect: tax documents, breeding records, some old photographs of horses I don't recognize. But one paper stops me cold.

It's a lease agreement. The document is old. Old enough that it has yellowed with age, the date across the top decades before I was born. And sprawled across the bottom, in fading ink, is my grandfather's signature. My eyes quickly scan the document. Then again, slower this time, because my brain won't accept what I'm reading.

Parcel 2847-B. Eastern section, 60 acres.
Lessee: Astor Fairfield...

Fairfield. As in our neighbors. The competition, our *enemies,* the man who has been making every auction a battlefield for as long as I can remember.

If this document is real, it rewrites everything. The land isn't theirs. It's *ours.*

My grandfather leased it to them...to Astor Fairfield, Warrick's father. It's a sixty-year lease, a year for every acre. I scan the document one more time. There's not much here; it's clear and concise, leaving no room for misunderstanding the terms. When I reach the bottom, I see it. The expiration period. In less than a year, the property will revert to us.

I sit back on my heels, the paper still firmly in my grip as I rub my hand over the stubble on my jaw. This has to be why he's been underselling us, Warrick's planning on moving. That must be why Asha hasn't been home. He doesn't want her getting attached to the land her mother loved...land she can't keep. Land he can't buy her.

I flip the lease over aimlessly in my hand. Warrick can't offer to buy the land; I already know that. I've known practically my whole life that Hale land can't be sold. As long as there are living heirs to claim the land, it stays in the family.

It's true, after the last time I saw Asha, I forced myself to let her go. Had to. Letting go meant letting go of a past that didn't work. You can't live there and still have a future. I buried it so deep I almost convinced myself it was just rivalry, just competition. Nothing more. For a while, I almost believed my own lie, but staring at this piece of paper, another realization is taking form.

This was always going to happen. It's always going to come back to her—back to us. Because she's mine. She was always meant to be mine.

For the first time in years, I have a date. There's no way her father will get away with moving off that land without her finding out, without her coming home to see it one more time, and you better believe I'll be there too, making myself unavoidable. I'll be standing between her and everything she's ever wanted, holding the deed to her dreams, and there won't be a damn thing she can do but deal with me. Face me. This time, I have something Asha Fairfield wants. Running is no longer an option, and I'm the only road home.

PART TWO

ASHA

CHAPTER 14

THE PROPOSAL

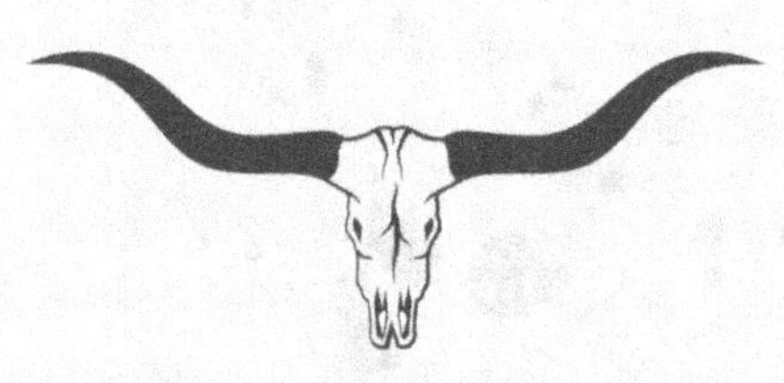

The bartender slides two tequilas across the polished mahogany just as his laugh cuts through the reception chatter. Deep. Smug. Unmistakable. I don't look.

"You okay?" Sydney bumps my shoulder.

"Peachy." I wrap my fingers around the shot glass.

"Liar." She follows my gaze in the bar mirror to where Trigger holds court with a cluster of guests. "I know this week is...complicated."

"Seven days, Syd. Seven days to either propose to that asshole or lose everything." I throw back the shot, welcoming the burn.

She shifts uncomfortably. "Have you talked to your dad about it? Maybe there's another way—"

"My dad?" I laugh bitterly. "You mean the man who wasn't even going to tell me about the lease? Who only came clean because I showed up with Laney, who needed an internship. I knew he wouldn't turn me away, because she was a student at Louisville."

"Asha—"

"No, seriously. Every time I came home...Louisville, the racetracks, random business trips. He made sure I was never actually at the ranch, and I went along with it because I loved him. Because I trusted him. Sixty years, a year for every acre, and it all goes back to the Hales. My mom's legacy...gone."

Sydney's face is carefully neutral. She knows my relationship with my father has been strained; she just doesn't know the depth. "Maybe he was trying to protect you."

"From what? The truth?" I signal the bartender for another round, as the sight of my father laughing across the bar grates on my nerves. *How can he laugh when we're on the verge of losing something so important to my mother?* "I've been planning my whole life around that ranch. Vet school, the horses, the business. Now I don't even know what I want anymore."

She's quiet for a long moment, fingers tight around her glass. "What are you going to do?"

"About the ranch? Or about him?" I nod toward where Trigger is now looking our way, that infuriating smirk on his face.

"Either. Both."

The DJ's voice booms across the reception hall before I can answer. "Alright, alright, do I have all my single ladies on the dance floor? Come on, don't be shy..."

I close my eyes. Great, now this.

"That includes you, ladies!" Laney's voice rings out, and suddenly, my best friend is at my elbow, radiant in white lace and tulle, eyes sparkling with champagne and happiness. "Come on! Maybe you'll catch it."

Maybe I don't want to catch it. Maybe I want to run for the hills and never look back.

But Laney is linking her arms through ours, and I'm sure if Trigger wasn't watching me before, I know he is now. I can feel his gaze like a brand between my shoulder blades. There's no way I can back out now. If I did, he'd know I cared about what he thought, and that would give away too much. Caring is a weakness. Caring gets you exploited.

The bartender does me a solid and quickly passes me the second shot I ordered. I toss it back and let the liquid courage settle hot in my chest.

"Let's do it," I say, forcing fake glee into my voice. I'm happy for my best friend—I am—but that doesn't mean I want to catch a bouquet.

She just married a Hale. Laney knows exactly what position I'm in. Hell, part of me thinks she might throw the bouquet right at me just to speed things along.

Laney was one of the first people I'd trusted in years. Maybe because I saw something broken in her, something familiar. Or maybe it was just the kindness she showed when I walked into class, soaked through, muddy boots tracking dirt everywhere, no supplies. I sat beside her and asked to borrow a pen. She gave me a genuine smile without an ounce of pity. We were fast friends after that. She's also how I gained my bonus best friend, Sydney. They were kind of a package deal since they grew up together.

Now, I have not one but two best friends. That title is not one I give easily. Everyone I've ever known has betrayed me somehow—even the people who were supposed to love me unconditionally. But I let Laney in because I saw that same wariness in her eyes, that same careful distance. She knew what it was like to build walls. And now she's married. Not just to anyone, but to *his* brother. The brother of my enemy.

I don't feel betrayed, not exactly. Laney didn't do this to hurt me, but that's almost worse. It proves why I'm content being a one-woman show, single for life. Even when people don't mean to leave, they still do. They find someone else, and you're left on the outside looking in. This loss just hits different because of the name now attached to hers.

She pulls us onto the dance floor and positions us right where she wants us before looking toward the head table, where her bouquet sits in waiting. "Don't move. Stay right here," she instructs.

"Yes, Mom," I tease.

Her eyes flash up to mine, and she smiles big. "I'm serious. This is serious. You have one week and—"

"Don't worry about me," I say. "This is your night."

"Tick tock, Mrs. Hale. It's time to toss that bouquet," the DJ announces, and for once tonight, I'm glad for one of his interruptions.

"You know she's going to nail you in the face with those flowers, right?" Sydney deadpans.

"Yep. And I'll use you as a human shield."

Laney glides to the table to grab her flowers, and I smooth my dress, suddenly hyperaware of every eye in the room. My heart begins to accelerate with the knowledge that another set of eyes is keenly tuned to my every move, and I can't help but wonder if he's praying I don't catch the bouquet.

Laney turns around, her veil floating around her shoulders, bouquet raised high above her head. "Ready, ladies?"

I'm suddenly a ball of nerves, my palms sweating, my breath coming too fast. This is ridiculous. It's just a stupid tradition. It doesn't mean anything, but I can't help but feel like my fate and the future of my mother's land lies somewhere in the knotted lace holding her bouquet of sunflowers together.

"One...two...THREE!"

Laney launches the bouquet backward with all the enthusiasm of a major league pitcher and immediately overthrows it. I watch in slow motion as the bundle of sunflowers and white daisies sail over my head, over the reaching hands of every woman on the dance floor, tumbling end over end through the air. Then, because fate loves a good joke at my expense, it nails Trigger Hale directly in the chest.

He catches it on reflex, and for one suspended moment, the entire reception hall goes silent. My body goes cold before every nerve catches fire. Unbelievable. Though, really, I should have seen this coming. Because why wouldn't the universe decide that even this, a stupid bouquet toss at my best friend's wedding, has to somehow involve him? Everyone's now staring at him, but his eyes are only on me. My face heats, but not from anger, from something else, something I've tried hard to keep tucked away. But that gaze...it's a dark storm that's always had the ability to see too much, remember too much.

The DJ's voice crackles over the speakers, dripping with amusement. "Well, folks, it looks like we just found our groom!"

The entire reception breaks out in laughter, and my feet are cutting across the dance floor before I can fully think through my next move. I'm suddenly too visible. Eyes bore into me from every direction, and it feels like they are all connecting dots they have no business connecting, as if they all know about the impossible choice I have to make and how it all comes back to this man and his arrogant, blasé indifference to my misfortune.

"Trigg, what the hell? Are you trying to cause a scene? A single woman is supposed to catch the bouquet." The words come out sharp, and my irritation almost falters the moment his cologne hits me. That damn scent, the same one that I once found comfort and safety in, the one that made me foolish enough to think he might be different.

A subtle tick pulses in his jaw before he says, "I'm not sure how I'm the one causing a scene. I'm practically at the back of the room. The flowers hit me. I wasn't diving across the floor to get them, but since they're so important to you..." He extends his hand holding the bouquet. "Take them."

It's not a suggestion. It's a challenge.

"You know what these represent, right?" I question with false patience, tossing the weight of the gesture back in his lap.

"I do," he answers.

Just that. Two words. No explanation, no elaboration. Like he's deliberately keeping me in the dark, watching to see how I'll react.

I hesitantly take the flowers from his grip and focus on keeping my hand steady as my heart thunders against my ribs, so loud I'm sure he can hear it. *Is this a game to him? Another way to twist the knife?*

"Are you proposing?" I arch an eyebrow, my voice dripping with sarcasm even as my heart hammers traitorously in my chest. Two can play at whatever game he's started.

"Am I?" He tilts his head to the side, and there's something in his eyes I can't read.

I thought I could swallow my pride. I thought I could pretend, but I can't. I refuse to be his entertainment for the evening.

"Whatever." I push the flowers back against his chest, harder than necessary.

His expression shifts, and something reminiscent of regret seems to appear, but it's gone before I can be sure. He's always been so damn good at hiding. I step around him, needing distance, needing air, but his hand darts out and captures my wrist. Not rough, but firm. Deliberate.

"Wait. Do you want me to?"

I stare at his hand on my wrist before forcing myself to meet his eyes. The contact sends electricity racing up my arm, and I hate that my body still responds to him like this. After everything. After nothing. He's serious.

I moisten my lips. "Depends."

"On?" he challenges, and there's an edge to his voice now, something raw breaking through that careful control.

"Conditions," I answer, my sigh full of nerves and frustration and years of unanswered questions. I'm giving him an out, a way to laugh this off, to prove that I'm right, that this is all just a cruel joke.

"Such as?" he presses, and damn him, he sounds genuinely interested. Like my answer actually matters.

God, I don't even know where to start. My pulse is racing. Is he serious right now? Are we really having this conversation? I scan his face for any sign of mockery, any hint that he's enjoying watching me squirm. Then laughter near the bar steals my attention. Bingo. At least that decision is easy. I don't need alcohol to make bad decisions, but it helps.

"Want a drink?" I nod toward the bar, watching him carefully.

He purses his lips in thought, and for a moment, I think he's going to refuse, going to drop my wrist and walk away and prove that this was all just him messing with me. "Only if you take the flowers."

I can't help but roll my eyes at his antics, even as something in my chest loosens just slightly. Before I can second-guess myself, I snatch the bouquet out of his hand, gripping it so tight my knuckles go white. "Drink now."

"As you wish," he says, and there's something in the way he looks at me, something warm and familiar and terrifying that makes my breath catch, but I don't let him see it.

Can I trust this? Trust him? I don't know. But I'm about to find out.

I slide onto a stool, placing the bouquet on the polished wood surface between us as he settles beside me, close enough that his knee brushes mine. The casual contact shouldn't affect me this much. But it does. And from the way his jaw tightens, the way his fingers tap once against the bar top, he feels it too.

"Tequila," I tell the bartender. "On the rocks with a twist."

I'm not usually a straight shooter, but I started the night with it, and I need something strong for this conversation.

"Make it two," Trigger adds.

We sit in charged silence until our glasses arrive—and even after that. I need the liquid courage warming my veins before I open my mouth. I take a long sip, then another, before finally turning to face him. "The land lease expires in one week."

"I'm aware," he says, his face impassive.

"Of course you are. You own it." My grip tightens on the glass. "Decades-old family feud, rival ranches..." I trail off the next words, catching in my throat. "It's all I have left of her," I laugh. "Must be quite satisfying for you. After all, I didn't make high school easy."

"You think I want this?"

"Don't you? Our families have been enemies for—"

"Twenty-five years," he interrupts, and I furrow my brow at the number. I have no clue where he pulled it from, and he doesn't give me time to figure it out before adding, "But we haven't. Not always."

His insinuation that we were ever more than enemies keeps me quiet, and I wait to see if he'll say anything more. I pulled off my mask at prom, and I'm certain he was the man behind the other, but I can't help but feel he's still hiding behind it.

"You left," he finally says.

"There was an accident," I say, eyes forward as I take a long, deep swallow, allowing the burn to do its job of uncoiling the tension wound inside of me just enough that I might actually survive this conversation.

As he raises his glass to his mouth, I can't help but wonder if his silence is purposeful. Maybe he wasn't referring to prom. We've crossed paths more than once since my best friend started dating his brother. Trigger made ignoring him impossible, playing games he knew would get under my skin. I made ignoring him an art form in return. But the fact remains: neither of us has brought up high school. Neither of us has mentioned that night.

I have my reasons for not calling him out. I wait. I can't help it. It's who I am. I believe every cause has a beginning, and I didn't know where his started. I didn't have the pieces I have now. I didn't know why there were years of silence, and now suddenly he's everywhere I am. So, I waited, and now I know. The lease.

"I called," he says, his glass hitting the bar with too much force. Liquid sloshes but doesn't spill.

"That's a lie." My laugh is sharp and humorless as I take another sip.

"How could you know that?" His body shifts toward me, his knee knocking against mine under the bar. The contact sends a jolt through me that I refuse to acknowledge. "You blocked me." He states it matter-of-factly, like it's evidence in his defense.

"You took too long." I pivot on my stool, turning fully to face him. Our knees brush again, but I don't pull back. I don't give him the satisfaction of seeing me retreat. His gaze holds mine, something flickering in those dark depths—regret, maybe, or anger that I won't make this easy for him. We're close enough now that I can count his breaths.

"I went to your house before that." His voice drops lower, rougher. "Your maid answered the door and said you were in Louisville." His lips pinch together before he adds, "You never left Louisville," accentuating the last four words like they're an accusation. Like, somehow, *I'm* the one who lied.

He's right. I didn't know he'd called, nor did I know he'd shown up at my ranch, asking about me, but I do know about his visit to my house in Louisville and the night he spent talking with Sydney, my bonus best friend that came as part of the Laney package. But his pointed charge now confirms he doesn't know I came back after that night.

The glass grows slick under my tightening grip, but I don't look away. I won't give him that either. "I don't care to dig up the past." I set my glass down with deliberate precision.

"Then remind me again, why are we having this drink?"

"You know why." I try to shove down the humiliation and anger battling inside me. "Maybe I should be asking why you're entertaining it?" I say, more for an underhanded jab than anything, but a good fucking question, nonetheless.

He shrugs. "I need a wife," he says plainly before taking another drink of tequila. I know him well enough to know when he's bluffing. He's not.

"Wait...you're serious."

His eyes snap to mine and tell no lies.

"What could you possibly need a wife for?" I ask.

"For a merger. They're an old, traditional family. The patriarch won't do business with unmarried men under forty. It shows a lack of commitment and stability."

Right. I drop my gaze to my glass. Of course, he has an angle. I'm not sure why I thought he wouldn't. I have one too.

"Why me?" I ask, trying to pull more information out of him, since he's not giving me much to work with. I know he's not telling me everything.

"It's practical. You need a husband to keep your land. I need a wife to secure my merger. We both get what we want."

"For how long?" I ask.

He furrows a brow. "What do you mean?"

"I mean, how long do we have to pretend to be husband and wife?"

"Oh, there's no pretending, sweetheart. You're taking my last name. That's forever."

There it is, that nickname that makes my blood boil as much as it makes me squirm in my seat, hating the way it slithers like a caress down my spine, but I shove it off.

"Absolutely not. One year. One year and we go our separate ways."

His eyes narrow in question. "I know you've read the lease, but did your lawyer fail to tell you about the deed? A year does nothing for you. If we divorce, you don't have any rights to the land. Hale land can't be sold. I can't give it to you. You have to stay or..."

"Or?"

"Or produce an heir. Our child would then be entitled to the land."

"You are literally insane. That's not happening," I say before finishing my tequila in one go and setting the empty glass down hard enough to get the bartender's attention, where I tap my glass for a refill. "One year gives me enough time to find another way. My dad kept this from me. If I had more time—"

"You think he hasn't already done everything in his power to keep it?"

"No, actually, I don't." I meet his gaze. "He never told me marrying a Hale was an option, so you'll have to excuse me if I don't think he's done everything in his power to ensure I don't lose the last pieces of my mother."

His eyes hold mine for a beat, and in them I see sadness. I quickly turn away. I don't want him to pity me. I don't need someone feeling sorry for me, and besides, we both know his childhood wasn't all rainbows either.

"Fine, a year," he agrees as he signals to the bartender to refill his glass too.

"But there will be conditions."

He holds up his finger, signaling me to wait as the bartender finishes pouring his new drink. With a full glass, he says, "Name them."

"Separate bedrooms. This isn't a real marriage."

His jaw tightens before he takes a slow swallow. "Agreed."

"No one can know it's fake."

"We can't go from not talking to head-over-heels and expect no one to bat an eye."

"Have you been with anyone?"

His eyes widen, and he brings his hand to his mouth to keep from spitting out his drink. "If you're worried I can't perform in the bedroom, don't be. One night, and I promise my name will be the only one you remember."

I give him a dramatic eye roll. "Please, did you forget condition number one? There will be none of that. I mean, have you been in a relationship since..." I clear my throat, suddenly a little uncomfortable, and pick up my glass, swirling the contents for a distraction. "Since high school?"

His knee bumps mine, drawing my eyes back to his. I watch his throat work as he swallows, but it's the contact. The heat from his knee burns, and my mouth goes dry. There's always this *dance* between us, this magnetic pull neither of us will acknowledge. The air between us crackles, charged with everything we're not saying.

"I'm more interested in your answer."

"I don't do relationships." I bring my glass to my lips. "I'm a solo act."

I take a drink and hold his eyes as they look so deeply into mine that it takes real effort not to fold.

"Same." He finally breaks our stare.

"If this is going to work, you have to be honest with me. You expect me to believe you haven't slept with anyone? You literally just gave me a rundown of your ability to please women."

"That wasn't the question. You asked me if I've been in a relationship, not if I slept with anyone."

"Fine. Have you?"

"Yes." He takes a slow sip, letting the silence stretch until I want to scream. "But nothing that mattered. Never the same person twice." He stops himself, jaw working like he's revealing too much. Then he just waits, watching me with those intense eyes.

"Good. Then we lie."

"Lie? I'm not sure I'm following." He leans in, resting his elbow on the bar.

"This needs to be real. No one can know I'm marrying you for anything other than love. It needs to be convincing. And when I say no one can know, I mean no one. Your brother, Laney, Sydney, and my dad —especially him—they all need to believe we are madly in love."

His eyebrows rise, and his dark eyes sparkle with genuine amusement, but he doesn't laugh. Instead, he runs a hand through his hair, once, then twice, the way he does when nothing is sitting right with him. "How exactly do you plan on selling the people who are closest to us that you and I are head-over-heels in love with our track record. Hell, you've gone out of your way to ignore me since you returned to Bardstown."

"Easy." I swirl the contents in my glass before taking a drink. "It's a tale as old as time. Two star-crossed lovers who fell in love the first time they met. Fate said our paths were meant to cross, but our circumstances, not a lack of love, have stood in the way."

It's not until he stops drumming his fingers on the bar top that I realize I leaned in too. My knees are now fully between his spread legs, my shoulders hovering above his thighs. I pull back sharply, putting deliberate space between us, and it doesn't go unnoticed.

His jaw tightens, and his gaze drops to where my hand grips the bar, white-knuckled as I try to ground myself. When he looks back up, something flickers in his eyes before his expression goes carefully blank.

"You know if you want people to believe the lie, you're going to have to act like you love me." He nods toward the bartender still hovering nearby, wiping down glasses close enough to overhear. Then, his hand covers mine.

I can't help but watch as it slowly envelopes mine. The callused pad of his thumb traces lazy circles on my wrist, and heat quickly crawls up my arm and spreads through my chest. He waits until my eyes find his, the air between us intensely charged as his other hand finds my knee. His palm sears through the thin satin of my dress. I pinch my lips together not only to quiet my protests but to silence the gasp building in my throat.

His teeth teasingly graze his bottom lip like he's actually enjoying touching my body. "You're going to have to get used to me touching you. You'll need to pretend to like it." His hand begins to drift up my thigh with an achingly slow pace as he leans closer still. Close enough that I can almost taste the tequila on his lips. "You're going to have to kiss me," he murmurs, his eyes dropping to my mouth where my lips part on instinct.

It would be so easy to lean in and take what he's offering. I lick my lips, and his eyes track the path of my tongue with predatory focus. Damn it, I hate that he's already so good at lying, how he already looks like he wants to kiss me. How part of me wants to let him. I can't let him see that he has the power to affect me, especially when he shouldn't.

I press my hand flat against his chest, putting needed space between us. "Does that mean you're saying yes?"

He draws in a sharp breath, and just like that, the haze breaks. He straightens in his seat, physically pulling himself back from whatever edge we were teetering on. Reaching for his drink, he takes a long pull as though he's using those seconds to rebuild his composure. "I agree, but I have a condition of my own."

I quirk a brow. "Name it."

"You marry me, right here, right now."

CHAPTER 15

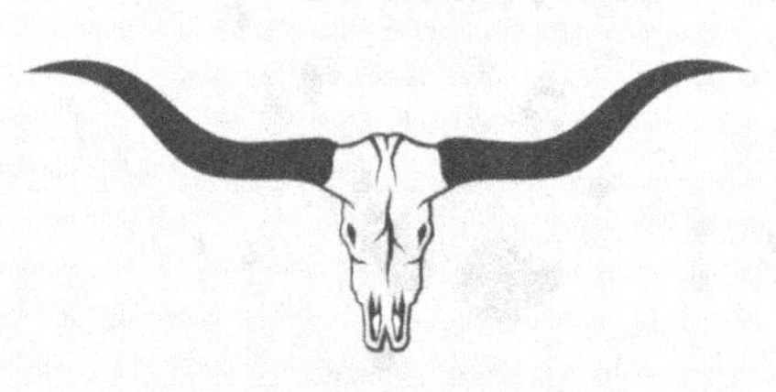

My hand jerks back from his chest like I've been burned. "What?"

"You marry me tonight." He says it so casually, like he's suggesting we order another round.

A disbelieving, laugh bubbles up. "You're joking."

His gaze doesn't waver. Doesn't even flicker with amusement. Oh, God. He's not joking.

My pulse kicks into overdrive, and suddenly, the bar feels too small. "Trigger, that's...we can't just..." I swallow hard, trying to organize the chaos in my head. Proposing this arrangement was one thing. A strategic plan with a conveniently vague timeline. But *now*? Tonight? I thought I'd have time.

"Why not?" He leans back, studying me with those knowing eyes that see too much.

"Because." I grab my drink, needing something to do with my hands. "Because this is *your brother's* wedding. Laney's wedding. Our best friends. We can't just hijack their night and make it about us. That's..." I shake my head. "That's unforgivably selfish."

"Is it?" He tilts his head, considering. "Or would we be making their night even more memorable? Think about it." He shifts closer, his voice dropping to something almost conspiratorial. "They'd get to share their celebration with us. Everyone we love is already here. The venue's decorated, the music's playing, there's cake—"

"That's *their* cake—"

"And an officiant who's probably having a drink in the corner right now." He's gaining momentum, and I can see the idea taking shape in his mind, becoming real. "All our friends and family in one place. No need for another gathering, another performance. We do it now, and it's done. Authentic. Spontaneous. The kind of love story people might actually believe."

My stomach flips. He's not wrong. The spontaneity would sell it. My hands start to tremble, and I press them flat against the bar. "Trigg, I can't... I need time to—"

"Time to what?" His voice gentles, but his eyes stay keenly tuned on mine. "Talk yourself out of it? Build up more walls? We both know what this is. You said it yourself; it needs to be convincing." He pauses then adds quietly, "What's more convincing than two people who couldn't wait another day?"

I stare at him, my heartbeat thundering in my ears. "They'll think we're crazy."

"They'll think we're crazy in love." The corner of his mouth lifts. "Isn't that the point?" He leans back in his chair and studies me, and I can tell by the look in his eyes that he believes this half-cocked solution to our problems is over before it's ever begun. That I'm all talk. "That's my condition, sweetheart. Take it or leave it."

"Fine."

"Fine, what?" He narrows his gaze.

"You know what," I bite back.

He quirks a brow, and the bastard actually looks *amused*. "I'm going to need to hear the words."

My face goes hot, but there's no shame in it, only white-hot anger. The nerve of this man, sitting there with that infuriatingly smug expression, waiting for me to spell it out as though I'm the only one who needs this arrangement. He said himself he needs a wife to secure his merger. However, it doesn't have to be me. I, on the other hand, only have one option for a groom.

I pull air through my nose and swallow my pride, reminding myself that this was my plan. My proposition. Only now, he's twisting it around, backing me into a corner, forcing me to either commit right here, right now, or walk away entirely.

"I'll marry you." The words somehow taste bitter, like defeat.

And the worst part? The absolute *worst* part is the way his eyes light up, just for a second, before he schools his features back into that mask of cool indifference. Like he's won something. The bartender appears, wiping down the section of the bar near us, and I realize how close we're sitting, how this must look. Two people huddled together in a dim corner, voices low, intensity crackling between us. From the outside, it probably does look like love. From the inside, it feels like I've just signed my life away with three words and a man who knows exactly how to get under my skin.

He raises his glass, that damnable smirk still playing at his lips. "To us, then."

I grab my own glass and drain it in one burning gulp rather than toast with him. The burn is still fresh in my throat as he takes my glass and sets it down before sliding off his stool and pulling me with him.

"What are you doing?"

"We're going to find the officiant," he says as though the answer is obvious.

His hand wraps around mine, warm, firm, possessive, and suddenly I'm being tugged away from the bar and deeper into the reception hall.

The bar was our quiet corner, our bubble of shadows and tension. Now we're moving into the heart of the festivities. The dance floor is packed with bodies, and he expertly winds us around the edges. My heels catch on the edge of someone's chair, and I stumble, but his grip tightens, steadying me without breaking stride.

"Trigg, wait—" I start as though my trip was some sort of sign that we shouldn't be doing this. But he doesn't wait.

We cut through the crowd, and my heart is racing, not just from the sudden movement but from the reality crashing down on me with every step. He spots the officiant near the back corner, a silver-haired man in his sixties nursing what looks like whiskey on the rocks. He glances up as we approach, his expression shifting from relaxed to curious.

"Officiant Reynolds," Trigger says, that easy charm sliding into place. "We have one more job for you this evening, if you're willing."

The man blinks. "Another ceremony?"

Trigger reaches into his jacket, pulls out a thick wad of cash, and presses it into the officiant's hand. "Meet us by the windows in five minutes." Officiant Reynolds looks at the money, then at us, then back at the money. Trigger squeezes his shoulder. "Remember, five minutes. Don't be late."

He doesn't give the man time to object before we're moving again. When I see he's pulling me toward the head table where his brother and Laney sit with their heads bent together in conversation, my stomach churns. Shit, this is the part where we ruin their night, where we tell them we want to get married too, but he doesn't stop at the table.

Instead, he reaches past a seated guest and grabs an empty champagne flute, then snags a butter knife from someone's place setting. The guest looks startled, but Trigger is already moving to the center of the dance floor, pulling me with him until we're standing in the middle of everything.

The music is still playing. People are still dancing and laughing when he raises the glass and begins tapping the knife against it.

Ting. Ting. Ting.

The sound cuts through the music. A few heads turn.

Ting. Ting. Ting.

More people notice, and the DJ stops the music. The dance floor clears as people step back, creating a circle around us. Conversations die down, all eyes turning toward the center of the room, toward us.

"I apologize for the interruption," he says, his voice carrying across the silent room. "I promise this isn't a best man speech—I already subjected you all to that earlier." A ripple of laughter moves through the crowd. "But I couldn't let this night end without sharing something." He turns slightly, pulling me closer to his side, and the warmth of him against me is the only thing keeping me from bolting. "See, my brother here..." He gestures toward the head table where his brother sits, looking thoroughly confused. "He's always been the romantic one. The guy who writes love letters and remembers anniversaries without a reminder. Wears his heart on his sleeve."

More laughter. Laney grins, nudging her husband with her shoulder.

"Meanwhile, I'm the guy who, in all honesty, has an exit strategy before the first date ends, keeps people at arm's length like it's my job, and has made a career out of not taking anything too seriously." There are a few knowing chuckles from friends who've clearly witnessed this firsthand. "My longest commitment before this was to my gym membership, and I still found reasons to ghost it half the time."

The room erupts in laughter. Even I feel my lips twitch despite the panic coursing through my veins.

But then his expression shifts, the lightness draining away. "Here's the thing, though, that was by design." His voice drops. "I had to keep things bottled up, had to keep my heart under lock and key, because it was never really available to give away."

The room has gone quiet again, hanging on his every word.

He turns to me fully, and the look in his eyes steals whatever breath I have left. "I gave it away a long time ago," he says, and his voice is soft enough that I almost believe him. Almost forget this is all an act. "And seeing all of you gathered here tonight, celebrating love, has inspired me. It's made me realize I don't want to spend another day pretending. Another day without my heart."

My throat tightens. This isn't fair. He's too good at this.

His gaze holds mine for one more beat before he turns back to the crowd. "When you know, you know. And I know I don't want to spend another day without calling her my wife."

A collective gasp ripples through the crowd. My face is on fire as every single person in this room is staring at us like we've lost our minds. Maybe we have.

The room is so quiet I can hear the soft clink of silverware, someone's nervous cough. From the head table, his brother, London, and Laney stare blankly. They are both very aware of my predicament and how marriage is the only solution to my dilemma, but I don't think either one of them actually thought this would happen, let alone like this, on their night. Then Trigger gives London a look. It's subtle, barely there, but I catch it. A slight tilt of his head, a raise of his eyebrows. *I'm doing this. Are you with me?*

He glances at Laney, who's watching with wide eyes and a hand pressed to her mouth. Then, he looks back to Trigger, and the corner of his mouth lifts, just barely, but I suppose it's permission all the same.

Trigger's hand tightens around mine, and suddenly we're moving again. He leads me through the parting crowd, and whispers follow as we pass. The wall of windows looms ahead, floor-to-ceiling glass overlooking

Hale Ranch. Officiant Reynolds stands there waiting with a kind smile and a small black book already in his hands.

"So without further ado," Trigger announces, his voice carrying across the room as we reach the windows, "welcome to part two of the evening. The part where I take Asha Fairfield as my wife."

The sound of glass slamming against wood cracks through the room like a gunshot. Every head whips toward the source.

My father.

He's standing at his table near the back, his highball glass slammed down so hard I'm surprised it didn't shatter. His face is a storm, dark eyes blazing with fury. He didn't just hear an announcement. He heard a declaration of war. Trigger didn't ask him, didn't come to him for permission, didn't request my hand, as tradition demands. And this isn't a traditional Indian wedding...no mehendi, no sangeet, no seven pheras around the sacred fire. But worse than all of that is the look in his eyes when they lock on mine. He knows.

My father has built an empire on reading people, on spotting a con from a mile away. And right now, standing there in his tailored suit, with his reputation on the line, he knows exactly what this is. A lie.

He takes a step forward. Then another. The crowd parts for him as my father storms across the reception hall, his gaze never leaving mine. Panic starts to claw up my throat. This is it. He's going to call us out. He's going to expose this whole charade before it even begins, and then everything I've been working toward will fall apart.

Unless...I step up. It's my turn to be convincing. My turn to sell this lie so thoroughly that even my father, the man who taught me how to spot deception, believes it.

I pull my hand from Trigger's and move to meet my father halfway, closing the space between us before he can reach the windows, before he can make a scene in front of the officiant, in front of everyone.

"Dad—"

"Don't." His voice is low, deadly quiet. The kind of quiet that's more terrifying than yelling. "Don't you dare."

We're standing in the middle of the reception hall now, surrounded by guests pretending not to watch while hanging on every word. I can feel their eyes on us, can hear the whispers starting.

"I know what you're thinking," I start.

"Do you?" He takes another step closer, and I have to fight the urge to retreat. "Do you have any idea what you're doing? What this looks like?"

"It looks like I'm in love." The words come out steadier than I feel.

He laughs without humor. "Love. You expect me to believe that? That you're suddenly marrying him, *tonight*, without so much as a conversation with your father?"

He's right. In any real scenario, I would have told him, would have brought Trigger to dinner, would have let my father interrogate him over masala chai while pretending to be casual about it. But the truth is, there's nothing normal about my father's and my relationship. Not anymore. We haven't been normal for years. My father has secrets too, and I'm determined to uncover every one of them.

"I'm telling you now." I lift my chin, meeting his gaze head on. "I'm in love with him, Dad. I have been for years."

"Years?" His eyes narrow. "Years, and you never mentioned it? I'm supposed to believe that?"

"You weren't supposed to believe anything, because I wasn't ready to tell you." My voice rises slightly, emotion and memories that have the ability to break me flooding in because some of this is true. The fear of disappointing him, the weight of his expectations, and the night I almost lost him to this senseless hate for a boy with the wrong name. "I knew what you'd say. What you'd think. That he wasn't good enough, that this wasn't the plan..." I trail off as the image resurfaces: a paramedic handing me my father's things while I sat in the waiting room, praying for the doctors in the other room trying to bring him back to me. A cracked phone screen couldn't hide what caused him to go off the road. He claims he wasn't distracted, but I know differently. If I want him to believe me now, it's time to show him one of my hands. "But my plan never looked like yours; a cracked screen wasn't enough to change it."

He stares at me, and I can see the pieces clicking together. Now he knows. My father's face hardens, and I watch as it shifts from anger, to hurt, and finally to the face he reserves for business—the one he's never once given me.

"Then you know exactly what you're doing choosing him, and nothing I say will change your mind?"

"Nothing," I confirm, schooling my face to ensure it tells no lies.

His hand runs over the dark, neatly kempt beard that peppers his strong jaw. He's still suspicious, but there's something else there too. Something I can't place. I know he's not entirely convinced, but it isn't until I feel Trigger's hand wrap around mine, his thumb gently brushing over the backs of my knuckles, and my father's gaze shifts, that I realize what's happening. My father may not be entirely convinced, but he's willing to let this go, to let this play out, at least for now, because this isn't over. Not for him. He's not staring at me. He's staring through me, plotting his next move. My father's gaze drops to our joined hands then lifts to Trigger.

The air crackles with an unspoken threat as the two men stare each other down. Trigger doesn't back down. He steps forward, bringing me with him, closing the distance until we're standing directly in front of my father.

"I'm going to marry your daughter now," Trigger says, without question but rather absolute certainty. "You can stand here and watch, or you can walk away. Either way, it's happening."

The boldness of his words steals my breath. My father doesn't respond, doesn't so much as blink. He's not threatened. Not even slightly. Trigger's words are washing over him like rain off glass, meaningless, because my father isn't really listening. His expression hasn't changed. His posture hasn't shifted, and I know that look. I've seen it before, in boardrooms and negotiations, right before he dismantles someone's entire world with a signature and a phone call. He's calculating. Not his response. Not his next words. His revenge.

My father is the kind of man who doesn't react in the moment. He plans. He strategizes. He waits. And right now, behind those dark eyes, I can practically see the gears turning. Every angle is being considered. Every pressure point is being identified. Every way to make Trigger regret this moment is being carefully, methodically mapped out.

Trigger doesn't wait for him to give a response. Instead, he turns and leads me back toward the windows where Officiant Reynolds stands waiting, that patient smile still in place. As we walk, the whispers start up again, a mix of shock and excitement over the star-crossed lovers who couldn't wait, who threw caution to the wind, and chose love over tradition.

We reach the windows and take our positions in front of the glass.

Trigger faces me, his hands taking both of mine now, and for a moment, just a moment, the lie feels almost real.

Officiant Reynolds clears his throat. "Well, then," he says, a hint of amusement in his voice, "shall we begin?"

I nod, but my throat feels too tight to speak.

"Dearly beloved," Reynolds starts, and there's a slight twinkle in his eye as he surveys the confused crowd. "We are gathered here tonight—somewhat unexpectedly, I might add..."

A ripple of nervous laughter moves through the reception.

"To witness the union of Trigger Hale and Asha Fairfield. Now, I've performed many weddings in my time, but I must say, this is the first where the guests thought they were just here for cake, dancing, and one wedding." More laughter, louder this time. Even I feel my lips twitch. Panic be damned. Reynolds looks between Trigger and me with that knowing smile. "But as I always say, when you know, you know. And these two clearly couldn't wait another moment."

This is insane. This is actually insane.

He's watching me with those penetrating eyes, and in the soft glow from the chandeliers, he's devastating. The sharp line of his jaw. The way his dress shirt fits across his shoulders. That slight curl to his hair that he probably spent twenty minutes trying to tame. And his mouth...God, his mouth.

Stop it. Focus.

"Not to be entered into lightly, but reverently and soberly..." The words Reynolds is speaking briefly register, only to fade again as Trigger traces slow circles on the back of my hand. "Do you, Trigger Hale, take this woman to be your lawfully wedded wife?"

Trigger's eyes never leave mine. "I do." His voice is steady, certain, like he makes life-altering decisions in front of crowds every day.

"Do you promise to love her, comfort her, honor and keep her, in sickness and in health, for richer or poorer, for better or worse, forsaking all others, for as long as you both shall live?"

"I do."

Two words. So simple. So binding. So completely false.

Reynolds turns to me, and suddenly, I can't breathe.

"Do you, Asha Fairfield, take this man to be your lawfully wedded husband?"

The room spins slightly. Trigger's hands tighten around mine, grounding me. This is it. The moment where I either commit to this lie entirely or lose everything I've been working toward. No going back after this. No undoing these words once they're spoken in front of everyone who matters.

I look at Trigger, really look at him, and something in his expression shifts. The practiced charm falls away for just a second, and I see something else there. Vulnerability, recognition that we're both about to cross a line we can't uncross.

His jaw is set, a muscle jumping there that betrays his own tension despite his steady voice moments ago. And those eyes...they're not mocking or amused now. They're...asking something. Checking in. Making sure I'm still in this with him.

"I do." My voice comes out quieter than I intended, but steady enough.

"Do you promise to love him, comfort him, honor and keep him, in sickness and in health, for richer or poorer, for better or worse, forsaking all others, for as long as you both shall live?"

Lies. All lies. This is a business arrangement. This is temporary. This is—

"I do."

The words hang in the air between us, and Trigger's eyes darken with something I can't quite name.

"The rings?" Reynolds asks.

Rings. We don't have... The thought I had is paused as Trigger reaches into his pocket and pulls out a ring. *Where did he get a ring?* He must catch my expression because the corner of his mouth lifts slightly, just barely. Always prepared. Always three steps ahead. The ring is simple, a thin band of gold that catches the light. Nothing elaborate, nothing showy.

Reynolds nods to Trigger. "Repeat after me: With this ring, I thee wed."

Trigger takes my left hand, and I watch as he slides the ring onto my finger. It fits perfectly. *How does it fit perfectly?*

"With this ring," Trigger says, his voice dropping lower, more intimate, "I thee wed."

The metal is warm from being in his pocket. Or maybe my skin is just cold. Everything feels surreal, like I'm watching this happen to someone else.

But then Trigger's fingers linger on mine for a moment longer than necessary, his thumb brushing over the ring he's just placed there, and the gesture is so unexpectedly tender that my breath catches.

Stop. Stop reading into this. It's an act. All of it.

But God, he's good at it. The way he's looking at me right now—like I'm the only person in this room, like this matters, like we matter—I almost believe it myself.

"By the power vested in me by the state of Kentucky," Reynolds says, and my stomach drops because I know what's coming next, "I now pronounce you husband and wife."

Husband and wife.

The words echo in my head, bouncing around like they're trying to find purchase, trying to mean something.

"You may kiss the bride."

Shit. Trigger's eyes meet mine, and I know he can tell I forgot about this part. He can see in all my plans that this is the one thing I left unaccounted for. I know he said I'd need to get comfortable with his touch, to learn to like it, that his mouth would have to cover mine if we were going to sell the lie. But with everyone watching, waiting, expecting, and my father still standing somewhere behind us, calculating, this isn't how I wanted it to happen. It's not how I wanted to learn to like it.

Then, surprising me yet again, Trigger doesn't miss a beat, pulling me flush against his chest, one hand sliding to the small of my back, the other coming up to cup my face. To the crowd, it must look like the beginning of a passionate kiss. But instead of closing the distance, he dips me away from the audience. His forehead presses against mine as he takes a second to gaze into my eyes, to let the weight of what just happened between us settle. For a second, it feels real, like we both actually want this, like maybe there doesn't have to be an end date.

He angles his head, his cheek brushing mine as his mouth hovers just beside my ear. "Relax," he murmurs, his breath warm against my skin. "I'm not going to kiss you."

My hands come up instinctively, fisting in his shirt. To anyone watching, it looks like I'm pulling him closer. Really, I'm just trying to stay upright as my knees threaten to give out. His fingers thread through my hair, and he tilts us just so. From every angle in the room, it would look like our lips are locked, like we're lost in a deep, intimate kiss. The crowd erupts in cheers and applause.

"Breathe," he whispers, and I realize I've been holding my breath. "Just a few more seconds. Need to make it believable, and I take my time."

"You're enjoying this," I accuse, my lips barely moving.

I feel his smile. "Immensely."

"I hate you."

"I know." His forehead presses against mine, and the gesture feels impossibly intimate despite the space between our mouths. "But they don't need to know that."

He holds us there for another heartbeat, then two, letting the moment stretch just long enough to be convincing before he slowly pulls me upright.

His eyes meet mine, dark and unreadable, and there's something in them that makes my stomach flip. Then he opens his mouth and ruins it. "Don't worry, sweetheart." His voice is low, meant only for me, with just enough edge to remind me exactly who I've married. "You might have my last name now, but I won't kiss you until you ask me to."

Heat floods my face. "That will never happen."

"We'll see." He pulls back, and there's a challenge in his dark eyes. "You never mentioned monogamy was one of the conditions."

My blood turns to ice then immediately boils. Perhaps it wasn't discussed, but it was implied, given we have to sell the lie. We have to make the people who are closest to us believe we are madly in love. How can we possibly sell that if he is sleeping around?

He mistakes my error for something it's not. "Jealous already, Mrs. Hale?"

"Practical," I correct. "If someone sees you with another woman—"

"They won't."

"The whole charade falls apart, and we both—" I stop, his words finally registering. "What?"

Trigger's hand is still at the small of my back, and he uses it to pull me infinitesimally closer. To anyone watching, we're lost in newlywed bliss. But his voice drops, and becomes something darker. "They won't see me with anyone else. Because, despite what you think of me, I don't do things halfway." His gaze holds mine, steady and certain. "When I commit to something, even a lie, I'm all in."

My breath catches.

"Besides," he continues, and now there's definitely amusement coloring his tone, "you're the one who'll be begging me for a kiss soon enough. I'd hate to ruin that moment by being seen with someone else."

"You're delusional."

"And you're my wife." He says it like a challenge. Like a promise. Like a threat. "So I guess we're both stuck with our delusions."

The crowd is still cheering around us, oblivious to the war we're waging in whispers.

"For now," I remind him, my voice sharp.

His smile sharpens to match. "For now," he agrees.

But the way he's looking at me—like he knows something I don't, like he's already three steps ahead in a game I didn't know we were playing—sends a shiver down my spine.

Trigger takes my hand, lacing our fingers together, and turns us to face the crowd. "Ladies and gentlemen," he announces, his voice carrying across the room, "Mr. and Mrs. Hale...again."

People are on their feet with applause, and all I can think about is the space that existed between our mouths moments ago. The kiss that didn't happen. The kiss he's now dangling like bait, waiting for me to break first.

I won't, I tell myself firmly. *I won't give him the satisfaction.*

As he pulls me through the reception, I feel a shift as his grip changes from performative to purposeful. Even his smile when he nods at well-wishers, doesn't quite reach his eyes anymore. Something's changed.

"Trigger—"

"Time to go." His voice is pleasant and easy, but his hand is already pulling me toward the exit.

"We can't just leave. Laney will—"

"Now, Asha." The pleasantness evaporates. He leans in close, his breath warm against my ear, and to anyone watching, it looks intimate. Loving. But his words are steel. "It's time to start playing the role you signed up for. Wife."

The word sends a chill down my spine. The way he says it, not teasing like before, not challenging. Final. Possessive. Real in a bone-deep, terrifying way.

"What are you talking about?" I try to pull back, but his arm slides around my waist, holding me against his side as we move through the crowd.

"Smile," he murmurs. "Wave. Look happy."

I do, because what choice do I have? People are watching, congratulating us, but my heart is hammering against my ribs.

"Trigger, stop." I dig my heels in as we reach the corridor. "Tell me what's happening."

"What's happening," he says quietly, his dark eyes locked on mine, "is that you're my wife now. Legally. Binding. You wanted everyone to believe we're madly in love. Well, that starts now. Tonight. No more plans and negotiations." His thumb brushes my bottom lip. "From this moment on, you're mine. In every way that matters."

"That wasn't the deal—"

"The deal," he interrupts, his voice dropping even lower, "was that we get married and make it look real. Did you think 'real' meant we'd go back to our separate lives?"

The corridor suddenly feels too small, too dark. "Where are we going?"

"We have a plane to catch, and you have a role to play."

"I didn't agree to..."

A door slams open behind us. Voices echo down the corridor. It's my father's, angry and commanding. Trigger's expression shifts, urgency replacing the cold calculation. "Time's up. Choose now, Asha. Come with me willingly, or I'll carry you out. Either way, you're leaving with your husband."

My husband.

The word feels like a trap closing around me. Behind me, I hear footsteps and my father's voice calling my name. But if I let my father interfere, everything falls apart. The plan. The arrangement. Every carefully constructed plan I've yet executed, answers I still need. This can only go one way.

"Fine." The word tastes like surrender.

Trigger's hand finds mine, and this time when he pulls me toward the exit, I don't resist. A black car waits at the curb, engine running. The door is already open.

"Get in."

I do, and Trigger slides in beside me. The door shuts with finality as the car pulls away, and I catch a glimpse of the entrance. My father bursts through the doors, his face a mask of fury, but we're already turning the corner, the taillights disappearing into the night.

Trigger's hand rests on my thigh, possessive and warm through the thin fabric of my dress.

"Relax," he says, but there's no comfort in the word. "You're exactly where you agreed to be."

TRIGGER

CHAPTER 16

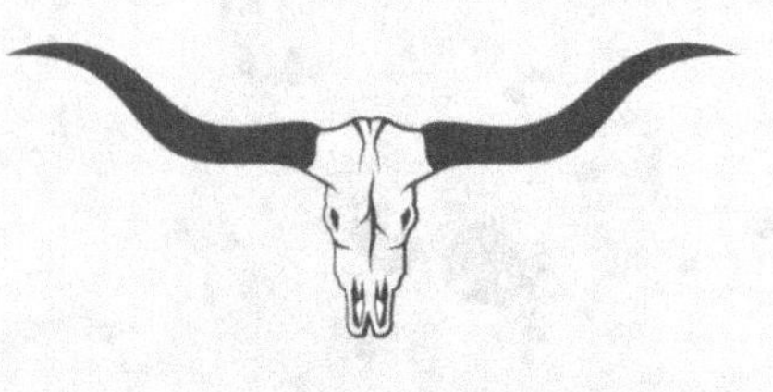

"What aren't you telling me?" London asks as I stare at Asha sleeping across from me on the plane, her head tilted against the plane's window, her arms crossed as if she needs to keep her guard up. There's a small crease between her eyebrows, like she's fighting something even in her dreams. Probably me. "You really expect me to believe the two of you are jet-setting to enjoy a romantic honeymoon?"

"Actually, yes," I sigh. I'm not thrilled about lying to my brother, but it's not just me I have to look out for anymore. I have her. My wife. For a year. That was the deal, anyway. Three hundred and sixty-five days, then we both walk away. She finds a way to save her land, my merger goes through, and everyone gets what they want. Except, I'm not walking away. Not in a year. Not ever. "It must be in our blood or something," I add, as my eyes study every curve of her face. "We fall, and we never stop." I toss back a truth he can't argue.

I hear the anxious breath he takes, his frustration evident before he says, "So this trip—"

"You mean honeymoon," I correct so that he starts to wrap his head around my new normal.

"No, I mean trip. Tell me which circle of hell I'm going to be dealing with when you get back."

Asha's eyes start to flutter open as she wakes up.

"I'm not sure what you mean. I'm on my honeymoon. See you when I get home." I cut the call without another word.

I turn to find Asha watching me, sleep still softening her features even as wariness sharpens her gaze.

"How long was I out?"

"Three hours. We have about five more to go."

She sits up straighter, tugging at the blanket I draped over her. "Five hours to where, exactly?"

"You'll see when we land."

"Trigger." Her tone is a warning. "I agreed to marry you. I didn't agree to be kidnapped."

"Legally, I don't think it counts as kidnapping when it's your husband." I reach for my coffee. I should sleep, but I can't shut off my brain. I'm still trying to wrap my head around the fact that last night fucking happened.

She looks furious and rumpled and entirely out of her element. It's a nice change from her usual immaculate control.

"Keeping me in the dark wasn't part of the plan. I didn't agree to this." She unbuckles her seatbelt, and I can see the moment she harnesses her anger and starts calculating. "Appearances matter, Trigger. If you want this marriage to win over your partners, it needs to look real, and this might be news to you, but couples talk. They share things. If I show up on your arm completely unaware, they'll know it's fake."

I know she's right, and I do plan to fill her in, but letting her in on my future business plans requires trust. She took a big first step last night, not once but twice. First, when she agreed to marry me on the spot. The second, and maybe even bigger move, was when she chose me over her father. But I don't want blind trust, and I don't want momentary trust, the kind that fails when things truly get hard. I want unconditional.

"Share things," I muse over the rim of my coffee.

"Yes, things. Information. Plans. The basic building blocks of a functional partnership." She's fully awake now. "Unless you'd prefer I smile blankly when your business associates ask about our life, our future?"

Our future. I like those words coming from her mouth. Those are the ones I'd like to discuss in detail, but since we're on the topic of sharing things, there is something that has been needling me since the words were uttered. Something I haven't been able to piece together.

"What did you mean last night when you told your father a cracked screen wasn't enough to change your plans?"

"Nothing." She averts her gaze out the window, which may have been borderline convincing were it not for her hands.

"Right, so you're cutting the circulation off in your fingers for nothing," I say as I watch them turn whiter by the second, which is a feat in itself, given her warm complexion. "Sharing works both ways, sweetheart."

She closes her eyes and presses her head into the seat. "Fine. I guess if anyone should know what those words mean, it's you." Her voice comes out quiet, almost detached, as she stares out the window.

I set down my empty coffee cup, the ceramic clicking against the wood console.

She's silent for a moment, her jaw working like she's trying to decide how much to tell me. When she finally speaks, she still won't look at me. "My father's accident, the one he was in the night of our senior prom... When he finally woke from his coma, the doctors asked him if he remembered any details from the night of his crash. His statement was he swerved to miss a deer crossing the road and lost control on the wet pavement..." She pauses, and I watch her fingers find the edge of the blanket, twisting the fabric between them before continuing. "But I know differently. I know because when the paramedics brought me his belongings that night, his cracked phone was among his things, and the picture on the screen was a photo of the student council prom committee."

My hand freezes halfway to the water glass on the console between us.

"You already know you are part of the reason I was sent away to begin with. They didn't want me going back to public school after I fell. I wasn't safe there." She finally turns to look at me, and I can see everything she's kept buried in those dark eyes. "He saw that photo, and it caused him to run off the road."

I shift to face her fully. "Are you saying he didn't know I was attending Ridgewood?"

"I never brought it up." She holds my gaze, unflinching, letting me see the truth. The question is what truth? I'm not sure why she never mentioned it to her father. I sure as hell know it wasn't for her undying love for me. She enjoyed having fun at my expense most days.

"Why?" I lean forward, elbows on my knees, needing more.

If she had brought it up, I'm sure it would have gotten her out of there. She wanted to go home. She never hid that fact. If I were the reason she was sent away, surely my presence at Ridgewood would have been enough for Warrick to bring her home.

"I answered your question." Her voice is steadier now. "Now it's time you answer some of mine, starting with where we are going."

I sink back into my seat and cross my leg over my knee at the ankle. "Somewhere warm."

She rolls her eyes, a trademark sign of her annoyance, one that's grown on me because even if she's thoroughly peeved with me, I'm still the one on her mind. It's still me making her feel something.

"More specific."

"Why are you so worried about it anyway?" I press, loving how easy it is to get her worked up.

"It would help to know if I packed the right wardrobe. You only gave me ten minutes."

"I said to pack something nice." I shrug, reaching for my water.

"You're such a man. You probably packed jeans, boots, and a few polos and called it a day. It doesn't work the same for women." She shifts in her seat, and sunlight breaks through the clouds just then, flooding the cabin with harsh light that catches the gold band on her left hand.

"You think I care what you wear?" I quirk a brow. "If you're asking, I'd prefer you wear—"

"Definitely not asking, but if we arrive and I don't have the right wardrobe, you're buying." My forehead creases as my eyebrows rise, her comment taking me by surprise. Asha is fiercely independent, so the fact that she's willing to take anything from me is somewhat shocking. "What?" She points toward my face. "What is that look for?"

"Just surprised, is all. I assumed I'd be splitting checks this entire marriage."

She rolls her lips and inhales deeply through her nose. "That's kind of hard to do, seeing as how I don't have a trust fund like you. I had a credit card with no limit, but since I just married my enemy without so much as discussing it with my father, I'm sure I've been cut off."

"My money is your money, Wife," I say a little too pridefully, drawing out that last word like it's something profane.

"I'll pay you back. I don't want to spend your father's money on my clothes."

"Not necessary. You won't be spending his. You'll be spending mine." I watch her process this, watch the war play out across her face, pride versus practicality versus whatever else she won't let me see. "The money in your trust fund wasn't earned by you, so yes, I'll be paying back every dime."

"I don't have a trust fund, sweetheart. I didn't go to college like you. Instead, I came home and started running the family business alongside my brother and my father. Every dime I have to my name is mine. The only thing my last name guaranteed me was land." I pause, letting that sink in as the clouds thin below us, revealing the deep blue hues of the sea. We must be getting close. "The only thing I inherited was enemies—including you."

I'm not sure what I see on her face. For a small second, she looks fairly impressed, but then a notable scowl appears before she snaps. "Good. I'll be sure to make it hurt," she says with a smile.

"I wouldn't expect anything less." I let my gaze drag over her deliberately. "But here's the thing, watching you spend my money on something that makes you look good isn't the punishment you think it is."

She turns back to the window, jaw tight, her interrogation seemingly put on hold. I know my responses are throwing her for a curve. It can't be helped. I want her to think about what it means to be tied to me now.

I didn't create this situation. Didn't manipulate it. I just...waited. Patiently. So patiently it nearly killed me. I waited for her to realize what I'd known the moment I found out about the land lease. I waited for her to exhaust every possibility, rage against the unfairness of it all. I waited for her to come to the inevitable conclusion: she needed me. For the first time in all the years I've known her, loved her, fought with her, she actually needed me. And then I waited for her to come to me.

The hardest part was knowing I could approach her and offer her this very solution, but also knowing she might just throw it back in my face if I did. She'd see it as pity, as me lording it over her, as a weakness on her part. It had to be her choice. Her decision. She had to be the one to swallow her pride and ask, and last night, she finally did.

She laid it out like a business deal. One year of marriage. I get the merger I need; she gets to save her land. Then we divorce and go our separate ways. I listened. Nodded. Asked the appropriate questions. All while thinking: she has no idea. No idea she just handed me exactly what I've wanted for years. The one thing I could never take by force: her.

I made her think I was considering it. Made her sweat a little, not to be cruel, but because she needed to feel like it was a negotiation. Like she still had power. Then I agreed. One year, a few poorly negotiated conditions. Above board, on her terms.

Except for the part where I have absolutely no intention of honoring the end date.

Asha made the choice. That's what matters. She came to me, she proposed this arrangement, then she stood up in front of all our friends and family and said "I do" of her own free will. No one forced her. No one manipulated her.

She chose this. Chose me. And now that she has, I'm never letting her go.

TRIGGER

CHAPTER 17

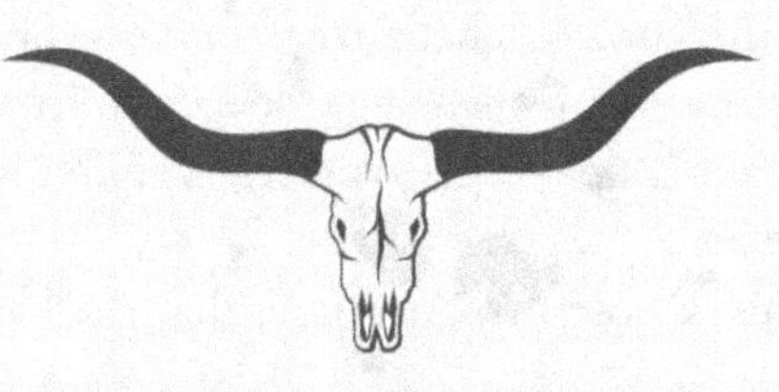

The door to our hotel suite clicks shut behind us, and I watch her take in the space. It's luxury, floor-to-ceiling windows overlooking the city of Granada, marble floors, expensive art on the walls, but none of that matters because her eyes are only focused on one thing: the single bedroom visible through the open doorway. I can see the moment she registers it. Her shoulders tense, and her fingers flex. Here we go.

"There's only one room," she says, her voice carefully neutral. She doesn't look at me, just wheels her bag forward with deliberate casualness. "I guess you'll be sleeping on the couch," she says, like it's already decided. Like I'm just going to nod and accept my place on the couch while she takes the bed. *Not a chance.*

"No," I say simply, setting my own bag down by the door.

She turns, eyebrows raised. "Excuse me?"

"I said no." I shrug off my jacket and drape it over the back of a chair. "I'm not sleeping on the couch."

"Our agreement—" she starts.

"Was separate sleeping quarters when possible," I finish for her. "Unfortunately, this was the only suite available on short notice. So, we'll have to make do."

Her eyes narrow. "Make do?"

"The bed's big enough for two adults to share." I meet her gaze. "We can put pillows between us if it makes you feel better. We both know you like walls. Build one."

"You're joking."

"Do I look like I'm joking?"

She stares at me for a long moment, and I can see the war happening behind her eyes.

"Fine." She turns on her heel, wheels her bag away from the bedroom entirely, and parks it next to the couch. "You take the bed. I'll sleep out here."

"Don't be ridiculous. You're not sleeping on the couch."

"Why not?" She's already unzipping her bag, pulling out what looks like sleep clothes. "Problem solved. You get the bed, and I get my separate quarters. Everyone's happy."

"You're my wife. You're not sleeping on a couch."

"Contract wife," she corrects, not looking at me. "And it's a very nice couch. I'll be fine."

I can feel my jaw tightening. This is exactly the kind of stubborn, infuriating thing she would do.

"This is childish."

Now she does look at me, and her eyes are blazing. "Childish? You want to talk about what's childish? You're the one who apparently booked a single room for a marriage that was explicitly supposed to have boundaries."

"I told you, this was the only suite."

"Sure it was." She crosses her arms. "How convenient."

She thinks I planned this. The thought sends a flash of something hot through my chest. She thinks I'm already playing games, already breaking the rules. She's not entirely wrong to be suspicious. I have no intention of honoring that divorce clause, but I genuinely didn't orchestrate this. The hotel situation is just...lucky timing.

"Believe what you want," I say, forcing my voice to stay level. "But you're not sleeping on the couch. It's uncomfortable. You'll wake up with a stiff neck, and we have meetings tomorrow."

"I'll be fine."

"Take the bed."

"No."

Stubborn woman. We're at an impasse, and I can see from the set of her shoulders that she's not going to budge. Fine. Let her sleep on the couch tonight. Let her wake up sore and uncomfortable. Maybe it'll teach her that being contrary for the sake of being contrary has consequences.

"Fine," I say, picking up my bag. "Suit yourself."

I close the bedroom door, but not all the way, and start unpacking a few things. Through the gap in the door, I can see her moving around the living area, and I take my bag of toiletries to the ensuite. I'm an unpacker. I don't like living out of a suitcase when I travel, and setting my things on the counter, giving them a space, will help unclutter my mind.

I've only taken my toothbrush and cologne out when movement out of the corner of my eye catches my attention. Asha is in my room.

"Change your mind already, sweetheart?" I say, emptying a few more items onto the counter.

"In your dreams. I'm here for your credit card."

I blink. "What?" I face her, only to find her sitting on the edge of my bed, her bare legs crossed, looking like all my dreams come true.

"I'm going shopping," she sing-songs. "You promised I could buy clothes if I didn't pack the right attire." She's completely serious, sitting there checking her manicure like some kind of spoiled schoolgirl. "We're in Spain. I'll look like an American."

"You *are* an American," I snap back.

"You know what I mean. I need appropriate clothes. You said—"

"It's late." I walk into the room, move my suitcase to the floor, and begin unbuttoning my shirt. "This is a new city. I don't want you going out alone."

"Too bad." Her voice is firm, unyielding. "I need to be alone with my thoughts after everything. Hand over the card."

I look at her—really look at her. There's something in her eyes, not just stubbornness, but genuine need. She needs space. Time to process whatever the hell the last twenty-four hours have been for her. *For both of us.* I'm too tired to argue. Too tired to fight this battle when there are so many more important ones ahead. However, I also can't just let her wander around Granada alone at night. I abandon my buttons and grab my phone off the bed.

"What are you doing?" she asks, immediately suspicious.

I don't answer, just pull up the hotel contact and hit the concierge services button. It rings once. "Yes, Mr. Hale."

"I need the butler assigned to our suite," I say, keeping my eyes on her. "My wife needs an escort for some late-night shopping."

"What?" She's off the bed. "No. Absolutely not. I don't need a babysitter."

"We can arrange that immediately, sir," the voice on the phone says. "Manuel will be at your suite in five minutes. Will you be accompanying Mrs. Hale?"

"Stop," she hisses, and suddenly she's right there, leaning over the bed, reaching for the phone in my hand. "Hang up the phone. Right now."

I pull it back, just out of her reach, which only makes her lean in farther. She braces one hand on the mattress, the other stretching toward me, and suddenly she's close enough that I can smell whatever soap she used on the plane. Something clean and citrusy that makes my head swim.

"Give me the phone," she demands, her voice low and dangerous.

Our faces are inches apart now. I can see the tiny sparks of gold in her eyes even in the dim light, can feel the heat radiating off her skin. My hand comes up automatically and lands on her wrist. For one loaded, dangerous second, neither of us moves.

This is what I've been waiting for. The electric moment of raw connection, a split second where the hatred between us dissolves. Her gaze meets mine with a vulnerability that cuts through our usual rivalry, and I see a glimpse of something deeper brewing beneath the surface, but then she pulls away.

"No, just my wife." I keep talking over her hissing protests. "Make sure he takes her anywhere she wants to go and stays with her the entire time."

"Of course, sir. And shall we—"

"Hang up the phone," she tries again, crossing her arms with a glare in her eye that threatens to murder me in my sleep if I don't obey.

I cover the phone with my hand, meeting her glare steadily. "You want to go shopping with my card in a new city without me? This is me meeting you halfway. Take it or leave it."

Her eyes flash with fury. "I said I need to be alone—"

"And I said I'm not letting you wander around Spain alone at night." My voice is firm, final. "Manuel will keep his distance. He'll carry your bags, make sure you get back safely. He'll stay out of your way, but he's going. It's non-negotiable."

"This is ridiculous."

"Take it or leave it," I repeat, removing my hand from the phone. "Are you still there?"

"Yes, Mr. Hale."

"Perfect. Have Manuel meet my wife in the lobby."

"Excellent. Will there be anything else?"

"No. Thank you." I end the call and look back at her. "You have five minutes to get ready if you're going."

She's seething. I can practically see the steam coming out of her ears.

"I don't need a babysitter," she says through gritted teeth.

"Then don't go." I pull my wallet from the nightstand, extract my card, and hold it out to her. "But if you do, Manuel goes with you. Those are the terms."

She stares at the card, then at me, then back at the card. I can see the war happening in her head. The need to defy me versus the need to get out of this room. Finally, she snatches the card from my hand.

"Fine," she bites out. "But if he hovers, I'm sending him back."

"He won't hover. He's a professional."

She takes the card from my fingers. "Don't wait up."

"Wasn't planning on it," I say, sliding off my boots. "Try not to bank-rupt me."

"Don't tempt me." She brushes past me to the door.

Stubborn, infuriating woman.

She can buy all the clothes she wants and have all the alone time she needs to process, because at the end of the day, she's still my wife. Still wearing my ring. Still bound to me for the next three hundred and sixty-four days, and by the end of those days, she won't want to leave. I hear the suite door open and close. She's gone.

Go ahead and run, sweetheart. Shop until dawn if you need to. You'll still come back to me.

ASHA

CHAPTER 18

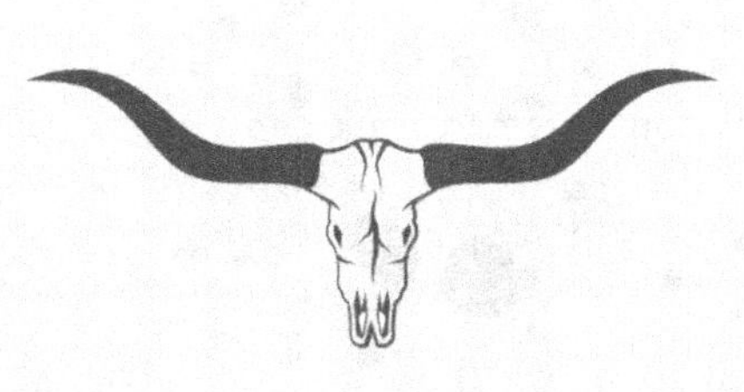

The Spanish sunrise is too beautiful for how I feel. I've been awake for an hour, maybe more, watching the light creep across the marble floors of this obscenely expensive hotel suite. My neck hurts, my back hurts, and the decorative throw blanket I used did absolutely nothing to counter the chill from the air conditioning. I slept like crap.

The past forty-eight hours have been a blur. I'm married, but for the first time in my life, I feel truly alone. I chose to marry my enemy, to lie to my friends, to go to war with my father. Alone has been my default since boarding school. Even the fakest of friends were still friends, someone to sit with, who needed me, even if it was for their own gain. I knew I had someone if I wanted to play the game.

Now, I have Trigger, my new husband, a new game, but the problem is I don't know if I can win this one. The way he looked at me during our vows. The way his hand was steady when he slid a ring onto my finger while mine trembled. The way he acts like this marriage is real. That's what terrifies me most.

He's not treating this like a business arrangement. Not really. Sure, he went along with all my terms, agreed to everything I demanded: separate quarters, professional boundaries, one year and done. But he doesn't act like a man who's planning to walk away in three hundred and sixty-four days. He acts like a man who's already decided I'm his.

The confidence in his voice last night when he said "you're my wife" like it was a fact of nature, not a legal technicality. The way he tried to insist we share the bed, not out of desire, but out of this possessive courtesy. Like, of course his wife wouldn't sleep on a couch. It was as though the very idea was offensive to him. Then there was the way he called the concierge, taking my request for space and bending it to his will while somehow still giving me what I wanted. *This is me meeting you halfway.*

I clench my fists, and my nails dig into my skin, the pinch of pain pushing out the thoughts that keep coming back to him. This can't happen. I can't let it. I have a plan. Get my land back, honor my mother's memory, fulfill the contract, and walk away. Letting him in or letting *anyone* in, for that matter, isn't part of that plan. Because people let you down; they don't stay. And even if they did, I have no room for anything else.

"Asha, we need to be on the road by—" Trigger's words die the second he sees me standing in front of the window. I see the way his eyes trail over my body, hear the subtle stutter in the intake of his next breath, and my heart skips a beat. *This can't happen.*

"You better stop looking at me as though you like what you see," I snap before dropping his gaze and cutting across the room to the kitchen. "Unless this outfit isn't suitable for today's meeting, I'm ready to go."

"Trust me, sweetheart, if I liked what I saw, you'd know it," he tosses back, walking toward the front door. Opening it, he holds it with his foot. "Your outfit is acceptable. Let's go before you ruin it by speaking again."

I grind my teeth. He truly knows how to get under my skin, but this side of him I can deal with. This side allows me to keep my walls intact.

Pausing in front of him, I say, "If you don't want me to speak, you'd better caffeinate me into submission."

Something dangerous flashes in his eyes. He bites the corner of his mouth, barely suppressing a smirk. "Submission. Noted." He leans in until I can feel his breath. "When I want you silent, I won't need coffee to do it."

I force myself to keep walking, ignoring the heat creeping up my neck. I hate how my skin feels too tight, how aware I am of him beside me. We're supposed to be playing the perfect couple, but this tension humming between us feels dangerously real. And that terrifies me more than anything he could actually say.

~

"WE SHOULD PROBABLY TALK ABOUT OUR STORY," I SAY, breaking the silence as we sit in traffic in the back of a town car.

"Our story?" he questions, not bothering to look up from his phone.

Of course he's not taking this seriously. "Yeah, our story... If you think these people aren't going to ask us casual questions about how we met, over lunch and as we tour their ranch, you're not as smart as I thought you might be."

"We already have a story. No need to change it," he states, like it's the most obvious thing in the world.

"Enlighten me, because I'm not sure why we actually went through with getting married if it was to come all this way and tell them we got married to seal the deal."

That gets his attention. Finally. He shifts slightly, and I can feel his gaze on me even though I'm staring straight ahead at the traffic.

"It's the same lie we already committed to telling our family. Star-crossed lovers, two kids who fell in love before they knew the meaning of the word, torn apart by circumstance, brought back together by fate," he recites.

Star-crossed lovers. The words make something twist uncomfortably in my chest. I hate how easily he says it, like it means nothing. Like *we* mean nothing. Which we don't. Obviously. This is business. *So why does it bother me?*

"Okay..." I draw out the word frustrated, feeling like I'm walking into this business meeting that he's expecting me to help him land blind. "Who are we meeting and why did we have to come to Spain for it?"

He puts his phone in his pocket, finally sensing I'm not going to let this go. "We are here to meet with Arora Heritage. They currently only operate in Spain. I'm looking to partner with them and expand their reach in the US."

"Why would you want to partner and split profit? Hale Ranch is already international."

"I need support. Bull breeding is new territory for me. I'm sure I'm ahead on the curve, considering Hale Ranch is an elite horse breeder, but—"

"Wait, back up. Bull breeding? Since when—why wouldn't your father and London come to this meeting?" I'm stuttering through my questions as I try to wrap my mind around this news.

"They don't know. My father refuses to give me his blessing, and I'm trying to keep London out of the crossfire. He and my father have their own projects, side hobbies that have become full-blown businesses. They left the horse operation almost completely in my hands. I have my Uncle Baylor keeping the books, but for the most part, I'm the one overseeing the day-to-day. It's what I was born into, and I'm not complaining. I've had a good life, considering it didn't start out so great, but that doesn't mean I don't want something for myself. Something I'm passionate about. Something that fuels my soul, something to feel connected to, something that's mine."

I understand this. I sympathize with this. I was born into this life too. It's what my family did, therefore it's what I do. Even if I tell myself I chose to be a vet because it's what I wanted, ultimately it was influenced by what I was born into. I love horses, but I also wanted to please my father, to carry on our traditions, and to continue building a legacy.

"I get that," I say softly. "But bulls... Why? Are you planning to ride again?" I ask, remembering the charity ride I watched him partake in. That night lives rent-free in my mind for countless reasons, but the top one is the way my heart felt like it stopped the second I saw him get kicked.

"I can't say I'll never ride again. There's something about being on the back of such a powerful animal, an inexplicable rush, a high that grounds you even as it lifts you up. You feel big and small all at once. It's a fleeting taste of power, yes, but also a sobering reminder of how small you are, how little control you truly have."

He crosses his leg. "But the plan is to breed them, not ride them. The business model is more sustainable than horse breeding. The selection process is rooted in genetics rather than performance, actual science, not tradition and ego. You studied genetics because you wanted to be a step ahead when picking horses. With bull breeding, that work would actually be quantifiable. You'd be focused on long-term herd improvement and sustainability, not chasing ribbons and reputations. Horse breeding is still decades away from breaking free of its performance-based hierarchy."

He has a valid point. Ironically, it's the same one I've been giving my father for years. *Genetics over performance. Data over gut feeling and family names.* The horse world won't change in our lifetime, not really. Too much money, too much tradition, too many egos wrapped up in the old way of doing things. But bulls?

I shift in my seat. "You make it sound simple."

I anxiously twist the gold band that now sits on my left hand, and my eyes catch his watching the thoughtless move. The weight of his gaze makes my skin prickle. The night he put this ring on my finger, I'd wondered how it ended up in his pocket, why he had it, who it was meant for, because its current resting place couldn't be where he'd intended it to be. The look in his eyes now seems distant, like he's thinking about the broken plans that now sit on my finger, and I can't take it.

"Whose ring am I wearing?" I ask, my voice sharper than I intend. I need to know what I messed up. I don't want secrets between us. I know I'm not his forever, but I don't need surprises when we get home and whoever this ring was meant for shows up.

"It was my grandmother's," he says, his voice void of any emotion.

That definitely wasn't the answer I was expecting, but it also wasn't the one I was after.

I swallow hard, fingers stilling on the ring. "Let me rephrase that. Who were you planning on giving it to? A man doesn't carry around his grandmother's ring in his pocket unless he planned on giving it to someone."

The air between us feels dangerously charged.

"I think I'll keep that to myself for now." His tone is clipped, final.

Coward. Heat flashes through me—anger, hurt, something I refuse to name. "Trigger, this isn't going to work if you're seeing someone behind my back. I have to know how to cover for you, and I don't need to be looking over my shoulder, worried about what woman wants to spill my blood because I took her man."

He shifts toward me slightly, and suddenly the backseat feels impossibly small. "I never said there was someone else—"

"Then why can't you just tell me why you had this ring in your pocket?" My voice rises despite my best efforts to stay calm. *Why does it matter so much? Why do I care?*

"I didn't say I wouldn't."

The words hang between us, heavy with implication. I spin the ring again, a nervous habit I'm developing, hating his silence on the subject because I have to stare at the reminder. I lean my head against the seat, and my eyes catch his hand. He's not wearing a ring. Unlike him, I don't carry spare rings for funsies.

"Fine, don't tell me," I say, my throat tight as I take it off. "You're not wearing one, so neither am I."

I hold it out between us.

"Asha, stop playing games." His voice drops lower, and there's an edge to it now that makes my pulse quicken. "You have to wear that ring. You're my wife."

"And you're my husband. I'll wear mine when you wear one."

The challenge sits between us like a lit fuse. His eyes darken, jaw working as he stares at the ring in my palm, then back up to my face. The muscle in his temple twitches.

"You're serious." It's not a question.

"Completely." I don't drop my hand, don't break eye contact.

"You didn't get me one," he bites out, and there's an edge to his voice that makes my stomach flip. "I can wait. You, however, can't. We have a meeting to attend, and that ring needs to be on your finger. It's part of our deal."

Our deal. The words sting more than they should.

"I agree, it's a bad look, but so is you not wearing one. If the Arora family is as traditional as you say they are, they'll expect both of us to be donning rings."

"I'm a rancher. These are working hands." He holds one up as if to prove his point. "It's perfectly reasonable that I don't wear a ring for that reason alone. Beyond the safety aspect, there's the cost of losing it, riding, mucking stalls, feeding, the list is endless."

Of course he has an answer for everything. My grip tightens on the ring.

I shrug, forcing casualness I don't feel. "Well, I'm a rancher's wife and a vet at that, so..." I set the ring on his thigh. "We can be untraditional together."

The ring sits there on the dark fabric of his pants, catching the light. Neither of us moves to touch it. The backseat of our car is humming with tension so thick it almost feels tangible.

There's a tick in his jaw before he says, "Put this back on and don't take it off again."

His voice is low, controlled, but there's something dangerous underneath it, something that makes heat coil in my stomach even as irritation flares in my chest.

He doesn't get to just order me around.

"Make me," I say before I can stop myself.

The words hang in the air between us, and I watch his eyes flash with surprise before something darker moves in. His gaze drops to my lips for just a fraction of a second before snapping back to my eyes.

Oh God, what did I just say?

The tension is suffocating now, the space between us charged with something that has nothing to do with business deals or fake marriages. My heart pounds so hard I'm sure he can hear it. He leans forward slightly, and I force myself not to retreat. His hand moves toward the ring on his thigh, fingers closing around it.

"Don't test me, Asha," he says quietly, his voice rough. "I always win."

But instead of handing it back, he reaches for my left hand. His fingers are warm, firm, as he takes my wrist, gentler than I expected given his tone, but with enough pressure that I feel trapped. Claimed. *Breathe. Just breathe.*

"Wear this, and I'll meet your terms." His eyes search mine as he waits for another objection. When I don't stop him, he takes my hand and slides the ring back on himself. His thumb brushes over my knuckles, lingering a beat too long to be casual. "Was that so difficult?"

I should pull away. I should say something cutting. Instead, I'm frozen, hyperaware of every point of contact between us and the way his eyes haven't left mine.

"Your turn," I manage, but my voice lacks conviction.

His thumb traces another slow circle on my wrist, right over my pulse. "As you wish," he says before his eyes flash outside the window. "Manuel, change of plans. Pull over; we have to make a stop."

He pulls away, and I straighten in my seat, my eyes darting out the window. There's no jewelry shop, just a few tiendas. That's when my eye catches the word *tatuajes.* My Spanish is rough, but I'm pretty sure that translates to tattoo.

My head snaps back toward him. "Have you lost your mind?"

"In more ways than you know," he answers somewhat cryptically.

"'Trigger, this is—" I start, but I don't even know how to finish. Insane... Extreme... Permanent!

That last word echoes in my head like a warning bell. This is a temporary marriage. A business arrangement with an expiration date. You don't get permanent marks for temporary things. He's already out of the car, heading toward the parlor.

By the time I catch up to him, he's already inside. The tattoo parlor is exactly what you'd expect: dark walls covered in flash art, the buzzing hum of machines in the back, the sharp scent of antiseptic mixed with ink. A woman with sleeve tattoos and a nose ring looks up from the counter.

"Can I help you?" she asks with a thick accent.

"Yes, wedding band," Trigger says, holding up his left hand.

Her eyes dart between us. "One or two?" she questions.

He glances over his shoulder like he's waiting to see if I'll take the same reckless leap. "I didn't ask you to do this."

He doesn't argue. Instead, he turns back and replies, "Just one. Will there be a wait?"

"No, not for a band. Easy tattoo," she confirms before adding, "Follow me."

Once he's seated in the chair, I can't help but point out the obvious under my breath as she prepares her tray. "This is permanent. We aren't."

The way he pushes his tongue into his cheek as though he doesn't like my comment has me shifting on the stool beside him.

"It's as permanent as I want it to be. Tattoos can be removed."

"Even if you get it removed, it could still leave a scar."

His eyes flick to mine, dark and intense. "Maybe I want the reminder. I have no intention of forgetting my first and last marriage."

First and last. I can't help it. Those words make my breath catch in my throat. I can't be sure what they mean. Does he mean he plans to keep me, or does he simply mean he has no plan to ever get married again? Neither makes sense, given that he was carrying a ring in his pocket the night we randomly decided to set this fake marriage in motion.

Here I am, overthinking again, letting my mind travel down roads that lead to inevitable ends. I stand abruptly, needing air, and hike my thumb over my shoulder. "I think I saw a coffee shop. I'm going to grab another. Want me to grab you one?"

"Sure," he says with a heavy sigh.

Did he feel it too? Or am I imagining things?

I'm almost to the door, my hand on the handle, when I remember I have no money. Heat creeps up my neck as I turn back. The worst part of all this might be that I have no money of my own. I've never worked—at least not a job that earns me a paycheck. I pull the card I never returned out of my pocket and hold it up.

"Mind if I use this?"

He doesn't even look up from where the needle is tracing black ink into his skin, but I see the corner of his mouth twitch. "My money is your money. You're my wife, sweetheart."

Sweetheart. The use of that nickname needles at my nerves because it feels like a power play. Like he's getting me back for walking away while he gets the wedding ring I requested tattooed on his finger.

"Don't call me that."

"Why?" Now he does look up, and the heat in his gaze pins me in place. "Does it bother you...sweetheart?"

"It's disingenuous," I manage, gripping the doorframe a little tighter than necessary.

"So is this entire marriage." He holds up his hand, showing me the half-finished band wrapping around his finger. "But here we are, making it permanent anyway."

The artist glances between us, clearly entertained.

"You're the one who suggested this," I point out, gesturing vaguely at his hand.

"And you're the one who demanded I get a ring." His eyes don't leave mine. "Seems like we both got what we wanted."

Did we?

"Two coffees, then," I say, needing to escape before I do something stupid like ask him what he really meant about this being his last marriage. "Black. No sugar?"

"You remembered." He sounds almost surprised.

Of course I remembered. I remember everything about you, and I hate myself for it.

"Don't read into it. I'm just a good actress."

"The best," he agrees, but something flickers in his eyes. "Almost had me convinced you actually give a damn."

I leave before I can respond, my heart hammering against my ribs.

This is just a role. Just a performance. So why does it feel like every word between us is carving something permanent into my chest, deeper than any tattoo ever could?

TRIGGER

CHAPTER 19

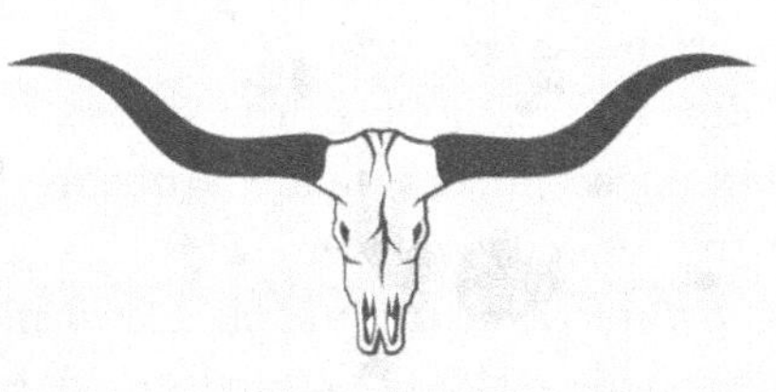

"Holy shit," Asha says in awe as the Arora Estate comes into view. "We are definitely breeding the wrong animals."

The heart of the nearly thousand-acre ranch comes into view. They built their house in the absolute best spot, situated on a hilltop with the mountains and a lake as a backdrop. It's definitely a jaw dropper.

"Fairfield isn't exactly slumming it," I say.

"Pfft, we might have high-end facilities, but we sit on less than a hundred acres. Without your sixty, we're barely forty."

"What would you do with all this land anyway?" I ask as I take in the sprawling estate through her eyes.

"Same as you, I suppose," she mutters before turning to me. "Start a dream."

We share a second of what feels like a moment that could be a shared dream, a shared reality, both of us letting go of all the circumstances and history that kept us apart, and then the car comes to a stop.

"Remind me again, who are we meeting with?"

"Originally, we were meeting with Dar, the owner, but plans changed on the ride over, and now Mateo, their ranch manager, is going to be giving us a tour. We will meet with Dar this evening for dinner."

She nods, and I unbuckle my seatbelt, squinting through the windshield. A figure is already descending the porch steps, broad-shouldered, wearing a faded denim shirt with the sleeves rolled to his elbows. The heat hits us like a wall when we step out.

Mateo closes the distance with his hand extended and a genuine smile beneath the shadow of his hat brim. "Welcome, welcome. You must be exhausted. That's a long drive." His handshake is firm and callused. "I'm Mateo. Sorry about the change in plans, but Dar had to be called away on business. You're in good hands, though, I promise," he says, the Spanish rolling warm through his voice.

He turns to Asha, and his smile lingers. "And you must be Mrs...?"

"Asha," she says, extending her hand.

He takes it, holding it a beat longer than necessary. "Asha. Beautiful name. Suits you." His fingers linger a moment too long before he lets go. "I hope the drive wasn't too rough on you."

Instinctively, I move into her space and place my hand on the small of her back, spreading my fingers wide. The thin fabric does nothing to hide the warmth of her skin, and when her spine straightens, I know she feels the claim in my touch, and when she plays the part, my mind can't help but short-circuit. *Mine.*

"We managed just fine," she confirms before glancing up at me with surprise or one of her scolding glares; I can't be sure because I keep my gaze keenly tuned to Mateo. It can't be helped. A man knows when another is admiring what he has, and I'm making sure he knows she's all mine.

"She's tougher than she looks." I pull her closer and feel her warmth against my side, the way she fits there like she was meant to. Her hip brushes mine, and the contact feels electric. "Aren't you, sweetheart?"

"Oh, absolutely," she says, her tone sweet and sharp as her hand comes to rest against my chest. The gesture looks affectionate to anyone watching, but I can feel the tension in her fingers. "If anyone had a rough ride, it was my husband, having to put up with being stuck with me for all those hours."

Stuck with her, as if that's what this is. As if the way I can't stop touching her, the way my body gravitates toward hers without permission, is some kind of burden. Her fingers curl slightly into my shirt, and I can feel my own heartbeat against her palm, hammering harder than it should be for a simple touch.

This is supposed to be for show, but the way my thumb unconsciously traces a small circle against her back, the way she doesn't pull away even as she cuts at me, coupled with the way we both seem to have forgotten to breathe properly, says different.

"Lucky man. Well, then, shall we get started? I promise to take good care of you both," he says, slipping deeper into his accent.

His words snap us out of the haze brought on by yet another one of our petty feuds that exist for reasons I can't name. We break apart, but instead of missing her touch, I'm already anticipating the next one. Because that's what tonight promises, an entire evening of her playing the devoted wife, and every time she does, every touch she manufactures for appearance's sake, every smile she forces for our audience...it chips away at that wall she's built between us.

The pleasantries continue, small talk about the drive, the weather, the ranch's history. I'm half-listening when something pulls my attention sideways. Across the garden, past the cluster of plants and the wooden fence line, a man stands on the far porch. Just standing there. Watching. The distance makes it hard to make out details, but it's the stillness that catches me. Everyone else on the property seems to have purpose, movement. This man has neither.

"...and we've got about two hundred head right now, though that fluctuates seasonally." I blink, turning back to Mateo, who's gesturing toward the stables. The man is probably just a ranch hand, curious about visitors.

"Sounds good," I say, falling into step as we head toward the barn.

Inside, the air is cooler, thick with the smell of hay and leather. Mateo walks us through the operation with the ease of someone who's given this tour a hundred times.

"Our main focus is breeding stock," he explains, running a hand along a stall door. "We've got some of the finest Angus bulls in the Southwest. Bloodlines going back three generations, all AI-certified. We lease out bulls for natural cover during breeding season."

"What's your turnover like?" I ask, watching a massive black bull shift in his stall.

"We keep our prime breeding bulls for about five to six years. After that, if they're still performing, they're sent to smaller operations or sold for beef. But the genetics is where the real money is."

"And day to day?" Asha asks, surprising me. She's leaning against the stall, genuinely interested. "What does that look like?"

"Early mornings," Mateo says, that warm smile back for her. "Feeding starts at five. We've got a rotation for pasture management, can't over-graze, especially in summer. The vet comes by twice a week to check breeding soundness and do collections. Then there's maintenance, fence repairs, and water system checks. We run AI classes here too, teaching other ranchers proper technique. It's good supplemental income."

"You mentioned Arora's sole focus is breeding stock, and I can tell most of the herd we've seen today is docile. Do you breed rodeo bulls?" Asha asks, and I can't help but wonder if she's asking because of my past, because of the story I told her about my father not wanting me to ride.

"We do. We keep them separate from this herd. The two are raised differently. Dar would like to walk through that part of the ranch with you," Mateo advises, extending his arm for us to continue our tour.

We continue to the northern pasture where Mateo points out their rotational grazing system, explaining how they move the bulls every two weeks to prevent overgrazing and maintain soil health. He talks about their water infrastructure, solar-powered wells, and a network of pipes that keep every pasture hydrated even in the brutal summer months. For the most part, he isn't saying anything I didn't already know. I have plenty of land to sustain and grow a herd; however, if I want to go big, I will need to look into solar-powered wells.

"Dar's invested heavily in sustainability," he says, kicking at a sprinkler head. "Pays off in the long run. Our grass stays greener longer, bulls stay healthier, and we can support more head per acre than most operations out here."

By afternoon, I've caught myself looking over my shoulder three more times, unable to shake the feeling of being watched, but not just in a passing sense, as you would someone in the store. It's that deep-seated feeling of being watched. Maybe it's just paranoia. I'm grateful for the tour, but I want to meet Dar and start talking to people who matter. I'm anxious to start strategizing and talking numbers.

"You alright?" Asha asks.

I realize I've stopped walking and am staring back toward the house. "Yeah," I say, forcing my attention forward. "Just taking it all in."

Mateo studies me for a moment then checks his watch. "Well, we've covered most of the operation. Why don't I show you to your room? You'll want to freshen up before dinner. Dar should be back by seven."

We walk back toward the main house, our boots crunching on the dry grass. The sun is lower now, but it's still warm. Inside, the house is cool, all thick walls and terracotta tile. Mateo leads us up a wide staircase and down a hallway lined with landscape paintings and old photographs of the ranch from various decades.

"You'll be staying in the blue room," he says, stopping at a heavy wooden door. "Private bathroom, and the windows face east, so you'll get good morning light. There are fresh towels in the bathroom."

"Oh, we aren't staying. We have a place in the city," Asha informs him.

Mateo frowns, and his face suddenly looks worried. "It's just to freshen up," I add. He must not have known we weren't staying, and I don't want to come off as an ungrateful houseguest.

He pushes the door open, revealing a spacious room with a four-poster bed, Southwestern textiles, and windows overlooking the front garden and the distant porch where I'd seen the man earlier.

"Dinner is at seven in the main dining room, back down the stairs and to your left. Cocktails at six-thirty if you want to join us early." He tips his hat again, that lingering look at Asha. "I'll let you two get settled."

When he's gone, I move to the window, scanning the property, and Asha flops onto the bed.

"What does AI mean? He kept using that term, and I couldn't for the life of me put it together," she asks, clearly flustered that she didn't have the answer to something for once.

"Artificial insemination," I answer evenly, turning from the window.

"Gah, I can't believe I couldn't come up with that." Palm to forehead, she adds, "I should have known that."

"Nah, you're used to horses," I say, unbuttoning the top button of my polo, for comfort. "Thoroughbreds still have strict laws against AI breeding. It's not something we often encounter every day in the arenas we work in."

She kicks her feet and pounds her fists against the bed like a small child throwing a tantrum. I've never seen her lose control. Even when she's on the attack, she does it with complete, practiced control, as if she knew her opponent's move before they made it. Asha is smart; she's smarter than smart. And while I think it's cute that something stumped her, I know that can only mean her attention is divided. She's here, but her mind isn't. *So where is it?*

Then calmly, she stares at the ceiling and asks, "What are we supposed to do for the next hour?"

"I'd be more than happy to walk through the differences between AI and natural conception. Maybe you need a refresher. Knocking off the dust might help bring it all back," I say, casually leaning against the bedpost. "I can take off my clothes or you—"

"You're joking, right?" she deadpans.

"Only if you want me to be," I say with a devilish smile. *Definitely not joking.*

She grabs her chest and mocks silent laughter.

"Laugh all you want. I just didn't want you to show up to dinner ill-prepared. I know how you hate it when you're not the smartest person in the room."

"Stop..." she exaggerates, the word drawn out with playful exhaustion before rolling to her side. Propping her head up on her bent arm, she studies me with those calculating eyes.

The playfulness between us dissolves into something heavier, and I can't hold her gaze.

"You should go freshen up," I finally manage, my voice rougher than I intended as I nod toward the bathroom. "I'll go after you."

She doesn't move immediately, just watches me with an expression I can't quite read. Then she slides off the bed, padding barefoot across the room. When the bathroom door clicks shut, I find my way to the loveseat and sit heavily before dropping my head back against the pillows and closing my eyes.

Temporary. That's what I agreed to, and I have to remember it, even if temporary was never my plan. I drag my hand down my face and lean back, but every stolen moment, every time she looks at me like maybe there's something more building between us, I fall deeper. If I can't earn her heart, if she walks away when this is over... The certainty hits like a fist: losing her might actually break me.

The water turns on in the bathroom, and my eyes flash open. *Get it together. You just have to earn her.* Somehow, I have to make her see that what we have is worth keeping. That this could never be temporary.

By six-thirty, we've both freshened up. I went through my emails, did some research on solar wells, and rodeo breeding vs fighting. Bulls are aggressive by nature. If anything, rodeo breeding makes them more docile as they become somewhat accustomed to human interaction, opposed to fighting bulls which are raised with minimal human interaction. All that matters is that at their core, both want bulls with energy, stamina, and strength.

"Ready?" she asks from the doorway, her tone clipped and businesslike.

Asha emerges from the bathroom in a simple sundress that Dar had sent up for her. I don't like the thought of another man dressing my woman for dinner—a fact I'm sure she saw written all over my face the second a maid brought it to the room. I didn't like it, therefore she did.

We make it halfway down the stairs before she breaks the silence. "Is the dress okay?"

Of course she's worried about the dress. About appearances. About playing her part perfectly for the cameras, for Dar and Mateo—for everyone but me. At the bottom of the steps, I stop and turn to face her, letting my eyes travel over every exposed inch deliberately, slowly, taking my time in a way I know will get under her skin.

She shifts her weight, that familiar fire sparking in her eyes. "Oh, come on, you saw it when I walked out of the bathroom, and you didn't say anything."

"Sweetheart," I draw out, letting the endearment drip with just enough edge to remind her how much she hates when I use it, "I wasn't looking at the dress. I was looking at you."

She tenses, and for a second, that careful mask slips. Then her chin tilts up, defiant. "Is that supposed to be a compliment? Because it sounds like you were ignoring my question."

"You want me to comment on the dress?" I step closer, crowding her space just enough to make her bristle. "Fine. It's blue. It fits. Happy?"

"You're an ass," she mutters, but there's color rising in her cheeks now, and we both know it's not from anger.

"And you're stalling." I lean in, lowering my voice. "What are you really asking me?"

Her eyes flash. "I'm asking if I look appropriate for a business dinner, not fishing for your approval."

"Right. Because God forbid you'd actually care what I think."

"Why would I?" she shoots back, but her fingers tighten on my arm, betraying her. "You've made your feelings about me perfectly clear over the years."

"My feelings?" I stare at her. "What the hell is that supposed to mean?"

"You know exactly what it means." There's old hurt in her voice now, buried under the anger. "I'm good enough to be your temporary wife, but I was never good enough to be—"

"To be what?" I press, but she's already shutting down.

"I'm not—" She cuts herself off, jaw clenched, and looks away. "Forget it. Let's just get through this dinner."

Men's loafers click across the terracotta floors. "There you are," Mateo says, coming down the hall. "I thought maybe you got lost, the two of you."

Asha smiles, "No, I just took a little longer changing. The dress Dar sent up for me is beautiful."

"No, Mrs. Asha, it's the woman who makes the dress beautiful," he says before extending his arm. "Come, have a drink," he says, motioning for us to follow him.

I let him get a few steps ahead before tightening my hold on my wife. "This conversation isn't over."

She doesn't give me her face, and even from the side, I can tell it wouldn't matter. It gives nothing away. We turn the corner, and the expansive living room comes into view. High ceilings crossed by exposed beams and windows that frame the property. A bar cart sits in the corner, and Mateo is there, pouring something amber into glasses. Two other men stand nearby—ranch hands, by the look of them.

"Whiskey okay? It's local, from a distillery about forty miles south," Mateo asks, handing each of us a glass.

"Perfect," I say. "Will Dar be joining us for drinks?"

"Yes," he says, "Will you excuse me for a moment?" His eyes flash over to someone else entering the room.

"How many people are coming to dinner?" Asha asks, taking a look around.

"I'm not sure," I say, flexing my left hand, the covering on my finger a little stiff.

"That might be too tight. Your hand looks slightly hued compared to your other."

Now she acts like she gives a damn. Hot and cold this woman is. I'm beginning to think her mood swings are intentional. She knows she's driving me crazy and enjoys watching every second of my suffering.

"It'll be fine," I say, taking a long drink of the whiskey Mateo handed me.

She nods toward the wall. "I'm going to look at the paintings. You should mingle and find out who these people are. If they're invited to dinner, they're likely important to Dar."

The conversation flows easily enough. A few of the men in attendance work on the ranch, and the other two couples are friends staying in town for the week. They've already recommended a few must-see destinations for us if we decide to extend our stay. I'm halfway through the story about our drive up when I see him again—the man who was on the porch this morning. The same one I could have sworn I felt watching me through the windows and across the garden.

He has that same stillness, but in the light, I can see his presence isn't as ominous as I originally thought. He can't be much older than me. Late twenties max, but with the shadows gone, there's something else I notice. He was never watching me. He was watching her.

I've just put the two together when I watch him stalk across the room to where Asha is standing beside one of the women visiting Dar on holiday. My hand tightens around my glass, and then my feet are moving.

"Excuse me, but I was curious if we've met before?" I hear him ask as I close the distance.

That's it. That's his pick-up line?

Asha's eyes narrow on him, and she takes a second to collect his features. "I don't think so, but you do feel oddly familiar."

"What's your name?" he presses.

"Asha," she answers. I instantly hate how she doesn't add my name to hers.

"Asha..." He draws her name out slowly. "Is it just Asha, or do you have a last name?"

"Hale. Her last name is Hale," I answer for her, stepping up to her back and eliminating any space that remained between us.

Fuck, wrong move. I'm instantly aware of the curve of her round ass pressed firmly against my groin. Every logical thought tells me to step aside and reposition myself. I'm supposed to be immune to my fake wife, but she can already feel that I'm not, and I'm about three seconds away from remembering why I need to be.

ASHA

CHAPTER 20

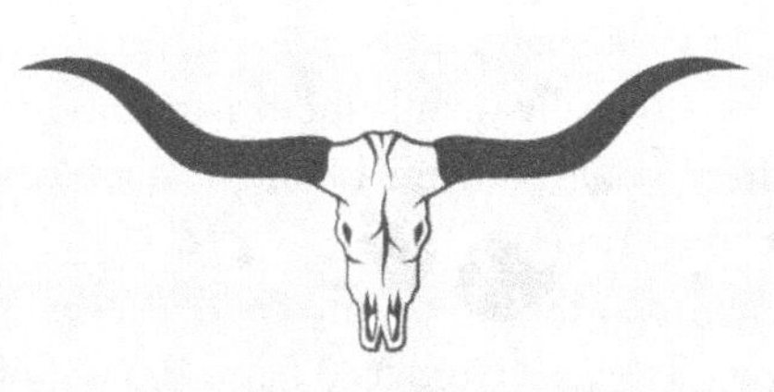

His warmth hits me before anything else. Then he's against me, his chest to my back, so damn close. Every inch of space I'd maintained all evening...gone. His hand slides around my waist possessively, and I have to remind myself to breathe, to stay relaxed and not stiffen, even though every nerve is screaming *This isn't us!*

"Yes, sorry. I'm still getting used to saying my new last name." The lie comes out smooth, easier than expected, given the way my thoughts are torn between his touch and the man standing in front of me. "This trip is somewhat doubling as our honeymoon. In fact, we left our reception to come here."

The man's eyes flick up over my shoulder, and something shifts in his expression. It could be hesitation, but it looks like suspicion. His gaze lingers on Trigger like he's trying to decide if he buys what we're selling.

I use the moment to actually *look* at him. Mid-twenties, maybe twenty-eight at most. Handsome in that effortless way some men are, sharp jawline, warm brown skin, dark eyes, and black hair. He looks like me—or we share the same roots, anyway. It's not every day I run into someone with Indian heritage. Maybe that's why he asked if we'd met before. We have the same skin. It has to be what's making him do a double-take, wondering if there's a connection he's forgotten.

His attention returns to me, and I realize I've been staring a second too long.

"Congratulations," he says, his tone polite, even though his smile doesn't quite reach his eyes. "This is quite the honeymoon choice," he offers, but the sarcasm is noted.

Trigger's fingers tighten at my hip, brief and deliberate. Right, I'm here for him. I have a job.

"I didn't catch your name," I say, keeping my voice light and curious.

"Rohan." No last name. No elaboration. His gaze drifts back to Trigger.

"Rohan, this is my husband—"

"Trigger," my new husband cuts me off, extending his hand in greeting while keeping the other firmly locked around my waist.

Rohan's eyes drop to his bandaged hand at my hip. "Already allergic to wearing your wedding ring?"

The comment hangs in the air, pointed and just shy of rude.

"Don't need one." Trigger's bandaged hand slides more firmly around me, pulling me back against him with unmistakable possession. "Got something more permanent instead. I play for keeps, needed to make sure everyone knows it's not coming off."

Heat floods through me. Not embarrassment, though I wish it were, because this somehow feels worse. I like his words too much. *Permanent. Playing for keeps.* I like the solid weight of him at my back, the way I fit against him. Logic abandons me completely as my head swims, and my body makes the decision my brain can't, and I lean back into him. Just slightly, just enough, and he notices.

I hear the sharp inhale he draws in, feel the way his chest expands against my spine, and then the unmistakable and devastating feel of his hard length pressing against my ass. *Fuck.* We're both frozen, caught in this moment that's spiraling far beyond the carefully constructed lie we're supposed to be selling. His fingers dig into my hip, not to pull me closer and not to release me. It's like he can't decide which impulse to follow.

Rohan's gaze flicks between us, but whatever response is forming dies as the heavy double doors at the far end of the room swing open.

"Dinner is ready," a butler announces.

The spell breaks, and the room stirs to life around us as guests head toward the dining room. But Trigger holds me back, his grip firm, keeping me exactly where I am for one more second.

His mouth drops to my ear, his voice low and rough. "You're a good actress, sweetheart." The words are edged with something dark, something that sounds like accusation and want tangled together. "For a minute there, you actually had me believing you liked my touch."

His hand begins to retract from my waist slowly like he's savoring the way I feel as his palm drags across my dress, leaving a trail of heat that makes my stomach tighten. By the time his hand falls away completely, I'm wound so tight I might shatter.

"No more leaving my side tonight." It's not a request. His hand wraps around mine possessively before he threads his fingers through mine and leads us toward the dining room. And I follow, because what else can I do? My words at the bottom of the stairs and now this... He knows. He knows I wasn't acting at all.

"A new face. You must be Trigger," a woman with rich, dark hair flowing in waves down her back and striking eyes greets us before we take our seats.

"I am," Trigg answers, releasing my hand to shake hers. "And you are?"

"Daruka." Her eyes sparkle with curiosity and confidence. "But you may call me Dar."

Well, that's unexpected. Trigger never mentioned that Dar was a woman, but her studied gaze now makes sense. He didn't know, and she's watching for a reaction. She wants to see if her gender makes a difference to him.

"This is my wife, Asha," Trigger responds, not missing a beat. If the revelation that his new business partner is a woman—and a stunning one at that—rattles him, his expression betrays nothing.

"Pleased to meet you." I extend my hand. "Your home is incredible."

"Thank you." Her hands envelop mine with surprising warmth, holding on longer than needed. "I want all my guests to feel welcome in my home." Before I can process it, she slides past Trigger and wraps her arm around me. "Come, sit here beside me." She guides me toward the head of the table, and I catch a glimpse of Trigger over my shoulder. His expression is unreadable, and I'm officially a ball of nerves. I expected to be a side character on this trip, an afterthought, not center stage.

"So how has Spain been treating you?" Dar asks as we settle into our seats. Her voice has a smoky quality, accented but impossible to place. "Well, I hope?"

"We haven't seen much yet." Trigger claims the chair to my left, his hand finding mine under the table with practiced ease before resting our joined hands atop. "Just arrived last night."

His callused palm is warm, and his touch quickly settles my nerves, and I resent it. I don't like feeling dependent, like he's somehow my medicine. I've been alone my whole life; letting people in has never worked out for me. People you let in eventually leave, or worse, they stay and ruin you. He might feel like safety now, but we both know the truth: we're oil and water.

"Last night?" Dar's dark brow arches as Rohan materializes at her side, setting a glass of burgundy wine before her. "Where are you staying?"

"A place in the city. The Alhambra," Trigger answers.

"Mateo." Dar's voice cuts through the low murmur of conversation at the far end of the table, where ranch hands have begun gathering. Mateo's head snaps up immediately. "Drive into Granada. Collect our guests' luggage from the Alhambra." She doesn't ask; she commands. "If you leave now, you'll return before they retire to their suite."

"That's really not—" Trigger begins.

"You are guests in my home." Dar leans forward, and I notice for the first time the thin gold chain disappearing beneath her collar. "Not just any guests, special guests. You will stay here. What better way to understand the land than to live on it?" Her eyes lock with Trigger's, and something unspoken passes between them.

Trigger's hand tightens around mine—a silent apology or warning, I can't tell. "Thank you. Your home is beautiful. We'd be honored."

"Good." Dar claps her hands once, and servers materialize from hidden doorways, carrying platters that smell of saffron and charred meat. "Now we eat."

The first course arrives, bowls of salmorejo so cold and smooth they might be velvet. Dar launches into a story about the property, something about water rights and a decades-old dispute with a neighboring ranch that she resolved with what she calls "creative negotiation." Her hands move as she talks, graceful and empathic, painting pictures in the air, and Trigger nods along, seemingly enamored.

I've sat through enough business calls with my father to know how to handle myself. Give me profit margins and distribution logistics, contracts, and projections, and I can hold my own. I'm good at that, the clean lines of numbers, the clear terms of deals. But this isn't that kind of dinner. There's been no talk of acreage or breeding programs, no discussion of timelines or investment structures. Instead, Dar asks about the property's history, tells stories about her grandfather, and asks Trigger about growing up in Kentucky. Personal stories. Family. Trust.

This dinner is about bonding. About proving we belong at this table, not as business partners, but as people worth knowing. Worth trusting. Which means I'm not here to negotiate terms. I'm here to sell a lie. To perform convincingly as Trigger's wife so that these strangers will want to tie their legacy to ours.

"So, Asha," Dar says, spearing a piece of steak and studying me with those warm, calculating eyes. "What is it that you do?"

"I'm a veterinarian," I answer confidently. "Equine, specifically."

Dar's eyes light up. "A horse doctor? How wonderful! And convenient." Her eyes flick over to Trigger before returning to mine as she leans forward. "What made you choose horses?"

I see where this is going. She must think he married me for my skill set, for this merger.

"They're honest," I say, and it's the first true thing I've said all evening. "They don't lie about what they're feeling. If something's wrong, they tell you. All you have to know is how to listen." I pause, running my thumb along the stem of my glass.

This dream wasn't always all mine. It was something I pursued to impress my father. It's why I hate the assumption she is forming about me because of the man sitting on my left. That I did this for someone besides me, and that's not the entire truth. If anything, I stayed for me because animals give me something people never could. Trust. I look up, meeting their gaze.

"I spent too much of my life trying to decode what people really meant, reading between the lines, wondering what they weren't saying. With horses, there are no lines. Just pure, unfiltered communication. A mare who's colicking doesn't care about my credentials or whether I had a bad day. She just needs me to understand her, to help her. And when you figure out what they're trying to tell you, and you make it better..." I stop, searching for the words. "That moment when the pain leaves their eyes...that's the most honest transaction I've ever been part of. No pretense. Just trust."

"She's brilliant at it," Trigger adds, his thumb drawing idle shapes across my hand. "I watched her single-handedly identify a case of strangles. Took her less than an hour to trace the outbreak back to a visiting horse whose trailer hadn't been properly sanitized during transportation. She moved through that barn like she could see what everyone else was missing. Checked water sources, feed storage, and tack room protocol. Had the entire facility locked down and a treatment plan in place before some vets would've even confirmed the diagnosis."

I don't know what to make of the pride I hear in his voice, but I try not to let it distract me from focusing on Dar's line of questioning. I think she's testing us. She knows we're newlyweds, and I don't have to know her personally to tell she's a master at reading people. In a lot of ways, I feel like I'm sitting at dinner with my father, his knowing gaze sifting through the truth in my lies. Lucky for me, that story was not a lie. I am good at my job. It's one of the few things I'm certain about.

"Is that so?" This time, when I look up, Rohan is definitely watching me. His eyes are dark, almost black in the candlelight, and there's an intensity there that makes my pulse kick up. Not attraction, something sharper. Assessment, maybe, like he's cataloging details, filing them away.

"We've been having trouble with one of our mares," Dar says. "She's pregnant, but something feels off. Our local vet says everything is fine, but a mother knows." She glances at Rohan. "Would you mind taking a look while you're here? Professional opinion?"

"Of course," I say. "I'd be happy to."

"My son doesn't talk much during dinner," Dar says, as if reading my mind. She glances toward Rohan with unmistakable maternal affection. "He prefers to observe. Don't you, mijo?"

Son. The word recalibrates everything. I'd assumed... Well, I'm not sure what I assumed. But looking at them now, I can see it: the same sharp cheekbones, the same way they both hold themselves like they own not just this table but the very air around it.

"Someone has to," Rohan says. His tone is teasing, but there's also an edge to it. "You talk enough for both of us."

Dar laughs. "He's very protective," she adds, turning back to me, something shifting behind her smile. "Of the business, of our land. Of family..." She lets the word hang there, weighted.

"Mother." Rohan tries to keep his voice even and light, but I can tell there's a warning in it.

"You'll forgive my son. He takes after his father, too serious, always thinking three steps ahead. I've told him a thousand times: business is important, but so is enjoying the moment," she says lightheartedly, but because I know her kind, I know it's anything but. She takes a long sip from her wine. "Did I miss the story about how the two of you met?" she changes the subject.

"We're neighbors," I answer.

At the same time, Trigger says, "At school."

Her eyes dart between us, and I feel like we've made a slip, but Triggers recovers without missing a breath. "We officially met at school, but our families have been neighbors for a few generations."

"Oh." Her eyebrows tug together. "I didn't realize you grew up in the States. Asha, it's a beautiful name. Sanskrit, isn't it? It means hope, if I remember correctly."

I swallow my wine. "Yes, that's correct. My father is Indian, and my mother was a mix of many heritages. She died when I was young."

Something in her gaze shifts, and for a moment, it feels like she's left us completely. "I'm sorry. I know how hard it is to lose people you care for deeply, especially parents. I lost my father when I was young too."

Silence settles over us, but it's not the comfortable kind from earlier. The air feels thick, and Dar's face has gone eerily still, her eyes fixed on some point beyond us, and when she finally moves, it's only to take a slow sip of her wine.

Then Mateo is back. "Sorry for the delay. There was traffic," he says, reclaiming his seat at the far end. "I had Noro take the bags to their room."

"Thank you, Mateo," she says, rising in one fluid motion. "You've all had such a long day between the drive and the tour. Let's get you to your room. There will be plenty of time to talk more over the coming days."

Days? I never asked how long this trip was supposed to last, but I suppose that's because I didn't expect it to last days. Usually, these types of deals are pretty much a sure thing before the meet and greet ever occurs. Both companies have vetted the other, thorough research has been done, and all that's left is a vibe check. First impressions can make or break a deal, and in some way, I can't help but feel like I'm somehow responsible for fumbling this.

"Thank you for the meal," Trigger says, rising from his chair. "Everything was wonderful."

"Yes, thank you," I add quickly, doing the same. "Goodnight, Dar."

She nods, but her expression remains unreadable. "Buenas noches."

As we leave, I glance back and see Dar still standing, perfectly motionless, watching us go. Our eyes meet across the distance, and I tense. There's something in her gaze, something achingly familiar that I can't quite place. It tugs at the edges of my memory like a half-remembered dream.

But I blink, and whatever it was is gone, and reality crashes back as Trigger's hand finds the small of my back. "I hope you're not tired."

My stomach tightens. The interrogation isn't over. It's just changing locations because I'm not retreating to my room, but *ours*.

TRIGGER

CHAPTER 21

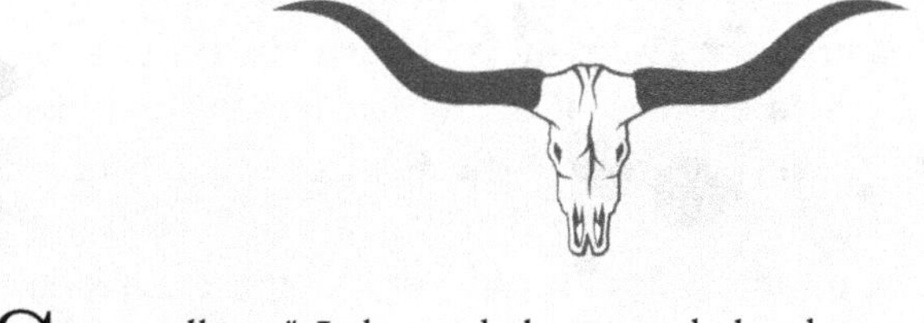

"Start talking," I demand the second the door to our room closes behind us.

"Dinner was unexpected. I didn't realize I'd be doing so much talking." She moves toward the bathroom.

I step in front of her, blocking her path. "I don't want to talk about dinner." My voice comes out rougher than intended. "I want to know what you meant when you said you're only good enough to be my temporary wife, but not good enough to be my...my what? My real wife?"

Her expression hardens, and she sidesteps me, putting the bed between us like a barricade. "Seriously, this is what you want to talk about right now?" She slips off her heels, kicking them under the bed with more force than necessary. "Not the fact that Dar is Daruka, a woman? Or that her son, Rohan, was watching me intently all night and not even being discreet about it?"

I rake a hand through my hair, pacing toward the window before wheeling back to face her. "I couldn't care less that Dar is a woman. It doesn't change anything. She's smart and clearly respected by her staff." I take a step closer, watching her retreat toward the armchair in the corner. "I don't know what to make of her son, but I don't care about him right now." Another step. "Right now, the only thing I care about is standing in front of me, deflecting." I plant my hands on the footboard of the bed, leaning forward. "So, I'll ask you again. What did you mean, Asha?"

She won't look at me. Instead, her fingers work at the clasp of her bracelet. "It's been a long day, and now here we are, officially stuck in one room together—again. A term that is strictly outlined in our agreement." The bracelet falls into her palm, and she sets it down with a soft click. "I just want to go to bed."

"Not happening." I straighten, my voice dropping to something dangerous and raw. "I'm not going to keep playing this game with you." I move around the bed. "I don't think you hate me as much as you'd like to, so what is this if it's not a game?"

"You're the one playing games, Trigger. Not me." She finally turns to face me, and the look in her eyes stops me cold. It's a mixture of sadness and something else, something that looks a lot like fear. *Is she scared of me?* Her voice cracks. "Answering these questions gets us nowhere. It doesn't change anything."

"Bullshit." I shrug off my sport coat and toss it over the chair, never breaking eye contact. "I know you felt something today." I take another step, watching her spine straighten in defiance. "You felt it when I shocked you and got this tattoo. I felt the way your pulse raced beneath my fingers at dinner tonight when I held your hand, and the way you relaxed against me when I was at your back." One more step. "I don't think you hate me at all."

She shakes her head, dark hair falling forward to hide her face as she turns her back on me. Her arms wrap around herself. "You never called."

The accusation doesn't make sense. *Why is she so scared of the truth?* "You already know that's a lie—"

"It was four months." Her voice is barely above a whisper, but it cuts through the room. "Four months after Hollis gave me your number that I finally blocked you." Her shoulders shake once, like she's fighting back something she doesn't want me to see. "You had time to ask, to try, and you didn't."

I close the distance between us, stopping just behind her, close enough to see her reflection in the window glass. "I could say the same about you. You had my number, and you didn't call."

"That's not—"

"Asha." I force my voice to soften as my frustration builds. "You already know what happened. My world was turned upside down when I got home. I went to your house. I expected to run into you in town, expected you to come home, and you didn't." My hands ball into fists at my sides to keep from reaching for her. "I came after you. I showed up at your father's house in Louisville." I pause, making sure she hears every word. "I know you know that. So don't sit here and pretend you believe I didn't try."

She remains stoic against the window, but I can see the rise and fall of her chest is more pronounced. "I came home after that." Her voice is hollow. "It was the week of the Winter Classic. I showed up." She pauses and pulls in a stuttered breath. "I watched you ride, and then I watched you exit the arena."

The memory rushes back, and my fingers curl so tight they ache. That night. The buckle bunnies giggling and hanging on my every word while my body screamed in pain, and my heart was somewhere else entirely.

"Yeah, well, clearly whatever brought you there that night wasn't enough to make you stay." I turn away from her, needing space, and pace the sitting area in front of the fireplace. "Because had you stayed, you would have seen that I didn't leave with any of them." I look up, meeting her reflection in the window. "I went home and soaked in a bath of Epsom salts—alone."

Her head shakes again, slow and steady, like she's not satisfied with my response. "And what about after that?" She finally turns, and her eyes are blazing now, all that fear replaced with something fiercer. "If it was important to you, if I meant anything, then why not say anything?" She takes a step toward me, then another. "You saw me at the auction house in Lexington a few months later and basically acted like I didn't exist."

The accusation stings because it's true—and because she doesn't know why. I close the space between us until we're toe to toe, until I can see the dark-brown flecks in her eyes and the way her chest rises and falls with each sharp breath.

"Because I showed up at your apartment a month before that." My voice is barely controlled, each word careful and precise. "I sat in my car, waiting for the rain to let up so I could see you again." I watch her eyes widen, watch the color drain from her face. "Instead, I watched you run into another man's arms." I lean in, my voice dropping to a rough whisper. "You drove off, and I let you go."

The silence that follows is deafening. Her lips part like she wants to say something, like she almost believes me, but something is telling her not to. Her eyes search mine back and forth, and with every pass, I can see her fortifying her walls.

"What you saw..." She takes a shaky breath. "It wasn't what you think, and you know that." Her voice gains strength, an edge of accusation cutting through. "You know that because there is no one at my side. There never has been." She takes a step back, then another, putting distance between us. "And for the past year that my best friend and your brother have been falling back in love, you never once brought up that night."

"Neither have you." The words come out more defensive than I intended.

She lets out a bitter laugh, the sound breaking somewhere in the middle. "I took off my mask that night." Her voice drops to something vulnerable. "You knew who I was. I let you see me. I let you..."

Her voice trails off, and she drops my gaze, turning toward the window again. I don't need her words to know where she was going. I know what she let me have. It replays in my mind like a fever dream weekly, the weight of her in my arms, the taste of her skin, the way her nails bit into my back like a prayer and a curse all at once.

"Asha—" I start, my hand reaching for her.

"Don't." She flinches away from my touch. She whirls to face me, and when her eyes come back to mine, they're blazing with fury and disappointment. "I know what I said that night. I told you not to speak, told you not to take off your mask, and you want to know why?" She advances on me now, each step deliberate and fierce. "Because I knew this would be our fate. Lies, pretending, hiding behind—"

"Behind what?" I challenge, standing my ground even as she gets close enough that I can smell her perfume. "Say it, Asha. What are we hiding behind?"

"Behind whatever this is!" Her hand waves between us frantically. "This thing we won't name because naming it makes it real, and making it real means—"

"Means what? That you might have to admit you feel something?" I take a step forward, and she retreats until her back hits the wall beside the window. I plant my hands on either side of her head, caging her in. "That you might have to stop punishing us both for something that happened when we were kids who didn't know how to—"

"Behind our families!" she cuts me off, her voice sharp and desperate. "Behind generations of Fairfields and Hales who can't stand to be in the same room together."

"That's bullshit, and you know it." I lean in closer, watching her pupils dilate even as her jaw sets stubbornly. "You don't give a damn about why our families hate each other."

"Don't I?" She ducks under my arm, finally breaking free, and storms toward the center of the room. "My father has spent my entire life warning me about your family. About how the Hales are snakes who take what they want and destroy everything else." She spins to face me, arms crossed defensively over her chest. "How they're charming and persuasive right up until they're not."

I know that last part is her own addition, another tick on the list of reasons she keeps to hate me, but it doesn't hold weight.

"So that's what you think I am?" I push off the wall, my hands flexing at my sides. "Just another Hale waiting to destroy you?"

"I think..." She stops, her throat working as she swallows hard. "I think it doesn't matter what I think. This fake marriage proves it, doesn't it? We're using each other. I find a way to keep my land, and you seal the deal on your merger. It's transactional. It's exactly what our families do."

"Using each other," I repeat the words slowly, letting them hang in the air. "Is that what prom was? A transaction?"

Her face pales, but she doesn't back down. "That night was a mistake."

Her words hit hard, and I have to take a breath before I can respond. "A mistake?"

"Yes," she says, but her voice wavers, and she turns away from me, pacing toward the window. "It was...it was weak. I was weak. I let my guard down and—"

"And what?" I close the distance between us in three strides, grabbing her wrist gently but firmly, making her face me. "You let yourself feel something? You let yourself want something that wasn't approved by your father or filtered through decades of family bullshit?"

"Let go." She tries to pull away, but I hold firm.

"Not until you admit the truth." I lean down, forcing her to meet my eyes. "You're not hiding behind the family feud because you believe in it. You're hiding behind it because it's easier than admitting you're scared."

"I'm not scared." But her pulse racing beneath my fingertips betrays her.

"Liar." I release her wrist and step back, running both hands through my hair in frustration. "You're terrified. You're terrified that if you let yourself care about me—and I mean really care—I might actually stay this time. And that scares you more than me leaving ever did."

Leaving, she planned for. Leaving, she expected. Staying, she doesn't know what to do with.

"You don't know what you're talking about." She wraps her arms around herself again, that defensive posture that's becoming all too familiar.

"Don't I?" I let out a harsh laugh. "You took off your mask that night. You let me see you, and then you ran. You've been running ever since, and now you're using our families as an excuse because it's convenient. Because it's safe."

"Safe?" her voice rises, anger flashing in her eyes. "There is nothing safe about any of this! Nothing safe about being in this room with you, about having to pretend to be your wife, about—" She stops abruptly, her hand coming up to cover her mouth, like she's said too much.

"About what?" I press, moving closer again. "About feeling something real for once?"

"Stop." She holds up a hand, keeping me at a distance. "Just stop. You want to know the truth? Fine. The truth is that our families hate each other for a reason, and whatever happened between us that night..." her voice cracks. "It was always going to end badly. This..."—she gestures around the room—"this fake marriage is proof of that. We can't even be real with each other. We have to hide behind contracts and clauses and business arrangements."

She's not wrong. I saw this as my opportunity to finally have her and capitalized on it. I hid behind the contract, used it as armor and invitation all at once, but only so I could have moments like this, have her alone, where she couldn't hide behind her father's opinions and a feud that has nothing to do with us.

"We don't have to." I keep my voice level, controlled, even though every instinct is telling me to close the space between us and make her listen. To make her see that the contract was never the point. She was. "We're choosing to. You're choosing to."

"I'm not choosing anything tonight except to be done with this conversation. I'm going to take a bath, and then I'm going to go to sleep in that bed alone." She pauses at the bathroom door, her hand on the frame. "I took the couch last night. It's your turn."

The door closes between us with a soft click that somehow sounds louder than if she'd slammed it. I hear the water start running as the tub fills, and I sink down onto the couch, elbows on my knees, and run my hands through my hair. I replay every word, every look, every crack in her armor, and what I keep circling back to is this: she never said she didn't want me.

She said it was always going to end badly. She said we can't be real with each other. She said our families hate each other for a reason. She threw up every excuse, every defense, every rational argument for why this can't work. But she never once said she didn't want it to.

I lean back against the couch, closing my eyes. Tonight, she fought me instead of shutting down completely. That's progress, and I have time. Three hundred and sixty-three days of closed doors, careful distance, and walls she thinks are impenetrable. A year of her trying to convince us both that this is just business, just a contract. But here's what I know: Asha Fairfield doesn't run from things that don't matter. She doesn't cry over things she doesn't care about. She doesn't fight this hard for something she's not terrified of losing.

And tonight, for the first time in years, she fought.

Tomorrow, she'll go back to being cold and distant. She'll avoid eye contact over breakfast and pretend tonight never happened, but I'll know the truth. I'll know that somewhere underneath all that fear and fury, there's a girl who took off her mask for me once. A girl who showed up to watch me ride. A girl who came to Lexington looking for something she was too scared to name. A girl who just spent twenty minutes fighting with me about why we can't work instead of simply walking away.

A girl who never said she didn't want me. And that's enough. For now.

TRIGGER

CHAPTER 22

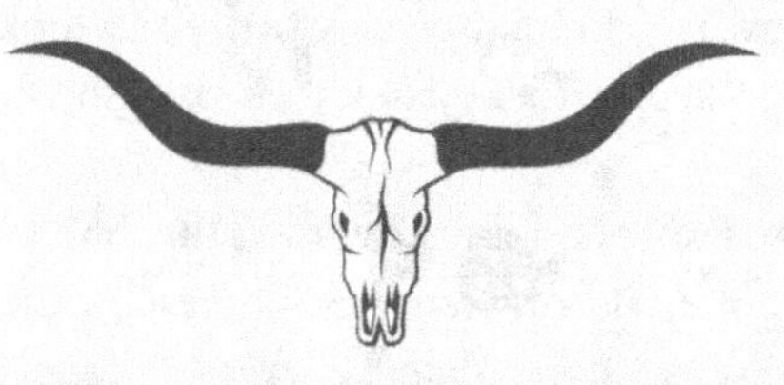

The knock at the door comes too early, sharp and insistent against wood.

I'm still half-asleep on the couch, my neck screaming from the awkward angle, when something hits me square in the face, soft but startling enough to jolt me fully awake.

"What the—" I start, but Asha's frantic whisper cuts me off.

"Get. Up." She's sitting up in bed, her hair a mess around her shoulders, eyes wide with panic. She's pointing at the door, then at me, then at the bed, her movements quick and urgent.

Another knock. "Hello? Anyone awake in there?"

"Just a second!" Asha calls out, her voice suddenly bright and cheery. She grabs another pillow, winding up like she's about to launch it at my head.

I hold up my hands in surrender, finally processing what's happening. "Alright, alright."

"Now, Trigger!" she whisper-yells across the room, her face flushed. "Get over here. Rohan's at the door!"

"You could've just said that instead of assaulting me with a pillow," I mutter, shoving the blanket off and running a hand through my hair. I'm in my boxers, and I don't miss the way her gaze flicks down to my chest before quickly looking away.

"I did say it!" She makes a frustrated gesture. "Just get in this bed before he thinks—"

"Before he thinks what? That we had a fight and I slept on the couch?" I cross the room in three strides, unable to resist the jab even as I'm moving.

"Exactly," she hisses, throwing back the covers on my side. "Get. In."

I climb into the bed, the mattress dipping under my weight, and she immediately shifts closer, eliminating the space between us.

"Put your arm around me," she whispers urgently, her breath hot against my neck as she tucks herself against my side. "And for God's sake, try to look like you didn't spend the night on the couch."

"Hard to do when I did spend the night on the couch," I murmur back, but I wrap my arm around her shoulders anyway, pulling her closer.

She shifts against me, her hip pressing into my side, and then she goes completely rigid. Her eyes widen as she feels exactly what morning and her proximity have done to me.

"Are you—" she starts, her face flooding with color.

"It's morning," I say simply, unable to keep the hint of amusement out of my voice. "Among other things."

"Oh my God." She tries to pull away, but I tighten my arm around her shoulders.

"You're the one who demanded I get in this bed," I point out, my lips quirking into a smirk. "What exactly did you think was going to happen when you pressed your half-naked body against mine?"

"I wasn't...I didn't..." She's sputtering now, and her face is reddening faster by the second. "Can you just...think about something else?"

"I'm trying, but you squirming around isn't helping." I let my hand slide down to her hip, holding her still. "So, unless you want to make this worse, I suggest you stop moving."

She freezes, her breath coming in short bursts. "This is not funny."

"It's a little funny," I murmur, leaning closer so my lips brush her ear. "You're all flustered."

"I am not flustered. I'm—" Another knock at the door cuts her off.

There's another light knock. "Hello? I have breakfast."

Asha's eyes go wide, and the next thing I know, she's throwing her leg over mine and draping herself across my chest in a way that both hides the situation and makes me bite back a groan.

"What are you doing?" I ask, my voice strained now for an entirely different reason.

"Fixing it," she whispers back. "Now shut up and look like a newlywed."

"That's not going to be a problem," I mutter, my hand settling possessively on her lower back.

She glares at me, but there's no real heat in it. "If you make one more comment."

"You'll what?" I challenge softly, enjoying the way her breath catches when I run my thumb along her spine. "Throw another pillow at me?"

"I'll—" Another sharp knock makes her jump. "Just...can you please try to look less smug?"

"I'm comfortable. Why would I be smug?" But I'm grinning now, and she knows it.

"I hate you," she whispers, but her fingers are curled into my chest, and she's not pulling away.

"Sure you do." I brush a strand of hair away from her face, letting my fingers linger against her cheek. "Ready to put on a show, Mrs. Hale?"

She pinches my side hard, and I barely suppress a laugh as she calls out, "Come in!"

The door swings open, and Rohan steps in carrying a covered tray, his expression pleasant and professional. His eyes are a different story. They're sharp, taking in every detail of the room with an assessing gaze that makes my instincts prickle.

"Good morning," he says, almost too cheerfully. "I hope I'm not interrupting."

"Not at all," Asha says, her voice remarkably steady considering she's still plastered against my chest.

I feel her try to shift away, but I keep my hand firm on her lower back, holding her in place. She shoots me a warning glance, but I just give her an easy smile, playing the part of the satisfied husband who's in no rush to let his wife leave the bed.

"I brought a bit of everything," he says, placing the tray of food on the table in the sitting area.

"It looks amazing," Asha says, finally managing to extract herself from my grip. She sits up, pulling the covers up, very aware that her nighttime attire is revealing. "Thank you, Rohan."

I prop myself up on one elbow, letting the sheets pool at my waist. If Rohan's going to scrutinize us, I might as well give him something to see. "Your mother's hospitality is top tier. Sending her son to bring us breakfast is next level," I call his visit to our room.

"She likes to take care of her guests." Rohan's smile is warm as he pours two cups of coffee with practiced efficiency, but when he glances up at Asha, there's something in his gaze, an intensity and curiosity that lingers too long. I reach for Asha's hand and lace my fingers through hers. His gaze follows the movement, studying her with his trademark intense focus. "I actually came to ask if Asha would be willing to take a look at Sahara this morning—the mare we discussed at dinner."

Asha's interest is immediately piqued. "Of course. How far along is she?"

"About seven months, we think. But she's been off her feed the last few days, seems uncomfortable." Rohan pauses, his eyes still locked on her face. "Our regular vet says everything looks fine, but given how valuable she is, both the mare and the foal, I'd feel better with a second opinion. From someone with your expertise."

The way he emphasizes 'your' makes something twist in my gut. It's not just professional interest; there's something else, something that feels too personal for a man talking to a married woman he just met.

"I'd be happy to examine her," Asha says, all business now. "Seven months and off feed could be several things. Give me thirty minutes to get ready."

"Perfect. The stables are just behind the main house. I can show you the way," Rohan offers.

"I'll come with you," I say immediately.

Asha turns to me, and there's a flash of irritation in her eyes. "You don't need to."

"Actually," Rohan interrupts, "my mother asked me to pass along a message. She'd like you to meet her out front in an hour, Trigger. She wants to show you the other side of the ranch, the training facilities, and the breeding program. Said she thought you'd appreciate seeing how we run things here, given your background."

The timing is too convenient. Way too convenient.

"The tour will take most of the morning," Rohan continues smoothly. "Mother's quite thorough when she's showing off the operation. And honestly, with a pregnant mare, Asha will need to take her time. It could be an hour, could be several, depending on what she finds. These examinations can't be rushed."

He's boxed me in, and he knows it.

"Sounds like we both have our mornings planned, then," Asha says, and I can't tell if she's relieved or annoyed that I won't be tagging along.

"Seems that way." I keep my eyes on Rohan, who meets my gaze with that same pleasant, unreadable smile.

"Well, then." Rohan moves toward the door. "I'll see you in thirty minutes, Asha. And Trigger, Mother will meet you out front. She's very punctual, so I wouldn't be late if I were you."

There's something almost like a challenge in those last words, like he knows exactly what he's doing by separating us. The door clicks shut behind him, and the silence that follows feels heavier than it should.

Asha immediately scrambles out of bed. "Don't start."

"Start what?" I sit up fully, running a hand through my hair.

"Whatever you're thinking." She's already pulling clothes out of her bag, not looking at me. "I can handle examining a horse without you hovering."

"That's not what I'm thinking." I stand, pacing toward the window. "I'm thinking it's awfully convenient that they've managed to split us up. You with him, me with Dar, both at the exact same time."

"Then what is it about?" She looks up at me, challenging.

I could tell her it's about the way Rohan looks at her like she's something to be figured out. About the way my gut is screaming that something's off. About the way the thought of her alone with him makes every possessive instinct I have roar to life.

But what comes out is: "Maybe if you weren't parading around in that..." I gesture at the silky camisole that's barely covering her and the thin straps that keep sliding off her shoulder. "He wouldn't be finding excuses to get you alone."

Her eyes widen then narrow dangerously. "Excuse me?"

"You heard me." I cross my arms, knowing I'm being an ass but unable to stop myself. "Did you see the way he was looking at you? He could barely keep his eyes off your bare shoulders."

"So now it's my fault he was staring? My fault he came to the bedroom I'm sharing with my husband?" Her voice rises, color flooding her cheeks.

"I'm saying maybe put on some actual pants before you go meet him in the stables."

"Oh, I'm sorry." She stalks toward her bag, yanking out clothes with more force than necessary. "I didn't realize I needed to dress for *your* approval. Last I checked, this is what I sleep in. You know, sleep—that thing I was supposed to be doing alone, in my own room, which was the agreement?"

"Yeah, well, plans changed."

"Clearly." She whirls back to face me, holding up the silk shorts and tank top set she pulled from her bag, somehow even more revealing than what she's currently wearing. "And for your information, I wear silk because I get hot when I sleep. Not because I'm trying to seduce anyone. Least of all you or Rohan."

"Could've fooled me. And apparently fooled him too, based on how he couldn't take his eyes off you."

She drops the clothes onto the bed. "You know what I think? I think you're jealous. And I think you don't trust me."

"That's not—"

"You were real quick to point out my flaws last night," she cuts me off, taking a step toward me. "How I don't let people in. How I hide because I'm scared." Another step, and now she's close enough that I can see the fury and hurt warring in her eyes. "But you can't trust me either, can you? Can't trust that I can do my job without throwing myself at the first guy who brings breakfast."

"Asha..."

"Tell me I'm wrong."

The challenge hangs in the air between us. I open my mouth, then close it, because what can I say? That she's right? That I am jealous? That the thought of her spending the morning alone with a man who looks at her like he's trying to solve a puzzle makes me want to punch something?

Her expression shifts when I don't answer. "That's what I thought."

She turns away, grabbing her clothes from the bed, and something in me snaps.

"You're not wrong," I say, my voice rough. "I am jealous, and it's eating me alive." She freezes, her back still to me. "But it's not because I don't trust you, Asha." I take a step closer. "I don't trust him, and I can't compete with someone who could actually offer you something real."

Slowly, she turns to face me, her expression unreadable.

"You want to know what I'm scared of?" I continue, the words coming out before I can stop them. "I'm scared that you'll realize you deserve better than a fake marriage with an expiration date. I'm scared that some guy like Rohan will show up and offer you exactly what you should have, something permanent, something that doesn't come with decades of family baggage attached to it." I pinch the bridge of my nose. "I'm scared of losing something I don't even have the right to claim."

Her lips part, and for a moment, she just stares at me. "Trigger..."

"You asked me to tell you if you were wrong," I interrupt, my voice dropping. "You're wrong about one thing. This isn't about me not trusting you. It's about me knowing that on paper, I'm your husband. But in reality?" I meet her eyes. "I don't have you. Not really. And the thought of watching you realize that someone else might be a better option...that's what's killing me."

The silence stretches between us, heavy and charged. Her clothes are still clutched in her hands, and I can see her throat work as she swallows.

"We're wasting time," she finally says, her voice tight. She won't look at me. "We both need to get ready. You have to meet Dar in..."—she glances at the clock—"forty-five minutes. And I need to be in the stables in fifteen."

"Asha..." I try.

"I said we're wasting time." She moves toward the bathroom. "I'm taking a shower." She pauses at the bathroom door, her back to me. "And for the record?" Her voice is quieter now, almost defeated. "It doesn't matter who I'm thinking about. It doesn't matter what I want. We have a year. That's it. That's what we agreed to."

It doesn't matter what I want.

I sink down onto the edge of the bed, running my hands through my hair. She's still running. Still hiding behind the contract, behind the expiration date, behind every excuse she can find to keep those walls up. And I just gave her exactly what she needed—a reason to retreat. My jealousy, my lack of trust in what we could be, my inability to just say what I mean.

Well, I'm done with that.

I'm done dancing around what I feel. Done pretending this is just business. Done waiting for the perfect moment or the right words or for her to magically decide I'm worth the risk. She'll run, she'll hide behind the contract and the feud, but it's my turn to show her that not everyone leaves, especially when they have something worth fighting for. It does matter what she wants. It matters because I think it's me.

ASHA

CHAPTER 23

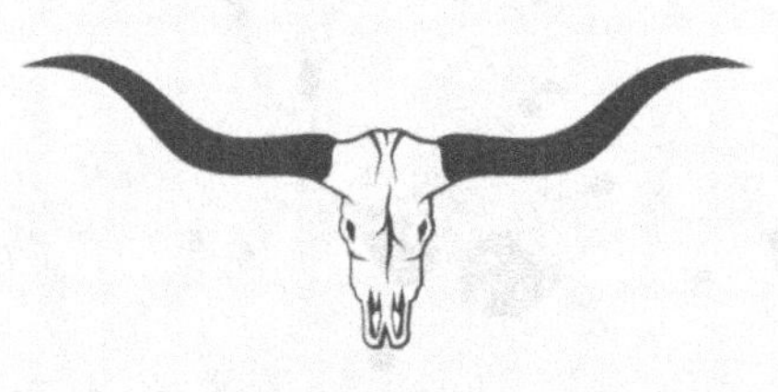

The stables are immaculate. Rohan leads me down the center aisle, past stalls housing some of the most beautiful horses I've ever seen. Arabians, mostly, with a few quarter horses mixed in. But I'm barely seeing them.

I'm scared of losing something I don't even have the right to claim.

Trigger's words keep replaying in my head, no matter how hard I try to focus on why I'm here. The raw honesty in his voice, the way his hands flexed at his sides like he was physically restraining himself from reaching for me.

I don't have you. Not really.

I adjust the bag on my shoulder. He's wrong...or maybe he's right. I don't know anymore. All I know is that hearing him say those things, admitting he's jealous, admitting he wants more than what the contract offers... It's everything I used to dream about hearing from him. And that's exactly why I can't trust it.

"She's in here." Rohan's voice pulls me back to the present. He opens a stall door at the end of the row, and I force myself to focus.

The mare is stunning, a dappled gray Arabian. She shifts her weight, and I immediately notice the slight favor of her back left leg, not the front left as Rohan said earlier. Interesting.

"Hello, beautiful," I murmur, approaching slowly with my hand extended. She sniffs my palm then allows me to stroke her neck. "How long has she been off her feed?"

"Three days, give or take." Rohan leans against the stall door, and I can feel his eyes on me, not the horse. "Started the same day she began favoring that leg."

I run my hands down the mare's shoulder, feeling for heat or swelling. "You said front left earlier."

"Did I?" There's something in his tone that makes me glance back at him. He's watching me with that same intense focus from this morning, like I'm a specimen under a microscope. "My mistake."

I don't think it was a mistake at all. Setting down the vet bag Rohan supplied, I pull out a stethoscope and begin a thorough examination. The mare stands patiently as I check her heart rate and respiratory rate and listen to gut sounds. Everything seems normal so far.

"Your father must be proud," Rohan says casually. "Having a daughter follow in his footsteps in business."

My hands still for just a moment. "I didn't follow in his footsteps. I'm a veterinarian, not a businessman."

"But you understand his world. Help with negotiations, I'm sure. Make connections." He shifts his weight. "That's valuable in its own way."

I move to examine the mare's legs, running my hands carefully down each one, feeling for heat, checking the joints. "I suppose."

"And Trigger, he's in rodeo? That must create interesting dynamics between your families."

"He's not in rodeo," I correct, my hands continuing their methodical examination. "He knows how to ride a bull, but his family breeds Thoroughbreds. Like mine." I pause, feeling the slight heat in the mare's left hind fetlock. "That's actually part of the problem between our families."

There it is again, that studying quality to his questions, like he's trying to piece something together.

"Our families have their differences. We make it work."

"Competing breeding operations. That must be complicated."

"It can be." I move to the mare's abdomen and palpate carefully. At seven months, the foal should be easily felt. "How long have you had her?"

"She was born here. Offspring of one of our prized stallions." There's genuine affection in his voice when he looks at the mare. "She's been part of our family since the beginning. One of our best."

I nod, continuing my examination. "She's beautiful. Excellent conformation."

"How large is Trigger's operation?" Rohan asks, shifting topics. "Compared to yours?"

I glance at him as I pull out a portable ultrasound. "Why do you want to know?"

"Just curious. Mother is always interested in successful breeding programs. Maybe there's room for this to be more than just a land use agreement." He shrugs, but his eyes are sharp. "What about your family? How many generations have you been breeding?"

"Just one," I say, moving the ultrasound wand over the mare's abdomen, searching for the foal. "Well, technically, our land has been in the family for three generations, but we've only been breeding for one. When my father married my mother, the land was a farm. They grew flowers and food, but my father had big ideas and converted the land into a ranch."

The silence that follows is heavy. When I glance at Rohan, his expression has changed. There's something razor-sharp in his focus now.

"Your mother's family," he repeats slowly. "What was her maiden name?"

The question sends a chill down my spine, though I can't explain why. Maybe it's the way he's looking at me. Maybe it's the sudden shift in his demeanor. Or maybe it's just that I'm on edge after this morning with Trigger, reading into things that aren't there.

"Why does it matter?" I ask, trying to keep my tone light.

"It doesn't. I'm just curious." But his posture has changed, and there's an intensity in his gaze that wasn't there seconds ago. "Please. Indulge me."

The foal's heartbeat shows up on the screen, strong and steady, and I focus on it, using the examination as an excuse not to look at him.

"Fairfield," I say finally. "My mother's maiden name is Fairfield. The estate has been in the Fairfield family for three generations before my parents married and my father took over managing the land."

Silence fills the space, and I look up from the screen to find Rohan's face has gone carefully blank. Not surprised, not shocked, just blank in a way that suggests he's working very hard to control his expression. His jaw is tight, and I can see a muscle ticking in his cheek.

"Fairfield," he repeats, his voice quieter now.

"Yes." I turn back to the ultrasound, suddenly uncomfortable with the weight of his stare. "Is something wrong?"

"No. Nothing's wrong," he says, though his tone says otherwise.

"I'm almost done."

"Good." He runs a hand through his hair, a gesture that mirrors Trigger so exactly it's almost jarring. "I'll wait outside. Let you work."

Before I can say anything else, he's gone, the stall door clicking shut behind him. I stand there for a long moment, my hands still on the equipment bag, trying to understand what just happened. The way his entire demeanor changed the second I said my mother's maiden name. The way he looked at me not like someone who's attracted to me, but someone who's just had a suspicion confirmed.

I finish the examination on autopilot, checking the mare's teeth and gums, taking her temperature, and examining the heat in her fetlock more closely. When I'm done, Rohan is leaning against the wall across from Sahara's stall, his arms crossed, his expression distant. When he sees me, he straightens, and I can see him physically composing himself.

"Well?" he asks, his voice carefully neutral. "What's the verdict?"

I run through the diagnosis and treatment plan, forcing myself to stay professional even when his studied glare is unnerving.

When I finish, he nods slowly. "Interesting."

"What is?"

"That's the exact same conclusion I told Mother yesterday."

The words hang between us, and I stare at him blankly while my brain tries to process what he just said.

"You're the vet, aren't you?" I say, handing him the bag I now believe is his.

His smile is slow, almost apologetic. "I am."

"Why didn't you tell me?"

"It was better this way." He straightens from the wall, his expression serious now. "I didn't want you second-guessing yourself or rewording your diagnosis because you were worried about offending me. I wanted your honest, unfiltered, professional opinion." He pauses, and something almost like respect crosses his features. "And truthfully? I wanted to see if another vet would reach the same conclusion I did. I'm competitive by nature."

"Are you sure that's all this was?" I ask skeptically.

His questioning, while cloaked in the guise of an easy conversation, felt more like digging. But digging for what? I don't see how any of those questions pertain to the merger, which is why I answered them.

Rohan's expression becomes more guarded, like he's weighing how much to tell me. "Let's just say my mother likes to be thorough when it comes to people who might be significant to our family's interests," he finally says.

"Significant? You're talking to the wrong Hale," I say, assuming he's referencing the merger.

"Am I?" He tilts his head, and there's something in his eyes that makes my stomach clench. "Tell me, Asha, does the name Daruka mean anything to you? Beyond my mother, I mean."

"Should it?"

"Can I show you something?" He's already moving toward the stable doors, not waiting for my answer.

Does the name Daruka mean anything to you? His words echo in my head, and I hesitate, but only a moment, until I match his pace stride for stride back to the house because I can't say no.

∾

"When I saw you yesterday, I knew you looked familiar, but I couldn't place it." Rohan leads me toward a mahogany shelf lined with framed photographs at the far end of what appears to be a private study. "And now I know why." He picks up an old photograph, his fingers careful on the worn frame. "I couldn't place it because the last time I saw you, you were small."

He holds it out to me. It's a framed picture of my family. I'm sitting on my mother's lap, maybe five years old, wearing a yellow dress I don't remember. My father sits beside us, but he's not looking at the camera. He's looking at my mother and me, his expression so full of love that my chest tightens. He's looking at us like we're his whole world.

The thought makes my heart pinch painfully. I don't remember this day, but I remember the feeling of being his everything. Like it was him and me against the world after we lost her. Somewhere along the line, that died. Somewhere between boarding school and summers spent anywhere but home, that look disappeared. It was replaced by distance, secrets, and a wall so high I stopped trying to scale it.

"How did you get this?" My voice comes out steady, even though my pulse is racing.

"So it is you?" Rohan moves closer, looking over my shoulder at the photo. "That's your mom and dad?"

"Yes." I force myself to meet his eyes, to keep my expression neutral even though my world is tilting sideways. "Now answer my question. How did you get this?"

"Your mother sent it to us." His voice is soft, almost gentle, and that somehow makes it worse.

The floor seems to shift beneath my feet. "My mother? When?"

"Around the time that photo was taken." He reaches out, his hand hovering over the frame, drawing my attention back to the image. Back to the family that no longer exists. "Asha, I don't know how else to say this, but your father is my uncle." He pauses, letting that sink in. "Our parents are twins."

The photograph slips in my grip, and I have to tighten my fingers to keep from dropping it. *Twins.* Which means Dar, Daruka, is my father's sister.

My head spins, though part of me isn't surprised. I've known for years my father was keeping secrets. I felt it in every deflection and every time I asked about family and got silence. I just didn't realize the secret was this big.

Why would anyone assume their father had erased an entire family from existence? My mother's parents died when I was young, leaving only Aunt Melly and Hollis on her side. I've always known my father was adopted. I spent summers with Grandma and Grandpa Stone in Connecticut until they died. That was supposed to be it. All the family I had.

But my father has a twin sister. A whole birth family he never mentioned. I love my father. I love him so much it hurts. However, that man in the photo, looking at my mother and me like we were his entire world...that's just a memory. After she died, something changed or broke, and slowly, piece by piece, I started to wonder why he kept me away.

Dark thoughts crept in, thoughts I'd push away because I didn't want to believe my father was the bad guy. Because he was all I had. If I let myself believe the worst, what did that leave me with? So I told myself boarding school was for the best. That his silence was grief, not guilt. That the walls he built were to keep pain out, not to keep me at a distance.

However, finding out about the expiring lease he hid from me, those dark thoughts flooded back in. It was proof that maybe my suspicions weren't paranoia. That maybe there was something fundamentally wrong I'd been too afraid to acknowledge. Boarding school ensured his secrets were kept. Keeping his secrets was easier if I wasn't around to unearth them.

I hand the picture back to Rohan. "That's it?" He takes the frame, his brow furrowing. "No comment? No questions?"

"I'm not sure what you want me to say."

He plants both hands on his hips. "You're either just as surprised as I am by this coincidence, or it's not a coincidence at all, and you knew exactly who my mother is." His eyes search mine, hard and assessing. "And you're here trying to hurt her."

The accusation snaps me back to the present. "Hurt her?" I take a step back. "Why the hell would I want to hurt your mother?"

"Because of your father." He sets the photo down with deliberate care. "Because of what he believes happened. What he blames her for."

A cold weight settles in my stomach. "You think my father hates his own sister?"

I don't even know if that's true. How could I? Her existence was news to me ten minutes ago.

"Yes." Rohan's voice is flat, certain. "He hates what he believes happened when they were kids. That their parents chose to save my mother over him."

The words don't make sense. I shake my head, trying to piece it together. "What are you talking about?"

His eyes search mine, and I watch something shift in his expression. Recognition. Understanding. "You really don't know, do you?"

I keep my face impassive, drawing on years of practice hiding my feelings from my father. From everyone.

"Of course you don't." He lets out a breath, and the suspicion in his posture eases slightly. "You can drop the act, Asha. I could tell last night that you had no idea who we are, but I had to ask. I had to be sure you weren't here to—" He stops himself and idly spins the watch on his wrist. "I had to be sure."

Rohan picks up the photo again, his thumb tracing the edge of the frame. "When our parents were kids, there was a flood." His voice is quieter. "The waters rose quickly. Unexpectedly. Our grandmother was feeding my mother when your father started crying in his crib down the hall. She called for help, and our grandfather tried to save him." He pauses, his throat working. "He didn't get to him in time and lost his own life trying."

My breath catches.

"The floods separated them. Your father's crib was swept away." Rohan looks up at me, and there's genuine sadness in his eyes now. "He was believed to be among the dead. They held a funeral. Mourned him. My mother was just a baby, but she grew up knowing she'd had a twin brother who died and that her father died trying to save him."

"But he didn't die." The words feel thick in my mouth.

"No. However, it wasn't until your mother sent us that photo that we found that out." Rohan's voice is careful. "She reached out to my mother years ago. Said she'd been doing research into your father's adoption, wanted to know if we might be family. That photo was proof."

My mother knew. She knew about the Aroras, about Dar, about all of it.

"When?" my voice cracks. "When did she send it?"

"A few months before she..." Rohan stops, his expression shifting to something gentler.

The room tilts again. My mother spent her final months trying to connect my father to the family he'd lost. Trying to heal something he refused to acknowledge was broken, and he never told me.

"Asha?"

I turn at the sound of my name, and Trigger is standing in the doorway of the study. His hair is windswept, his shirt dusty from the ranch tour, and there's dirt on his jeans. His hat is clutched in one hand, and his eyes are locked on me with an intensity that makes my chest tighten.

He takes one look at my face and goes still. "What happened?"

TRIGGER

CHAPTER 24

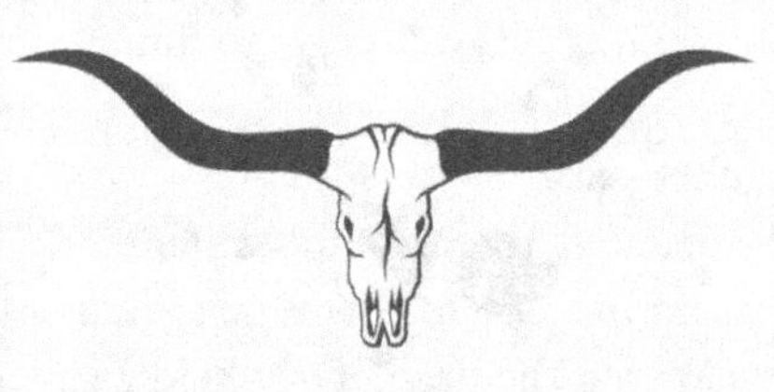

"Where is she?" I mumble to myself, the sharp clicks of my boots echoing my rising frustration against the terracotta floors as I search yet another room and come up empty.

I checked the stables first after Dar got called away, ending our tour. Then the main barn, our room, and still nothing. It isn't until I start heading toward the kitchen that the sound of hushed voices coming from the study catches my ear. One of them is unmistakably Asha's, low and strained in a way that makes my jaw clench.

I throw the door open, and my heart sinks. They're standing close, too close. Rohan is holding something, and Asha is right there beside him, close enough that their shoulders are nearly touching. Her head is tilted toward whatever he's showing her, and there's an intimacy to the moment that makes jealousy flare hot and instant in my chest.

"Asha?" My hands flex at my sides, and I'm about to say something I'll probably regret when she turns.

Our eyes meet, and everything stops, because I've never seen that look on her face before. Not once in all the years I've known her. She's not guarded. Not defensive. Not angry or annoyed or hiding behind that mask she wears so well. She looks broken. Shattered. Like someone just ripped the ground out from under her, and she's still trying to figure out which way is up.

My anger evaporates, and all I can see is the way she's looking at me like I'm the only solid thing in a world that's suddenly stopped making sense.

I'm across the room in three strides, my hands coming up to frame her face. "What happened?" The demand comes out rougher than I intended, but I need to know. Need to understand why she looks like this.

Rohan clears his throat behind us. "I'll give the two of you some space."

I don't take my eyes off Asha. Don't acknowledge him. Don't care about anything except her. The door clicks shut, and then it's just us.

"Talk to me."

She blinks, and I watch the walls slam back into place. Just like that, the vulnerability disappears, replaced by that careful blankness she uses to hide everything she's feeling.

"Nothing." Her voice is steady, controlled. "It's nothing. The mare is fine. Just some inflammation in her fetlock. Nothing—"

"Stop." I tighten my grip on her face slightly, making sure she can't look away. "I'm not asking about the damn horse. I'm asking about you. What did he say to you?"

"It doesn't matter."

"It clearly does matter." I can feel the tension in her jaw, see the way she's fighting to keep her composure. "Asha, you look like you've seen a ghost. What—"

"I said it's nothing!" She tries to pull away, but I don't let her. "Can we just go back to the room? I'm tired."

"No." My voice is firm, final. She's not going to do it my way, so I'll play it her way. "Don't tell me because I care; tell me because of our deal. Tell me because the future of my merger might depend on whatever just went down in here. I can tell by the look in your eyes that something big just happened, and I need to know if my wife just screwed up my deal."

Her eyes blaze, and I can tell I touched a nerve. *Good.* That was my goal. I need her to open up, and if playing the enemy accomplishes that, I'll play the role.

She jerks her chin away, her eyes burning with anger and defiance. "Dar is my aunt."

I deflate. "Asha, that's not funny—"

She silences me, pushing a picture frame into my hands. "See for yourself."

Suddenly, another question is on my lips, one I'd had but shelved as others took precedence. "Why did you choose me?"

After we said our vows and I dragged her out, Warrick came after us. She hesitated that night. She thought about going to him, then didn't, and it hasn't gone unnoticed that she's had her phone off since we arrived.

"What are you talking about? You already know why," she says exasperatedly.

"No, I'm not talking about why you said *I do*. I want to know why you chose me over your father in that hallway."

She turns away from me. "You gave me no choice. I could either come willingly, or you were going to toss me over your shoulder like a caveman and drag me out."

"I know when you're lying, sweetheart. Try again," I say with an annoyed bite because, apparently, we can't talk unless we're at each other's throats.

I saw the trepidation, the fear in her eyes over the choice she had just made. She looked at me like I was the devil, and then she got in my car. *Why?*

"Let it go, Trigg. It has nothing to do with you or this merger, so it's not your concern."

"Wrong." I step closer, close enough she can feel me at her back. "You wear my ring. You carry my name. That makes everything you do my concern. Your problems are my problems. Your enemies are my enemies. So tell me what happened, or I'll find out myself."

She whips around, her eyes locked on mine with defiance. "You really want to know? Fine. I chose the devil I know over the one I don't."

My brow furrows as my mind processes her words. If I'm the devil she knows, then that means... "Wait." My hand reaches for her wrist as she tries to step around me. "You don't get to tell me your father, the man you once referred to as your best friend, is the devil you don't know without an explanation."

She jerks her wrist out of my hand. "Do you ever think maybe I don't want to talk because giving voice to my thoughts makes them real?" She starts pacing in front of the built-in bookcase. "Right now, they're just shadows in my head. But the moment I speak them out loud, they take form. They breathe. They *exist* in a way I can't take back." She stops before looking me square in the eye and adding, "And I'm not ready to let them out of their cage."

"From where I'm standing, keeping them caged inside isn't working. They're eating you alive from the inside. They're already real, sweetheart. They're destroying you in silence. So tell me, what scares you more: telling me the truth or realizing you're giving these thoughts exactly what they want by keeping them locked away?"

She drops her head, and I watch her shoulders curve inward like she's trying to make herself smaller. When she finally speaks, her voice is barely above a whisper.

"My father sent me away after the accident. Both of my parents said it was to keep me safe." Her fingers twist together, and her knuckles go white. "A year later, my mother died, and I rarely got to return to Fairfield. When I would visit my father on breaks, it was always at our property in Louisville, or we'd vacation somewhere else. Anywhere but home."

She drops her hands to her sides and heads to the window. "For the longest time, I didn't question it. I missed everything: my mom, the ranch, the life we had. And because I missed it so much, I assumed he did too." She presses her palm against the glass. "I thought being there was just as hard for him. That's why whenever I'd bring up my mother or ask about the year she died, he'd shut down, change the subject, because remembering was too hard."

"But?" I prompt, moving to the other side of the windowsill.

"But that excuse only works for so long, doesn't it? After high school, after the accident..." She wraps her arms around herself. "It's felt like more than grief. The fact that he's been adamant, almost borderline obsessive, about keeping me away from the ranch. Now I know part of it was because of the lease, but even without that..." her voice cracks. "He's different with me. Like we're strangers living in the same house. Passing ships in the middle of the night."

So much of who she is and why she's so addictively stubborn makes more sense the more she talks, and I hate that she won't let me in. I want to be the one to help her, but fuck, I understand why she doesn't want help. Why she doesn't trust it?

"And now this." She laughs, but there's no humor in it. "He practically hid a whole existence from me."

I close the distance between us, needing to be closer even if she's not ready to be touched. "You still haven't told me what you think he's hiding."

She meets my gaze, and for the first time since we started this conversation, I see real fear there. "My mother's death certificate." Her voice is steady now, too steady, the kind of calm that comes before a storm. "Coroner reports. All her medical files." She takes a breath. "They're sealed."

"Sealed." I shake my head, not following why she'd even go down that rabbit hole. "I thought you knew how your mother died."

"I was told she died in her sleep from a stroke. I only started looking after my father shut me out one too many times. I wanted to know if she was sick. What she was like before she died. Was she happy. And when I started looking, that's what I found." She lets out a sigh like she's glad to finally speak the words that have been gnawing away at her sanity for more years than she's probably letting on. "Why would they be sealed unless someone has something to hide?" She moves past me, agitation rolling off her in waves.

Fuck. I've always known Asha Fairfield had layers, but this...

"You think your father had something to do with your mother's death?" I let out a long slow breath. "That's why you asked me to lie. Why you wanted this marriage to look real. You want to break him so you can get your answers."

She spins to face me, and the truth is there in her eyes. Her father hates me. Really hates me. Not the way she does, which feels performative at best. This runs deeper. This is the kind of hatred that roots itself in a man's chest and never leaves, and she married me to exploit it.

"I don't know what I think anymore!" Her hands shake as she throws them up. "All I know is I've been questioning how much I really know the man I call Dad for months—years, even—and now there's this." She gestures wildly at nothing and everything. "And I don't know what's real anymore. What if everything I remember about them, about us, is a lie?"

There it is. The real fear. Not that her father is guilty, but that her entire childhood was built on deception. I move closer and feel the charge in the air between us. Her eyes flick between mine, wide and wary.

"This right here, right now, us." My voice drops lower. "This is real."

"No, Trigg. It's fake. One—"

"Stop." The word comes out rough, and I watch her breath catch. I run my hands down the sides of her arms and feel her shiver beneath my touch, and I don't know if it's from anger or something else entirely. When I reach her shoulders, my fingers flex, holding her in place. "You don't get to put me in the same category as everyone else who's hurt you."

She tries to look away, but I'm not having it.

"Penn was a coward who didn't deserve you. Emma was a snake who'd sell her own mother for social currency." I step closer, eliminating what little space remains between us. Her chest brushes against mine with each breath she takes, and I can feel her pulse hammering beneath my fingertips. "Your mom? That wasn't a choice; she didn't leave you. She was taken. And you still have Laney. You don't get to write her off just because she married my brother and life got complicated."

My thumb and forefinger catch her chin, tilting her face up to mine. Her skin is soft, warmer than I expected, and when her lips part slightly, it takes everything in me not to get distracted.

"And the jury's still out on your father."

Warrick Fairfield has done nothing to earn me giving him the benefit of the doubt, but I'm not doing this for him. I'm doing it for her. I don't want the woman I care about to lose the one person I know she loves so deeply. Her love for her father is why she's hurting now, and I refuse to let it break her.

"Maybe I'm not the guy you pictured standing beside you through this. This whole situation is fucked up and messy and not what either of us planned." My other hand slides up to cup her jaw, my thumb brushing across her cheekbone. "But I can be the one person who doesn't lie to you."

She looks at me like she wants to believe me but doesn't know how. "It's never that simple."

"It doesn't have to be hard," I say, leaning deeper into our closeness, drawn in by her fear and the need to erase it. "I'm not going anywhere." I lean in until I can feel her breath on my skin. "You keep waiting for me to become another person who hurts you, but that's not who I am. Stop pushing me away. Stop fighting me and making me the enemy." My forehead touches hers. "Let me in." My thumb drags over her bottom lip, and her eyes drop to my mouth. "Let me prove we can be something else." My words are barely a whisper as her mouth is so close I can practically taste the kiss she hasn't granted me.

Then she closes her eyes, and the gloss of her lips barely grazes mine before the door to the study opens. "Oh, I'm sorry," a man who looks like he might be one of the ranch hands says, removing his hat. "I was looking for Dar."

She doesn't pull away, but I know whatever stolen moment we just shared is gone. But gone for now isn't gone for good.

ASHA

CHAPTER 25

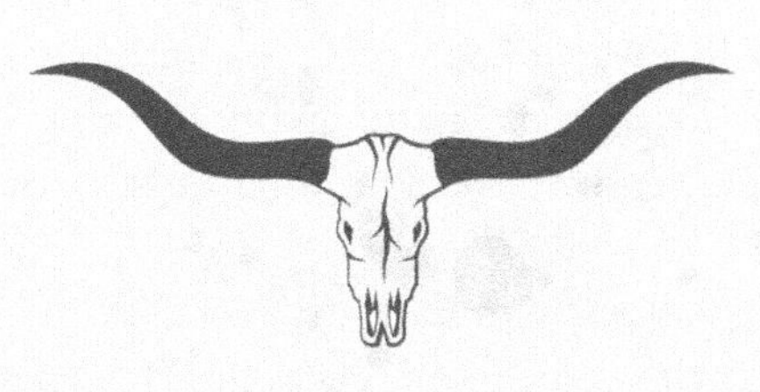

I almost kissed him.

My fingers drift to my lips as I stare at the woman reflected in the mirror. Yesterday, I almost kissed Trigger Hale, and God help me, I wanted it. I *wanted* him. The memory alone makes my skin flush. The way his hands felt on my jaw, the heat of his body pressed against mine, the rough timbre of his voice saying all the right things. I still want it. That's the part that terrifies me. Because wanting him and trusting him are two very different things, and damn it if everything I've unearthed about my father isn't the exact reason I can't afford to blur those lines.

You can trust me, he said. *You don't get to make me into someone I'm not.*

Logically, I know he's not wrong. But logic and a lifetime of conditioning are two separate beasts, and my father did a hell of a good job making me believe the Hales couldn't be trusted. Even now, as I stand here questioning everything I thought I knew about my father's character, I can't shake what I've been conditioned to believe. It's maddening. How can I doubt him on one hand and still let his poison about the Hales dictate my reactions on the other? How can both things be true at the same time?

My reflection doesn't have any answers, just the same wide eyes and lips that ache, betraying exactly how close I came to giving in yesterday.

I've never lied to you.

My brain had stumbled over those words when he said them as I tried to reconcile them with the narrative I'd built. I had to separate my hurt from the actual truth: he didn't lie. Not about prom. Not about us. Not about any of it.

I made assumptions. I let those assumptions root into facts because he was the enemy, and enemies don't get the benefit of the doubt. Of course, prom night was calculated revenge for all the hell I'd given him in high school; that's what made the most sense when he didn't call. When I came home from college and saw him with someone else, her hand on his arm, his smile easy in a way it had never been with me. And then again, this past year, when he kept his careful distance, playing nice because his brother and my best friend are irrevocably in love, and someone had to be the mature one.

I'd filled in every blank with the worst possible explanation because that was what I'd been taught to do. Hales lie. Hales manipulate. Hales take what they want and leave destruction in their wake. But what if I was wrong? What if the only liar in my life has been the man I trusted most? The thought makes my stomach turn. I grip the edge of the sink, maybe Trigg was never the villain. Maybe I just needed him to be one because wanting him since I was fifteen scared me more than hating him ever did.

There's a knock on the door, shattering my spiral, but I don't say anything. I can't. Not yet. I just need a few more seconds because, if I'm being brutally honest, the reason I almost kissed him yesterday wasn't that I trust him. It's because part of me doesn't care if I should.

"Asha, are you ready?" I turn toward the closed door and the voice that's echoed in my head nonstop for more nights than I can count. "We're supposed to be down—"

His words die when I open the door. For a moment, he just stares.

His gaze travels down my body and back up, slower the second time, like he's memorizing every detail. The crimson dress hugs every curve before flaring at my hips. It has off-the-shoulder sleeves, and my hair is pinned over one shoulder in loose waves. It's bold, feminine, and completely different from anything he's seen me wear. But we're in Spain.

"Trigg?" My voice comes out smaller than I intend. His silence is unnerving.

His eyes linger on my collarbone before snapping back to my face. "Christ, Asha."

It's not a complaint.

"Too much?" I smooth my hands down the fabric nervously, suddenly self-conscious under the weight of his stare. "The event coordinator said traditional Spanish formal wear, and this was what—"

"Don't." He steps closer, and I can see the muscle ticking in his jaw. "I'm just... I thought... I mean..." He clears his throat. "It's perfect."

I can see the genuine compliment in his eyes. He likes what he sees, and what he sees is me. My chest tightens, and I'm not ready to face whatever this is. I dramatically roll my eyes and press my hand against his chest to push past him into the room for my shoes.

"What were you about to say?" I ask as I walk toward the closet, where one of the maids must have unpacked, hung, and organized our things while we were out touring the property yesterday.

"I thought you might have changed your mind about dinner," I hear him say. I take a seat on the ottoman inside the walk-in closet to put on my shoes.

"That's not part of the deal," I tell him evenly, although the thought of not attending passed my mind many times.

"We don't have to. We can leave," he says, and my hand pauses on the clasp of my ankle strap.

"You'd do that?" I ask, my eyes finding his. "You'd walk away from the deal for me?"

"If that's what you want," he says without hesitation. "Arora Heritage isn't the only bull breeder out there. I can find another partner." He shrugs. "You can help me land that deal."

My heart skips a beat from his admission. I know how much this deal means to him, and knowing he'd walk away for me... I stop myself from processing the thought. It's too heavy.

"But you chose Arora because they're the best?"

The way he scrubs his hand over his jaw, I know I'm right, and whatever words he gives me will be a downplay for my sake. "It doesn't matter. I don't want you to feel uncomfortable. If this deal goes through, there will be visits. Dar and Rohan will come to Bardstown."

I pause, my fingers freezing on the strap of my other heel. I hadn't thought that part through, not fully. But I did weigh walking away.

After we left the study yesterday and retreated to our suite, we didn't leave. Not for dinner, not even after the sun went down and the house was quiet. Trigg worked on his laptop, jaw tight with concentration, while I sat curled in the chair by the window, watching him when I thought he wasn't looking. This morning, I finally turned my phone back on.

The voicemail box was full. Over a hundred missed texts. The work I'd started back home at Fairfield, organizing the evals and updating our records software, all of it on pause. After sifting through the chaos, one glaring truth remained: I don't want to go back to the way things were. Which means seeing this through. Seeing *us* through, whatever that means.

I drop his gaze and focus on strapping my other heel, hyperaware of him watching me. "I'm sure Rohan told Dar about the picture in the study. How I confirmed I'm the little girl standing next to her mother." My fingers fumble with the tiny buckle. "How Warrick Fairfield is my father."

With my shoe secured, I stand and walk to the full-length mirror, needing distance and the excuse to look anywhere but at him. "That might make all of this harder to pull off. I have no idea if Dar wants anything to do with me now that she knows I'm Warrick's daughter." I smooth my hands over the crimson fabric. "And even if that doesn't give her pause, I'm not sure she'll buy that all of this"—I gesture between us —"is truly one big coincidence."

"So, we're doing this?" His voice is closer now, and when I glance up, I catch his reflection. He pushes off the door frame, and his eyes drag over me achingly slow. What I see in his expression makes my pulse stutter because it looks a lot like pride and possessive satisfaction. When his eyes catch me watching, he bites his bottom lip, but not before I see the heat there.

I turn to face him. "Unless you're having second thoughts..."

"No." The word comes out clipped, almost harsh, and I watch his hands flex at his sides like he's restraining himself from reaching for me. Then his brows tug together, worry creasing his forehead. "But there's something I haven't been able to work out since last night, and I feel like I'm missing a puzzle piece that I need if this is the choice *we're* making."

We. Like it wasn't going to happen if I'd said no. Like my answer actually mattered to him beyond the business arrangement. The word snags my breath; it's warm and terrifying all at once.

"What piece?"

"If the land and the business dealings were your father's doing..." He takes a step closer, and I have to tilt my head back to hold his gaze. "What reason would he have to hurt your mother? What would he gain?"

The question hangs between us, heavy and unavoidable.

"The land belonged to my mother."

He frowns. "I don't understand. The lease agreement was between my grandfather and Astor Fairfield."

"Yes, Astor was my mother's father, my grandfather. My father took my mother's name when they married." I watch as understanding starts to dawn on his face. "He was adopted, had no deep connections to his last name, so he took hers. The Fairfields were known in the community; they already had a reputation. It made sense for him to take her name."

It made sense for him to become someone he wasn't.

I see the exact moment it clicks. The way Trigg's face changes. The last shred of innocence he might have reserved for my father dissolving like smoke. His jaw clenches, and something dark and protective flashes in his eyes.

"Asha—"

"Don't." I grab my clutch from the dresser, needing to move, to do something before I completely fall apart in front of him. I've already let him see too much. "We have a dinner to get to."

I brush past him toward the door, pausing just long enough to glance back. "Try not to look like you've been sleeping on the couch. You're supposed to look thoroughly satisfied. We're newlyweds, remember?"

Then I'm out the door before he can respond, my heels clicking against the terracotta floor as I head toward whatever's waiting for us downstairs.

Behind me, I hear him follow, his low voice carrying down the hall. "Keep talking like that, and it won't be an act." Then, quiet enough that it sends a shiver down my spine: "You're playing a dangerous game, and we both know you're not ready for me to stop playing along."

His words burrow under my skin. Part of me wants to prove him wrong, to show him I can handle whatever game we're playing. But a bigger truth sits heavy on my chest: I'm not playing anymore. And neither is he. That's what scares me most.

~

Two hours into dinner, and the wine has done nothing to settle my nerves. This isn't like me. I was raised for this, trained to be poised under pressure, to smile through anything. My father made sure of that, but tonight, composure feels impossible.

Across the table, Dar laughs at something her husband says, her hand resting on his arm. She's effortlessly beautiful, warm brown skin, dark hair in an elegant twist, eyes that crinkle when she smiles. My aunt.

Santiago has been telling stories about his trip to Seville, where he'd taken two of their younger bulls to novilladas this morning, and my mind is everywhere but present.

"The smaller one, Valentín, he showed real promise," Rohan is saying, leaning forward in his enthusiasm. "Brave, noble. The young matador barely had to work for it."

Beside me, Trigg's hand finds my thigh under the table, a steady pressure that grounds me. He hasn't said much tonight, content to let me take the lead, but I can feel him watching me.

"More wine?" Rohan asks, already reaching for the bottle.

"She's good," Trigg says smoothly, his thumb stroking a small circle against my leg through the fabric of my dress. A gentle warning that I am decidedly not good.

The dinner has been pleasant—almost too pleasant. Surface conversations about the vineyard, the merger, Spain's wine country, Santiago's trip to Seville. Nothing about the photograph in the study. Nothing about my mother. Nothing about the fact that I'm sitting across from family I never knew I had while my father kept them hidden like a dirty secret.

Why? The question circles my mind on repeat, fueled by wine, confusion, and hurt. Why would he do this? What reason could he possibly have for cutting Dar out of our lives? For cutting me off from the only connection I have left to my mother? I feel a million different things and can't settle on one.

I reach for my wine glass again, but Trigg's hand intercepts mine, his fingers threading through mine instead. When I glance at him, there's a question in his eyes. *You okay?* I'm not, but I nod anyway.

Then Dar's eyes settle on mine across the table, and the pleasant buzz of conversation around us seems to fade. She sets down her fork with a deliberate care that makes my stomach clench.

"Maybe we should have started the evening with this," she says, her voice quiet but clear enough to cut through the ambient noise. "But honestly, I didn't know how." Her gaze holds mine, and I see something there, recognition, uncertainty, maybe even hope. "It's not every day a niece you've never met walks through your front door."

The table goes silent. My heart hammers in my chest, and I'm suddenly, painfully sober despite the wine coursing through my system. This is it. The moment I've been dreading and desperately needing all night.

"I..." My voice comes out rough. I clear my throat and try again. "I didn't know you existed until yesterday."

The confession hangs in the air between us, raw and honest and devastating, before I force myself to straighten in my chair. "We understand if you no longer want to partner with Hale Ranch. We didn't come here to deceive you."

Dar holds my gaze, silent and assessing. "I believe that's true," she says finally. Then she pauses, her fingers tracing the stem of her wine glass. "But I can't say the same is true for me."

Beside me, Trigg goes very still. Under the table, his grip on my hand tightens.

"What does that mean?" his voice cuts through the silence, sharp and demanding.

Santiago clears his throat, drawing our attention. "What my wife means to say is she was well aware that Hale Ranch bordered Fairfield. It's not a coincidence that we took an interest in partnering when we heard through the grapevine that you were looking to diversify, no?"

I feel the blood drain from my face.

"How could you have known I was married to Trigg?" Confusion bleeds into my voice as I try to make sense of the timeline. "The partnership discussions started before..." I stop myself before I say too much.

"She didn't." Trigg's voice is calm, measured, his eyes focused on Dar as if he's already worked everything out. "She didn't know we were married. That part is truly the coincidence." He leans back slightly, though his hand remains locked with mine. "She wanted to partner with me so she would have a reason to come to Bardstown. A reason to accidentally run into Warrick or maybe even you."

The table falls silent again, and I watch Dar's face carefully. She doesn't deny it.

"Is that true?" I ask, though I already know the answer from the way she's looking at me.

Dar sets down her wine glass with care. "I've never spoken to Warrick. Not once." Her voice is steady, but there's an undercurrent of old pain there. "Your mother was the one who sent me that picture." She pauses, her eyes meeting mine. "She was searching for his family, not him. She was so excited when she found us. Warrick wasn't. The last time I spoke to your mother, she told me he would come around. That he just needed time." Her voice drops. "But then I stopped hearing from her too."

My chest constricts, the wine turning sour in my stomach because I know exactly why she stopped hearing from my mother.

"Maya passed away shortly after that picture was taken," Trigger speaks for me.

"Yes," Santiago says quietly, his accent softening with sympathy. "After months went by with no response to any of our exchanges, I did a little digging and found her obituary online."

The silence that follows is suffocating even though we're outside. Around us, the Spanish countryside stretches into darkness, the ranch below barely visible now except for scattered lights dotting the landscape like fallen stars. The terrace where we sit is lit by warm string lights that cast everything in a golden glow, intimate and almost romantic if not for the weight of what's being said. A warm breeze carries the scent of fresh dirt, rustling through the olive trees that frame the stone terrace. I can hear the low calls of cattle settling for the night, a sound that should be comforting and familiar, but instead feels like it belongs to someone else's life.

"Listen," Dar finally says, her voice stronger now, steadier. "I know your trip was supposed to wrap up tomorrow. Tonight was supposed to be spent discussing terms over a meal and drinks, and we can still do that if that's what the two of you want." She pauses, looking directly at me. "But if you can, we'd like it if you could stay through the weekend."

The request hangs in the air between us, weighted with possibility.

"It would give us some time," she continues, "not just to speak as partners, but as family. If you're open to it, Asha, I'd like to get to know you as my niece."

I try to speak but can't get words past the lump in my throat.

"Can you give us a minute?" Trigg asks, feeling the tension coiled tightly in my hand.

Dar nods, understanding in her eyes. "Of course. Take all the time you need."

She and Santiago rise from the table, and Rohan follows their lead. For a long moment, I just sit there, trying to hold myself together. My breathing is coming too fast, too shallow, and there's a pressure building in my chest that feels like it might crack my ribs.

"Hey." Trigg's voice is soft, closer than before. "Come here."

He doesn't wait for me to move. Instead, he shifts his chair closer and gently pulls me toward him. I go willingly, pressing my forehead against his shoulder as he wraps his arms around me.

"I've got you," he murmurs into my hair. "I've got you, Asha."

And just like that, every wall I've built crumbles. The fakeness, the pretense, the careful distance we've been maintaining...it all disappears. In this moment, he's not my fake husband. He's the only solid thing in a world that's tilting sideways.

I bury my face in his chest, my hands fisting in his shirt as I try to breathe through the storm raging inside me. He just holds me, his hands stroking my back in slow, soothing circles. He doesn't tell me to stop, doesn't tell me it's going to be okay. He just lets me feel all of it.

"She wanted to know me," I finally manage, my voice muffled against his shirt. "All this time, and he kept her away. He kept *family* away from me."

"I know." His arms tighten around me.

"Why would he do that? What else has he lied about? What else don't I know?"

"We'll figure it out." His lips press against my temple, and the tenderness of it makes something crack open inside my chest. "Whatever it is, whatever we find, you're not alone in this. Not anymore."

I pull back just enough to look at him, and what I see in his face steals my breath. There's no calculation there, no careful distance. Just raw concern and something fiercer, something that looks almost like...

"Trigg," I whisper.

His hand comes up to cup my face. "Yeah?"

His eyes search mine, dark and intense, and I've never felt more seen, more understood.

"Kiss me." The words escape before I can think better of them.

He goes very still, his hand freezing against my cheek. "Asha..."

"Please." I lean into his touch, my fingers clutching his shirt tighter. "I need—"

"Not like this." His voice is pained. He shakes his head slowly. "Not when you don't know what you want. Not when you're messed up inside like this."

"Trigg, I'm asking you to kiss me." My hand covers his where it rests against my face, holding it there. "You're right. I'm lost. So help me feel something real. Help me feel anything other than—"

His mouth captures mine before I can finish. The kiss isn't gentle. It's desperate and consuming, like he's been holding back for too long, and my words shattered whatever restraint he had left. His hand slides from my cheek to tangle in my hair, and he tilts my head to deepen the kiss. The move pulls a sound out of me I don't recognize, half sob, half moan.

I kiss him back with everything I have, pouring all my grief and confusion and need into it. I pull him closer, and when his tongue sweeps against mine, I forget how to breathe. He tastes like wine and something darker, something that's purely him. His other hand grips my waist, fingers pressing into my side through the thin fabric of my dress, and I arch into him, chasing more contact, more of whatever this is that's making my head spin and my heart race.

When he pulls back just enough to change the angle, I actually whimper at the loss. But then he's kissing me again, harder this time, more demanding, and my hands slide from his shirt to his shoulders, to the back of his neck, threading into his hair.

"Asha." My name comes out broken against my lips. He doesn't pull away, though, just kisses along my jaw, down to that sensitive spot below my ear that makes me shiver.

"Don't stop." My voice is breathless, needy, and raw. "Please don't stop."

A low sound erupts from his chest, one that I feel more than hear, and then his mouth is back on mine. This time, when he deepens the kiss, it's slower, more thorough, like he's memorizing the taste of me. His hand tightens in my hair, and the slight tug makes heat pool low in my stomach.

This is fire and hunger and years of complicated history burning between us. This is every argument we've ever had, every heated glare across a room, every moment of tension that I told myself was hatred but was always something more. This is real in a way nothing else has been, no pretense, no performance, just raw want and need and something that terrifies me because I don't know how to name it.

The sound of the back door breaks our kiss. We're both breathing hard. His forehead rests against mine, and I can feel his heart hammering beneath my palm where it's pressed against his chest.

"Oh, I'm sorry. I didn't mean to interrupt," Dar says, her voice carrying across the terrace before she gestures apologetically to the table. "I left my phone."

"It's okay," I manage, my voice still breathless. She gives a curt nod, quickly retrieving her phone from beside her abandoned wine glass.

As she disappears back into the house, I let out a shaky breath and mutter under my breath, "Well, that was perfectly timed."

I feel Trigg go rigid against me. His hands, which had been holding me so tenderly moments ago, loosen their grip. When he pulls back, there's something shuttered in his expression, something cold that wasn't there before.

"Yeah," he says, his voice flat. "Perfect timing."

He releases me completely, leaning back in his chair and putting distance between us that feels like miles. His jaw is tight, and he won't quite meet my eyes.

I blink, confused by the sudden shift. "Trigg," I start.

"We should probably head in soon," he cuts me off, his tone now detached. "Figure out if we're staying for the weekend or not."

The warmth from moments ago has evaporated, and in its place is a chill that has nothing to do with the night air. I don't understand why, don't understand what just changed, or what I said wrong. All I know is the walls are back up in his eyes, and I feel like I lost something I didn't know I had.

ASHA

CHAPTER 26

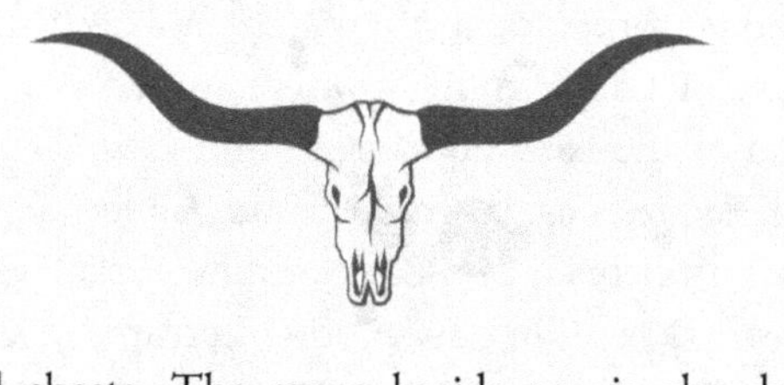

I wake to cold sheets. The space beside me is already empty, the indentation in the mattress the only proof Trigger was ever there. It's been like this ever since we kissed. Ever since I not only asked him to kiss me but let him into my bed—with conditions, of course. No touching and no crossing the wall of pillows.

He's honored those conditions religiously. Perhaps to a fault.

I'd extended the olive branch after hearing Santiago mention wanting to see him ride. There was no way I was going to let him continue sleeping on the couch, not when I know how brutal bull riding is on the body. I didn't want him climbing onto two thousand pounds of rage already wrecked because he got shit sleep on a decorative couch. Honestly, I expected I'd be kicking him out, peeling him away from my space. Instead, he arrives after I've gone to sleep and leaves before I wake, leaving his avoidance unmistakable.

A muffled shout shatters the silence, and then I hear Santiago's gravelly voice carrying through the air. I throw off the covers and cross to the window. When I wrench open the thick curtains, sunlight floods in, and my stomach knots.

The training pen sits halfway up the hillside, a circle of weathered wood fencing. I squint as my eyes adjust to the sunlight, and sure enough, it's him. Trigger is in the pen with a bull, a massive black beast with horns that could gore a man in half, but this time, he's not on his

238

back. No, this time he's on foot, planted in the center of the ring with nothing but a red cape between him and two thousand pounds of pure muscle and fury.

Shit. I don't remember moving. One second, I'm at the window; the next, my lungs are burning as I stomp up the hill. When I finally reach the pen, I'm ready to tear into him, to scream until my throat is raw about his recklessness, his stupidity, his apparent death wish. However, when I reach the fence, the words die on my tongue.

He's...beautiful.

Trigger moves with grace and precision. The bull charges, and he pivots, the cape sweeping low. Every muscle in his body is tensed, but he's ready and more alive than I've ever seen him. The bull thunders past, close enough that its horn tears through the cape's edge, and Trigger doesn't even flinch. He's going to get himself killed, and he looks more at peace than I've ever seen him.

"He's a natural, huh?" Santiago appears at my side, one weathered boot hiked up on the lowest fence rail.

"He's insane," I mutter, unable to look away.

We watch in silence as Trigger executes another pass and then another. The bull tires, but he's still no less deadly.

"How does this end?" I ask, keeping my voice low.

Santiago doesn't look at me. "You know how it ends, *mija.*"

"He's going to kill it?" My stomach drops. "Trigger, *stop!*" The words rip out of me before I can stop them.

His head snaps toward me, those stormy eyes finding mine. For one suspended heartbeat, the world narrows to just us. Then the bull moves.

It happens so fast. His massive head twists, and the horn slices through the air where Trigger's ribs were a fraction of a second before. He throws himself backward, stumbling, eyes wide as saucers. Then he's running, cape forgotten in the dirt, scrambling for the fence. His boots find the rails, and he vaults over, landing on the other side just as the bull slams into the wood hard enough to make the whole structure shudder.

I'm already moving, rounding the pen at a dead sprint. He's standing when I reach him, chest heaving, hand braced against the fence. There's a wildness in his eyes that hasn't faded yet, that primal rush of surviving something that should have killed him.

"What the hell do you think you're doing?" I shove him, hard, and he barely moves.

He's breathing fast as adrenaline floods his system. "What does it look like?"

"You were about to kill it!" I punch his shoulder, needing to feel something solid, needing to confirm he's real and whole and still breathing. "That's what you wanted? To slaughter something for sport?"

Something shifts in his expression. "Glad to know where your concern lies." He shakes his head, jaw tight, and starts toward the barn. Just...walks away, like I'm not worth the argument. Like the past few days of carefully constructed distance has turned into something permanent.

"You're not getting back in there." I follow him, my boots kicking up dust with each step.

"That's not your call to make." He doesn't slow down, doesn't look back.

I pick up my pace and cut him off, planting myself directly in his path. He pulls up short to avoid colliding with me. We're so close I can smell him. His sweat and earth and that cedar soap Dar keeps in all the bathrooms. I can see the pulse hammering in his throat, the green flecks in his dark eyes that I've cataloged against my will during too many sleepless nights.

"I'm your *wife*." The words come out louder than I intended, sharp enough to echo off the barn walls, gaining a few looks from farmhands.

Our eyes lock in challenge. He doesn't hate the claim I just made, but he's not happy about it either. The emotion flickering across his face is something darker, more complicated. Hunger mixed with resentment. Want twisted up with frustration. *Why?*

He's the one who's been telling me he'll prove me wrong. Who swore he'd show me this marriage could be more than a business arrangement. However, if the last few days have proven anything, it's that letting people in never works out for me. I kissed him, opened myself up for one reckless moment, and then he iced me out so thoroughly I might as well be living alone.

"Yeah, you're playing the part perfectly." His voice drips with contempt.

"What's that supposed to mean?"

Another backhanded jab. He agreed to stay longer so I could get to know my family, which has meant helping Dar prepare for the festival this weekend. Prepping recipes handed down for generations and hanging paper lanterns in the courtyard. I've put everything else on mute so I could have this, but not him.

"It means exactly what I said." He runs a hand through his hair. "Now, if you'll excuse me, I'm actually out here working."

"Is that what this is about?" my voice rises. "Is this why you've been acting like this? Because of the contract? If you're worried about it, let's sign it today. Right now. We can drive into Granada, find a notary, and get it done."

Something flashes across his face. "It's not about the contract." He tries to step around me, but I grab his wrist. Touching him sends heat spiraling through my veins. I miss him. The realization hits with devastating clarity. I miss what we had that night.

I feel the exact moment he registers my touch. His whole body goes taut, every muscle tensing like I've put my hand on a live wire. I see the way his jaw sets, that familiar stubborn clench that means he's fighting something internal. But I also feel the way his pulse kicks up beneath my fingers, betraying everything his expression is trying to hide. That has to mean something.

"It doesn't matter." His voice comes out rough, strained.

"*Trigger!*" Santiago's shout cuts through the moment. We both turn, my hand still wrapped around his wrist, to see him waving from another pen on the opposite side of the barn. He's standing with two of his most experienced hands, and even from this distance, I can see another bull, this one brown and rangy, pawing at the ground.

Trigger pulls his wrist from my grasp. "Go put some clothes on." His eyes drop briefly to my chest, and I suddenly remember what I'm wearing—or rather, not wearing. The thin silk of my sleep dress does nothing to hide the way my body has reacted to this confrontation—to him. My nipples are clearly visible through the pale fabric, hardened and practically on display for him and every single farmhand within eyeshot.

I cross my arms over my chest, catching a fleeting second of what looked like satisfaction on his face, knowing how my body reacted to him that way, and then it's gone. "Don't worry." He puts deliberate distance between us. His eyes are hard again, that brief moment of vulnerability gone. "None of your precious bulls die today."

Then, turning on his heel, he walks away, his stride long and purposeful across the dusty yard. The farmhands scatter like birds, suddenly very interested in their work. Santiago claps Trigger on the shoulder when he reaches the pen, already talking animatedly as I stand there in my nightgown and boots, my wrist still tingling from his touch.

If he wants to ice me out, fine. I'll remind him who he's playing with. I agreed to play the role of wife to help him land this merger. It doesn't mean I have to make it easy.

TRIGGER

CHAPTER 27

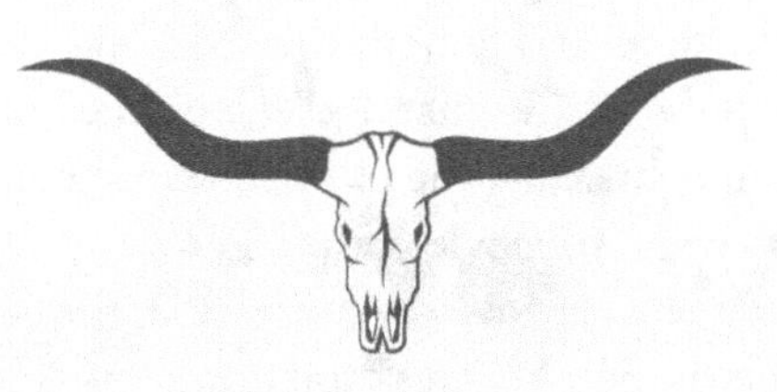

The first thing that registers is warmth. My body aches in places I'd forgotten existed, every muscle protesting yesterday's work in the pen. Those damn bulls nearly trampled me twice, but I want this. It makes me feel alive. My sore body is a reminder that I was not only alive but living intentionally. I draw in a slow breath, my mind still caught in that hazy space between sleep and consciousness, and that's when I feel it. The weight across my hip. The steady rise and fall of breathing that isn't my own. Soft hair tickling my jaw. *Shit.* My eyes snap open.

Morning light filters through the gaps in the curtains, and the pillow wall Asha constructed with military precision last night lies scattered across the floor. Her arm is draped possessively across my chest, and her leg is hitched over my thigh, her knee pressed dangerously high. I draw in a deep breath. I should move. It's what I've done every day since she proposed this arrangement, and every day, she unknowingly breaks it. But usually that's a good hour or two before now.

Asha is a heavy sleeper. It's how I've managed to put everything back together every morning before I leave, but I know my window of getting out unnoticed has passed. And my body has other ideas. I don't want to get up, not really. I'm exactly where I want to be, even if my mind is fighting it.

She shifts against me, and I go perfectly still, barely breathing. Her face is buried against my chest when cool air assaults the spot where her mouth was.

Is that drool?

My mouth twitches, and then she stirs again. I feel the moment consciousness returns. Her body goes rigid, and her breathing changes. Then slowly, she lifts her head, her eyes meet mine, still sleep-hazed with dreams before awareness sharpens them into accusation.

"What do you think you're doing?" Her voice is rough with sleep.

I raise an eyebrow, not moving an inch even though her leg is still very much tangled with mine, her body pressed along the length of me in ways that make my pulse kick. "What does it look like I'm doing?"

"It looks like you're breaking the rules." She pushes up on one elbow. "You're supposed to be on your side of the bed."

"I am on my side of the bed, sweetheart." I let the endearment drawl out, knowing it'll needle her. My eyes drop to where her leg is still thrown over mine then back up to her face. "It's your leg hiked up over mine and your drool on my chest, not the other way around."

Color floods her cheeks, and she snatches her leg back like I've burned her. "I don't drool."

"Evidence suggests otherwise." I tap my chest where the damp spot is clearly visible.

"You—" She sits up fully now, the sheets pooling around her waist, and I force myself not to notice how her tank top has ridden up, exposing a strip of skin at her hip. "You could have moved."

"I was comfortable."

"Comfortable." She laughs, sharp and bitter. "Ever since this sleeping arrangement started, the sheets on your side of the bed have remained cold every morning. Now, when I..." She pauses as if to redirect her words. "I was asleep. This doesn't mean anything."

And this is why I've slipped out of bed. She's not ready to admit she has feelings, and I don't want to hear her rejection. After the kiss, the kiss that meant fucking everything to me and nothing to her, she's been hard to look at. Letting her wrap herself around my body like I'm something she actually wants is masochistic. So, I slipped out—until now.

"Didn't say it did."

"Good," she snaps.

"Great."

We stare at each other, and the air between us shifts into something electric. My heart constricts, and I'm acutely aware of every shallow breath she takes. My eyes drop to her mouth and the lips I've spent nights trying to forget. I drag my gaze back up to meet hers. The anger there is barely masking something else, something hungry that makes heat coil low in my gut.

"The pillows—" she starts, but her voice wavers.

"You knocked them over."

"I did not—"

"Asha." I drop my voice. "Your side of the bed is pristine, and mine looks like this." I gesture to the crumpled sheets and pillows, and the evidence of her gravitating toward me in sleep. "You want to keep pretending, go ahead, but we both know the truth."

"Oh, you want to talk about the truth now. That's rich coming from you," she says with a bite, which makes me think the past few days of intentional distance I put between us were not only recognized but felt. If she even feels a pang of the hurt I felt after she dismissed our mind-bending kiss, chalking it up to a show for my merger...good.

"Yeah, I do," I say, leaning in closer, close enough to feel the heat radiating off her skin, and blood rushes south at the memory of her softness pressed against me. "You spent the night wrapped around me, loving every inch."

"Did not." She leans in, challenge in her eyes. "But the situation in your pants can't hide the fact that you more than enjoyed it."

"Your silk pajamas are just as revealing." I let my gaze drop slowly, taking in the evidence of her arousal before dragging back up to her face. My voice comes out rougher. "Tell me, do all women wake up with hard nipples, or is that just a *you* thing?"

She rolls her eyes, but I see the way her breath hitches, the flush creeping up her neck. "You're infuriating."

"And you just got caught looking," I point out, unable to keep the satisfaction off my face. Knowing exactly how she'll react, I can't help but deliver my next provoking line. "You know, if you want to, I'll even let you touch it."

Her cheeks turn rosy, her eyes darken to almost black, and Christ, I want to catalog every second of this reaction. The flush spreads over her chest, blooming across her collarbones, and I'm mesmerized by it. Her mouth can tell lies all day long, but her body? Her body never can. That truth settles in my chest like a brand.

"That's never going to happen. It was in our agreement."

"Was it?" The words come out almost as a growl. I'm so hard it hurts, and the space between us feels thick enough to choke on. "You mentioned separate sleeping quarters, but beds aren't the only place you can bounce up and down in my lap."

She scowls, but I see it, the flash in her eyes, the way her lips part slightly. She's envisioning it, imagining exactly what I just suggested, and the knowledge sends a bolt of pure want straight through me.

"You really expect me to stay celibate for a year?" My voice is rough, raw with frustration and desire that's been building for years.

"What are you suggesting?"

The distance between us feels eliminated, nonexistent. I can feel the whisper of her breath against my skin.

Heat floods through me. "I think you know exactly what I'm suggesting, Wife." I draw out the word deliberately, making it clear she agreed to the title, agreed to being mine.

"I think that's why God gave you hands," she says seductively, my cock noticing before my brain can register what she's said. The sultry expression that was written all over her face is gone like it was never there, and cold air rushes between as she pulls away and adds, "Use them." She smiles sweetly, innocently, but her eyes glitter with triumph. She knows exactly how she just played me, and she's enjoying every second of watching me realize it.

My jaw tenses as understanding crashes over me. This was payback for the distance I put between us, walls I erected because of her, because of stunts just like this one. I should have seen it coming. If I push, she pushes back. She always does, and fuck if it doesn't make me want her more.

My fists clench in the sheets, and she already has one leg off the bed, grabbing her robe, when my phone rings. The name on the screen gives me pause, but it doesn't surprise me.

"It's your father."

"Don't answer it."

"It's one a.m. there. It could be important," I tell her before answering on speaker phone. "Hello." A pillow slams into my face before I can finish, and I catch it one-handed.

"I want to speak to my daughter," Warrick's voice comes through the speaker, hard and demanding.

I raise an eyebrow as Asha stomps her foot and motions for me to hang up, to which I silently mouth back, *No.*

This isn't me choosing sides. If I had to pick one, it's always hers, but we aren't going to figure anything out by building walls and holding onto resentment. I know why she's avoiding everyone back home. She's scared, and there's no room for anything else when fear controls you. She can't think about an actual future with me when she's too scared to let anyone close, scared of losing them, scared of betrayal. That's why I answered. It's time to start chipping away at the fear. And I have to take that advice too.

When she sees I'm not going to give in to her demands, she puts a knee on the bed and snatches the phone from my hand. "Why are you calling me on Trigger's phone?"

"You're not answering or returning any of my calls." Static crackles through the line with his irritation. "You're not even responding to your friends."

"And how would you know that?" She's pacing now, bare feet padding hard against the hardwood, the phone gripped white-knuckled in her hand.

"I ran into Sydney at the coffee shop in town and asked if she'd heard from you. I don't need to fill you in on how the rest of the conversation went. I'm sure you can guess."

I roll my lips. His response does not sit right with me. I've had my own suspicions about Warrick since he and Asha returned to Fairfield. None of them are remotely related to Asha's suspicions, which is why they've stayed tucked away, but his supposed run-in with Sydney out of all her friends. Sydney—the same friend who stayed at their Louisville estate over the holidays, the same friend with a trust fund that rivals the one percenters we attended boarding school with—stayed in Asha's family home instead of checking into a hotel or, better yet, getting another temporary residence while their place was worked on.

Asha's theories and my suspicions may have nothing to do with each other, but they are definitely shading the same picture. Warrick has secrets.

"There's a reason for that. I have nothing to say to you," Asha says simply, but her free hand curls into a fist at her side.

"Asha, this is ridiculous." His voice rises. "You need to come home. We're not losing anything by giving those acres back to the Hales."

"You knew the ranch was important to me. That's why you kept me from it." Her voice cracks just slightly, and she stops pacing. "You were going to let it go right under my nose."

"You're my daughter, Asha!" His voice explodes through the speaker, loud enough that I can hear it echoing on his end. The anger radiating through the phone is so intense it makes Asha flinch. "I would never make you marry someone over a land dispute."

"It wasn't your choice to make."

A rough exhale filters through the phone, the kind meant to rein in fury. "Your mother's house is built on land I own, land you will eventually own if you end this and come home." His tone shifts, softer now, almost coaxing, which somehow makes it worse.

"Are you threatening me with Mom's house?" Her voice rises, disbelief and rage mixing together. "Why is it so hard for you to accept that maybe this is what I want? What I've always wanted."

"Because it's not!" There's a loud CRACK through the speaker, the unmistakable sound of a palm slamming against wood. The violence of it makes Asha jerk back a step. "It's not what you want, Asha. You're doing this to punish me."

I'm on my feet before I realize I've moved, crossing to her. Her whole body is coiled tight.

"Maybe you deserve to be punished," she shoots back, but her voice wavers. "Did you ever think of that?"

Another sound comes through, something heavy hitting the floor. "I'm your father. Everything I've done has been to protect you—"

"Protect me?" Her laugh is sharp and bitter. "You've been controlling me. There's a difference."

"Asha, that's not—"

"No." Her hand is shaking now. "I'm done. Don't call again."

She ends the call, and the sudden silence is deafening. She tosses the phone onto the bed like it's burned her.

"Asha—" I start, taking a step toward her.

"Don't." The word comes out raw, but she doesn't step away from me. "I'm upset, but I don't know which reason is harder to swallow: feeling like I'm losing my dad or knowing he's still keeping things from me."

I'm close enough to see everything she's trying to hide, her fear, her fury, her hurt...it's all there, bleeding through the cracks. She finally lifts her eyes to mine, and the devastation there nearly levels me.

"It's working, you know."

"What is?" I ask softly.

"Marrying you." She lets that sit between us for a beat then continues. "He just slipped. Said something he shouldn't have. Fairfield is every bit mine as it is his. Turns out we have more in common than you thought. My mother didn't leave me money, but she did leave me land. He doesn't know I've seen the title. He's again lying to control me."

Her eyes stay locked on mine, and for one unguarded moment, I see it—the war raging behind them. The need to run warring with the need for something solid to hold onto.

I chose the devil I know over the one I don't. Her words from before echo in my head. She's terrified of everyone, including me.

"I'm going to take a shower." Her voice is steadier as she steps around me. "You should get ready. We have that tantric yoga class with Dar in an hour." I can hear her walls snapping back into place as she finds something else to focus her mind on instead of addressing the root of her pain.

I hate it. I hate that she feels like she has to be this way with me. But I give her space because, truth be told, I need a minute too. I've gone from incredibly aroused, to angry and hurt, and now I have to push all that out because, on top of everything, I'm here to work. To close a deal.

"Yeah, about that. What is tantric yoga?"

"Yoga," she says dismissively with a shoulder shrug. "Wear sweatpants. You'll survive." And then she closes the door to the bathroom.

I exhale hard, scrubbing both hands over my face. My body still aches from yesterday's work with the bulls, but that's nothing compared to the frustration burning in my chest. She can put the walls back up all she wants. I've seen what's behind them, and I'm not going anywhere.

A rough laugh escapes me despite everything. Leave it to Dar to schedule something called "tantric yoga" right after the morning we just had. The universe has a twisted sense of humor. In a few minutes, Asha will come out of the shower, composed and acting like nothing happened.

I look down at the sweatpants in my hands and shake my head. Tantric yoga with my wife who just edged me into oblivion for revenge, then almost shattered from a phone call, then locked herself away again. This is going to be one hell of a morning.

TRIGGER

CHAPTER 28

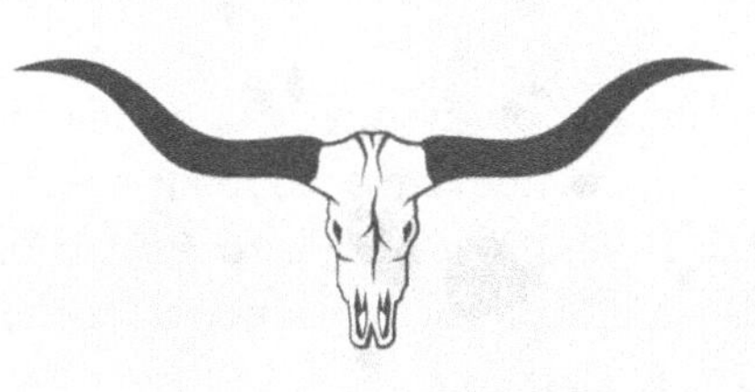

Twenty minutes into this torture, and I'm barely holding it together. Dar's private gym is all exposed beams and floor-to-ceiling windows that look out over the southern pasture. The morning light streams in, making the polished wood floors glow golden. Sandalwood incense burns in the corner, and some kind of meditative music plays softly from hidden speakers.

The instructor, a woman named Valeria, moves between the two mats with the grace of someone who's never experienced sexual frustration in her life.

"Beautiful work, Dar and Santiago," Valeria says, observing them in some complicated twist where they're back to back, arms intertwined. They move like water, completely in sync. Santiago's dark eyes are closed, peaceful, while Dar looks like she's reached some kind of enlightenment.

Meanwhile, Asha and I just finished a pose where I had to lift her by the hips while she arched backward over my thighs, her hair brushing the mat, her body a perfect curve of tension in my hands. I'm still recovering.

"Next, we'll move into Yab-Yum," Valeria announces, settling onto her own mat at the front. "This is a sacred tantric position. It represents the union of wisdom and compassion, of masculine and feminine energy."

I watch Santiago settle into position, easily crossing his legs and straightening his spine. Dar climbs into his lap like she's done it a thousand times, wrapping her legs around his waist, her arms looping around his neck. They look comfortable, nothing like what Asha and I are about to look like.

"Trigger," Valeria says gently. "Legs out, please."

I extend my legs, and Asha's eyes meet mine for the first time since we stumbled through the last pose. Her cheeks are flushed, her breathing still elevated, and there's a thin layer of sheen on her collarbone. This session is clearly affecting her too. The question is, in what way?

"This is the fourth pose," she mutters. "How many more does she have planned?"

"I don't know, but I'm pretty sure your aunt is trying to make a point." I keep my voice low, but across the room, I see Santiago's mouth twitch in a suppressed smile. Yesterday, he overheard us arguing by the pens. I'm sure that argument got back to Dar, and that's why we're having this intimate yoga class now.

"Asha," Valeria prompts. "Whenever you're ready."

Asha takes a breath then swings her leg over my lap. She settles onto my thighs, her legs wrapping around my waist, ankles crossing at my lower back. Every muscle in my body goes taut.

We've done three poses before this: a standing pose where she had to trust me to hold her weight as she leaned back, a seated twist where our legs tangled and hands clasped, and that backbend that nearly broke me. But this? This is different. This is her in my lap, chest to chest, with nowhere to hide.

"Arms around each other," Valeria instructs. "Create a circle of energy. Let your connection flow."

Asha tentatively sets her hands on my shoulders, and I wrap my arms around her waist. My thumb rests against her bare skin, and I have to resist the urge to trace the curve of her spine. Her eyes are fixed somewhere over my shoulder, but I'm acutely aware of every point where our bodies are close.

"Foreheads together," Valeria says. "Eye contact is necessary for this pose. Breathe as one."

She leans in slowly, and our foreheads connect. The contact sends electricity racing down my spine. This close, I can see everything: the gold buried in her brown eyes that are currently trying to avoid mine, the freckle just above her lip, the way her pulse hammers in her throat.

"Breathe," Valeria says softly. "Let go of whatever you're holding onto. The past, the future, the stories you tell yourselves. Just be here. Now. With your partner."

Asha's breathing is shallow. I can feel her trembling slightly, though whether it's from exertion or something else, I can't tell. My hands flex on her lower back, and she makes a small sound in the back of her throat. Then something shifts.

Her weight settles more fully into my lap, like she has finally stopped fighting the position. The defiance is still there, but underneath it is something else. Something that has me holding my breath.

"Breathe together," Valeria says somewhere in the background, but her voice is just noise now. "Let yourself sink into the connection."

Asha's next inhale is deeper, slower. I match it without thinking, and suddenly, we're locked into the same rhythm. She slides her hands from my shoulders to the base of my neck and threads her fingers through my hair. The touch is intimate and sends heat cascading down my spine. This is the closest we've been since prom night.

The memory hits without warning. Her wrapped around me like this, legs locked around my waist, hands tangled in my hair. Gasping as I pressed her against the wall. Her voice breaking as she begged me not to stop. One night where everything felt right before it all came crashing down.

My hands tighten on her lower back, pulling her closer. She shifts in my lap, adjusting her position, and my body responds, instantly hardening. There's no hiding it. Not with her pressed against me like this, not with the thin fabric of our workout clothes as the only barrier between us. I wait for her to pull away. To scramble back like she did this morning. To throw up those walls again. But she doesn't.

Her eyes widen slightly when she feels my hardening length pressed directly against her center. I watch awareness flash across her face, see her breath hitch. But she doesn't retreat. Instead, she stays exactly where she is. Then she shifts again, barely, just a fraction of an inch, and this time I know it's deliberate. She's testing it, testing me. The pressure increases between us, and I have to bite back a groan.

"Asha," I breathe her name, a warning and a question all at once.

Her breathing quickens, and those pretty pink lips I've tried to forget part slightly, and I watch her tongue dart out to wet them as her gaze drops to my mouth before darting back up to my eyes, and what I see there nearly undoes me. Want. Pure, undisguised want.

She rocks against me wordlessly, acknowledging what I know she feels. A slow, deliberate grind that has my vision blurring. For a second, the girl from prom is back. The one who looked at me like I was everything. The one who wasn't afraid to take what she wanted. I can feel her heat against my length, feel her body telling me everything her mouth won't: she wants this, wants me.

Another rock of her hips, and I choke back a groan. My hands grip her tighter, and she makes a soft sound in the back of her throat that goes straight through me. Her lips are so close to mine, a hairsbreadth apart, when her eyes snap open. I see it immediately. Panic floods in as reality comes crashing back in. Her entire body goes rigid, and the spell shatters.

"I'm sorry." The words come out breathless, rushed. "I'll be right back."

She's off my lap before I can respond, unwrapping her legs and scrambling to her feet with none of the grace from before. She doesn't look at me, doesn't look at anyone. Just grabs her water bottle and heads straight for the door. I sit there on my mat, chest heaving, body screaming with unfulfilled need, trying to process what just happened. Trying to calm the racing of my heart and the ache low in my gut.

When I turn my head, Dar and Santiago have stopped their pose, both of them looking at me with matching expressions of concern. Valeria has her back turned, giving us privacy as she organizes her things at the front of the room.

"Is she alright?" Dar asks quietly.

I run a hand through my hair. "I don't know."

Santiago and Dar exchange a look, some silent communication passing between them.

"Give her a minute," Santiago says, but his tone suggests I should probably do the opposite.

I push to my feet. Every nerve ending in my body is still firing, and I can still feel the phantom pressure of her against me, still feel the heat of her breath on my lips.

"I'll go check on her," I manage, my voice rougher than I intend.

I head for the door she exited, my heart still pounding because I know what just happened in there. We both gave in. For just a moment, we stopped fighting and let ourselves feel everything we've been avoiding. And it terrified her enough to run. Again.

"Open the door, Asha." My voice comes out strained as I stand outside the only other door in the hallway. I knock once, twice. Silence. Just the sound of running water on the other side. She's not going to answer.

I press my forehead against the door, trying to get my breathing under control. I know she's worked up. Hell, I know exactly what I was doing back there in that pose, what we were both doing. But it couldn't be helped. It's not my fault; I like the way Asha feels pressed against me. I wasn't about to hide my reaction to having my wife wrapped around me, grinding against me like she couldn't help herself. She's supposed to like how I feel. She *is* my wife.

The memory of her in my lap crashes over me again, the way her eyes went dark and heavy-lidded, the way she rocked against my hardness with unmistakable intent, the soft sound she made in the back of her throat when she felt exactly what she was doing to me. The way her fingers tightened in my hair like she was about to pull me into a kiss right there in front of everyone. Then she ran.

I open my eyes, jaw clenched, and look up. Running my fingers along the top of the doorframe, I feel for what I'm hoping is there. Sure enough, a small key. Old farmhouse trick. Every interior door has an emergency key somewhere. The lock clicks open, but she doesn't hear it over the sound of running water. I slowly push the door open just enough to slip inside. Steam fills the hallway bathroom, but the shower isn't running. It's the sink, the water is pouring full blast, like she's trying to drown out any other sound.

When I turn the corner, I freeze.

She's bent over the counter, one hand gripping the marble edge so hard her knuckles are white. The other hand is down the front of her leggings, her arm moving in a rhythm that makes my cock twitch violently in my joggers. *Fuck.* The sight of her touching herself because I got her this worked up almost brings me to my knees. Every muscle in my body goes taut, and I have to clench my fists at my sides, taking a deep breath to contain myself.

I don't want her to stop. I want her to give in to this. To give in to me. Her eyes are closed, head dropped forward, breathing hard. She hasn't noticed me yet, too lost in whatever she's chasing. Her hips rock forward slightly, seeking more friction, and a soft whimper escapes her lips.

The sound destroys me, and I move forward on instinct, closing the distance between us. My hands slide slowly around her waist, and her entire body jolts.

"Don't stop," I murmur, meeting her startled gaze in the mirror. Her eyes are wild with arousal and shock. "I like it when you touch yourself while thinking about me."

"Who said I was thinking about you?" She yanks her hand out of her leggings, her chest heaving, but she doesn't pull away from me.

I press my hard length firmly against her ass, letting her feel exactly what she does to me. "Then who?"

Her eyes widen in the mirror, and she bites that plump bottom lip. "I have a schedule. You messed it up this morning. This has nothing to do with—"

"With me?" I lean in, my lips brushing her ear. "So it wasn't the feel of me pressed against your pussy in the other room that had you running in here?"

"No." Her voice wavers, and her hips press back against me involuntarily.

"Liar." My hands slide down to her hips, holding her against me. "Your body's telling me a different story, sweetheart."

"It's just biology," she breathes, but I can see her walls crumbling in the mirror. "Physical stimulation. It doesn't mean anything."

"Biology." I rock my hips forward, and she gasps. "That's why you're trembling?"

"I'm not—" She cuts off when my hand glides down the back of hers.

"You are." My fingers slide over hers, then lower, slipping beneath the waistband of her leggings. When I feel how wet she is, we both groan. "Fuck, Asha."

"It wasn't because of you," she insists, but her eyes are fluttering closed, her body melting back against mine.

"No?" I slip one finger through her folds, coating myself in her arousal, and her hips buck. "Then why are you soaked?"

"I told you...my schedule..." Her words break off when I slide my finger inside her. Her pussy clenches around me immediately, and her hand slams against the mirror to brace herself.

"Right, your schedule. You took a long shower this morning...." I pump her slowly, letting the insinuation hang between us. "I think we both know you maintained your schedule." I tuck away the fact that my wife likes to touch herself first thing in the morning for later. "So you're going to have to give me a better reason for why you're grinding against my cock now." I watch her face in the mirror as she comes undone.

"I'm not—" But she is. Her ass rocks against my hardness with every thrust of my finger, seeking more.

"You are," I add a second finger, and she gasps. "Stop lying to yourself. To me. You want this."

"I don't— I can't—" Her head falls back against my shoulder, and I can see the moment her last defense crumbles. "Trigger..." Her tone is a curse and a plea all at once.

"Say it." I curl my fingers inside her, finding that spot that makes her legs shake. "Tell me who you were thinking about."

She doesn't answer. Just stares at me in the mirror, breathing hard, her lips parted. But she doesn't tell me to stop either. That's answer enough. I pump my fingers deeper, slower, and her hips rock back against me. My cock throbs against her ass so hard it's painful. I grind forward, and she moans like she wishes it were more.

"Trigger," she gasps my name, and the sound destroys what's left of my control.

"I know, baby. I know." I establish a rhythm. My fingers pumping into her pussy, my hips grinding against her ass. It's not nearly enough, but it's everything. Her other hand reaches back, gripping my hip, pulling me harder against her. The movement presses my cock right between her ass cheeks, and even through the layers of fabric, the pressure is exquisite torture.

"Fuck," I breathe against her neck. Sweat beads on my forehead, slides down my spine. The bathroom is thick with steam and heat and the scent of her arousal.

She moans, soft and breathy, and I can feel her getting wetter, coating my fingers, dripping down to my palm. Every thrust of my fingers is met with a rock of her hips, and she's moving against me like we're fucking. Like there's nothing between us. Fuck, I wish there was nothing between us.

I imagine shoving her leggings to her ankles and sinking into her, feeling her tight walls around my cock instead of my fingers. The thought makes me grind harder against her, and she whimpers, both hands now on the mirror again, fingers splayed, leaving streaks in the condensation.

"Please," she gasps, and I don't know what she's begging for, but I'll give her anything.

"I've got you," I add a third finger, stretching her, and her back arches, pushing her ass more firmly against my length. The friction is maddening. I'm humping her like a teenager, unable to stop myself. Every thrust of my fingers is matched by a grind of my hips. We're both panting, both sweating, moving together in a rhythm that feels inevitable. Her moans grow louder, less controlled. Little gasps and whimpers that she can't hold back. I can feel her thighs trembling, feel her pussy fluttering around my fingers.

"That's it," I growl, my free hand gripping her hip, holding her steady as I work her harder. "Let me feel it."

In the mirror, I watch her lips part, and I revel in the way her eyes are glazed with pleasure. She's so beautiful like this. Undone. Mine. I imagine her coming apart on my cock instead of my fingers. The fantasy makes me thrust harder against her, and she cries out.

"Oh god—oh god—" Her words dissolve into moans, her entire body starting to shake.

"Come for me," I demand, curling my fingers and grinding the heel of my palm against her clit. "Let go, Asha."

But I don't make her say it. Don't force the words from her. Because her body is already telling me everything I need to know. She wants this, wants me, that maybe she's always wanted me, even if she won't admit it out loud.

She shatters, her entire body convulsing around my fingers, and when the tremors finally subside, she sags against me, breathing hard. For a moment, she's completely pliant. Then she straightens, pulling away from me and adjusting her clothes with shaky hands.

"Don't look so smug," she says, not meeting my eyes in the mirror. "It's been a while. A vibrator would've gotten the same reaction."

I watch her smooth down her tank top, tuck her hair behind her ear, anything to avoid looking at me. A smile tugs at my mouth despite the ache still throbbing in my joggers.

"Right," I say slowly. "A vibrator. That's why you were moaning my name."

Her eyes snap to mine in the mirror. "I didn't."

"You did." I step closer, and she tenses. "But keep telling yourself whatever you need to, sweetheart. We both know the truth."

She whirls on me, eyes flashing. "The truth is this was a—"

I cut her off. "Don't." It comes out sharp, my tone a clear warning. I refuse to let her downplay another one of our moments.

She must hear my warning, because she doesn't finish what she was about to say. "It won't happen again."

"We'll see about that."

She shoves past me toward the door, and I let her go this time, watch her yank it open and disappear into the hallway without looking back. I brace my hands on the counter where hers were just minutes ago, staring at my reflection. My hair is a mess from her fingers. My shirt is wrinkled where she gripped it. And I'm still hard as stone, my body screaming for release she didn't give me. But that's okay.

Because I felt the way she came apart in my arms, heard my name on her lips even if she wants to pretend she didn't say it. She can throw up every defense she has, but I know better. I felt the way her pussy clenched around my fingers like she never wanted to let go. Felt the way she ground back against me, seeking more. Heard those soft, desperate moans that she couldn't control. She wants me. She's wanted me this whole time, even if admitting it terrifies her.

And now that I've had a taste of what it's like to break through her defenses, to feel her come undone in my arms? I'm not stopping until every wall between us is rubble.

I adjust myself in my joggers, still painfully hard, and head for the door. Time to face Dar and Santiago and pretend like I didn't just finger fuck my wife in their bathroom while she tried to convince us both that it didn't mean anything.

ASHA

CHAPTER 29

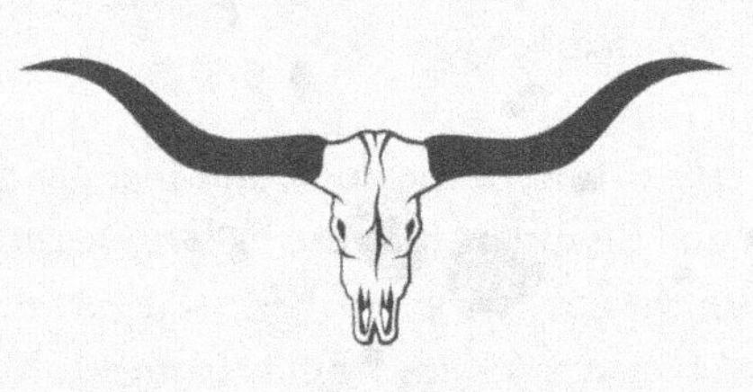

The kitchen smells like cumin and ghee, warm spices that should comfort me but instead feel like a betrayal. Dar is teaching me how to cook authentic Indian dishes—something I've always wanted to learn, but now that I'm not talking to my father, it feels pointless. Everything feels pointless.

My head is a fucking mess. If you asked me what color the sky was right now, I'd tell you it was red. I press the rolling pin hard against the dough. I'm mad at my father for keeping secrets. Mad at Trigger for making me feel everything. Ultimately, I'm mostly mad at myself for not seeing a rational way through all of this.

"Like this, Asha," Dar says softly, demonstrating the proper wrist movement.

I nod, trying to mirror her grace, but my movements are stiff, mechanical. Outside, I can see Trigger's silhouette moving past, and my stomach clenches. I've never been this way. I'm not easily ruffled, and right now I feel like the walls are literally closing in. I wanted to call him out this morning, on his silence, the bull riding, his plans for the merger, all of it, and I didn't. Because somewhere between the anger and my undeniable attraction for this maddening man, I've lost my footing entirely.

The night we kissed, I opened a door. I let him see something I don't show anyone: my vulnerability, the parts of me that aren't armor and ambition. And he shut me out. At least, that's what it felt like. That's what I've been telling myself. Then this morning... Heat creeps up my neck just thinking about it. My legs clench involuntarily, and I roll the dough harder, feeling it tear slightly under the pressure. *Damn it.*

This morning, what the fuck was that? It's what we do: we get each other worked up, push boundaries, and play with fire. But the way he was holding me, the way his hands gripped my hips like I might disappear. The look I saw in his eyes when our foreheads were pressed together, when the world narrowed to just breath and heartbeat and the impossible space between wanting and having. He looked at me like I was everything to him. Like I was truly something precious.

And it's that look I haven't been able to stop thinking about. I can't stop thinking about it because it feels so utterly contradictory to everything that's transpired up until that moment. How can he look at me like that and still hold pieces of himself back? How am I supposed to trust what I see in his eyes when everything else feels like a transaction, a negotiation, a carefully orchestrated merger of convenience?

"Do you want to talk about it?" Dar asks, snapping me out of my thoughts.

"Hmm?" I look up from the dough, realizing I've been staring at it without seeing.

She smiles knowingly, nodding toward my hands. "If you roll that dough any thinner, it won't hold our filling."

"Oh." I glance down. The dough is nearly translucent. "Sorry."

"Don't be sorry." She wipes her hands on a towel and moves around the island toward me. "This is what aunts are here for. Cooking and sharing stories." She takes the rolling pin from my hands and sets it aside. "You know, I remember what it was like to be newly married."

I gather up the overworked dough, pressing it back into a ball.

"There's a lot of hunger and excitement," Dar continues, adding seasoning to the pot on the stove. "But there's also a learning curve, one that can make two people who are madly in love feel like they're speaking different languages."

She rounds the counter to join me, her shoulder brushing mine as she starts forming her own piece of dough. The simple intimacy of it, cooking side by side, makes my throat tight. This is what I've been missing. What my mother should be here to teach me.

"Speaking different languages is giving us more credit than we deserve," I say quietly, dividing the dough into smaller portions.

"Is it?" She glances at me sideways. "I see the way that man looks at you, the way he watches you when you're unaware. You're the center of his world, Asha. He came here for business, but do you know, since we discovered our connection, he hasn't brought it up once?"

My hands still. "No. I didn't know that. I assumed—"

"You assumed because he was learning our ways that he was talking shop." She shakes her head, reaching for more flour. "He hasn't. And you want to know why?"

My eyes meet hers. "Why?"

"Because he's letting you lead. Someone in love will never hold you back. They won't douse your flame to make theirs burn brighter." She places her hand over mine, stilling my nervous movements. "You're his fuel, Asha. Without your happiness, this means nothing."

That's one way of looking at it. The other is that he married me specifically to land this deal. He has to play by my rules now more than ever. I hold the cards. Or at least I thought I did. However, hearing Dar's perspective, threading her words with the things he's said and the way he touches me, how he looked this morning...it has me questioning my fear again. That old, familiar fear of abandonment. The one that's had me pouring everything into my studies and work, into anything that busied my mind, anything that kept me from feeling. Because feelings never worked out for me. And now, here I am, terrified I'm catching them for the one man my father always told me not to.

"Then why doesn't he just say that?" My voice comes out smaller than I intended because I didn't mean to say the words aloud.

She smiles, that patient smile of someone who's lived longer, loved harder. "Because he's a man. Men rarely express what's on their hearts the way we want them to. Sometimes you just have to know. He wouldn't have chosen you to be the person by his side, the mother of his children, his forever, if you weren't everything he wanted."

My hands go clammy instantly at the words *children* and *forever*, spoken in reference to me and Trigg. I wipe them on my apron and reach for the tequila she poured earlier. *Well, at least she thinks this is all very real.*

"We definitely aren't having kids anytime soon," I say, taking a drink and welcoming the burn.

"That's not always in our control." She laughs. "Rohan was a surprise. In fact, I'm pretty sure he was conceived during angry sex."

I cover my mouth to avoid spitting out my tequila, choking on laughter and liquor.

"Don't be shy." She waves her hand dismissively. "I'm sure if your mother were still with us, she would be having this conversation with you. We can learn from the women who came before us, watch how they made things work, how they weathered the storms." She rolls out the last piece of dough. "It doesn't mean we walk the same path, but sometimes we see that we're not as alone as we think we are. And sometimes what we think is failure, what we think is rejection, it's just love. Messy, imperfect, human love."

I watch Dar's hands as she works, wondering what it's like to have that kind of certainty. To know someone that deeply.

"What do you and Santiago do when you disagree?" I ask.

My father never remarried. He's never even had a serious girlfriend. I know he hasn't been celibate, but if there are women in his life, they aren't anyone he's kept around long enough for me to meet. I've never watched a love story unfold. I've never witnessed the mortar it takes to keep the walls standing.

"We talk," Dar says simply, turning to check the dal, stirring slowly. "Even when it's the last thing we want to do. When we know it might hurt, we talk. And then..." Her voice trails off with a knowing smile, implication hanging in the steam-filled air.

"Right." *Makeup sex.* I take another drink, feeling the warmth spread through my chest. "I don't think I need help with those details."

She laughs again, and the sound makes me ache for something I can't name. For the mother who should be here. For the father who used to be present before secrets carved him hollow.

"Talking," I murmur, more to myself than to her. "It seems so obvious."

And though I feel like it's what I was trying to do this morning, I was also letting my own insecurities get in the way. My fear of being too much or not enough. My terror of opening up only to find there's nothing on the other side but empty space.

But what if there isn't empty space? What if there's just...him?

I start forming the samosas, folding the dough around the spiced potato filling. The kitchen is warm now, almost too warm, and I can feel sweat gathering at the base of my neck.

"Dar," I say slowly, pressing the edges of a samosa to seal it. My heart is suddenly pounding. "Can I ask you something?"

"Of course."

I set down the samosa, my hands trembling slightly. The question has been sitting in my chest since I arrived, growing heavier with each passing hour.

"Why do you think my father refuses to speak to you to this day?"

Dar's hands still over the samosa she's forming. For a long moment, she doesn't speak, just stares down at the dough. Then, softly, she says, "Fear."

Fear. Such a simple word, yet a devastating truth. I stand there, my own hands frozen mid-fold, and suddenly, I can see it so clearly. My father and I are not opposites. We're mirrors. Reflections of the same crippling ailment, the same poison running through our veins. We're more alike than we are different.

First, he lost his family, then he lost my mother. The love of his life, gone, and he was left holding a daughter who had her eyes, her smile, her spirit. Every day was a reminder of what he'd lost. So, he did what he knew how to do. He built walls. He poured himself into work, and he taught me to do the same, to be strong, independent, to need no one. To feel nothing. And I learned the lesson all too well.

My throat tightens. I can feel Dar watching me, but I can't look at her. I'm too busy seeing my father differently, not as the distant, cold man who kept secrets, but as someone drowning in the same fear that's been strangling me. The fear of losing someone. The fear of being left. The fear that if you let someone in, if you love them, if you need them, they'll be taken away, and you'll be left with nothing but the unbearable weight of their absence.

The kitchen door swings open behind me, and I hear his footsteps before I hear his voice. I know the sound of his walk, confident, purposeful, the slight scrape of his boot heel against tile.

"Hey, need any help in here?" Trigger asks. "Something smells incredible."

I freeze, my back still to him, desperately trying to compose myself.

"We're just finishing up the samosas," Dar says warmly, but I can hear the careful note in her voice. The way she's giving me a moment.

I force myself to turn around. The moment my eyes meet his, I watch his entire expression shift. His smile falters then disappears completely. He takes a step forward, instinctively, like his body has a will of its own when it comes to me.

"Asha, what's wrong?" I can hear the genuine concern in his ask.

Everything. Nothing. Everything. Because I can see it now. Everything Dar said...it's right there in his eyes. The way he's looking at me isn't polite concern or the practiced care of someone playing a role. It's raw. It's real. He's looking at me like seeing me upset physically hurts him.

His gaze sharpens, and I watch him glance at Dar, then back to me, clearly trying to assess the situation, and I pull him by the wrist over to the pantry, unable to hear him ask me, *what's wrong* one more time with that gentle voice that twists me up inside.

"Did something—"

I cut off his question, rising on my toes and sealing my lips over his. For a heartbeat, he's still, shocked, and then he's kissing me back with an intensity that steals the breath from my lungs. His hands come up to frame my face, thumbs stroking my cheekbones, and I melt into him. My hands slide up, tangling in the hair just above his collar, and God, it feels good. So good.

Just like the kiss we shared days ago, when his mouth is on mine, everything floats away. All the noise, all the fear, all the questions. It's just me and him, and I feel safe. I feel happy. I feel at home. His tongue sweeps against mine, and I make a sound I don't recognize, pressing closer. His hands slide from my face to my waist, gripping, pulling me flush against him. I can feel his heart hammering against my chest and the way his breathing has gone ragged. The pantry smells like him, leather, soap, and something uniquely Trigger that makes me dizzy.

Then reality crashes back in. The clinking of pots and Dar's soft humming fill the air. We're not at home. We're not alone. I pull back, gasping, my forehead resting against his. His eyes are still closed, his lips parted, his hands still gripping my waist like he's afraid I'll disappear.

"I'm sorry," I breathe, blinking away the haze of yet another insanely intimate kiss with my fake husband.

His eyes snap open. His brow furrows, and I watch his face morph from confusion into something harder, colder. He drops his hands from my waist and takes a step back, the loss of his warmth immediately devastating.

"You're sorry," he repeats flatly, his jaw tight. "For what, exactly? Kissing me?"

His hands move to his hips, and his whole body goes rigid. He shuts down, and reality smacks me in the face. This is the same way he reacted after our last kiss. He pulled away, and I thought he was the one closing the door, but now I can see that wasn't it at all.

"That's it," I say. "That's why you've been mad at me."

"Who said I was mad at you?" he asks, truly confused.

"Tell me you're not hurt." I step closer, closing the distance he just created. "Tell me I didn't hurt you."

"Asha, I don't think this is the place to get into this—"

"I wanted to kiss you then." The words tumble out. "I wanted to kiss you now. And not for any other reason than I wanted to."

He stares at me, his chest rising and falling with heavy breaths. "You wanted to kiss me?" His voice is careful.

"Yeah." My heart is in my throat. "It's one of the perks of being married. I get to kiss you anytime I want."

His eyes search mine, looking for the lie, an angle, and expecting a catch, but I hold his gaze, letting him see me. Really see me.

"How much have you had to drink?" His eyes flick past me toward the counter where I know the tequila bottle sits, still mostly full.

"Stop," I draw out, pressing my hand against his chest.

He looks back at me, jaw set, waiting. I know exactly why he thinks I'm crazy. Hell, I *am* crazy. I pull him in and then push him away. I opened up the night we kissed then made a flippant comment that made him think it was for show. And just now, I apologized like it was a mistake. This morning... God, this morning at yoga, pressed against him, wanting him so badly I could barely breathe, and then what happened after...I pushed again.

The man doesn't know how long I'll let him have me before I cut the cord. Before fear wins and I run. That's why I have to get this out. All of it.

"I kissed you because it felt right. Because I wanted to." My voice is steady and certain. "It was never part of keeping up the act. That kiss was real. The first one, this one, all real."

He stares at me, trying to decide if he believes me. I can see the war happening behind his eyes, the want to believe warring with the evidence of every time I've shut him out.

Then, slowly, something shifts in his expression. The corner of his mouth quirks up, just barely. "So you get to kiss me anytime you want, huh?"

A slow smile spreads across my face, matching his. "Yes," I answer, letting the coyness creep into my voice, feeling the tension shift from painful to electric.

His hand reaches for my waist, fingers spreading against my hip as he pulls me close. The move sends heat racing through my veins. Our bodies align, chest to chest, hip to hip, and I have to tilt my head back to hold his gaze.

"Does that work both ways, then?" His voice has dropped to that low rumble that does things to me, and his thumb traces small circles against my waist through the fabric of my shirt. My breath catches, and suddenly, the pantry feels impossibly warm. I can feel every inch of him pressed against me, can see the heat in his eyes, the slight flush on his cheekbones. His eyes drop to my mouth. "Because if you let me," he murmurs, his voice rough and low, sending shivers down my spine, "I might not ever stop."

I still can't speak. Can't think. Can only feel the rough pad of his thumb against my hip, the solid warmth of him, the way my heart is racing, the way every nerve ending in my body has come alive. So I don't say anything. I just look at him, let him see everything I can't put into words written across my face: the want, the fear, the decision to stop running.

His mouth crashes against mine, and this kiss is different from all the others. It's not tentative or questioning. It's claiming, consuming, like he's been holding back, and finally he doesn't have to anymore. His hand tightens in my hair as he angles me right where he wants me to deepen our kiss.

I kiss him back with everything I have, my fingers fisting in his shirt, pulling him closer. His other hand slides from my waist to the small of my back, pressing me against him until there's no space left between us.

He tastes like mint and possibility, and when his tongue sweeps against mine, my knees actually go weak. He must feel it because his arm tightens around me, holding me up, holding me to him.

I'm drowning in him, in the sensation of his mouth on mine, the way his hand has moved to cradle the back of my head, the solid strength of him surrounding me. Everything else fades away. There's no merger, no secrets, no fear. Just this. Just us. His lips leave mine to trail along my jaw, down to that sensitive spot just below my ear, and I gasp, my head falling back to give him better access.

"Asha," he breathes against my skin, and the way he says my name makes my stomach flip.

"Tri—" I start, but then his mouth is back on mine, and whatever I was going to say dissolves into another kiss.

I lose track of time. Of where we are. Of everything except the taste of him, the feel of him, the way he kisses me like I'm oxygen and he's been suffocating.

"Dinner is ready!" Dar's voice cuts through the haze, warm and amused, carrying clearly through the pantry door.

We break apart instantly, both of us breathing hard. Trigger's forehead drops to mine, his eyes still closed, his hand still tangled in my hair.

"Fuck," he whispers, and I almost laugh because it's exactly what I'm thinking.

"We should—" I start.

"Yeah." But he doesn't move. Neither do I.

I can still feel the ghost of his lips on mine, can still taste him. My heart is hammering, my skin flushed, and I know I must look thoroughly kissed.

"They're going to know," I murmur.

His eyes open, meeting mine, and there's heat there still but also something softer. Something that looks a lot like happiness. "Good," he says simply.

"Good?"

"Yeah." His thumb traces my swollen bottom lip, and I have to fight not to kiss him again. "You're mine, sweetheart." His eyes search mine for an objection, and when it doesn't come, he says, "Come on." His hand slides down my arm to catch my fingers, lacing them with his. "Before she comes looking for us."

TRIGGER

CHAPTER 30

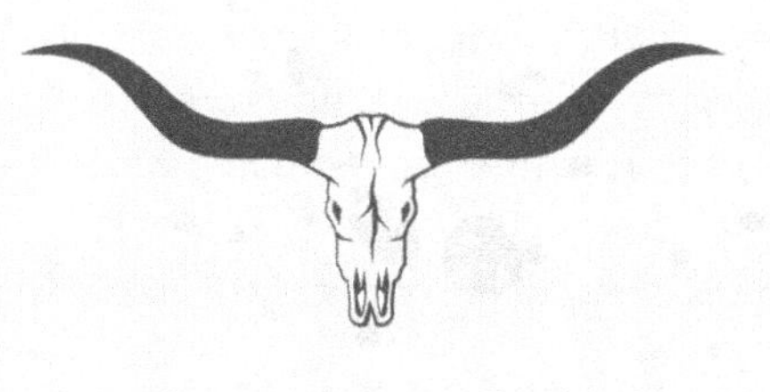

I settle back into my chair as Santiago finishes his story about Rohan's first attempt at bullfighting when he was twelve, something about a neighbor's goat and a red tablecloth. Even Asha is laughing, and I let myself enjoy the sound. We've both been a ball of nerves since we said our vows, and hearing her laugh feels like a weight has been lifted. Her laugh is my happiness, and on the heels of that kiss we shared in the kitchen, I can't help but feel hopeful that things are changing between us.

"These are perfect," Asha says softly, breaking off a corner of the pastry. "Just like—" She stops herself and glances at Dar.

Dar gives her a knowing smile. "Just like I taught you," she finishes for her.

I can't be sure what they were talking about before I entered the kitchen, but I know whatever it was must have been intense. It was written all over Asha's face when I walked in. It was why I wasn't convinced when she kissed me that she did it for any reason other than to keep up appearances. However, the way I watch something pass between them now...I know it must have been about her father or maybe even her mother. They've been separated by an ocean and family drama for years, and I'm only beginning to understand how deep that must be for her.

"This evening has been..." Asha pauses, setting down her napkin as she finds the right words. "Everything. Thank you so much for opening your home to us in this way."

"We wouldn't have it any other way," Santiago says. "It's not often we get to—"

"Actually," Dar interrupts, reaching down beside her chair. She pulls out a portfolio, and I feel the shift in the air immediately. "If the two of you are ready to sign, I'd like to get this out of the way so we can truly enjoy what time we have left together this week and not worry or stress about this merger."

She slides the contract across the table, and I reach for it, holding it so that Asha can review it with me. I flip through the pages, scanning the terms we've already negotiated via email and video calls. Everything looks in order. Standard partnership agreement, profit sharing, and operational oversight. I'm about to reach for the pen Dar's offering when Asha goes still beside me.

Her hand wraps around my wrist. "My name is on it," she says quietly.

Dar's brow furrows, confusion flickering across her features. "Is that a problem?"

I look down at the contract again—really look this time. There it is, my name and Asha's, listed together.

Trigger and Asha Hale, co-owners.

Asha's face has gone carefully blank, that mask she wears when she's about to bolt. I've seen it enough times now to recognize it. Hot and cold, this woman. Fire and ice. And I can't get enough of her particular brand of crazy. But this time, I see something deeper. The way her hand is applying firm pressure around my wrist is a warning. This isn't just about her father not knowing Dar is her aunt, though that's certainly part of it. This is about us. About a contract that will tie her to me long after our one-year arrangement ends.

I cover her hand with mine, feeling her pulse jump against my palm. "Can you excuse us?" I say, keeping my voice even. "We need a minute. We haven't talked about how this affects things when we get home."

It's vague enough. Dar doesn't need to know that Asha still hasn't told her father she not only knows he has a sister, but that his sister is my new business partner. Santiago doesn't need to know our marriage has an expiration date. Nobody needs to know that I've fallen for my fake wife, and she's simultaneously kissing me and running from me in the same breath.

"Of course," Dar says, though her eyes narrow slightly.

Asha's already pushing back from the table, mumbling apologies. I follow her into the hallway, pulling the heavy wooden door closed behind us.

"Asha, what's—"

"I can't sign that," she says, her voice tight. She's staring at a painting on the wall, like it holds the answers to all her problems. "We can tell them I'm not comfortable having my name on the contract because of my father. I'm fine with admitting he and I haven't talked and that he doesn't know Dar and I have found each other."

I step closer, unable to help myself. "Is that what you really want?"

"Trigger, what kind of question is that? This is your merger, not mine. This contract lasts longer than our arrangement, which means—"

"I know what it means," I interrupt her. She finally looks at me, and there's something raw in her dark eyes. "So, I'll ask you again. Do you really want your name removed?"

Her lips part, and for a second, I think she might answer honestly. Might tell me what's really going on in that brilliant, complicated head of hers. But then she shakes her head. "You don't understand. When my father finds out about Dar, about this whole thing, he's going to..." She breaks off. "And now my name is on a contract that makes me your business partner on top of your wife? He's going to lose it. You thought he hated you before; that will be nothing compared to what comes after this."

"I'm not worried about what your father may or may not do. I'm worried about one thing and one thing only." I place my hand on the wall beside her head. "You."

We stand there in the hallway, close enough that I could kiss her again if I wanted to. If she wanted me to. And God help me, I think maybe she does. I think maybe that's what scares her most.

"What are you really afraid of?" I ask softly. "Your father finding out about Dar? Or the fact that, when this year is up, you won't want to walk away?"

Her breath catches. Bullseye.

"Asha, I'll be honest with you; I have no idea what I'm doing here.

You run hot and cold so fast I get whiplash. One minute, you're kissing me like the world's ending, and the next, you're looking at me like I'm a stranger. But I'm drawn to you anyway. All your crazy, all your complications...I can't get enough of it. Of you."

She stares at me, something wild and terrified in her expression. "You don't know what you're saying."

"I know exactly what I'm saying."

"We have a deal," she attempts to make excuses.

"Screw the deal." I cup her face, making her look at me. "I'm not talking about the deal. I'm talking about this. Us. What happens in this hallway when nobody's watching and we don't have to pretend."

"There is no us," she whispers, but her hand comes up to cover mine, holding it against her cheek. Her skin is warm, soft, and I can feel the slight tremble in her fingers. "There can't be."

"Why not?"

"Because," her voice breaks. "Because in one year, this ends. You go your way, and I go mine. That was the agreement. That was safe."

"And the contract in there?" I nod toward the dining room. "That's not safe?"

"No," she admits. "It's not. Because it means we're tied together after. And I don't..." She closes her eyes. "I don't know how to want something I can't keep."

"Who says you can't keep it?"

Her eyes open, locking onto mine, and God, I hate the fear I see in them. That raw vulnerability she tries so hard to hide. It's that hate, that desperate need to erase it, that has me pressing on.

"I can't promise it will be easy," I say, brushing my thumb across her cheek. She leans into the touch almost unconsciously. "I've never done this, never had what I feel for you with anyone else. All I know is I don't want it to go away." Her eyes soften, and that wall she keeps between us cracks just slightly. "I want to try something." My other hand finds her waist, and she doesn't pull away. Doesn't run. My eyes search hers, looking for permission, for any sign I should stop. "Tell me I can."

She nods, barely perceptible, and that's all I need.

I close the distance between us, my hand sliding from her cheek to tangle in her hair. She rises on her toes to meet me halfway, and when our lips connect, it's like something inside me ignites. This isn't like the careful kisses we've shared before, the ones we could blame on the act, on maintaining appearances. This is raw, and honest, and completely us.

She hums softly as her hands slide around my waist, sending delicious tendrils of heat straight to my cock as she pulls me closer. I back her against the wall, my body pressing against hers, and she opens for me, deepening the kiss until I forget where I end and she begins. She tastes like the sweet chutney from the samosas and wine, and I want to drown in it.

Her fingers dig into my hips, and I swallow the gasp that escapes her when my thumbs brush over the bare skin where her shirt has ridden up slightly. Heat radiates between us, and I can feel her heart hammering against my chest, matching the wild rhythm of my own. I want more. Want everything. Want to lift her up, feel her legs wrap around me, find out if she makes those same sounds when... No. I force myself to break away, resting my forehead against hers as we both struggle to breathe. My hands are still on her waist, her fingers still tangled in my hair, neither of us willing to let go completely.

"If you can tell me you felt nothing," I manage, my voice rough, "that that kiss isn't worth the risk, we'll go in there and remove your name."

She's quiet, her chest rising and falling rapidly, her lips swollen and parted. I can see her trying to regain her bearings, trying to rebuild that wall. Her eyes are dazed, unfocused, and I know she felt every second of the passion we just shared. I can still taste her on my lips, still feel the phantom pressure of her body against mine.

But she doesn't comment on the kiss, doesn't acknowledge what just happened between us.

I wouldn't expect anything else from her. This is who Asha is: brilliant, complicated, terrified of vulnerability. She can't just shut that off, can't suddenly become someone who wears her heart on her sleeve just because I kissed her senseless in a hallway. But little by little, she's trying. Little by little, I'm breaking down those walls, and each time I do, they might go back up, but they aren't as tall. I can see it in the way her hand still hovers near her lips, like she can't quite believe what just happened. In the way she hasn't stepped away from me yet, hasn't put the safe distance between us that she usually would. Progress. It's progress.

Instead, in true Asha form, she focuses on the contract. "I have one condition." Her voice is steadier than I expected, though I can still hear the breathlessness underneath. "One condition, and I'll keep my name on that contract."

"Name it, sweetheart." I'm still close enough that I could kiss her again. Part of me wants to. Part of me knows if I do, we won't make it back to that dining room.

"No killing bulls." She swallows, and I watch the wheels turn behind her eyes. "What I saw the other day, with you in that pen..." She trails off, and there's real fear in her eyes now. A different kind. I know what she thought was going to happen, and after she automatically assumed the worst, I didn't correct her. "I never want to see that at home. These are their traditions. I don't want my name tied to that."

"Done." The answer comes easily. I'd agree to anything right now if it means keeping her close, keeping her name next to mine on that contract.

She slips under my arm, breaking our connection, and reaches for the door handle. Her hand trembles slightly as she grips it.

"Oh, and Asha?" I say, my voice low.

She glances back, her hair slightly mussed from my fingers, her lips still red from our kiss.

"It's *our* name."

TRIGGER

CHAPTER 31

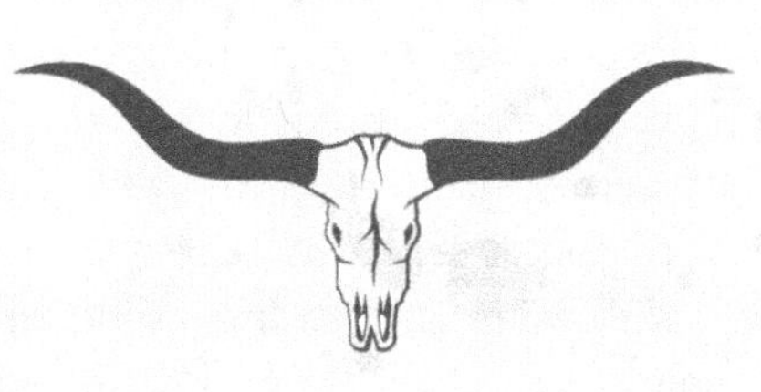

"Yes, just like that, sweetheart," I say as my cock throbs in need of release. It's been too damn long since a hand other than my own has stroked it. Her hands are sliding slowly down my chest.

"Is this what you want?" she whispers against my neck, her breath warm, her body pressed against mine in the darkness of our room.

I can't speak. I can only feel her fingers tracing the lines of my abdomen, her mouth on my jaw, my throat. My hand tangles in her dark-brown locks, her scent wraps around me, and I thrust against her hand.

"Don't stop," I pant. Except, when I squeeze my eyes shut, there's light around the edges, and the pleasure, her touch, her smell, it all starts to ebb. "No," I grind out. "Not again." Not another dream. This can't be a dream. It felt too real.

Then, as if the gods heard my plea, the warmth returns. Soft warm curves envelop me, lips press against the side of my neck, soft and plush. "Fuck yeah," I hiss, returning to the dream I never want to leave. The one where my wife wants me back. The one where she finally lets herself have what she wants. The one where she stops fighting me and gives in.

"Tell me what you need," she murmurs against my skin, and her voice is different—softer, vulnerable in a way she never allows herself to be when we're awake.

"You," I rasp, my hands sliding down her sides, feeling silk and skin. "Just you. Always you."

She shifts, straddling me now, and I can feel the heat of her through the thin fabric between us. My hands grip her hips, and she rocks against me once, twice, drawing a groan from deep in my chest.

"Like this?" she asks, and there's something almost shy in her voice, like she's testing the waters of something forbidden.

"Exactly like that." My fingers dig into her thighs. "You're everything I want."

She leans down, her hair falling around us like a curtain, and finally her mouth finds mine. The kiss is hungry, desperate, all the tension we've been holding onto for weeks spilling out in one devastating moment. She tastes like honey and sin, and I'm drowning in it.

"I want you," she breathes against my lips. "I've wanted you since—"

"Since when?" I need to hear her say it.

Her eyes go dark with want, and her hand slides down between us. Then light starts creeping in again, the warmth beginning to fade.

"No," I grit out, trying to hold onto the dream. "Not yet. Please, not yet."

But the darkness is dissolving, and the last thing I feel is her body pressed against mine, real and solid. *Wait.* My consciousness surfaces slowly as I cling to the remnants of the dream. The warmth, her scent, the feel of her pressed against me. It's all still there. For a blissful, disoriented moment, I think I'm still dreaming. Then cool air hits the wetness that's seeped through my boxers, and my eyes flash open. She's *here*, on my side of the bed, her body curved into mine as the pillow wall lies scattered across the floor like a broken promise.

I go completely still, my mind scrambling to piece together the fragments of the dream with reality. Fuck. It felt real because part of it was real.

I feel the moment her breathing changes, and I know she's awake. For a few agonizing seconds, neither of us moves. Then her fingers flex, freeing her hand from my boxers. She spreads her fingers, evidence of my arousal coating them, as awareness sets in.

Her eyes snap up to mine. "Did you..." Mortification covers her face. "Did I..." She sits up and pulls the covers around her, shielding herself from me like I'm some sort of beast. "Why didn't you stop me?"

The blame in her voice cuts deep. I don't like how she keeps me at a distance, how even after everything last night, the kisses, the admissions, agreeing to keep her name on the contract, and she still put that damn wall of pillows between us when she came to bed. I'd come up late, after drinks with Dar and Santiago, to find her fast asleep on her side of the divide, like nothing had changed. I try to remind myself that she is giving me more than she ever has, but that thought is hanging on by a thread. This push and pull is fucking draining. She's looking at me right now, like I'm a fucking monster who took advantage of her, like I orchestrated this somehow.

"I was asleep," I defend. "Forgive me for not maintaining constant vigilance against my own wife."

"Don't call me that."

"It's what you are," I point out, and I can hear the edge creeping into my tone.

She flinches, and I hate that too. Hate that we're here, in this moment, taking steps backward when we'd finally moved forward.

"How long?" she asks, unable to look at me. "How long were you awake before...before you..."

I'm off the bed, unable to sit still with the accusation she's throwing at me. I pace to the side of the bed, running both hands through my hair, trying to breathe through the frustration building in my chest.

"Jesus, Asha." I turn to face her. "You think I, what? Laid there and let you..." I break off, shaking my head. "I woke up maybe ten seconds before you did. I was dreaming, and our bodies..." I gesture helplessly between us. "We're married. We've been sleeping in the same bed for two weeks, and if you touch me, I'm going to react."

"You should have stopped me the second you realized—"

"I barely realized what was happening before you woke up!" My voice rises, and I have to force myself to stay calm. I don't want to fight. "You crossed to my side of the bed, Asha. You. I didn't pull you over here. I didn't touch you first. I was asleep on my side, where I've stayed every single night, respecting your precious pillow wall."

She looks away, her jaw tight. "I know. I just—"

"Just what? Needed someone to blame?" The words come out harsh. "I'm trying here. I'm trying so damn hard to give you space, to let you set the pace, to be patient while you work through everything. But you can't keep doing this. You can't kiss me like you did last night, agree to tie your-self to me in business, and then treat me like I'm taking something from you every time we get close."

"I'm not."

"You are, and that's fine. You can hate me the way you always have, hate our situation—fuck, hate all of it—but I never agreed to hating you. I never could because I never have." The words hang between us, and her lips part like she might refute it, but no sound comes out. I grab the towel from the chair, my movements sharp. "I'm taking a shower."

I don't wait for her response. I can't. Instead, I let the bathroom door click shut behind me with finality and flip on the cold water before ripping off my boxers. The cold water does absolutely nothing. I brace my hands against the tile, letting the spray beat down on my neck, my shoulders, but all I can feel is the weight of her body against mine. All I can smell is jasmine. All I can hear is her voice from the dream, *I want you.*

"Fuck," I mutter, my forehead pressed against the cool tile.

I switch the water to hot and reach down, because what's the point of pretending anymore? My hand wraps around myself, and I'm already so close it's pathetic. A few strokes and I'll be done, and maybe then I can think clearly. Maybe then I can face her without wanting to...

The bathroom door opens, and my hand freezes.

"Leave," I grind out, but the shower door opens, and she is there in her silk nighty that leaves little to the imagination. But it's not her body that has my chest tightening; it's the look in her eyes, the one that mirrors mine.

"I'm not letting you do this alone," she says, and her voice trembles slightly. "Not when I started it."

"Get out," I rasp, but it comes out weak because it's the last thing I want. But I can't be another one of her mistakes. Not with this.

"No." She steps closer to the shower's edge, and I can see her pulse racing in her throat. "You said you never hated me."

"I meant it."

"Then let me finish what I started." Her eyes drop, taking in my hand still wrapped around myself. "Please."

"You don't know what you're asking."

"Yes, I do." She reaches for the hem of her nightgown. "I'm done pretending I don't want this."

The nightgown hits the floor, and my brain short-circuits. God, I've imagined this so many times, but nothing prepared me for the reality of her standing here, bare and vulnerable. The curve of her waist, the swell of her hips, the way her hair frames her face. She's devastating.

"Last chance," I manage, my voice barely recognizable. "If you come in here, I'm not going to be able to stop."

"Good," she says and steps into the shower.

The water soaks her immediately, plastering her hair to her shoulders, running in rivulets down her body between her full breasts, over the plane of her stomach, following the curve of her thighs. She's close enough to touch now, close enough that I can see the goosebumps rising on her skin despite the steam. Close enough that I can count each breath she takes.

"I didn't cross that pillow wall by accident," she says quietly, and there's something raw in her voice, something honest that makes my chest tight. "I woke up on your side because it's where I want to be, because I'm tired of fighting what I feel."

"What do you feel?" I need to hear her say it. Need the words.

"Like I'm going insane." Her hand reaches out, fingers trailing down my chest, leaving fire in their wake. "Like every night in that bed is torture. Like I married my enemy and somehow fell for him anyway."

I catch her wrist, my thumb pressing against her racing pulse. "You don't fall for people you hate."

"I know." Her eyes meet mine, and they're darker than I've ever seen them, pupils blown wide with want. "That's the problem. I never actually hated you. I just hated how much I wanted you."

Something inside me snaps. I pull her against me, and she gasps as our bodies collide, skin on skin, wet and slick and perfect, nothing between us now. My mouth finds hers, and the kiss is brutal, desperate. Weeks, months, years of pent-up frustration pouring out all at once. She kisses me back just as fiercely, her hands sliding up my shoulders, into my hair, and when her nails drag over my scalp, every nerve ending in my body sparks to life.

I break away to breathe. "Tell me to stop," I say against her lips, giving her one more out.

"You better not."

My hands slides down her sides, over her hips, and over her round ass, where I fill each hand with a heady amount of cheek and squeeze hard. She arches into me with a gasp that I swallow with another kiss. "Tell me what you want."

"Everything," she breathes, her voice breaking on the word. "I want everything. I want..." Her hand wraps around my hard length, and my vision goes white. "I want to feel you come apart. I want to know I'm the one who does this to you."

Then, before my mind can put together a response, she's sinking to her knees on the wet tile.

"Wait..." I start, but her mouth is already on me, and the word dissolves into a groan that echoes off the tile walls. Coming in here was one thing, but getting on her knees for me is another.

"Fuck, sweetheart," I exhale sharply. My hand finds her hair, tangling in the wet strands. She looks up at me through her lashes, water streaming down both of us, her lips stretched around me, and the sight alone nearly destroys me.

She takes me deeper, hollowing her cheeks, and my head falls back against the wall. Her hands grip my thighs, her nails dig in, and my cock twitches, already feral that she's leaving a mark for me. The soft sounds she makes vibrate through me with every stroke, and I'm on the verge of insanity.

"God, yes," I pant, my hand tightening in her hair. "Just like that. You're so—fuck—so good at this."

She hums in response, and the sensation makes my knees almost buckle. I'm getting close, too close, pleasure building at the base of my spine like a coiled spring. My hand tightens in her hair, and I'm fucking her mouth. Tears stream down her cheeks as she chokes on my length, and still she doesn't pull away. She takes it, takes everything I give her.

"I'm going to come," I warn her, and she doubles down, her hands gripping me tighter as her tongue does something that makes stars burst behind my eyelids, and I'm right there, right on the edge, about to fall, and I pull her up by her hair. She comes up with a gasp, her lips swollen and red, her eyes dark with arousal.

"Why?" The word is almost a whine, and seeing her like this, wanting me, frustrated that I stopped her, is almost as devastating as what she was just doing.

"Not here," I rasp, my voice completely wrecked. "Not like this."

"But I want—"

"I know what you want." I capture her mouth, tasting myself on her tongue. "But the first time you make me come..." I pull back to look at her, needing her to see how serious I am. "It's going to be inside you where I can watch you fall apart."

"Then take me to bed."

I don't need to be told twice. I lift her, her legs wrapping instinctively around my waist, and carry her out of the shower. We're both dripping wet, leaving a trail of water across the bathroom floor.

"We're making a mess," she says breathlessly.

"I don't give a damn."

I shoulder through the doorway, and we're back in the bedroom. The morning light filters through the curtains, illuminating the room and the scattered pillows still on the floor where they fell. I lay her down on the mattress, and she looks better than any fantasy I've ever had.

"No more walls," I say, settling between her thighs.

She pulls me down to her. "No more pretending."

"No more running," I add, and she nods.

"I'm done running." Her hand cups my face. "I want this. I want you."

I kiss her deeply, slowly, pouring everything I haven't been able to say into it.

"Then let me worship you properly," I murmur against her lips. "Let me show you what it means to be mine." I kiss her again, deeper, claiming her mouth in a way that leaves no room for doubt. When I pull back, I brush wet hair from her face, studying her. "You're scared."

She doesn't deny it this time. Just holds my gaze, and I can see the vulnerability there, the fear warring with want.

"You're already trying to figure out how to pretend this didn't happen," I say softly, tracing the curve of her jaw. "How to rebuild your walls after." Her eyes flash with something not quite defiance. She opens her mouth to protest then closes it. "Too late, sweetheart." I kiss her throat, feeling her pulse race beneath my lips. "Way too late."

"Arrogant," she breathes, but her hands are sliding up my back, pulling me closer despite her words.

"You knew what I was when you married me." I work my way down, kissing the valley between her breasts. "Knew exactly what you were getting into."

"This wasn't part of the arrangement."

"No. This is so much better." I take a nipple into my mouth, and she arches into me with a sultry moan. "This is real, and it terrifies you." She doesn't respond with words. Instead, her eyes meet mine, and in them I see the admission. This terrifies her, but she's here anyway. "That's my girl," I murmur against her skin, and I feel her shiver.

I work my way down her stomach, pressing kisses to each trembling muscle, and when I settle between her thighs, she doesn't protest. Just watches me with dark, hungry eyes.

"Look how ready you are," I murmur, pressing kisses to her inner thigh. "Your body knows who it belongs to."

She could snap back at me. Instead, she just bites her lip, a tiny, almost imperceptible movement that sends heat straight through me.

I lower my mouth to her, and the first taste nearly undoes me. My tongue traces her slowly at first, learning the shape of her, but my restraint fractures when she gasps my name. I dive deep, my tongue pushing inside her as she arches off the bed. I thought I could go slow, savor this, but I've wanted this too long. She tastes like everything I've been craving.

Her hand finds my hair, fingers threading through and tightening when I find a rhythm that makes her thighs quake. She's not directing, just holding on, anchoring herself as soft, desperate sounds spill from her lips and drive me insane.

She's close already. I can feel it in the way her thighs tremble against my shoulders, the way her breathing becomes shallow and erratic, the way her hips roll, seeking more. But I don't let her fall. Not yet. Every time she gets close, when her body goes taut and her breath catches, I pull back, gentling my touch to featherlight brushes until she's writhing beneath me, her fingers flexing in my hair, wordlessly begging.

Unable to take the sweet torture, she pants, "Please." The word is barely audible, but it's everything.

"Please what, sweetheart?"

She stares at me for a long moment, pride and need battling in her expression. Then something shifts, a conscious choice, a surrender. "Please make me come."

"As you wish," I say before spearing her with my tongue, a reward for her admission. I plunge in deep, and I know she feels the groan that rumbles up from my chest. Her back arches, and I suck her bundle of nerves hard, and she explodes. For seconds, I'm delirious, unsure what's better, the taste of her coming apart on my tongue or hearing my name fall from her lips like a prayer. I lick her through the aftershocks, savoring every drop until she's pushing weakly at my head, oversensitive and trembling.

When I crawl back up her body, her eyes are glazed, unfocused. I catch her chin gently, making her look at me.

"Stay with me," I say softly. "Don't hide from this."

For a moment, I think she'll retreat anyway, but then she cups my face, pulling me down into a kiss that's tender and honest. No walls. No games. Just Asha.

Then, pulling back, she bites my lip. "I'm not hiding. You have a job to finish, husband."

"Fuck, yeah, I do." My tone is pure gravel. She just claimed me and asked for my cock in one sentence. I reach between us, positioning myself at her entrance. "Last chance to change your mind."

Her legs wrap around my waist in answer, pulling me closer until I push inside her slowly, and we both groan at the sensation. She's impossibly tight, impossibly perfect, and for a moment, I can't move, can't think, can't do anything but feel.

"God," I grit out. "You feel—"

She silences me with a kiss, her nails digging into my shoulders. When she pulls back, her eyes are dark with need. "Move," she whispers, not a demand but a plea.

I pull almost all the way out and thrust back in, and she gasps against my mouth. I do it again, finding a rhythm that has her clutching at me, all that careful composure dissolving.

"Look at me," I say, and she does. She holds my gaze even as I drive deeper, harder. "Let me see you," I pant as beads of sweat gather across my shoulder blades.

The sound of her wetness pulling me in echoes around the room like a siren song, and there's no denying she more than wants every second of this. She could close her eyes. Could hide. Instead, she keeps them locked on mine, letting me see every emotion flickering across her face: pleasure, vulnerability, something that looks dangerously close to a four-letter word.

The thought has me widening my legs and changing the angle, with a need to drive in deeper to conquer depths no man ever has, to leave my mark. She cries out, the pinch of pain catching her by surprise, and then her eyes roll back in pure euphoria.

"That's my girl, taking everything I give her like a good little wife."

She's shaking now, her whole body trembling as pleasure builds. Her mouth opens like she wants to say something, but no words come out. Just small, desperate sounds that drive me wild.

"That's it." I watch her face transform. "Let go for me. I'll catch you."

Her eyes search mine, and whatever she sees there...trust, desire, promise...it's enough. She shatters with a cry, and the feel of her pulsing around me drags me over the edge with her. I bury myself deep as I come hard, my face in the crook of her neck as I work to steady my racing heart. When the world finally stops spinning, I collapse beside her, pulling her against my chest. She comes willingly, tucking her head under my chin, her fingers tracing idle patterns on my skin.

"Don't," she says quietly.

"Don't what?"

"Don't make me regret this." Her voice breaks on the last word. "Please don't make me regret finally letting you in."

I tighten my arms around her. "Never, sweetheart."

We lie there in silence, hearts gradually slowing, reality waiting at the edges. I can feel her thinking, processing, but she's not running. Not building walls. She's here, in my arms, choosing to stay.

"The pillows are still on the floor," she says finally, and there's the faintest hint of amusement in her voice.

"So they are."

"If we stay in this bed all day... it still only counts as once, right?"

I know what she's asking. We don't do relationships. We don't sleep with the same person more than once. It's safer that way. Cleaner. Things don't get messy.

But I want messy. I want beautiful, complicated, earth-shattering messy with her. And this will be happening again and again today, tomorrow, every day after, until the day I die, because she is mine. Whether she's ready to fully accept that or not, we are happening. So, I'll give her this fiction. This temporary safety net while she adjusts to the reality of us.

"Yeah," I say, my hand sliding down her spine. "It only counts as once."

She's mine now. Completely, irrevocably mine.

ASHA

CHAPTER 32

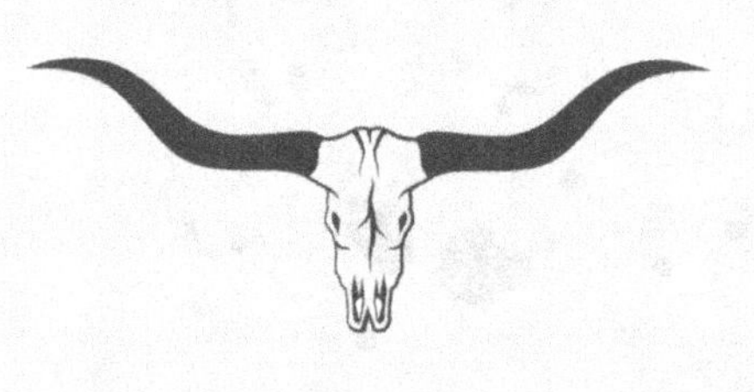

My eyes flick open with sudden alertness. Morning light filters weakly through the heavy curtains, leaving most of the room in darkness. Something woke me. I reach for Trigger, and my arm protests, its own weight almost too much exertion, but it's nothing compared to the weight on my chest when I find his side of the bed cold.

Insecurity and hurt flare inside of me. We spent the entire day in bed, exploring, charting new paths, each of us intent on leaving our mark. Yesterday meant something, and I was certain it meant something to him too, but if that were true, I don't see how he left.

I close my eyes, and that's when another sound registers. The shower is running in the bathroom. That must have been what woke me up. He didn't leave. Relief floods through me, and the way my entire body physically uncoils from the stress of believing he left, even if it was just to tend the animals, tells me there's no going back. I can't be halfway with him. There's no going back. It's all or nothing with us.

I stretch, and my body literally groans, bones popping as I arch my back, when I hear a soft knock at the door. Shit. That's probably Dar.

"Just a sec," I say as I sit up and look around the room for an article of clothing. I'm out of bed, tossing pillows aside to find something to put on, when I spot my robe on the loveseat in the sitting area. I pull it on, tying it loosely, and pad to the door.

One of Dar's maids stands in the hallway, a garment bag draped carefully over her arm.

"Buenos días," she says with a warm smile. "Mrs. Dar asked me to bring this up for Mr. Hale."

I take the bag and automatically note its weight. It's heavy. "What is it?"

"That's Mr. Hale's outfit for the fights today. Mrs. Dar had it specially tailored for him."

My smile freezes. "Oh. Thank you," I say, giving her a curt nod. She disappears down the hallway, and I close the door slowly, my heart starting to pound.

The fights. No. No, I must have misunderstood. Maybe she meant… maybe it's just nice clothes for watching—spectator attire. My mind flicks through all the possible options, but my hands are already shaking with a knowing sense of dread.

Laying the garment bag down carefully, I send up a whispered plea. "Please let me be wrong about this."

I unzip the bag slowly, and the fabric inside catches the morning light streaming through the window. Sequins. Gold and crimson, intricate embroidery along the shoulders and down the sleeves. The unmistakable cut of a bullfighter's jacket, a traje de luces—a suit of lights.

The betrayal pierces my chest. He promised. When I finally agreed to keep my name on that contract, I only had one condition. He looked me square in the eye and promised. *No killing bulls*. He said, "Done," without hesitation, like it was nothing, like it was easy. And I believed him.

The shower is still running. He's in there, completely unaware that I know. Probably planning how to tell me—or maybe he wasn't going to tell me at all. Maybe he was just going to slip into this costume and go do the one thing I asked him not to do. This is exactly why I don't let people in. This is why I keep my walls up, because the moment you trust someone, make yourself vulnerable and believe their promises, they prove you were right to be afraid all along.

I'm biting the side of my thumb, ready to storm into the bathroom and confront him, when something else ignites beneath the heartbreak. Something cold and calculating. Something that feels like the old me, smart and strategic, someone who doesn't just react, but who plans and stays three steps ahead.

I turn from the bathroom door, every move already mapping out in my head. Last night, he uttered the words, '*You knew what I was when you married me.*' Time to remind him who he married. This was his first mistake, and I'll be damn sure it's going to be his only one.

TRIGGER

CHAPTER 33

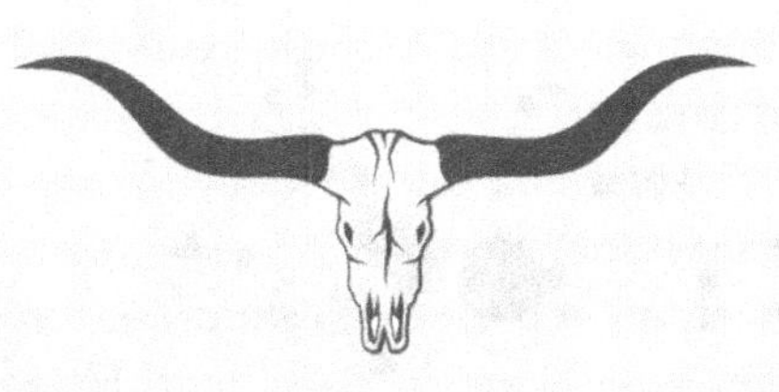

"Have you seen, Asha?" I try to keep my voice steady, even though I'm out of breath and panicked after walking out of the shower this morning to an empty room. When I got in the shower, Asha was still sleeping. When I walked out, all that remained was my unzipped garment bag on the bed I had left her in.

I scan the suite and nothing. She's not here either. I'm half convinced the maid got it wrong when I asked if she'd seen Asha. She told me I'd just missed her and that she requested a ride into Seville. It's the only reason I'm here and not at the airport. She's running.

"The traje de luces suits you well," Dar praises, taking too much time to admire the suit she had tailored for me to wear this weekend.

"Dar, I'm not trying to be rude, but it's important I find my wife," I say, trying to hurry her along.

"Is everything okay?" Her expression morphs to worry.

"Yes," I try to sound less panicked. "I just want to see her before I get out there."

Her eyes look past me and scan an area across the arena. Then she points. "She is with Rohan at the stables under the north entrance."

Shit. That's literally on the other side of the arena. "Thanks," I say before rushing out of the room.

I'm shouldering through the crowd, sweat already soaking through my shirt as bodies press in all around me. There's a bottleneck at the gates

289

when the ring official's voice crackles over the speakers, announcing the start of ceremonies, and my stomach knots. *Damn it.*

I break left, and the roar of the crowd swells just as I reach the tunnel reserved for performers. When I round the corner into the dim passageway, my heart stops completely. Near the front of the tunnel, I see her immediately, and she's not alone. Another man has his arms around her waist, but that's not even the part that has my heart pounding in my ears. It's what she's wearing.

I push through the cluster of banderilleros adjusting their capes, past the picadors checking their lances. Someone curses as I elbow by, but I don't care. None of it matters.

"What the hell do you think you're wearing?" I say, my hands tightly gripping the saddle she just mounted.

She looks down at me, and the dim light of the tunnel does nothing to hide the fire in her eyes. "What am I wearing?" Her eyes drift over my suit. "I could ask you the same thing, but I'd probably just get more lies."

"What are you talking about? I've never lied to you."

"You looked me in the eyes and promised." Her voice cracks, just slightly, but she corrects it with anger. The horse shifts beneath her, sensing the tension.

"So that's what this is." Heat floods my chest. "Once again, you made me an enemy. After everything we shared last night, you still ran."

I can see my words are touching a nerve. She wants to believe them, but then her eyes narrow. "Did you forget what you're wearing? You can tell all the lies you want, but your outfit doesn't."

I shake my head. "I'm not fighting. I made you a promise, and putting on this suit doesn't break it. I'm not going out there as a matador. I'm going out there as a banderillero." I can see the moment she realizes her error. Confusion and then the realization wash over her face, and something twists in my chest, but there's no time to savor being right, because she's still mounted, still wearing white, still recklessly holding the reins.

I spin toward Rohan. "Who put her up there?" I bark. "She needs to get down. Now."

"I'm not getting down, Trigger. I'm riding." Her voice is steel. Stubborn.

"Like hell you are." The words rip out of me.

I turn back to Rohan, blood pounding in my temples. "She can't go out there. Find whoever was supposed to ride this horse."

"It's my horse." He shrugs, maddeningly calm, like this is no big deal. "Your wife can be very persuasive."

"I'm going out," she cuts in. "I grew up riding horses, Trigger."

"Not horses with their eyes and ears bound." I practically spit the words; my hands still locked on the saddle. "You've never trained to take a hit from a half-ton bull."

The tunnel erupts with movement as a door handler appears at the massive wooden gates with one hand raised. *"Diez segundos!"* his voice echoes off the stone.

Ten seconds.

"It's too late," Rohan says quietly, backing up before the gate opens, and everyone rushes out.

The crowd's roar doubles, a wall of sound that reverberates through my bones.

"Asha!" I desperately shout her name, one last plea for her to end this madness, but we're out of time. The gates swing wide, and the crowd's roar becomes a physical force.

The bull charges into the center of the ring, and the arena explodes into controlled chaos. Picadors fan out, adjusting positions. Banderilleros are spreading along the barrier, and the air quickly fills with dust kicked up by hooves and boots. I spin, searching for white among all the movement. Nothing.

My heart is pounding so loud it nearly drowns out the crowd as I watch the bull circling the center of the ring. A group of picadors crosses in front of me, blocking my view of the far side. When they clear, I'm scanning desperately. Then, finally, I spot her near the far curve of the barrier. Her white shirt catches the sun, and I'm able to take a breath, but not for long. She's positioned too close to the bull's line of sight, and my relief instantly transforms to fear.

This isn't how tonight was supposed to go. I had no intention of fighting a bull. An occasional distraction to help a matador, maybe...that was the plan. But the second that gate opened and she took the field, all my plans went to shit. Now, I'll do whatever it takes to keep her safe.

My heart is lodged in my throat as I watch her circle toward the bull. The first picador makes his pass and the bull charges straight toward

Asha, hitting the padding of her horse with a sickening *thud*. Her horse staggers, and she manages to hold on, but she's holding her lance wrong if he comes back around. That's when it occurs to me. *She's going to miss. On purpose. Every single time.*

I get it. She's not here to hurt an animal. Hell, I even bet she justified getting on that horse with no training, believing she could protect it more than Rohan because she cares deeply about its well-being. I know she's here to prove something, but the thing about missing a bull on purpose is you still have to get close enough to make it look real.

The matadors and banderilleros fail to distract the bull. I can't be sure if it's her or the horse; either way, it doesn't matter. The bull is fixated on her, and I see the fear in her eyes the second she realizes he's about to charge. Whatever revenge she was seeking just got very real.

It charges. She holds her position too long, pulling the horse hard right at the last possible second. When she brings her lance down, the tip skates across the bull's shoulder, not enough to wound, but enough to make it wheel back toward her.

"Move!" I'm screaming, already spurring forward. The bull is coming around for another pass, faster this time, and her horse is too close.

I'm driving between them, my cape already unfurling, the magenta fabric snapping in the air. "Toro! Eh, toro!" The bull's head swings toward me, momentarily confused by the new target, but only for a second before it charges me instead.

I pivot, and his horn catches my cape, ripping through the fabric, and the crowd gasps. I look up to find Asha is clear, repositioning near the far side, but her eyes are locked on me. Even through the dust and distance, I recognize the look. It's sharp and unmistakable: fear.

The bull circles back to center, its head swinging to Asha, but I'm already moving, cape out, screaming at the top of my lungs, when he locks onto me instead. Two other picadors make their passes as he surges forward; they hit their mark, but it does nothing to slow his speed.

He comes at me full force. I plant my feet and hold the cape low, every muscle coiled. Time slows, and I can hear her voice, somewhere behind me, shouting my name. Then just as the sound of my own pounding heartbeat silences all the noise, the bull hits my cape like a freight train. I spin with it, and the momentum carries us both before it's past me.

I'm still standing, adrenaline coursing through my veins louder than ever when I find her. She's still mounted, and we're both somehow still alive when the trumpet sounds, signaling the end of the tercio. My legs feel like Jell-O, and I have to use every ounce of strength I have to put one foot in front of the other and get out of the arena.

The gates close behind us, shutting out the sun and the crowd, plunging us back into the relative cool of the darkened tunnel. We make it only a couple of feet before I stop her horse to help her down. Her boots hit the ground, and before I can process what's happening, her hand is fisted in my jacket, pulling me sideways into one of the holding stalls.

The door slams shut behind us, and suddenly, we're in near darkness, the only light streaming in through the thin slats of the weathered wood. My back hits the wall, and she's right there, palms flat against my chest, her face inches from mine.

"That was incredible," she breathes.

"Incredibly *stupid.*" My voice is rough, loaded with stress and worry. "You could have been killed."

"But I wasn't." Her eyes are wild as she works to steady her breathing. "Now I get it. I get why you love it." She steps closer. "It's a total rush. Everything fades away when you're out there. I've never felt more alive."

Her hands slide up my chest, their heat serving as a reminder that she's still here, uninjured and whole. I revel in the reminder, and then her mouth is on mine. The kiss is hungry and desperate, charged with all the chaos coursing through my veins since I walked out of the bathroom and found she had left.

My hands find her waist, pulling her flush against me, and her gasp melts into mine. The relief of having her here, alive, solid, and real in my arms after thinking I might lose her crashes over me like a wave. I pull her closer, my fingers threading through her hair as I tilt her face up to mine, deepening the kiss until I can feel her breath become mine. She makes that sound in the back of her throat, the one that always undoes me, as her fingers start working at the buttons of my vest. And for a few seconds, everything disappears. All is right again.

The fight. The fear. The anger. It's all gone, and there's only her lips on mine, her body pressed against me, her heart racing against my chest, but then reality slams back into me. This is what she does. I catch her wrists and pull back, breathing hard, my lips still tingling from the kiss. She tries to follow, to close the distance again, but I hold her away.

"No." The word comes out sharp, and I see her flinch. "No, I'm not going to keep letting you do this."

"Do what?"

"This." I release her wrists and step back, putting space between us even though every cell in my body is screaming to close the distance. "You pull me in, and then when things get hard, you push me away. We have one perfect night together, and then you wake up and convince yourself I'm the enemy again."

"That's not—"

"It is." My hands are shaking from adrenaline, from fear, from years of this cycle repeating itself. "You keep putting me in the same category as everyone who's hurt you before. Your ex, your father, your so-called friends, anyone who made you a promise and broke it. But I'm not them."

She opens her mouth to argue then closes it. Her eyes are bright with unshed tears.

"I have never lied to you," I continue, my voice cracking. "Not once. I told you I wouldn't fight as a matador, and I kept that promise. I put on this suit, and you immediately assumed the worst. You didn't ask. You didn't give me a chance to explain. You just decided I was like all the rest."

"I know." Her voice is small. "I know, and I'm sorry."

"Sorry isn't enough anymore." The words taste bitter. "I need you to trust me—actually trust me. Not this version where you trust me until you get scared and then run."

She moves toward me, reaching up to touch my face. "Please, I'm sorry. I was wrong. I..." She rises on her toes, trying to kiss me, but I catch her shoulders, stopping her just before our lips meet.

"I can't." The confession comes out broken. "I love you too much. It was never fake for me, Asha, not for one second. I never had any intention of letting you go, but I'm starting to think I have to. You'll survive losing me, but I won't survive you."

"You love me?" she whispers, as if she's unsure she truly heard those words.

"Watching you out there nearly killed me." I pull her closer, making her look at me, ensuring she hears every word. "I love you so much it terrifies me."

"Trigger..." her voice breaks, tears spilling over.

I step back, needing space to get this next part out, my shoulders hitting the rough wood of the stall wall. "But I can't keep doing this. I thought I could. I thought I could pretend until you finally realized what I've always felt in the depths of my soul...that we were inevitable." I drag my hand through my hair and tug hard. "I thought I could survive off your sharp tongue, knowing your words meant you felt something for me. I thought it would be enough, but after what happened out there..."

The words die in my throat, because watching that bull charge her all but stopped my heart. The memory rushes back, the massive black body closing the distance, her in white, the whole world narrowing to that single moment of terror. She takes a step toward me, but I hold up a hand, needing to finish.

"You were reckless, and I drove you to that. If you got hurt to prove a point, to get back at me for some petty rivalry that we can't seem to outrun..." my voice cracks. "I couldn't live with myself if things turned out differently today. But I can let you go. I'll suffer through a life without you if it means you'll have a tomorrow."

"It's not fake." She swallows hard and slowly brings my hand to rest over her heart, palm flat against her chest where it's still racing. "When I touch you, when I kiss you...it's never once been fake."

"Then what is it?"

"It's the only time I'm not scared." A tear spills down her cheek, cutting a clean line through the dust. "You're as close to real as I've ever felt. When I'm with you like that, I can forget that I don't know how to do this."

"Do what?"

"This." She gestures between us helplessly. "Let someone love me and be brave enough to tell them I love them back."

"No," I shake my head. "Don't you dare tell me you love me. A stronger man can swallow that lie, but I'm not him."

"It's not a lie." She steps even closer, and now we're almost chest to chest, her breath mixing with mine in the dusty air. "I've loved you since the day I told you I hoped you hated strawberries."

I bark out a laugh that's more pain than humor. "That's a hell of a way to show love."

"When you showed up at Ridgewood, I didn't hate you because my father told me to." She pauses when I quirk a brow, not buying it. "Okay, maybe a little, but that piece wasn't as big as the other piece." Her hand comes up to my face, and her fingers trace my jaw. "You were a living, breathing piece of home, and memories of my mother were tied up in you. I never hated you. I only ever wanted to because you made me feel, and that scared me. If I didn't have you, I couldn't lose you."

The confession breaks something open in my chest. "So you kept me at arm's length."

"I tried to." Her thumb brushes across my lower lip, and I can't stop the sharp intake of breath. "But you wouldn't stay away. You kept pushing. Kept showing up. Kept making me feel things I didn't want to feel."

"I couldn't stay away." My voice is barely above a whisper. "Even when I should have. Even when you hated me. Even when loving you felt like the stupidest thing I could do."

"You love me?" she asks again, like she still can't quite believe it, like hearing it the first time wasn't enough.

"Yes." I turn my head, pressing a kiss to her palm. "God help me, yes. I love you. I've loved you for so long I can't remember what it feels like not to."

Her hands slide around my neck, and she's pulling me down, rising on her toes, and this time when our lips meet, I don't pull away. She tastes like salt and dust and coming home. Her hands are everywhere in my hair, on my shoulders, sliding down my chest to work at the buttons of my vest, and I don't stop her. I need her more than I need air.

"This doesn't fix everything," I murmur against her mouth, even as my fingers find the hem of her shirt. "I'm still furious about that stunt you just pulled."

"Furious, huh?"

She's pulling at my shirt now, untucking it, and a low groan escapes my throat when I feel her hands on my heated flesh. She bites my lip hard, and I'm sure it draws blood.

"Yeah." I walk her backward until her back hits the opposite wall.

"Then why don't you stop talking and make me feel it?" she challenges.

"Sweetheart, you have no idea what you're asking for." I kiss her hard, our tongues hungrily battling to prove to each other that we're all in. That this is real. "Turn around."

She hesitates for just a second, and I see the flash of vulnerability beneath her boldness, before she relents. Turning, she faces the wall, her palms pressed flat against the rough wood.

I step in close behind her, and my lips are at her ear when I ask, "You want to know how angry you made me?"

"Yes." Her voice is barely a whisper now.

My hands slide around to the front of her riding pants, my fingers working the button. "Then I'm going to show you." I ease the fabric down slowly over her hips and down her thighs until it pools around her ankles. Her breathing changes, and she can't hide the way her body trembles with anticipation. She's unsure of what she just asked for, but her obedience tells me she wants whatever I have to give.

I place one hand on the small of her back, steadying her, before I unleash my anger.

"This is for thinking I lied to you." My other hand comes down sharp against her ass, and the sound echoes in the small space.

She gasps then moans, her fingers curling against the wood.

"This is for making me the enemy." Another slap, harder this time, and her whole body arches.

"Trigger." My name comes out broken.

"This is for running." The third lands in the same spot, and I watch the way her muscles tense and release, the way she pushes back into it instead of pulling away.

My girl would love getting spanked.

"This is for being reckless." The fourth makes her cry out, a sound somewhere between pain and pleasure. "For getting on that horse and almost getting yourself killed."

"I'm sorry." She's trembling harder now, and I can feel the heat radiating from her skin.

I lean in close, my lips brushing her ear. "And this last one..." My hand comes down a fifth time, harder than all the others. "This is for making me wait so long to have you. Not just the pieces. All of you."

Her body is still trembling from that final slap, and I lean in close, my chest pressed against her back, my lips at her ear. "Still think I'm holding back?"

"No." Her voice is wrecked, breathless. "God, no."

I can feel the heat radiating from her skin, see the marks blooming where my hand connected. My hands slide up her sides, and I can feel every shiver, every tremor coursing through her. "You wanted to feel how angry you made me?"

"Yes." She presses back against me, and the friction makes us both groan.

"Then keep your hands on that wall." The sound of my belt buckle is loud in the enclosed space. "Don't move them."

I free myself, one hand gripping her hip to hold her steady. With the other, I run my tip through her wetness in one slow, teasing stroke. She's soaked, and the knowledge of what I do to her nearly breaks my control.

"God, you're so wet for me," I breathe against her ear.

"Trigger, please—"

Before she can finish, I slam into her in one brutal thrust, burying myself to the hilt. The breath leaves her lungs in a rush, and we both let out guttural moans that echo off the wooden walls. I hold there, deep as I can go, feeling her pulse around me, both of us trembling with the intensity of it.

"Fuck," I groan, my forehead dropping to rest between her shoulder blades. "You're mine."

A desperate moan is her only response, her hips rolling back against me, seeking movement.

"Patience," I grit out, though I'm barely holding on myself. I pull back slowly, catching her wetness coating my cock on one of the streams that's casting light into our stall, and my cock jerks. I'm not going to last. My girl just told me she loved me and then asked me to punish her, which is something I didn't even know I needed. Smacking her ass unlocked something inside of me. It healed a part of me I didn't know was broken. I thrust in hard again, bottoming out, slow and steady three more times, wanting to draw this out, the thrill of getting caught, the adrenaline rush of almost losing her, and our surrender. It's fucking everything.

My hands grip her hips, and I set a rhythm that has her gasping and the stall walls rattling as she steadies herself to take each punishing stroke. It's utterly intoxicating, and I'm pretty sure a few shadows have lingered outside the stall. Let them listen. She's mine, and I want the world to know it. My hand slides from her hip around to her front, finding that spot that makes her whole body arch.

Her nails scrape against the wood as a broken cry escapes her lips.

"Don't ever stop," she manages to gasp out between moans.

"Not a chance." I pick up the pace, each thrust harder than the last, letting her feel every ounce of frustration and fear and desperate love I've been holding back. "You're mine. Say it."

"Y-yours." The word comes out broken between pants.

"Again."

"Yours." Louder this time, dissolving into a moan. "Always—"

The angle, the words, the way she's falling apart in my arms...it's too much. My rhythm falters, becomes more desperate, more demanding.

"I love you," I growl against her neck, my teeth scraping over her skin. "So goddamn much."

She moans in response, her voice breaking as I hit that spot deep inside that makes her whole body tighten before she comes apart with a cry that I'm sure they can hear halfway to the arena. The way she pulsates around me pulls me over the edge, and I bury my face against her shoulder, muffling my own groan as I follow her into a perfect, blinding release.

For a long moment, we just stay like that, her pressed against the wall, me pressed against her, both of us breathing hard, hearts racing in sync. Then carefully, I pull out and turn her around.

I cup her face. "You okay?"

She nods, still catching her breath, and manages a soft, satisfied smile, no walls or defenses. Just her. She rises unsteady on her toes to kiss me, slow and sweet this time, pouring everything she can't say into the press of her lips.

"No more running," I murmur against her mouth.

She shakes her head then whispers, "No more running. I'm ready to go home."

Outside, the crowd roars to life as another fight begins, but in here, in the small space, I can finally say we've stopped fighting each other. Now, I just have to make damn sure going home doesn't change that.

TRIGGER

CHAPTER 34

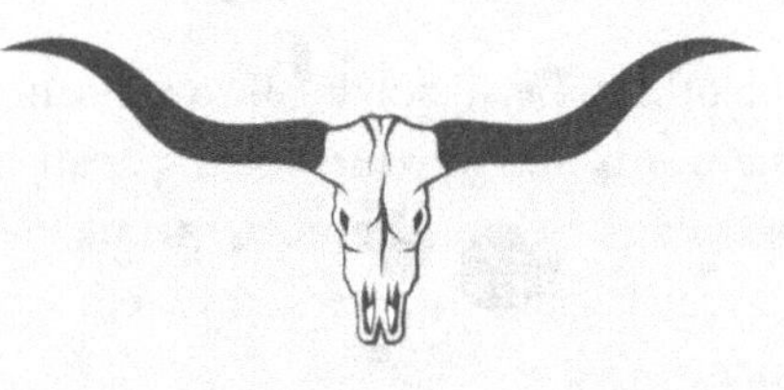

"So, a ring tat?" London says, eyeing my left hand. "For the girl who threw a milkshake on you your first day of freshman year." He takes a long drink, eyes fixed on my hand.

Hollis nearly spits his beer back into the bottle. "Strawberry, right?" He's leaning over the table now, shoulders shaking with laughter. "All down the front of his shirt in front of the team?"

Someone cheers at the game playing on the screen behind us, but my brothers don't even glance over.

"She hated you," Hollis tacks on, shaking his head, still smiling at the memory.

"Nothing says 'soulmate' like someone who knows exactly how to ruin your day." London's voice drips with mock sincerity.

I rest my tattooed hand flat on the table between us. "All that energy was just foreplay." I flash them my cockiest grin. "I like to take my time."

"Dude, she's my cousin." Hollis straightens, his face sobering.

"In all seriousness, married life looks good on you." London's glass clinks against mine, the sound bright and celebratory despite the tension coiling in my shoulders.

We've been so busy since we got home from Spain that Asha and I have been working nonstop, between finding a place to stay and preparing for our first bull delivery. Luckily, London has stepped in—in a big way—with the horses. Right now, breeding Thoroughbreds is still paying the bills.

"I think he looks constipated," Hollis chimes in, though he's not looking at me; he's looking at Sydney.

I pulled him from the girls' table ten minutes ago, and he's obviously butthurt about it. Asha needed time with her friends. The three of them haven't got together since we got back, and I know exactly what kind of interrogation is happening right now. They want every detail: when, how, and *why the hell* weren't they looped in before our surprise nuptials. I'm ninety-nine percent certain I even caught Sydney asking about my performance in bed. I've already made a mental note to ask Asha later what she whispered, because Sydney squealed, and Laney gasped.

"He's not constipated." London swirls his drink. "He's waiting to see what hand his new father-in-law is going to play tonight."

Sydney's voice cuts through our speculation as the girls drift over from their cocktail table, with three empty glasses. "What makes you think he's playing games?"

"How is he not? He won't let Asha on the property unless she is there to speak to him. He blocked off our access to the road, forcing us to excavate a new one, and then demanded Asha attend tonight to keep up appearances."

"You forgot the part about how he shut off the electricity to the back sixty," Asha offers up bitterly. "I'm not asking for a handout. He's just making everything difficult. I'm his only daughter. It could have been a conversation."

"But you refuse to see him, so how could it be?" Sydney's tone is careful, but the implication still slaps.

"Whose side are you on, Sydney?" Asha scowls. "My father may have extended an invite, but it hasn't included Trigger. He still thinks this is a game. If he really wanted to talk, he would include my husband."

Sydney's shoulders drop. "I'm not trying to upset you." She straightens. "I'm going to get another drink."

"I'll go with you." Hollis is already moving, following her toward the bar.

Laney seizes the moment, shaking her empty glass at London with a sweetness that doesn't quite hide her exhaustion. "London, I want another Ranch Water, but my feet are killing me. I'm going to call and check in on Grace."

He leans down and presses a kiss to her forehead. "One Ranch Water coming up."

I step behind Asha, wrapping my arms around her waist, and she melts back against me. I can feel the rapid flutter of her heartbeat through the thin fabric of her dress, and it instantly soothes me. "You good, sweetheart?"

She exhales slowly. "I don't know. I'm just flustered. I feel like we shouldn't have come here tonight."

"Are you saying you're not going to try to sneak into the house tonight?"

One of the reasons she accepted the invitation tonight was that she knew Warrick would be distracted, and she wanted to sneak into her room to grab a few things. The other reason was hoping that showing up would get him to back off and stop making things difficult for us.

"Sydney said she would go with me and create a distraction if my dad happened to come inside while I was there, but I can tell she had reservations about it, so I didn't bring it back up. She's been acting strange for a few months now. Ever since she went back to school to get a master's degree, she's been different. At first, I thought it was just the stress of going back. This time, she's up there alone since Laney and I are done with school, but now I don't know... In some ways, it feels like we are drifting apart."

My heart rate kicks up a notch as I try to swallow my own theories—ones that don't do anyone any good. Around us, the party continues, but it all feels distant, like we're caught in our own pocket of tension.

"We don't have to stay," I murmur against her hair. "I already told you I'm not worried about your father. We can leave right now."

"No." She shakes her head, determination settling into her voice even as her fingers tremble against my forearm. "We're both here. What Sydney said pissed me off because some part of me knows she's right, even if it's only partially. You can't fix your problems by avoiding them. I need to talk to my dad."

She turns in my arms, rising up on her toes. Her lips brush mine. "But another drink would do wonders for my nerves."

"Whatever you want," I promise, meaning it down to my bones.

Then I catch her chin, tilting her face up to mine. "But it's going to cost you first."

I cover her mouth with mine, and everything else falls away. She kisses me back like she's drowning and I'm air. Like every word Sydney said, every game her father's playing, every doubt creeping into her mind... none of it matters as long as we have this. As long as we have each other.

When I finally pull back, we're both breathing hard. Her eyes are glassy, and there's a vulnerability in her expression that guts me. But there's something else too—a fierceness, a determination that wasn't there before.

"I love you," she whispers.

My thumb traces over her bottom lip. "I love you too." I nod toward the bar. "I'll be right back."

When I reach the bar, I step up next to London, who's still waiting for his drinks, one hand drumming against the bar top. I use this moment alone to ask the question that's been burning in my chest all night.

"Do you remember coming to this party last year?"

His eyes narrow, head tilting slightly before the corners of his mouth curl up. "How could I forget?"

I can't contain the grin that takes over my face at the memory. I know exactly what he's remembering.

"I'm not talking about you crawling under the table to win back Laney..." I pause, biting my lip as heat creeps up my neck. "Actually, I am."

His eyes narrow to slits.

"I know you were a little occupied," I continue, leaning one elbow on the bar, "but do you remember the conversation I was having with her while you were down there..." I draw off as another guest slides up on my left.

"You're going to need to be a little more specific." He shifts his weight, crossing his arms. "You were doing a bang-up job of sabotaging me that night."

Cheers erupt behind us as one of Fairfield's horses comes on the screen. I wait for them to drop before leaning in.

"The part about Sydney," I say, lowering my voice. "What I said about her disappearing act. How she and Warrick seem to vanish at the same time."

He visibly pulls in a deep breath, shoulders tensing. The topic is clearly touchy for him too. His wife has been friends with Sydney even longer than Asha. When he exhales, it's slow and measured. "I've noticed things, yes." He rubs the back of his neck. "But I don't know if I notice them because they're actually there, or because you pointed it out and now I can't unsee it."

"What the hell does that even mean?"

"It means I haven't witnessed anything firsthand." He spreads his hands. "I haven't seen anything with my own eyes, but I notice things. Little things." He pauses, glancing toward the yard where laughter spills from the sitting area. "After you and Asha eloped at my reception and then took off, there were two other guests who disappeared right after. Initially, I thought maybe Syd went with you, but when Warrick didn't come back inside either..."

He lets the sentence hang in the humid night air, leaving me to fill in the blanks.

"Has Laney ever mentioned anything?"

"We talked about it last year after you inferred something was going on." He frustratedly shakes his head. "To my knowledge, Laney hasn't flat-out asked her, and I don't think she will."

The bartender returns and slides two glasses across the bar. London picks them up, condensation already dripping down the sides, and turns to face me fully.

"Look..." His tone is serious. "I've known Sydney my whole life. Her brother is my best friend. She's loyal as fuck, and the people she loves, she loves hard. Asha is one of those people." His eyes lock on mine, unflinching. "The last thing she would ever do is hurt her."

"That doesn't answer my question." My voice comes out firmer than I intended.

"Doesn't it?" His gaze holds mine, intense, almost challenging me to read between the lines. The string lights flicker above us, casting shadows across his face. "Being with Warrick would hurt Asha," he finally says. Then he nods toward the table, where I can see Laney's silhouette against the patio lights. "Laney's waiting for her drink."

As I watch him walk away, I hear the words he didn't say loud and clear: *What Asha doesn't know can't hurt her.*

London doesn't have the answers any more than I do. But he never flat-out denied it's a possibility, and that silence speaks volumes. I've left it alone and kept my now-wife in the dark about my suspicions for over a year, but keeping it to myself even if I don't have proof feels like a betrayal.

Silence isn't love. Secrets are just the truth waiting for their moment to surface.

Maybe Warrick's secrets aren't as dark as Asha believes. Perhaps this war has nothing to do with control or manipulation at all. People do fucked-up things in the name of love, things that look like deception from the outside but feel like survival from within. If I'm right, it's possible Warrick has kept Asha busy, deflected her questions, danced around the truth, not because he wanted to deceive her, but because he didn't want to lie. Because once you say it out loud, there's no taking it back.

How the hell is he supposed to tell his daughter he's sleeping with her best friend?

"What can I get you?" The bartender sets a napkin in front of me, professional smile in place.

"Whiskey neat and an Aperol Spritz."

He nods, already reaching for the bottles.

"There you are."

The voice comes from directly beside me, too close, too familiar, and my entire body goes rigid. I turn, and she's right there, invading my space like she has every right to it. Blonde hair and big blue eyes are locked on mine with an intensity that makes the hair on the back of my neck stand up.

Cassidy Miller. She's a local. Her father owns a tack shop in town, so our paths have crossed many times, and she's never been shy about her interest in being more than just acquaintances.

"I've been looking *everywhere* for you, Trigger Hale." Her smile doesn't reach her eyes. "We need to talk."

"What about exactly?" I ask, unsure where all this is going.

"Bourbon Trail, five months ago...you ran into me in the parking lot..." My brow furrows as I try to recall spending any amount of time with her outside of the occasional run-in at the tack shop. That's when my eyes drop involuntarily, and slight panic starts to set in.

She's pregnant. Visibly, unmistakably pregnant, maybe five-six months along, and the fitted dress she's wearing does nothing to hide the swell of her belly. My brain scrambles to make sense of what I'm seeing, timelines, and her words. *What the hell is happening?*

"Are you trying to tell me..." The words die on my tongue. I can't even get them out. How is this even possible? My hand covers my mouth. If I don't say the words, they can't be true.

"Yeah." She rubs her belly. "I know it seems far along, like I should have told you sooner, but honestly, I wasn't sure how you'd react, and I knew I was keeping my baby no matter what."

"I'm sorry," I say, my voice barely above a whisper. "I need..."

My feet carry me of their own accord. I wind through tables, past clusters of people whose conversations blur into white noise. I don't stop until I reach the fence line at the edge of the property, where the mani-cured lawn gives way to pasture. My hands grip the top rail, knuckles going white.

I can't breathe. My chest is tight, constricted like someone's tied a rope around my ribs. The horizon tilts, and I feel like I might actually pass out.

Five months ago. The Bourbon Trail. I was there. We were all there. I got shit-faced because Asha was thoroughly icing me out, and then I proceeded to flirt with the bartender. I don't remember seeing Cassidy; my focus was on Asha all night until I couldn't take it anymore and left the bar. The problem is, while I don't remember leaving with Cassidy, I have a fuzzy image of a blonde with a familiar voice in my truck. *Fuck.*

TRIGGER

CHAPTER 35

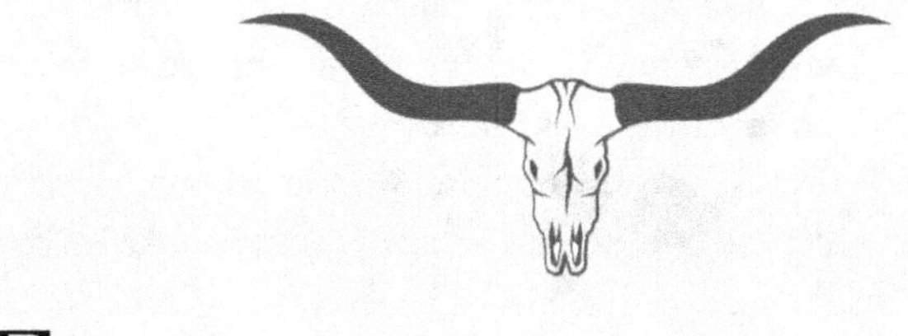

"Trigger." Her voice behind me makes my shoulders tense. She followed me. Of course she followed me.

"I need you to leave," I manage, still gripping the fence. "I need... I need to think."

"I know." Cassidy's footsteps stop a few feet away, giving me space but not leaving. "I know this is a lot. I'm sorry. I shouldn't have ambushed you like this. I just... I didn't know how else to tell you."

My hands slip from the fence, and I turn to face her fully. When I do, the evening light catches the tears gathering in her eyes.

"I didn't come here to ruin your life," Cassidy continues, her voice wavering. "I came because you deserve to know. Because he deserves a chance to know his father, even if his father doesn't want anything to do with him."

"That's not..." I start, but what can I even say? I don't know what I want. I don't know anything right now except that my entire world was just turned upside down.

"I just wanted you to know." She takes a shaky breath, wiping at her eyes with the back of her hand. "It's your choice if you want to be part of his life or not, but to make that choice, you have to know he exists."

I hear the sharp intake of breath before I see her. Asha.

She's standing ten feet away, frozen in place like she's been struck. In her hands are two drinks, the whiskey and Aperol Spritz I'd ordered what feels like a lifetime ago. Her face has gone pale, her eyes wide and glassy.

She heard. She heard everything.

"Asha—" I start toward her, but she takes a step back.

"Don't." The single word stops me cold. Her voice is barely above a whisper, but it cuts deeper than any scream.

"I'll leave you two alone," Cassidy says, turning on her heel.

"Asha, let me explain—"

"Explain what?" her voice rises. "Explain that you have a child? That you—" She can't finish, and I watch as the realization crashes over her.

"I didn't know," I say desperately, moving toward her again. "Asha, I swear to God, I didn't know until two minutes ago—"

"But you *did* it." Tears spill over, tracking mascara down her cheeks. "You slept with her." She looks in the direction Cassidy walked. "By the looks of it, maybe five or six months ago." Her eyes swing back to mine. "Is she the reason you carried that ring in your pocket? Am I wearing her ring?"

"What?" The word comes out strangled. "Why would you ask me that? That ring was always meant for you."

"Don't fucking lie to me," she says sharply before tossing the drinks in a bush.

"I'm not." My hands reach for her, but she flinches back. "I told you the ring belonged to my grandmother. That wasn't a lie. I started carrying it in my pocket a week after I found that lease."

She shakes her head, her bottom lip trembling, and something inside my chest actually *breaks*. I can't watch her fall apart like this.

"You expect me to believe you carried a ring around for almost a year on the off chance I might propose."

"Sweetheart, that ring was going to make it on your finger by the time the lease expired, whether you asked me or not. It was only ever yours."

"If that were true and I was the only person in your heart, you wouldn't have slept with her," she says, right before she takes off.

"Asha, wait!" I lunge after her, but she's already sprinting. "Asha, let me explain! I didn't know."

She rounds the corner and runs smack into London.

"Hey, hey..." He grabs her shoulders, steadying her before she can fall. "What's going on?"

"Let me go." She tries to twist free, but he holds firm.

Laney appears at his side, her eyes cutting to me like knives. "What did you do?"

"He knocked up another woman," Asha says with an empty tone that cuts deep.

"*What?*" London and Laney ask in unison, their faces mirrors of shock.

"When?" Laney's hand flies to her throat. "How... how is this even *possible?*"

"It doesn't matter." Asha wrenches herself from London's grip.

I start talking before she can walk away. She may not want to hear it. I know it's not an excuse, but I need her to know I didn't consciously choose someone else over her.

"It was the night we all went to Red Door, to celebrate London and Laney coming home from Texas as a couple. You hated that I was there and proceeded to flirt with the bartender all night." My throat tightens. "I don't remember talking to Cassidy. I was completely wasted—"

"That doesn't make it any better." Her eyes blaze.

"Wait, wait, wait." London holds up both hands, his jaw working as he processes. "Cassidy is telling you that was the night? That specific night?"

"Yes," I rasp out.

London and Laney exchange a loaded look.

"Then, unless you banged her in the bathroom," London says slowly, "that baby isn't yours."

My head spins. "I didn't fuck her in any bathroom, but I can't be sure what happened after I left the bar. I woke up in my truck the next morning, and I have this vague, blurry memory of a blonde in my passenger seat."

"That was me." Laney's voice cuts through the chaos in my brain.

London bites his lip hard, and she swats his arm.

"I'd rather have him know the truth than watch them destroy each other over a lie." Her eyes lock onto mine. "London followed you outside to take your keys so you wouldn't drive drunk. He put you in the backseat and came inside to get me. We got in the truck with you and considered driving you home, but then..." She smooths her hands down her dress, color rising in her cheeks. "We had other plans."

"Other plans?" Asha's voice drips with skepticism. "There's still unaccounted time where he was alone."

"We didn't leave," she answers. "We had other plans." She emphasizes each word through clenched teeth.

The pieces slam together, her words, the blurry blonde, that foggy memory. "You two fucked in my truck while I was passed out in the backseat."

London actually laughs, and Laney's face goes crimson.

"In my front seat." I force a laugh that sounds broken even to my own ears. "That's messed up, man. You owe me a detail." The attempt at humor falls flat because, inside, I'm still drowning in the whiplash of almost-fatherhood as I bend over and grab my knees that are threatening to give out.

"I'd say we're even. I just saved your ass," London tosses back. "You have an alibi for that entire night. We passed out and left when the sun came up. You came strolling into the house about twenty minutes after us. I'm pretty sure when we slammed the truck door, you woke up and drove home."

I pull in one last breath, filling my lungs to calm my racing heart, but when I look up, I see my girl. Asha's arms are wrapped around her middle like she's physically holding herself together. Her eyes shine with unshed tears, and I hate that I somehow put them there. Hate that I allowed myself to be in a situation where a mistake could have happened.

"Sweetheart." The nickname leaves my lips on a whisper. "Come here." I close the space between us in two strides. "I'm sorry," I murmur into her hair, pressing my lips to the crown of her head. My hands shake as they settle on her back.

"You have nothing to be sorry for." Her voice muffles against my chest. "I'm the one who—"

"Who needed a minute to breathe after her world just got rocked." I cut her off because I know she's about to apologize for running, and she has nothing to apologize for. That news didn't just shake her. It brought her to her knees the same way it did me.

"Wait a second." Laney's voice cuts through our moment. "Why would Cassidy falsely accuse Trigger if she knew damn well he wasn't the father?"

The question sits heavy in the silence, unanswered and damning.

Asha goes rigid in my arms. Then she pulls back, her jaw set in that way I know means trouble.

"I know who." Her voice is cold, deadly calm.

"What?" Laney leans forward.

"My father." Asha's hands curl into fists at her sides. "He's been trying to break us up since we got back. This is exactly the kind of thing he'd orchestrate."

"Asha." I reach for her, but she's already moving.

"No." She holds up a hand, her eyes blazing with a fury I've never seen before. "No, I'm done letting him control my life."

She turns on her heel and stalks back toward the party, her stride purposeful.

"Shit." London exhales. "This is about to get ugly."

We follow her up the hill, past the pristine white fencing that cuts across the manicured lawn of the estate. There's a crowd gathered near the massive outdoor screen, everyone watching the races in tailored suits and cocktail dresses, but still Asha doesn't slow, doesn't hesitate, even though whatever words she's about to deliver are going to be in front of an audience.

She cuts straight through the crowd like a woman on a warpath, and that's when I see him. Standing by the bar with a whiskey in hand, laughing with a group of men in expensive suits, is Warrick Fairfield.

"Dad," Asha's voice cuts across the space.

He turns, his smile not quite reaching his eyes. "Asha, I was wondering when you'd come over to say hi." His gaze flicks to me over her shoulder before sliding back to her. "Enjoying yourself?"

"Did you pay Cassidy to lie about Trigger being the father of her baby?" The words detonate across the patio.

Warrick's expression doesn't change, but I notice the way his hand tightens around his glass. She hit a nerve. "I don't know what you're talking about."

"Yes, you do." Asha takes a step closer. Her voice shakes, but she doesn't back down. "You've been trying to sabotage my relationship from day one. The electricity, the road, blocking me from entering my mother's home, the invites for one, as if your words weren't enough. I know you hate Trigger, but this...paying someone to claim he's the father of her baby. That's a new low."

"That's a serious accusation." His voice drops dangerously low. "You might want to reconsider making it in front of all these people."

"Is it an accusation if it's true?"

A muscle ticks in his jaw. "You're being hysterical."

"I'm being *honest*." Her voice rises. "Something you clearly know nothing about."

He drains his whiskey in one swallow and sets the glass down with a sharp *crack* against the bar. "This conversation is over."

"No, it's not—"

"I said it's over." His eyes cut to mine, cold and calculating, before sliding back to Asha. "You think you can stand here and accuse me? In my home? In front of my guests?" His voice drops to something lethal. "You're walking a very dangerous line, Asha."

"Dangerous?" her voice shakes, but she holds her ground. "Are you sure that's the word you want to use?"

Something flashes in his eyes—surprise, maybe, or the first crack in his control. His jaw tightens. "Watch it," he warns.

"You're not even going to deny it," Asha's voice fractures.

"I don't owe you an explanation for how I protect my family." His tone is ice.

"Protect?" Asha shakes her head. "You tried to destroy the man I love because you can't control me anymore. That's not protection. That's manipulation."

"You're making a scene."

"Good." Her voice doesn't waver. "Let them see exactly who you are."

"I've given you everything. Every opportunity. Every advantage. And this is how you repay me? All these years, I thought I was raising a daughter who understood respect, who valued what she had. Instead, I raised an ungrateful child."

I snap and step between them. "You don't get to speak to her that way."

Warrick's eyes cut to me. "Excuse me?"

"She's my wife," I cut in, my voice dangerously low when I add, "And you and I are going to have a real problem if you keep disrespecting her."

For a long moment, he just stares at me. The small crowd around us has gone silent. Then his mouth curves into something that might be a smile on anyone else, but on him it's a threat.

"Your wife." The words come out flat. He looks at Asha, and for just a second, something raw flashes across his face. "She's my daughter. My only family. We were all each other had." Then his expression hardens again. "And that husband title? It means nothing. You're not her partner. You're her revenge. A means to an end. Remember that when this all falls apart."

He turns on his heel and walks toward the house, his stride measured and controlled despite the fury rolling off him in waves. The crowd around us parts, and no one dares to meet his eyes. As I watch him go, my jaw is clenched so tight my teeth ache. A man like Warrick doesn't lose control without purpose. He plans. He orchestrates. Which means he saw this confrontation coming. Every word was calculated, designed to burrow into our heads and fester. Plant doubt. Drive wedges. Break us apart from the inside.

But why?

There has to be more to this feud than my father's letting on. Warrick is too smart to waste this much energy on pride alone. He knows my father's hands are tied when it comes to our land. So what's really driving this? What does he think he'll gain by destroying his own daughter's happiness?

Unless breaking us apart isn't the goal and we're just collateral damage in whatever game he's really playing.

Movement catches my eye near the house, and a shadowy figure steps from the porch as Warrick approaches. They exchange words before Warrick disappears inside, but not before a gust of wind reveals the shadowy figure is wearing a dress. I scan the party for answers, and sure enough, I find Hollis sitting across the yard, beer in hand, but Sydney is no longer at his side. Shit.

I pinch the bridge of my nose, hating the shit hand Warrick is dealing my wife and feeling helpless to stop it. I don't want to be at war with her father; I don't want her to choose a side. I just want her to be happy, and I don't understand why he doesn't want the same thing.

Laney's voice breaks through my thoughts. "You okay?" she asks Asha.

"No." Asha's voice is small. Broken. "But I will be."

The words gut me. I move to her side, and this time, when my arms come around her, she doesn't pull away. She collapses into me, her face buried against my chest, and I feel the moment she stops holding it together. Her shoulders shake with silent sobs.

"I've got you," I murmur into her hair. "I've got you, sweetheart."

Around us, the party starts to resume, but I can feel the weight of their stares, their whispers. Let them look. Let them talk. All that matters is the woman in my arms and the fact that her father just confirmed everything without saying a goddamn word.

ASHA

CHAPTER 36

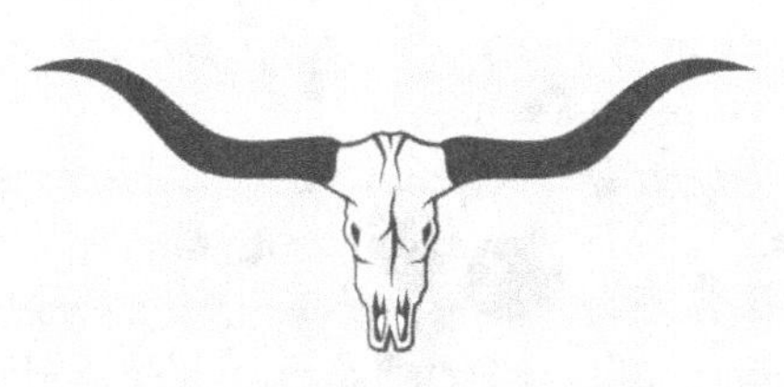

I'm quietly pulling down a coffee cup after getting out of the shower, trying not to wake Trigger or Hollis, when hands glide around my waist, and I instinctively jump.

"I'm sorry," Trigger mumbles against my neck. "I didn't mean to scare you, but I'm getting tired of my wife sneaking out of our bed every morning." His lips connect with my skin, sending delicious shivers down my spine. "If I knew having Hollis staying with us was going to mean I stopped getting to take care of my wife in the morning, I would have arranged a hotel for him."

"That has nothing to do with it," I say as his hand slips inside my robe, where he lazily drags his thumb over my nipple.

"No?" he questions before squeezing it between his fingers, simultaneously making my teeth sink into my lip and my thighs clench.

I wrap my hands around my coffee mug to ground myself. "I've just had a lot on my mind since the watch party, the future of the merger, my dad, what Cassidy claimed about the baby." My throat tightens around each word. "It's been a lot to wrap my head around."

The mug clinks as Trigger sets it on the counter and spins me around, his hands firm on my shoulders, giving me no choice but to meet his eyes. "You're still thinking about her accusation?" His gaze searches mine with an urgency that makes my stomach knot. I get sick thinking about that night. "Does that mean you don't believe me?"

"No." I press my palm against his chest. "I believe you. I just..." I swallow hard. "I don't like how it made me feel. I don't like the thoughts I had, and I hate not knowing if my father truly had anything to do with setting this up."

The memory of that trip into town plays on repeat in my mind. We'd gone to Cassidy's father's store the day after, demanding answers about why she'd tell such a vicious lie. But when we'd asked where Cassidy was, her father shrugged and said she'd left for Florida late the night before and didn't know when she'd be back. The timing wasn't lost on me. Her accusation, followed by a convenient disappearance, reeked of a paid setup of my father's manipulation.

"Talk to me." Trigger's voice pulls me back. He brushes a strand of hair behind my ear. "Tell me what's really bothering you."

"I was so upset, the betrayal that seeped into my veins..." I pinch my lips, hating the memory of how I felt like my whole world was collapsing. "Trigg, I haven't been with anyone since I came back to Bardstown almost a year ago. Sure, I flirted, but that was intentional. I knew doing it would draw a reaction out of you, so I did." I twist the belt of my robe between my fingers. "But I could never have taken it further than that. You were the only person I wanted."

His hands slide around my waist, and he pulls me flush against him. "I've felt that way about you since high school," he says, his voice rough with emotion. "No one was ever going to measure up. There was no point in even trying. They were never going to be you."

His lips cover mine in a kiss so sweet and delicate it steals my breath and makes my knees weak. Every secret I've just handed him, every truth I've laid bare, and he's answered by confirming that none of what I felt was in my head. Every charged moment between us was real. Every look, every touch, every word...all of it real.

His kiss heals wounds I thought were destined to destroy me as he backs me against the island, his tongue demanding more as his hands glide into my hair. But I need to finish this. I need to purge the ugliest parts of myself before we can move forward. I pull back, breathless.

"Sweetheart," he growls against my lips, "I want to do a lot more than kiss my wife right now."

"There's something else." My voice comes out weaker because what I'm about to say is shameful. It makes my heart look ugly and petty, and I absolutely despise this about myself. But I need to get it out. "I didn't want you to have a baby with her."

"I know," he says gently, like he fully understands the depth of my statement, but he doesn't. He couldn't.

"No." I shake my head and step back, running my fingers through my hair and tugging at the roots. "You don't get it. I was so *mad*, Trigg. Jealous, possessive, manic, you name it, and in that moment, I felt it. Pure rage." My hands are shaking now. "This deep-seated hate for a girl I don't even know. Logically, I know that you having a baby with someone else didn't have to mean we were over, but if I'm honest?" I force myself to look at him. "I don't know that I could have stood there..." My words come out broken because I don't want a future without him, and yet, these terrible thoughts consume me. "How could I watch you be a father to a baby that wasn't—"

"Stop," he cuts me off, pressing his finger over my lips.

"It was so selfish—"

"Shhh," he silences me again. "I would have done the right thing. If that boy had been mine, then he was mine. Period." He lowers his hand but steps closer, eliminating the space I'd created. "But if you think the thought of having a child with anyone but you doesn't make me physically ill, you're wrong." His voice drops, becoming almost reverent. "It's why I chased you for so long. Why I carried my grandmother's ring in my pocket for a year, just waiting for the right moment." He cups my face in both hands. "I couldn't stand the thought of you having a life with someone else that should have been mine all along. Don't beat yourself up for wanting all my firsts, for wanting my forever, because it's been here all along, patiently waiting for you to take it."

"Trigger, I love you." The words are barely out of my mouth before he silences them with a kiss that tastes like forgiveness and promises and home.

His hands slide down to my hips, then lower, pulling me harder against his hardening length. I gasp into his mouth, wanting everything I feel, but I swat at his chest. "Trigg, stop. Hollis is right around the corner in his room."

"Don't care," he murmurs against my lips, walking me backward toward the small island.

"I'm serious!" I laugh breathlessly, trying to push him away even as my fingers curl into his shirt. "If my cousin walks in here and sees us—"

"Then he'll turn around." Trigger grins wickedly, capturing my mouth again.

Somehow, I find the strength to pull my lips away from his, even though I want everything he's offering, and I turn, giving him my back so he stops this maddening pursuit. "We have to get ready. We have a long day ahead, and the crew will be here soon to shoot."

"It can wait. My wife is stressed, and it's my job to take care of her," he says, his lips finding purchase on the back of my neck as he pushes my hair aside.

"We can't," I try again, even as I tilt my head, granting him more access.

His fingers gently drag over the backs of my thighs, leaving a decadent trail of goosebumps before both hands squeeze my ass hard.

"You're not going to win this one, sweetheart." He nips my earlobe before adding, "I'm in my kitchen, with my wife, and I'm hungry." The words vibrate through me as his fingers slip beneath the hem of my robe, finding me bare. "No panties." The smack that lands against my bare cheek echoes through the downstairs, and I gasp before biting my lip to stay quiet.

"I was coming right back upstairs to get dressed," I feebly attempt to argue.

"You should never come down here dressed like this with guests in the house." His middle finger glides through my folds with agonizing slowness, and every muscle in my body clenches. He teases me, the tip of his finger dipping inside, though not nearly enough, before withdrawing completely. "Now I have to teach you a lesson."

The loss of contact makes me whimper, but the sound dies in my throat when both palms come down hard on my cheeks with a crack that reverberates through the quiet room. I brace myself against the island, the unexpected sting catching me off guard. Then he's pulling me open, and I can't hold back my groan when his tongue traces between my cheeks.

His mouth is everywhere, claiming, tasting, owning. Sure, we've done this before, but his mouth has never been there. The intimacy, coupled with the fact that we could get caught any second, has me feeling utterly exposed. For long seconds, I can't do anything but feel him take what he wants. It's filthy, intoxicating, and empowering all at once. I just brought a man to his knees because he can't get enough of me. He loves me so much that there's not a crevice on my body he doesn't want to claim, and to be loved like that is hypnotizing.

His tongue spears me deep, and I drop my head into my hands, stars already dancing behind my eyelids when—

"Good morning."

My head flies up, and there, standing between the living room and kitchen, is Hollis. Behind the island, Trigger goes completely still, his breath hot between my thighs.

"Are you okay?" Hollis asks, concern creasing his brow.

I know my face must be crimson. I can feel the heat in my cheeks.

"Yeah, why?" My voice comes out strained.

"Your face is red. You look flushed."

"Oh." I clear my throat, gripping the counter edge. "The shower was a little too hot, is all. I should have eaten fir—"

My words cut off in a strangled sound as Trigger resumes his task, his tongue running slow and deliberate through my folds like he's not hidden between my thighs behind our ridiculously small island while my cousin makes small talk.

Hollis's eyebrows raise. "Should we get you a snack?"

"No!" The word comes out high-pitched and desperate as he takes a step toward the pantry, which would bring him around the counter. "I'll be fine. Just need a minute to cool down..." My voice trails off as Trigger does something he's never done before, his tongue dragging with torturous slowness from front to back, intimately exploring places no one has ever touched.

I dig my nails into the wooden countertop.

Hollis's brow furrows, and then he glances at the coffee pot. "I'm just going to grab a cup of coffee." He takes another step, and he's too close to discovering exactly what's going on.

"Here!" I thrust my empty mug at him too eagerly. "Use this one. I need to empty the dishwasher."

He takes the mug and studies my face. "Okay..."

The moment he turns toward the coffee maker, I reach behind me and swat blindly at Trigger's head, trying to push him away. Instead, he captures my clit between his lips and sucks hard. My knuckles turn white as I grip the island, and I have to disguise the moan rising in my throat as a cough.

"You sure you're alright?" Hollis glances back over his shoulder.

"Fine," I squeak then force my voice lower. "Totally fine."

Behind me, Trigger's tongue flicks mercilessly, and I feel him smile against me. *The smug asshole is enjoying this.*

Hollis checks his watch as he pours his coffee. "The film crew is still coming at 9 a.m., correct?"

"Yeah." I nod vigorously, only to freeze as Trigger slides two fingers inside me while his tongue continues its work. My vision blurs, and my whole body trembles, barely able to stay upright. "Nine o'clock. Sharp."

"And we're filming—" Hollis starts to turn fully toward me.

"Outside!" I practically shout, leaning farther over the island to block his view, praying he can't see my white knuckles or the trembling in my arms. "We're filming outside. Not the kitchen. Definitely not the kitchen."

"Right..." Hollis drags out slowly, giving me an odd look. "I was going to say the main barn."

"Yeah, obviously," I agree, rolling my lips as Trigger's fingers curl inside me, hitting that spot that makes my knees threaten to buckle. My toes curl so hard they almost cramp, and I know my breathing is too erratic when I add, "The main barn."

"Are you sure you don't need to sit down?" Hollis takes a step closer, concern etched across his face.

"No!" I hold up a hand to stop him, my voice strangled. "I mean, I'm good standing. Really good with standing."

His phone buzzes loudly in his hand. "It's my mom." He's already heading toward the front door. "I need to take this. We'll go over the shoot schedule when I get back."

"Take your time!" I call after him. "Really long call! No rush!"

He shoots me another puzzled look over his shoulder before stepping outside, the door clicking shut behind him.

The second it does, Trigger's low laugh rumbles against my most sensitive flesh, and I nearly come apart from the vibration alone.

"It's not funny," I gasp, my fingers tangling in his hair.

"You're right." He pulls back just enough to speak, his breath hot against my clit. "It's hot as fuck eating my wife's pussy while she tries to hold a conversation." His tongue drags slowly through my folds before he grips my hips and pulls me harder against his mouth. "Watching you struggle not to scream my name."

My knees buckle, and I brace myself fully on the counter as he flips up the back of my robe, exposing me completely. Cool air hits my heated skin for only a second before his mouth returns with renewed hunger. His thumb presses against my puckered hole, and my entire body jolts, a strangled sound escaping my throat.

"You like that, baby?" His voice is muffled as his tongue works relentlessly against my pussy.

I can't form words. Can only whimper and grind shamelessly against his face, chasing the pressure building inside me like a storm about to break.

The tip of his thumb breaches that tight ring of muscle, just barely, just enough, and I detonate. The orgasm crashes through me so hard my vision whites out. I clamp my hand over my mouth to muffle the scream as waves of pleasure tear through every nerve ending, leaving me boneless and completely wrecked.

Trigger doesn't let up, his tongue still working me through every aftershock until I'm trembling so violently I can barely stand. When he finally emerges from beneath my robe, his lips are glistening, and his eyes are dark with possession.

"You're so damn beautiful." His voice is rough as he rises to his feet, fingers already working the belt of my robe. It slides off my shoulders and pools at my feet, leaving me naked and on display with morning light streaming through various windows.

Before I can catch my breath, he sweeps me up and carries me the few steps to the dining table, laying me across the smooth wooden surface like an offering.

"Hollis is right outside," I breathe, even as my legs fall open for him.

"You want me to stop?" He's already freed himself, his thick length heavy in his hand as he runs the tip through my folds, coating himself in my wetness. His thick head catches at my entrance, and my hips lift involuntarily. "Say the words, and I'll stop."

When I don't, because I can't, he slides in with one long, deliberate thrust, and we both groan at the exquisite fullness.

"That's what I thought," he growls.

His jaw goes slack as he pulls out torturously slow, his length glistening with evidence of my arousal. Then he slams back in hard enough to make my breasts bounce, and the table shifts beneath me.

"Yes!" the moan tears from my throat, loud and reckless.

"That's right, sweetheart." His grip on my hips tightens as he sets a devastating rhythm. "Let him know my wife wasn't flushed from a hot shower, but because her husband was between her legs, making her come."

Something about knowing someone could be listening, could walk in and see me spread out and desperate, amplifies every sensation. I clench hard around him, and his eyes darken further.

"You've been keeping secrets from me, Wife." He punctuates the word with a particularly brutal thrust that makes me cry out. His hands grip my ankles, bringing them up to rest on his shoulders. "First, the holding stalls in Spain, now our kitchen table." Another deep stroke that hits something devastatingly deep inside me. "You like an audience, don't you? Good thing I like the world knowing you're mine."

He sets a punishing pace, each thrust driving the table farther across the floor. The obscene sounds of skin on skin, of my wetness and desperate moans, nearly drown out the scrape of table legs dragging across the stone floor.

Then he slows, almost stops, and I whimper at the loss of friction.

"Look at you." His hands release my ankles, letting my legs fall to wrap around his waist as he leans over me, one hand possessively sliding up my ribcage. "Spread out on our table like a fucking feast." His thumb brushes the underside of my breast, and I arch into the touch. "These perfect tits bouncing every time I thrust into you."

He cups both breasts, his thumbs circling my nipples until they're painfully hard. "I could stare at you all day, sweetheart. Watch the way your body takes me, the way your pussy grips my cock like you were made for me."

"Trigger, please," I gasp, rolling my hips, trying to get him to move faster.

"Please, what?" He pinches one nipple, and I cry out. "Tell me what you need."

"More. I need more."

His grin is wicked as he lowers his head, his tongue circling one peaked nipple before he draws it into his mouth and sucks hard. The sensation shoots straight to my pussy, and I clench around him.

"Fuck, I love when you do that." He releases that breast with a wet pop before moving to the other, his teeth grazing the sensitive bud. "Love the way these pretty nipples get so hard for me." He sucks harder, and my back bows off the table.

His hips start moving again, slow and deep, while his mouth continues its assault on my breasts. One hand slides down my stomach, his fingers splaying across my lower belly. "Love watching myself disappear inside you. Watching this tight little pussy stretch around my cock."

"Oh God," I moan, my hands fisting in his hair, holding him to my breast.

He releases my nipple and straightens, his eyes hungrily raking over me.

"You're a work of art, you know that?" His hand trails back up, fingers ghosting over every curve, every dip. "These hips I hold onto when I fuck you from behind." His palm cups my breast again. "These perfect breasts that fit in my hands." His thumb traces my jaw. "This mouth that screams my name when you come." He punctuates each observation with a deep thrust that makes my eyes roll back. "And this pussy..." He pulls almost all the way out before slamming back in. "This sweet, perfect pussy that's mine. Only mine."

"Only yours," I gasp, my nails digging into his forearms.

"That's it, sweetheart. Fill this house. Fill this house with those intoxicating moans so everyone knows you're taken."

His mouth captures mine in a bruising kiss as his pace becomes relentless. I can taste myself on his lips, and somehow that makes everything hotter, filthier.

"Trigger," I gasp against his mouth, my body starting to shake. "I can't — I'm going to—"

"Then come," he commands, his fingers pressing harder against my clit, his hips driving into me with perfect precision. "Come on my cock and let the world hear what I do to you."

I shatter with a scream I don't even try to muffle, my body convulsing around him.

"Fuck, yes," he groans, his rhythm faltering as he follows me over the edge, spilling inside me with a guttural sound that makes me clench around him again.

For long moments, we stay like that. A tangled, breathless mess of limbs. Then, his forehead drops to rest against mine, and a satisfied smile plays at his lips.

"Now," he finally says, pressing a soft kiss to my mouth before slowly pulling out, "you can get dressed."

I let out a breathless laugh, my legs still trembling as I sit up. "Now I'm going to be late."

His grin turns absolutely wicked as he tucks himself back into his boxers. "And it was worth it."

I slide off the table on unsteady legs, acutely aware of the evidence of him sliding down my thighs. "You're impossible."

"You love it." He hands me my robe, his eyes still dark and hungry as they trace over my naked body one more time.

"I do," I admit, slipping the robe back on. "Even when you make me late."

From outside, I hear Hollis's voice wrapping up his phone call.

Trigger catches my wrist and pulls me in for one more kiss. "Go," he murmurs against my lips, "before he comes back in and sees my cum dripping down your thighs. That's for my eyes only."

My cheeks flush hot as I dart toward the stairs, his low chuckle following me all the way up.

ASHA

CHAPTER 37

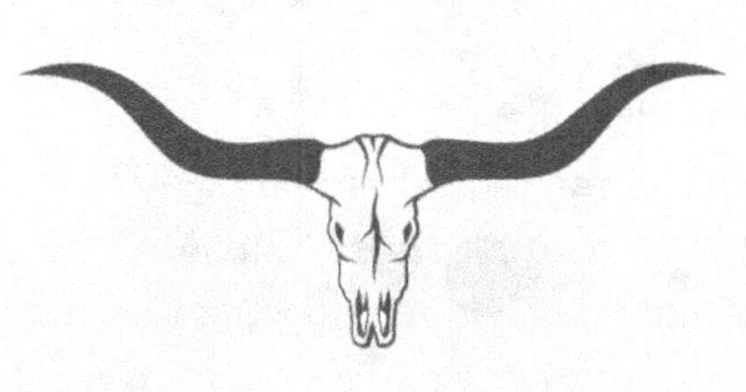

"You're alive," Hollis says when I step outside, dressed and ready for a day full of finding the perfect shot for our website.

The morning sun is already brutal, and Hollis is standing by the barn entrance, barefoot, an empty coffee mug dangling from one hand.

"Why wouldn't I be?"

"All that screaming..." He gestures inside with his mug. "I genuinely thought someone was dying."

My face ignites. "Do shut up."

"'Oh god, yes'—'right there'—'don't stop,'" he mimics in a high-pitched voice, grinning like an asshole. "Very convincing death throes."

"I hate you."

"Oh, now you're shy." He sets his mug on the windowsill, clearly enjoying himself. "Didn't seem shy twenty minutes ago when I was trying to drink my coffee in peace."

"Are we really having this conversation? You want to give me a play-by-play of my sex life?"

"Not a play-by-play. Just wanted to return the awkwardness." He gestures at his bare feet. I didn't realize he wasn't wearing shoes when he grabbed his coffee. "Standing out here like some kind of creeper, waiting for the main event to wrap up." He runs a hand through his hair. "Not how I saw my morning starting."

A laugh escapes before I can stop it.

He grins wider. "For sanitary purposes, is it the kitchen table or the makeshift island I need to avoid touching later? Because I heard furniture moving."

"We're newlyweds... If you're worried about surfaces, you might want to avoid all of them."

"Seriously." He drags a hand down his face. "I'm bringing someone home tonight. Just to traumatize you right back."

"You are not bringing some floozy back to my house."

"You're right, I'm not." He leans against the barn door. "But Sydney and I are going out tonight, so...fair's fair."

I freeze. "Sydney? Like a date?"

"Yeah." His expression shifts. "That a problem?"

Is it? Dating one of my best friends shouldn't be a problem. But I hate the thought of anything coming between us when—not if—things don't work out. And Sydney's idea of long-term is making it to a second date.

"Just be careful," I finally say.

"Is there something I should know about Sydney? Does she have some crazy, stalker ex?"

His question goes unanswered as we both turn toward the truck racing down the road my father blocked off.

"Is that your dad?" he questions, eyes wide, as a car kicks up dust coming down the gravel road that he blocked off.

"Yep," I say as we both cross the driveway to meet him.

He slams his door and pulls a large sign out of his backseat before marching toward us. "Asha, what the hell is this?"

"It's a sign."

"Don't be smart with me."

"Fine. It's a sign advertising our new partnership," I add, closing the distance between us and snatching it out of his hand. "One you had no right to remove since it wasn't on your property."

"Do you think this is a joke?" my father questions, fury raging through every feature.

"You're going to need to be a little more specific. My marriage, our new business venture—"

"Arora Heritage," he vehemently cuts me off. "You went behind my back, married a Hale, and now this. You had no right."

"No right? Do you hear yourself? Your family is my family too. Just because you cut them out of your life doesn't mean I need to do the same."

"You have no idea what you're talking about. No idea why I kept you away from them."

"You're right, because you refuse to let me in. Maybe you don't want family, but I do. I always have."

"I'm your family," he grinds out.

"Only when it's convenient for you." The words taste bitter, but they've never felt more true. "Only when I do exactly what you want."

His jaw works. "This ends now. You're acting like a child throwing a tantrum. You want to talk? Fine. Come home, and we'll talk."

"I tried talking." My voice rises. "I tried for years, and instead of letting me in, you buried me in work. Kept me so busy I wouldn't ask questions."

"Asha." He steps closer, and I can see he looks tired. "I am your father. I've provided for you, protected you, your entire life. Everything I've done—"

"Has been behind a wall. You won't let me in. You won't tell me anything real."

"You have no idea what you're talking about," he says, his hands falling to his hips.

"Then tell me!" I shout as tears threaten to steal my strength. I don't want to fight with him. I just want my dad. "That's all I've ever wanted. Just tell me. Tell me something that isn't a deflection, or an excuse, or another closed door." My hands are shaking. I clench them into fists. "I'm your daughter. I deserve to know you. Not just the version of you that shows up with instructions and expectations. The real you."

His face hardens. "Some things are better left in the past."

"For who? You? Because keeping me in the dark hasn't protected me. It's just made me feel like I don't matter enough to trust."

"That's not..." He stops, looks away. "It's not that simple."

"It could be." My voice cracks. "It could be if you'd just let it."

Gravel crunches as the marketing team's vehicles pull up behind us. My father's eyes flick toward the vehicles, and he visibly pulls in a deep breath.

"Get in the truck, Asha. I'm not doing this here."

"We're not doing it anywhere. That's the problem." I take a step back. "Every time I get close to something real with you, you shut down. Change the subject. Send me on another errand."

His jaw sets as his eyes flick back to the cars. He pulls himself up straighter, tension locking every muscle in his body. I've seen my father face down business rivals, navigate crises, and handle impossible situations, but I've never seen him look uncomfortable. Not like this.

"Hey, are you guys ready?" Sydney walks up to us and stands beside Hollis, completely unaware of the hot mess she just stumbled upon.

"I didn't know you were coming for this." Hollis grins as she wraps her arm through his.

"I wasn't, but I saw the van pulled over on the side of the road and noticed the signs were missing." She shrugs. "So I figured I'd show them to the barn."

I turn to glare at my father, whose eyes aren't on me but Sydney and Hollis.

"Stop sabotaging my life because you don't like my choices. You need to leave. I have work to do, and you're not welcome here."

"Asha, that's a little harsh," Sydney says, her tone less gentle than it has been.

"No, it's perfectly fitting. I'm done waiting for him to trust me. Done being shut out of his life while he tries to control mine."

"This has never been about control," my father tries again to get me to see it his way.

"It doesn't matter anymore. You want to keep your secrets? Go ahead, keep every one of them. This is my home now."

My father opens his mouth then closes it again. For once, he has nothing to say. *Good.*

I turn away from him and head back toward the van. Each step feels heavier than the last, but I keep moving. I hear Sydney say something to him in hushed tones, but I'm already too far away to make out the words. The crunch of gravel follows me across the empty driveway to where the van sits waiting, and I've never felt so alone.

Just how he wants it.

TRIGGER

CHAPTER 38

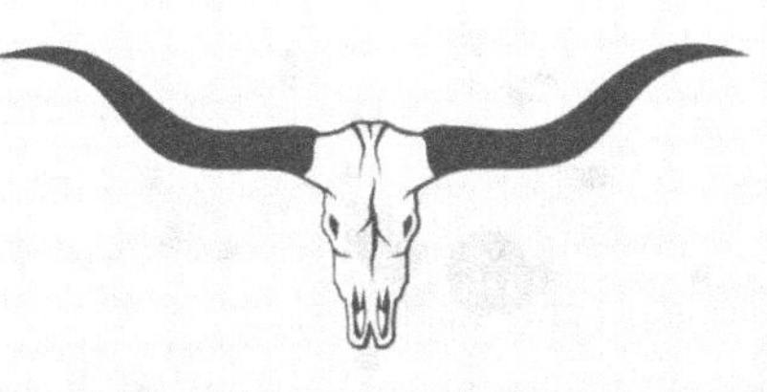

A door slamming followed by my father's raised voice, saying, "I didn't say you could come in," has my hands pausing on the manila folders I was rifling through in pursuit of property lines.

Who the hell has him all riled up now?

"We need to talk, and if I wait for an invite, I'll be six feet underground." Warrick's voice is tight.

I could announce myself, but doing so would be counterproductive to the other reason I stopped by today: find out what my father knows about the Fairfields. When I arrived, he was in the stables with Fisher and London, going over records for the next auction in Lexington, so I stopped in the house first.

"Well, get on with it, then. I ain't got all day," my father says, already exhausted by his presence alone.

"You need to help end this marriage," Warrick demands.

"That ain't gonna happen, so if that's all you came here for—"

"Was it you?" Warrick cuts him off, his footsteps suddenly sharp against the hardwood. "Did you send the Miller girl to my party?"

I press my back against the wall. Wait a second. If Warrick is asking my dad about Cassidy, that must mean he didn't put her up to that lie. Which also means Asha jumped to a very wrong conclusion, one that only puts more distance between her and Warrick. *But if it wasn't him, who? And why would he think my father would do something like that?*

"If you continue to push me, you're not going to like it when I push back. Maybe I can't touch your land, but I have other ways of bringing men to their knees," Warrick threatens.

I take three steps toward the door, my fists clenching, ready to give him a piece of my own mind. He doesn't get to keep fucking over the people I love. But my father's response stops me cold.

"I thought you were here to talk, not sling empty threats. Maya's probably rollin' over in her grave watchin' what's become of—"

"Keep my wife's name out of your mouth," Warrick's voice explodes across the room.

Heavy footfalls echo off the floors as he starts pacing.

"I knew it was you," Warrick continues. "You're trying to take Sydney, just like you tried to take Maya, but this time the gloves are off. Maya's not here to defend you and change my mind."

Take Maya? My stomach drops. Is that what all this hate is about? My father and Warrick loved the same woman?

Something slaps onto a surface—papers, maybe—and my father asks, "What the hell is that?"

"You started this war," Warrick grinds out. "First, by meeting with my wife and trying to get her to change her mind. Then you sent your son to Ridgewood, knowing it was where we sent our daughter to keep her safe —safe from you. And now this..." his voice drops lower. "You let him find that lease, you let him plant the seeds in her head, just like you did Maya. You hate that women don't willing choose you first. Trigger's mother despised you so much that she went as far as to hide an entire pregnancy from you and then put your son up for adoption just to keep him away from you. And then, Maya chose me, a man with colored skin, no money or title...a bastard. You can't—"

"Enough!" my father shouts, and I even startle. My father rarely raises his voice. Even when he's livid, his words will sting, but he delivers them evenly. "You have no idea how wrong you are. I'm not in the habit of telling my business, because it's mine. You have no right to it, but maybe I'll accomplish something your wife never could, and perhaps you'll hear it for the truth that it is." I hear him shift, and I imagine him facing Warrick head-on. "Trigger's mother was a young teen mom who made a mistake. Her mistake cost me missing out on the first five years of my son's life, but you should thank her for making it, because if I didn't know what it felt like to miss out on his life, I wouldn't be entertaining this conversation now."

"Please, do spare me your sob story." Warrick's words are clipped, dismissive. "I don't give a damn."

"And that right there is why you're losin' your daughter." My father's voice sharpens like a blade. "This ain't got nothin' to do with you and me, and you know it. You've kept too much from her, and now it's catchin' up with you."

He's hit the nail on the head. That's exactly why Asha has pulled away. She's tired of being lied to. The question is, what lies is Warrick keeping?

"I'm only here to warn you." Warrick's footsteps move closer to the door and closer to the wall concealing me. "That folder is just the beginning. Keep coming after me, Hale, and I'll make certain you regret it. One more stunt like the other night and all bets are off."

My father laughs. He actually fucking laughs, and I couldn't be more confused and prouder at the same time. He might be riled up, but he's not scared of Warrick Fairfield. Fear comes from a lack of knowledge and understanding, which tells me something else: I was right about my assumptions at the party. My father knows what makes Warrick tick.

"The Miller girl was your doin', not mine, but I guess I'll take the blame for that too. I can live with that. My table will be full tonight with my son, my brother, their wives. I'll sleep just fine." He pauses, letting the words land. "You, however, will be in a cold bed, alone with your fear."

"Don't pretend to know me." Warrick's voice is defensive now. "This has nothing to do with fear or how I choose to warm my bed."

There's silence, and I can't help but wonder if it's because my father is sizing him up, choosing which battle to fight next. The tension between the two of them, the words they're sharing now...at the center of it all is Maya.

"It's got everythin' to do with fear," my father says quietly, dangerously. "Don't forget, I know things too. Not only do I know where the bones are buried, I know the stories they tell."

Fucking hell. If I didn't know better, it sounds like my father just gave credit to Asha's dark suspicions about her father surrounding Maya's death.

"I reckon we're done here. I don't know what's in that folder. You can come after me, bankrupt me all you want, but we both know you'll lose more than just Asha in the process."

My brain is in overload, trying to fill in the missing pieces and read between all the things my father isn't saying. *Who else would Warrick lose besides Asha?* He has to be referring to Sydney. There's no one else. If Warrick takes down our operation, Fisher and Sydney lose business too. Hale Ranch has had a shared partnership with the Downs family for decades. They own the tracks. We breed the horses that will eventually race on them. Sure, we aren't the only breeders out there, but our families have history. However, history aside, if he takes us down, he hurts Sydney in the process.

"We'll see," Warrick says before heavy footfalls strike the wood floor, and the front door opens and closes with an echoing click.

I know where the bones are buried.

What the hell have I just stumbled into?

For a long moment, there's nothing but silence. Then I hear my father exhale a long, heavy breath. Now, probably isn't the best time to ask twenty questions, but the way I see it, there never will be.

"What was that about?" I ask, stepping out of the office, and I find him standing in the middle of the living room, staring down at what I now know is an envelope.

"Just your new father-in-law stoppin' by with well wishes," he says, his tone dripping with sarcasm as he works to open the envelope Warrick dropped on the table.

"Don't lie to me. Warrick does enough of that. I heard what you guys were talking about."

My father's eyes flash up to mine, but in them I don't see surprise. I see knowing. He knew I was listening.

"What do you know about Cassidy?" I ask, feeling like it's the lighter question to start with, considering the dark note his conversation with Warrick ended on.

"I hear the town gossip." He doesn't look up from the envelope, his fingers working at the seal. "You don't think I pay attention when I hear my son's supposedly gonna be a father?"

"I'm not," I start.

"I know." He holds up his hand and starts toward the kitchen.

"And?" I prompt impatiently, following hot on his heels. "That's all you're going to say about it?"

"Warrick's been lookin' for more land for some time now, knowin' the lease was expirin'," he says, setting the envelope down on the granite. "Rumor has it he looked at the Miller farm. It ain't no secret that Warrick Fairfield's held a grudge against this family since he rolled into town." He moves to the bourbon cabinet, pulls down one of his small-batch labels. "The Miller family needs to sell to keep their business runnin'. I think Cassidy took it upon herself to tell stories in hopes of gainin' a sale."

He pours two fingers of bourbon and examines the amber color in the light.

"If she split the two of you up, I reckon she thought she'd win Warrick's favor and land that sale." He caps the bottle and sets it aside. "But because he can't stand the thought of him bein' the reason he's losin' his daughter, it's my fault." He raises the glass to his lips and pauses. "Just like it was all those years ago."

"What does that mean?" I press incredulously, moving around the island to face him. "All those years ago with Maya?"

He takes a long drink instead of answering, his eyes closing briefly.

"It means I hope you love her, son," he says quietly, his accent softening with the weight of his words. "Because he's gonna pull out everythin' in his arsenal to break you two apart." He slides the envelope Warrick left across the granite island toward me. "If I don't help him end your marriage, we ain't goin' to Lexington next week."

I snatch up the envelope and pull out the documents, my eyes scanning rapidly. A formal HPA complaint concerning Hale Ranch.

"This is garbage," I fume as I look over the list. "Painful treatments, misrepresentation of horse health, sub-par facilities... Is he joking?"

"It doesn't matter if he is. An active investigation would keep us out of the auction." He sets his glass down. "Could tie us up for months, maybe longer."

"This has gone too far." I slam the papers down on the counter. "You need to tell me what you know. What really happened between you two? This isn't just about land or business. I heard what he said in there. About Maya, about you trying to take her from him."

My father's hand tightens around his glass. "That ain't—"

"Don't." I cut him off, my voice sharper than intended. "Don't brush me off. Not this time. I'm not a kid anymore, and Asha is my wife. Whatever history you two have, it's affecting my marriage now. I deserve to know."

He studies me for a long moment, his face unreadable. Then he lets out a slow exhale, and I feel its weight.

"You're right," he admits, surprising me. He picks up the bourbon bottle again and pours another finger into his glass. "You deserve to know. But it ain't a simple story, son. And it ain't all mine to tell." He swirls the bourbon. "I keep my word. And I gave it away a long time ago." He pauses, his jaw working. "I ain't keepin' Warrick's secrets. I'm keepin' hers. It's her secret that haunts him, that owns his fear."

He takes a slow sip, his weathered hands steady on the glass.

"And as much as that man gets under my skin, I leave it alone because I understand it," he says, his voice heavy with something I can't quite name. "Once you know his fear, you can't unknow it." Then, lifting his eyes to mine, he holds my gaze with an intensity that makes my chest tighten. "And you'll share it."

His words settle over me like a death sentence. Whatever Warrick Fairfield is so desperately trying to hide, whatever drove Maya to make my father swear his silence, it's the kind of truth that doesn't just change everything. It destroys it.

ASHA

CHAPTER 39

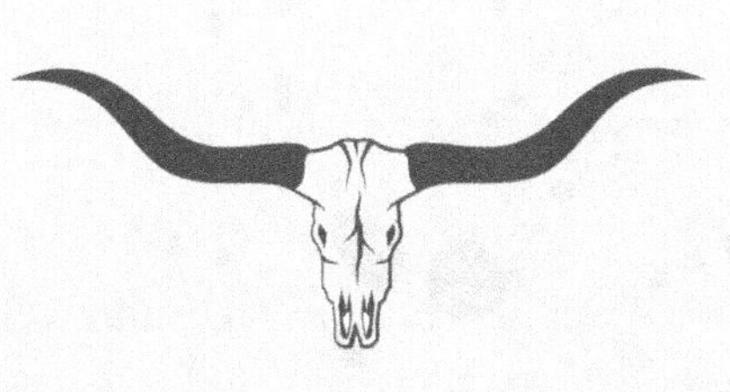

"Are you going over there now?" Trigger asks when I step outside. "Are you sure you don't want me to come with you?"

"No, it's fine. I'm not scared of my dad." Even I don't believe the words coming out of my mouth.

Then, the way he pulls my chin to him so I can't hide confirms he doesn't either. "Then why do you sound like that?"

I roll my eyes and release a long, controlled breath. "I put pressure on my father, pushed his buttons because I wanted answers. Now that I might get them, I'm questioning everything. His confrontation here the other day, and the one you overheard at your father's place... I don't know, maybe he was right, and some things need to be left in the past."

"So what are you going to say to him? Are you going to ask about your mother and what happened, or do you want to call a truce?"

Trigger told me about his father's relationship with my mother, how our families were friends, and Baylor's parents and my mother's parents hoped for a union between my mother and his father, but they never saw each other romantically. However, they were really good friends.

The way Baylor tells the story, my father was intimidated by that friendship. He didn't think men and women could be friends. In his eyes, one, if not both, always hoped to gain something more out of the rela-tionship. My memories of my mother are fading, and my father's refusal to talk about her doesn't help keep them alive. But the woman I do remember was kind; she wore her heart on her sleeve and taught me to be brave, fierce, and loyal. It's that last trait that had me blindly trusting my father, believing that the people who love us the most will never hurt us, but that's just not true.

"A truce would be nice, but I know history will repeat itself if I don't get the answers I seek. I'll be happy until I'm not. It just sucks feeling like I may never look at my father the same, that I may lose him altogether."

"You don't have to lose him just because you learn a truth you don't want to hear. It just might take time to forgive him," he says, placing a chaste kiss on my forehead.

"How do I forgive someone who might be the reason my mother is gone?"

"We don't know that."

"Don't we?" I step back and run my hands through my hair. "What secret could possibly drive my father to try to break up our marriage and bankrupt your family if not one that could put him behind bars?" My eyes snap to him. "Your father said, *Not only do I know where the bones are buried, I know the stories they tell.*" I throw my arms wide. "What the fuck else could that possibly mean?" I say, practically yelling now.

His face drops as he takes a deep breath. "I don't know, but let's say you're right, that would mean my father is covering up a crime, and while you don't know what to believe about Warrick, I don't think my father would do that, especially after hearing about his friendship with your mother."

I sigh as the tension in my body eases down a notch. He's right, or at least I think he's right. Baylor wouldn't cover for my father, and if by some chance he was, I think the threats my father hand-delivered the other day would push him to his breaking point, and he'd do something about it.

"I have to do this. I saw things going differently when I started this war with him. I thought he'd see he can't control me, that he can't keep me in the dark, that I'm not the little girl he sent away all those years ago. I knew marrying you would get under his skin, but I hoped he'd also see that I get to decide what I want, that my choices are mine and mine alone. And when I chose to ignore his invitations to talk, I saw him coming through my front door with an apology and a truth because the alternative was a future without me." My voice cracks with emotion. I know my father can be ruthless; he's built a damn empire. But I thought when it came to me, I wouldn't be just another transaction.

When he wraps his arms around me and just holds me, I fall more in love with him. It's what he did the first night I asked him to kiss me, and he's never stopped. For all the hell my father has put us through, Trigger has always let me lead. He doesn't pile on his own frustrations or opinions about my father, because he knows the weight I'm already carrying is enough. If anything, he defends him, and I hate it. Sometimes you just want someone to validate your anger, but I know why he doesn't. He understands how important my father is to me, even when I can't see it myself. I might be quick to burn it all down, but he's not. He holds me steady.

"I don't want you to worry. Laney is going to be there, so if for some reason things do go south, I won't technically be alone."

When I agreed to meet with my father, I set a condition: I wanted to get things out of my room.

"Sweetheart, I'm not worried." He pulls back his hands framing my face. "I'll become your father's worst nightmare if he so much as puts the look of hurt in your eyes." His eyes search mine with an intensity that promises retribution. "You're mine to protect now."

The words hang between us, heavy with promise. Then he closes the distance, capturing my lips with a desperation that matches the fear I've been trying to hide. I melt into him, my hands sliding around up his sweat-riddled chest, as if he can somehow transfer his strength directly into my bones. It's not gentle; it's a vow, a brand, a reminder that I'm not alone in this.

"I love you," I say as I head toward the truck. "Also, I'm taking your truck. I know you didn't like that the last time I did it, so..." I taunt.

"The last time you did it, you stole it, and you weren't my wife. What's mine is yours, sweetheart," he says, and I swear his abs literally glisten in the sun. So unfair. When that man is naked, he could tell me to rob a bank, and I'd ask which one.

I slide into the driver's seat, hands gripping the steering wheel tighter than necessary. Time to face the conversation I've been avoiding for years.

~

"Is this box ready to go out to the truck?" Sydney asks as I toss one of my journals on top.

"Um, not yet," I say, looking around my room. "I know I have an album somewhere around here that I want to put in that box."

She gets off the floor and brushes her hair out of her face. "Well, it's not under the bed."

"Why were you under my bed?" I quirk an amused brow.

"You said you couldn't find your mother's locket. I remember you used to keep it on your nightstand." She places her hands on her hips and shrugs. "Thought maybe it fell underneath the bed."

She's dressed down like she came prepared to work, and her skin glistens with a thin layer of sweat since she volunteered to take every box to my truck while I made piles I wanted to take back to the barn. We haven't been seeing eye to eye lately, and I can't help but feel like that's partly my fault. She's defended my father, and it's infuriated me. Yet, I've given Trigger a pass for the same thing, convincing myself he's only staying neutral to protect my relationship with my father, while I've refused to show her that same understanding. It's not fair, and I know that, but when she started talking to Hollis, another layer of emotions was thrown into the mix. I can only fight so many battles, and hers wasn't one I had energy for, so I was quick to be dismissive and unforgiving.

"Thanks for coming today. I appreciate you helping me," I say, folding one of my shirts and tossing it onto the bed.

"Don't thank me; it's what friends do."

"Yeah, well, we both know I've been a shit friend."

"Asha, please don't apologize to me. Friends mess up; we make mistakes. We're only human. Friendship means friends stay friends, and the mistakes..." Her fingers twist, and I can tell all of this has tested her too. "Mistakes stay mistakes."

We hug, and it feels like everything has been forgiven, at least for now, and for now that's good enough for me.

"Have you started on the bathroom yet?" she asks, starting toward it. "Want me to grab your makeup?" she asks, switching on the light as I follow her in.

I take a look around, and most of what's in my bathroom is towels and soap, but it's the soaker tub that steals my focus. God, I can't wait until I can take a long, hot bath again. We only have a small shower at the barn.

The sound of her pulling open one of my drawers draws my attention back to the task at hand.

"I'll go grab a small box," she says, rifling through the contents. "No sense in leaving stuff your dad won't use here."

She pulls something out and sets it on the counter with a soft thud. A box of tampons. My vision tunnels; everything else in the bathroom blurs except that blue-and-white box. When did I last...? My mind scrambles backward, counting days, then weeks. The realization slams into me like a freight train.

Oh God.

Why can't I remember the last time I used one of those? Not just from that box, from *anywhere*. My purse. The glove box. The spare I keep in my makeup bag.

My hands fly into my hair as I start pacing in the bathroom. "Think. Think," I mumble frustratedly.

Eight weeks since the wedding, but I've been stressed. The entire month before London and Laney's ceremony, I was a mess. Their wedding meant I was closer to my own deadline, closer to losing everything, and out of options that didn't include shackling myself to Trigger Hale.

Stress can do that. Throw everything off. Right?

"Are you okay?" Sydney's voice cuts through my spiral as she re-enters carrying a box. "You look like you're going to be sick."

"That's because I might be."

"Do you want me to get you something to eat? Water?" Her concern feels distant, muffled, like I'm underwater.

I sink onto the edge of the tub to keep from falling, as everything feels like it's tilting sideways.

"Asha, you're scaring me. What's wrong?"

My gaze locks on the box. That stupid blue-and-white box.

"I can't tell you the last time I used one of those."

Her brow furrows as she works to decipher my words. Then, her gaze follows my line of sight. "One of...*oh*." Her hand flies to her mouth. "You think...you think you might be pregnant? I thought you were on the pill?"

For half a second, relief floods through me. "I am." But then reality crushes back in, and I release a shaky breath. "But I missed two weeks when we went to Spain. Trigger gave me ten minutes to pack. I was so focused on grabbing clothes, I didn't..."

I don't tell her I didn't think I'd *need* them. That this was supposed to be temporary. That he was never supposed to end up in my bed, under my skin, and thoroughly wrapped around my heart.

"I refilled it when we got home, but—"

"But for two weeks, you were having unprotected sex." She finishes what I can't.

I nod. "Yep."

I've never told Sydney and Laney the whole truth about my marriage. I don't think they completely bought the story we sold that night at the wedding, but the roots don't matter anymore. I love him. I'm not leaving him.

"So what are you going to do?"

"I need to take a test." I stand, my legs still shaky. "I'll reschedule with my dad."

"*What?*" Sydney's voice spikes. "Why would you do that? You're already here."

I don't know why she's so insistent that I have this conversation today. You'd think that out of the two of us, she'd care the least about me confronting him. I blink the thought away.

"I can't talk to him with this hanging over my head. My mind will be anywhere but in that room. I have to *know*." I move past her toward my bedroom.

"Wait," she practically screeches.

I turn and find her biting the edge of her thumb, her face pale. "I have a test."

The words land like stones.

"You have a test?" I question carefully. "Why do you have a pregnancy test?"

"I wasn't supposed to say anything." The words tumble out too fast, like she's nervous. "That's why I'm here instead of Laney. She got sick this morning and asked me to pick one up for her. Please don't tell her I told you."

She's already crossing to her purse, digging through it before I can form a word, but something doesn't fit. I watch her fumble with the zipper, and a certainty settles in my gut. Sydney has known Laney since they were *children*. She was there the day everything changed, and we held our friend as we heard the news that there most likely won't be a next time. There's no way Sydney forgot that. Which means this test was never meant for Laney.

She pulls the box from her purse and crosses to me. Our eyes meet for just a fraction of a second, and in that look, there's something raw and unguarded, before she glances away. I take the box without a word. Whoever this test was *really* meant for, I'll find out when she's ready to tell me. Or I won't. That's her ghost to carry. Right now, I have my own.

She nods toward the door, backing away like she can't leave fast enough. "I'll give you a minute."

"Yeah. Okay."

The door clicks shut, and I'm alone. Just me and a piece of plastic that holds more future than I can process.

TRIGGER

CHAPTER 40

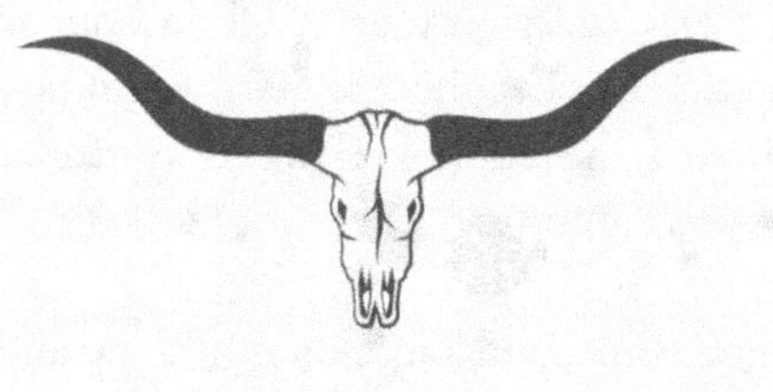

Sneaking into Warrick's house wasn't nearly as complicated as Asha made it out to be. I walked right in through the back door. The staff isn't as familiar with my face as they are hers. I could be a trainer, stable hand, guest, or any number of people who frequent the property.

I head toward the west side of the house, remembering that Asha mentioned his office overlooks the west lawn. As I move down the hallway, my senses go on alert. I hear two people speaking in hushed tones. I stick to the wall, scanning every corner as I inch closer. The voices become more distinct with each step.

My fists ball on instinct; it can't be helped. I hate being right, but more than that, I hate the deception. I hate it for my wife.

The library stretches before me, floor-to-ceiling mahogany shelves lined with leather-bound volumes that probably cost more than most people's cars. And there, standing in the shadows beside a ladder propped against the far bookcase, stand Sydney and Warrick.

"Aren't you supposed to be helping my wife?" The words come out sharp, edged with irritation I don't bother to hide.

Sydney's eyes flick to me. Her arms are crossed, and while they might not be doing anything more than talking, it's clear I walked in on an intimate conversation. They are standing too close to be anything more than two people who have Asha in common.

Warrick's jaw ticks before he straightens, taking a deliberate step away from the bookcase, his dark eyes that miss nothing never leaving mine.

"I don't recall today's invitation including you," he says coolly, putting more space between himself and Sydney as he rounds a leather reading chair.

I move farther into the room, my boots heavy against the polished wood floor. "Yeah, well, I'm sure my wife didn't come over expecting her father and her best friend to be rendezvousing in dark corners either." I stop beside a drafting table and turn to Sydney, my glare pointed. "Tell me, where exactly does my wife think you are right now?"

Her eyes widen as color floods her cheeks, something new for Sydney, who's one of the most confident, non-insecure humans I know. She shifts her weight, fingers tightening around her own arms. She usually owns whatever she does, even when it's outlandish. I think she enjoys the shock value of it all. But this...this is different. If she owns this, she hurts someone she cares about.

Before she can respond, Warrick cuts in. "What goes on in my house is none of your concern." He moves to the windows, his back to us now.

I angrily run my hand over my beard and bite my tongue so I don't say something I'll regret—not for Warrick, but for Sydney.

"You're right. It's not my house." I pace a few steps, unable to stand still with this much adrenaline coursing through me. "You can do what you want. But it is my concern when what you do hurts my wife."

He turns from the window, and afternoon light catches the sharp angles of his face. "What is it that you think you know?" he asks, each word measured.

"I have eyes. I see things." My gaze flicks between them before I add, "I notice things."

Sydney crosses the room toward me in quick strides. "I should get back to Asha." She pauses in front of me, and I can see a story there. I'm not wrong to have suspicions, but there's something else too. "Whatever you think you know, you don't." Her tone is certain, but there's vulnerability written all over her blue gaze.

"Sydney." Warrick's voice is sharp as he takes a step forward, his shoe clicking against the walnut floor. "That's enough."

She looks at him over her shoulder, and something passes between them, an entire conversation in a glance, filled with unsaid things–things I need answers to.

"There's nothing to tell," she says quietly, still looking at Warrick. "Maybe there once was, but there's not now."

And before anyone can say another word, she squeezes past me and slips out the door.

Warrick pulls in a deep breath, and I can see the tension beneath his perfectly pressed button-down. For just a moment, his composure cracks as he raises his hand to adjust his already perfect tie.

He drops his hands and turns to me, his dark expression unreadable. "You need to leave."

"I can't do that. Not when I know what's at stake," I say, taking a few steps farther into the room. His eyes narrow on mine as he processes their meaning. "I talked to my father—" is all I manage before he pulls an audible breath through his nose and clenches a leather wingback chair he's standing beside hard.

"And what did he say?" he asks through clenched teeth.

"I know about the audit you're holding over our heads and the ultimatum you gave him."

"The man who prides himself on telling no secrets sings like a canary for his son." He crosses the room to a decanter on a side table beside a leather couch and pours himself two fingers of bourbon.

"He didn't tell me those things." I supply evenly, watching him carefully. "You did."

He turns to face me, the glass already at his lips. "You were there..." He takes a long pull from the glass, downing the spirit in one go before adding, "In the house."

"I was. I heard everything you said. It's one of the reasons I'm here now." I pause, letting the weight of that sink in. "You might hate me, but we have something in common. We both love Asha."

"You still haven't told me what it is you think you know." He pours another two fingers of bourbon and swirls it in the glass, a tell that he's calculating. "If it has anything to do with what you think you saw walking in here today, then you've wasted your time."

I study him, the man who's built an empire on control and precision, who's never caught with a hair out of place or an emotion out of check. He's getting close to his breaking point; not only can I sense it, but I can see it in his movement. He's too tense, too controlled, too tight. He's riddled with anxiety because he knows we're close, even if we don't have the full story. We have pieces, and he doesn't like it.

"I know you're lying, but here's the part that might surprise you. Right now, I don't care. That lie has nothing on the one your daughter suspects you're telling." His eyebrows lift fractionally.

Then, his eyes snap to mine with an intensity that would make most men step back, and I feel my lips tug up at the corner slightly. *Good. I have his attention.*

"It's got everything to do with fear," I start, turning away from him to walk casually toward the tall windows overlooking the west lawn and paddocks. *"'Don't forget, I know things too. Not only do I know where the bones are buried, I know the stories they tell,'"* I finish with the words my father gave him.

The silence that stretches between us is short but suffocating.

"You gave Asha those words?" His voice is low, but I hear the hiss of anger threading through it all the same.

"I did." I move away from the window. "I don't keep secrets from my wife."

"Well, we both know that's not true." He sets his glass down with a sharp click against the table. "You're selective with your secrets. You keep the ones that don't advance your agenda."

I raise a brow, genuinely not following his claim. *What the hell is he getting at?*

"You haven't told her about your suspicions." He gestures vaguely toward the door Sydney left through, and there it is—an accusation, a challenge.

"I haven't told my wife that I suspect her father is fucking her best friend, because I didn't have proof." The words come out profane, and he rolls his lips, clearly not happy with the way they sound out loud. *Good.* "Outside of witnessing Sydney walk out of this house early on the morning after the watch party, all I have are coincidences and timely disappearances. So yeah, I haven't thrown a grenade in my wife's life when I don't have solid proof." I take a breath, forcing myself to rein in my anger that's threatening to boil over. "You'll have to excuse me for thinking my time is better spent focusing on how to help her see her father didn't commit murder."

He stiffens, his entire body going rigid. My words clearly hit a nerve, but not the one I expected. I anticipated defense, sharp words, threats, maybe even a demand that I leave. Instead, what I see in his eyes looks disturbingly like defeat. His shoulders slump almost imperceptibly, and suddenly, he looks older, more human. *This isn't the reaction of a man protecting a lie. This is the reaction of a man who's just realized how broken things really are.*

"And what do you think?"

"I think my father has honored whatever vow he gave to your late wife," I say, my voice softer. "Possibly to a fault, but I don't think he'd cover up a murder." He pulls in a stuttered breath, and I watch his knuckles practically turn white at his sides. He didn't know his daughter believed he was capable of murdering her mother.

"Whatever it is, it has to end here, today, when she comes to talk to you." I move closer, my voice urgent. "You have to tell her the truth. You can't keep this from her."

The words have barely left my mouth when the door to the library pushes all the way open.

"Tell me what?"

Asha steps fully into the room, her eyes darting between both of us, reading the tension thick in the air. Her brow furrows with confusion and maybe suspicion as we both stand frozen, both of us too scared to move after being caught on the heels of such a heavy discussion. *Fuck. How much did she hear?*

"Trigger, why are you here?" Her voice is confused. "I told you I need to talk to my father alone."

I take a step toward her. "I know, but—"

"Do you really think so lowly of me, Asha?" Warrick cuts me off, his voice rising with a rawness I haven't heard from him before. His face pinches with pain, and every carefully maintained line of composure cracks. "You think I'm so evil that I could stoop so low as to hurt your mother?" His voice breaks on the last word. "To kill my wife?"

"You told him?" She whips toward me, and the look of pure betrayal in her eyes feels like a knife straight to my heart, twisting with each second she stares at me. "Why would you tell him?"

"Asha—" I start, but my throat tightens. I can't stand her believing I'm doing anything other than trying to help her.

"So it's true, then?" Warrick steals my words, his voice hollow. He takes a step toward her. "You actually believe I could do that?"

Asha swallows hard before accepting defeat and throwing her arms wide. "What else am I supposed to think?" The question comes out somewhere between a shout and a sob.

She begins to pace, her movements shaky with emotion. "You sent me away and never let me come home. You kept me away from here and all of her memories. You stopped talking about her, and even when I'd point-blank ask you questions, you'd either shut me down or give me half-ass answers that were clearly not the whole truth."

Her voice rises with each accusation as years of hurt spill out. "Then, this past year, with the sale of the property, you hid it from me. You've hidden everything from me." She stops pacing, spinning to face him head-on. "How come I never knew Mom was friends with Baylor growing up? That the Hales and the Fairfields weren't always enemies? Those are just a few of my glaring questions, but I have a million more, small details I've collected over the years."

Warrick opens his mouth to speak, but she's not done.

"You tried to hold this house over my head to scare me. I know my name is on the title. I know Mom left it to me and you."

"How do you—" Warrick attempts to ask, genuine shock breaking through his pain.

"It doesn't matter how!" She throws her hands up, her voice cracking. "All that matters is you lied."

"I didn't lie," Warrick cuts in. "I just didn't tell you."

She rolls her eyes, a bitter laugh escaping her throat. "You of all people know an omission is a lie dressed in sheep's clothing."

"But that's nothing compared to your biggest omission, the one that makes you a murderer." She says it flatly, like she knows for a fact it's the truth.

Jesus, Asha.

"You've been lying to me my whole life. I don't think Mom died in her sleep at all." Her voice drops lower. "A man doesn't order his wife's medical records and death certificate sealed if he's not trying to cover up a crime."

Warrick doesn't respond. He simply stands statue-still, arms crossed, staring at Asha like he's still trying to determine if whatever he's holding onto is worth giving up. His dark eyes are unreadable, but it's his lack of automatic response that has my blood turning to ice.

She just accused him of murder, and the accusation alone isn't enough to make his lips move. What the hell could be worse than that?

The silence stretches on for what feels like an eternity, and I keep my eyes glued on Warrick, waiting for a tell, something that says we have it all wrong. I see the moment something inside him breaks. His eyes close briefly, and when they open again, they're glassy with unshed tears. He releases a long, shuddering sigh, and the tension in his shoulders drops like the weight of whatever he's been holding onto is finally too much to bear. Without a word, he moves to the leather couch beside the bourbon decanter and sits heavily. Then, he opens the drawer beneath the side table.

We watch in absolute silence as he pushes on one of the corners, and the false bottom pops up with a soft click, revealing a pile of envelopes underneath. The paper looks old, yellowed slightly at the edges. He takes them out carefully, his fingers gently thumbing over the corners like they're made of glass. For a long moment, he just holds them.

"I didn't murder your mother." His voice is rough with emotion. "I loved her, and because I loved her, I kept her secret."

His eyes finally lift to connect with Asha's, and when they do, I see nothing but pain, raw, unfiltered anguish that's been festering for years.

"I didn't lie when I said I sent you to boarding school to keep you safe, but I did lie about the reason." He pauses, his Adam's apple bobbing as he swallows hard. "It wasn't because we worried about you getting hurt at school. It was because we worried about you getting hurt at home."

Asha's brow furrows, confusion replacing some of the anger. "I don't understand." Her voice is gentler now, uncertain.

"Your mother was sick." His voice breaks on the word 'sick.' "We sent you away so you wouldn't be here to witness her death."

Asha's fists clench at her sides, not from anger this time, but from sadness and the sudden understanding of what was intentionally taken from her. I'm at her side in an instant, wrapping my arms around her. She doesn't pull away, but she doesn't lean into me either. She's frozen as she processes his words.

Warrick traces over the handwriting scrolled across the top of one of the envelopes, and when he angles it toward us, the writing becomes visible. Asha's name is written across the front.

"She wrote these for you." He says it so quietly I almost don't hear him, still not bothering to look up from the stack.

"What do you mean she wrote me letters?" Asha's voice is strangled with a mixture of anger and sadness. "How come you never showed them to me?"

Warrick's fingers tighten around the envelopes, and for a moment, I think he won't answer. "Because I was scared of what they might say," he admits. "She wrote one for every milestone. College. Birthdays. Your wedding." He finally looks up at her, and the devastation in his eyes is almost unbearable to witness.

The next thing I know, Asha tears out of my arms and crosses the space between her and her father in three quick strides. She grabs the letters from his lap, clutching them to her chest like they might disappear if she doesn't hold them tight enough.

"What was so bad that you'd go to such great lengths to keep me from knowing?" Her voice rises, desperation bleeding through. "What did Mom die from?"

Warrick pinches the bridge of his nose and rises slowly before meeting her eyes. "Your mother died from ALS."

The confession feels like a punch to the stomach. *Fuck.*

"What?" Asha gasps, the envelopes pressed tightly to her chest. "How could you keep this from me?" Her voice rises to a near scream. "That is something I need to know!" Panic edges into her tone.

"I didn't tell you because I didn't want you to know!" His voice matches hers now, loud and desperate and full of years of justification. "That was the deal your mother and I made. She didn't want you to watch her deteriorate from a disease that may or may not take your life. She didn't want you to live in fear, and I didn't want to get you tested."

He takes a breath, forcing himself to calm down, to explain. "So the deal was she'd agree to no testing if I agreed to send you to boarding school to spare you from watching her die." His voice softens, becoming almost pleading. "Your mother's gene mutation was sporadic and rare. Fifty percent of people with the gene will live their entire lives and never develop the disease. You've already lived longer than her and—"

"It doesn't matter how rare it was or that I've already lived longer!" she screeches, backing away from him. "I could still have it!"

"But why would you want to know how or when you might die?" Warrick's voice splinters with emotion, his hands outstretched toward her like he's begging. "I never wanted to know that information. I didn't want you to know and live anything less than a full, happy life. I didn't want that cloud hanging over you."

He takes a step toward her, but she matches it with a step back.

"Could you stand there and tell me you would have accomplished all that you have if you knew your last breath might be taken at age twenty?" His voice drops, becomes almost gentle. "Would you have gotten married?" he trails off, his eyes briefly flicking over to me before swinging back to her. "Or would you have prepared for a funeral?" He reaches for her arm, but she jerks away from his touch.

"That's why I kept those letters from you," he continues, his hand falling back to his side. "I couldn't be sure what they said. What if she told you? What if reading them made you want to know?"

Asha's head whips toward me so fast I flinch. "You knew?"

Her eyes are full of sadness and betrayal, searching my face for confirmation of her worst suspicions.

"What?" My heart hammers in my chest. "Sweetheart, how could I know that?"

"You've defended my father this whole time. Baylor was friends with my mother. He told you." She's putting pieces together now, pieces that don't actually fit but make sense to her in this moment of pain and confusion. "I could tell when you were telling me what you overheard Baylor and my dad fighting about the other day. You were holding back. You were holding back because you knew."

She slowly backs away from both of us, and it's like watching something break in real time.

"I heard you say as much when I walked in," she continues, her voice breaking. "*You can't keep this from her.* That's what you were discussing, right?"

A tear runs down her cheek, and I've never felt more helpless in my entire life.

"Asha, that's not what we were talking about. I fucking swear it." The words come out desperate, almost frantic. I take a step toward her, my hand outstretched. "I've never lied to you."

"Then tell me." She shrugs, tears now streaming freely down her face. Her voice is quiet, defeated. "Tell me what you were talking about."

My gaze instinctively flicks to Warrick, and I see him stiffen, see the warning in his eyes, and I hesitate. Not because I don't want to tell her, but because now feels like a really fucking terrible moment to add one more betrayal to the pile. My indecision lasts only a second, but it's a second too long.

"That's what I thought," Asha says, her voice flat now, emotionless.

She reaches into her back pocket and pulls something out. My eyes track the movement, not understanding what I'm seeing until she slams it down on the coffee table with a sharp crack. A blue-and-white test.

My entire world tilts on its axis as every certainty I had dissolves.

"You should have told me," she says, her voice hollow. "Congratulations. You're going to be a father."

My heart drops to my stomach, and I have to command every cell in my body not to fall to my knees. It feels like the air has been sucked from the room. I can't breathe. Can't think. Can't process anything beyond those two pink lines and what they mean.

"Asha." Her name comes out choked.

But she doesn't waver as she moves toward the door, the letters still clutched to her chest, as I try to make my legs move, but they won't. They're rooted to the floor.

"Asha, wait!" I finally force the words out, taking a stumbling step forward.

She pauses at the door, one hand on the frame, but she doesn't turn around.

"Don't follow me," she says quietly, and there's a finality in those words that terrifies me more than anything else that's happened in this godforsaken library. "I need to be alone." And then she's gone.

I'm frozen, staring at the space she no longer occupies. Another empty hallway, just like before. I need to run after her, need to chase her down and explain, but then I blink, and my eyes catch on the coffee table and the test she left there. My legs unlock, and in three strides, I'm there, snatching it off the table. My hands shake as I stare at it. It's real. We're having a baby. Joy and terror collide. This should be the best moment of my life, but instead, I'm standing on a cliff's edge.

She's pregnant. And she's alone.

I clench the test tightly. I'm her husband. I don't care if she told me not to follow her. She needs me, and fuck if I don't need her.

"Don't." Warrick's voice is sharp when I reach the door. "Let her go," he says, his tone softer. "Give her time to process and read those letters. She needs her mom, and right now she has pieces."

My grip tightens around the knob until my knuckles turn white as I stand there, torn between the door and the man who's already lost his daughter once. I know he's right, and Lord knows I can wait. I've done it for years.

So why does it feel like waiting might be the biggest mistake of all.

TRIGGER

CHAPTER 41

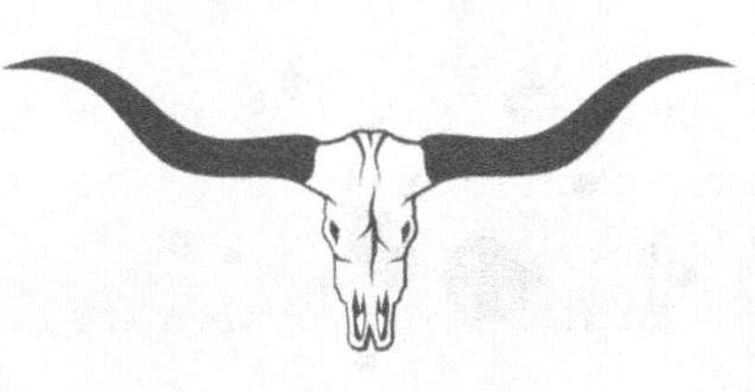

FORTY-EIGHT HOURS LATER

It's midnight, and I've already knocked on every damn door I know.

Forty-eight hours ago, my world was literally turned upside down. I spent the afternoon busying myself with chores around the ranch, things that needed to get done before the bulls arrived, because she asked for time. Space to be alone with her thoughts. I hated it, but it's why I tried to keep my hands moving and my mind occupied until she came home.

By dinnertime, I was pacing the loft. By bedtime, I was calling every one of our friends, trying to figure out where she'd gone. I didn't sleep. *How could I after the bomb that was dropped on me?*

By morning, I was checking every one of our credit cards in hopes of finding her. Did she go into town to buy coffee? Where did she eat dinner? Where did she sleep? Nothing. After putting an alert on all transactions, I got in her car and drove to everyone's house. I had to be sure they weren't lying to me just to cover for her.

That turned out to be a terrible idea. Everyone wanted to ask me twenty-one questions, and I couldn't answer any of them. Then, I drove through town, looking for my truck. Again, nothing.

It's why I'm here now, standing in the pouring rain at midnight in front of the last door I want to knock on. My last stop and my last hope. I walked. I left her car at the barn and followed the gravel path that cuts through the back of the property because I needed the time. I needed to stretch out these last minutes of believing she'd be here. Every step down that dark path, gravel crunching under my boots, rain turning the road to mud, bought me more time to hope. The longer it took to arrive, the longer I could hold onto a possibility. The longer I could tell myself that when I finally knocked on this door, she'd answer.

My clothes are plastered to my skin, and my boots are caked with mud, and somewhere between the barn and his front door, I stopped feeling the cold. Stopped feeling anything except the desperate need to find her.

I bang on the front door again, hard enough that my fist aches. "Please be here." I send up one last prayer.

The door swings open.

"What the hell—" Warrick's words die when he sees me soaked to the bone on his doorstep.

"I know she's here." My voice comes out rough and desperate.

"Who?"

"My wife!" The words explode out of me as I refuse to hear anything that's not a confirmation.

"She's not here," he says, but my hands are already finding his chest, pushing him aside as I barge my way into the house. Water drips from my clothes onto his pristine hardwood floors.

"She has to be." I'm already moving deeper into the house, my boots squelching with each step. "Asha, come out! I know you're here!"

I hear the front door close behind me with a solid thud.

"I'm telling you, she's not here." Warrick's voice is calm, too calm, and it grates against every frayed nerve I have.

I spin to face him. "I don't believe you. Where's her room?"

He sighs, running a hand over his face before nodding across the living room. "Down the hall."

I charge across the space, my wet boots leaving a trail of mud.

Let her be here. Please, God, let her be here.

"Which door?" I call over my shoulder.

"Two doors down." His footsteps follow behind me, measured and steady.

When I reach her door, I throw it open, expecting to catch him in a lie, expecting to find her sitting on her bed, surrounded by her mother's letters, red-eyed and hurting but *here*, alive and safe. Instead, I find darkness and boxes.

"Have you tried calling her?" Warrick asks, like I haven't tried the most obvious solution.

I pull her phone out of my pocket. "She left without it."

"When was the last time you saw her?" he asks quietly.

"Same as you. Two days ago."

The breath I hear him take could fill a room, but when I turn around, he simply nods. One slow nod, like everything isn't upside down.

"That's it?" I question, unbelieving of how he can be so unfazed. "How can you be so calm about this?"

His jaw tightens, and for a moment, something flickers across his face. "This isn't the first time someone I love received life-changing news," he says quietly.

The statement hangs in the air between us, heavy with meaning. He holds my gaze for a beat longer then turns and wordlessly walks down the hall. *He's right. He's lived through this before.*

I follow him, my emotions a tangled mess. Every feeling bleeds into the next until I can't tell where one ends and another begins. I can't stand waiting, but what's worse is not knowing where she is or what she's thinking. I've tried hard to hold it together, to not let my mind spiral into worst-case scenarios—*ones that end with her taking my choice in all of this away.* The thought makes my stomach turn.

Warrick pulls down a blue-and-white bottle of tequila and two glasses, setting them on the granite counter with a soft clink. He pours a sizable amount in each and, without asking, slides one across to me.

"What are you thinking?" he finally asks, leaning against the counter opposite me.

I stare down at the glass, watching how the crystal reflects the overhead lights. "Right now, I'm torn between hating you and hating that I understand you."

The words come out more honest than I intended. I take a long pull off the tequila, welcoming the burn that tears down my throat. He responds with another slow nod then takes his own measured drink. His jaw works as he swallows, and for a beat, we just stand there in silence, two men drowning in different decades of the same fear.

"Did you know Maya was sick before you married her?" I ask, needing to understand how he survived this.

"No." He sets his glass down with deliberate care and stares blankly across the kitchen, his dark eyes unfocused, like he's watching a memory play out on the wall. "We were young. I met her on a family trip. My parents came to Bardstown with friends for the summer, for a vacation."

"In Bardstown?" I raise a brow. "There's nothing here but bars and land."

His lips quirk into the ghost of a smile. "That's what I told them when I said I wasn't going." He picks up his glass again and swirls the liquid. "At eighteen, this place had nothing for me. But one of my father's friends wanted to look at buying land. He was a businessman with a vast portfolio and convinced my parents they should look into investing. Told them if they sat on it long enough, it would be worth enough to retire them when this place became the next hot spot."

He pauses to take another drink. "On one of the many property tours, I met Maya. While my parents spent the next month looking at land they didn't plan to buy, I spent my time falling for the farmer's daughter." A soft smile tugs at his mouth. "And then a few months later, after I returned home, she called me. She was hysterical, crying, and apologizing because she was pregnant."

I watch his fingers tighten around the glass.

"By the end of that week, I packed up the car my parents had given me for my birthday, and I moved to Kentucky." He looks up and meets my eyes. "She was so scared, and I'd just found out I was going to have a family."

She was scared, and I just found out I was going to have a family. The words echo through my mind, and my chest tightens. I'm in the exact same shoes he was. History is repeating itself in the worst possible way. I down the rest of my tequila and push my glass toward him. He refills it without comment.

"We were young, had no clue how we were going to make ends meet," he continues, his voice growing distant. "When her father found out, he was upset. He didn't like the idea of his daughter falling pregnant so young, but what could he do?" He shrugs. "He needed help on the farm. I needed money and a place to stay. So, I worked relentlessly. For every problem he had, I identified a solution. Built on his legacy."

He takes another drink, and I notice his hand isn't quite steady.

"By the time Asha was five years old, we'd made our first million-dollar sale on a Thoroughbred. We were on cloud nine. All the hard work we had been putting in had finally paid off," he says, before his expression darkens. "Later that year, Maya received her diagnosis."

Of course she did.

"She thought she was overdoing it around the ranch, working too much, not getting enough sleep. The symptoms she had in the beginning went hand in hand with a hard day's work. But when her speech started to slur..." He trails off, his jaw clenching. "I knew something was wrong. A lot of things went downhill quickly from there. We were able to hide it from Asha in the beginning, but we knew it wouldn't be long until we couldn't."

He drains his glass and pours himself another, heavier this time.

"She had fast-acting juvenile ALS, and we had hard decisions to make."

I grip my glass tighter, and a chill that has nothing to do with my wet clothes runs down my spine. "That's why you used the accident at school to send Asha away." The pieces are clicking into place. "But why did you make me the enemy? Why my father?"

Warrick's shoulders tense, and he turns away, bracing his hands on the counter.

"Maya was friends with Baylor. Admittedly, I was always jealous of their friendship, even though deep down I knew she loved me. But I'm human. My insecurities are no different from yours. They had a history, a relationship for years, before I ever came into the picture. And when I found out she confided in him about her diagnosis..." He stops and pulls in a shuddered breath. "I lost it. I questioned if she only loved me because we accidentally got pregnant. When she gave him something so personal, I worried it was because he was the one she wanted. Not me."

"My father said they never had romantic feelings for each other," I say quietly. "I believe him."

"I know." Warrick turns back to face me, and there's something raw in his expression now. "But I think you can relate a little bit to how I was feeling then, given what you're going through now." He leans forward, his dark eyes boring into mine. "If you found out Asha was sitting in another man's arms right now, seeking comfort with something so deeply fragile and personal instead of you, her husband, how do you think that would make you feel?"

His words strike a chord. *I'd lose my fucking mind.* It's taken every ounce of my sanity to keep my shit together and not go off the deep end. I'd fall apart if I knew I wasn't the only person she wanted in this moment.

"It wasn't her fault," Warrick continues, his voice rough with regret. "It was mine. I didn't handle the news well. Finding out my wife had months to live wasn't an easy fucking pill to swallow." His hands flatten against the counter. "I loved her, but my heart wasn't the only one about to be broken. I had a little girl who was about to lose her mother, a little girl who might be destined to live the same fate."

He looks down at his glass, and I see the pain he's kept to himself all these years.

"I couldn't talk about it. I couldn't talk about it because it was taking everything I had to hold it together and be strong for her. I was weak, and in that weakness, I pushed her into your father's arms." His lips pinch together with regret before he adds, "She couldn't talk to me. So she talked to him."

The silence that follows is heavy. I set my glass down, the sound too loud in the quiet kitchen. "And that's why you didn't want Asha and me to be friends. You were worried he'd tell her the truth about Maya."

"Yes." The word comes out flat, honest. He meets my eyes without flinching. "It's the reason I was distracted and wrecked my vehicle during your senior year." His voice drops lower. "I didn't know Baylor had sent you to Ridgewood, and when I saw the two of you in that picture together..." He closes his eyes briefly. "My mind went from zero to fear in the blink of an eye. I wasn't paying attention to the road. Just kept thinking about how close you were getting to her, how you'd eventually be the link, how it would all unravel."

He pauses, his fingers drumming once against the counter before stilling. "I thought if I could keep you apart, keep our families separated, I could keep the secret buried."

Fuck. He nearly killed himself over this. I suppose this isn't news. Asha told me she suspected it as much, but hearing it for the truth it is from his mouth hits different. It was a man enraged. It was a man crippled by fear.

"But regret and hate, they eat you alive from the inside out." His voice is rough, weighted with years of mistakes. "They almost stole my little girl from me. I pushed her away, trying to protect her, and I nearly lost her completely because of it." He straightens, his dark eyes finding mine across the counter. "I'm hoping what I've done is forgivable. That she can understand why I made the choices I did, even if she doesn't agree with them." He pauses, and the sound of rain hammering against the windows fills the silence until he adds, "But I know she'll come back." His gaze sharpens and locks onto mine. "I know she'll come back for you."

The words land like a promise, a promise I can't feel through my fear.

Because what if he's wrong?

I stare at the man who's already lived through losing everything once. What if this time, she doesn't? What if this is the thing that finally breaks her? Not the lies. Not the secrets. Not even the disease, but all of it.

What if I've lost her?

TRIGGER

CHAPTER 42

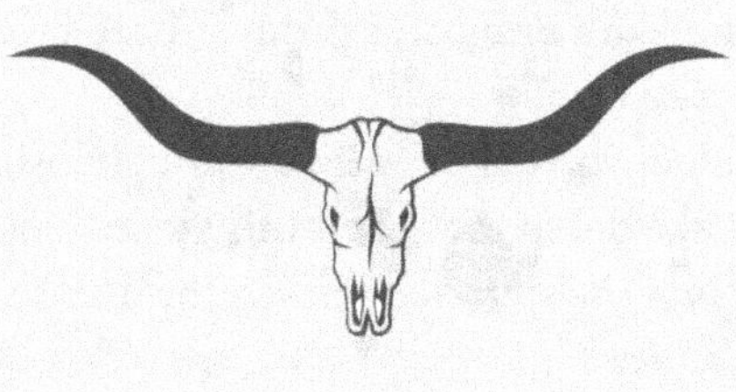

FIVE DAYS LATER

"Why don't you call Dar? Maybe Asha reached out to her," Hollis says as I slam the clamshell into the ground as I install the last post.

I wipe sweat from my forehead before it drops in my eyes. "No passport. No cards. And her phone is on the kitchen table." Each word drops like a hammer. "She doesn't want to be found." I clench my jaw on the last word because it feels like chunks of my heart are being removed from my chest, one piece at a time, and there's nothing I can do to stop it. I understand she needed time. But this? She's left me alone in this. Her words told me she loved me unconditionally, the same way I love her, but the longer she stays gone, the more I question whether they were ever really true.

"Rohan will be here in three days, when the bulls arrive. If necessary, I'll ask him then. For now, I don't want to concern them with this."

My reasons for leaving them out have nothing to do with our partnership and everything to do with protecting my wife. *God, I can hear myself turning into Warrick with every other thought.*

"I checked with my mom and casually asked if she had heard from Asha." He unscrews the lid of his water. "Made up a story about her wanting one of her recipes." His voice lowers to something apologetic. "She hasn't called."

"You don't have to stay. I know your dad needs you back home." I'm winded, wrestling the post into place with blistered hands. "I can handle this."

"Bullshit, you can handle it." His voice sharpens. "You're not eating or sleeping. I don't know what the hell is keeping you vertical right now—adrenaline, spite, both. Which is exactly why I'm not going anywhere." He pauses. "Look, I know you don't want to talk about what happened, but if you'd just—"

"I can't tell you." The words come out strangled as I lean heavily on the wooden post to keep from collapsing into the dirt. "I can't."

"Okay. Okay." His hand finds my shoulder, steadying me or bracing to catch me, I'm not sure which.

"It hurts, Hollis." My voice breaks. "It hurts so fucking bad I can't—" I can't finish. Can't breathe.

"Hey, come on, let's go back to the house. You might not want to eat, but I'm starving, and Sydney said Laney dropped off a casserole."

"I need to finish—" I straighten up, but the world tilts sideways, trees and sky trading places.

"Screw this." Hollis is at my side, steadying me. He yanks the post from the ground and hurls it aside. "That's it. We're done." He drapes my arm over his shoulders, bearing most of my weight. "You want her back? You gotta stay alive long enough to be here when she comes home."

I DON'T KNOW HOW LONG I'VE BEEN STARING AT THE CEILING of our loft. Every heartbeat feels like a lifetime. I don't want to be alone with my thoughts, and I can't give them to anyone. It feels like I'm trapped inside my own personal hell, made worse because there are no bars. I can leave, but I can't escape.

When I roll over, Sydney is there.

"You literally have to eat this. It's been five days, and Hollis says you haven't touched anything."

"That's not true. There was an orange peel in my old-fashioned yesterday," I say flatly.

"Doesn't fucking count," she says evenly. "Now sit up. I don't cook, and I made you an egg sandwich. You're going to eat it."

"That's a terrible sales pitch," I say, my voice void of any emotion. I don't care if I eat. Nothing matters without her.

"Don't be an ass. I said I don't cook, not that I can't." She slaps my arm. "Now sit up."

She sits beside me, and the movement carries the smell of the sandwich to my nose. My stomach rumbles, and for the first time in days, food doesn't make me want to throw up.

I sit up and plant my feet on the floor. I'm tired, angry, and depressed. At least if I eat the sandwich, I won't be hungry on top of it.

I pick it up and take a big bite. The flavors immediately burst on my taste buds, instantly killing my hunger pangs. "Mmm," I groan as I swallow my first bite.

"See, it's good," she says, pleased with herself.

"Cardboard would probably get the same reaction right now," I grumble around another gigantic bite.

"Hey." She punches my arm.

"Why are you here, Syd?"

"What do you mean? The people I care about are hurting right now. Where else would I be?"

I swallow the bite in my mouth and meet her gaze. "I mean, why are you here when you're one of the people doing the hurting?"

"She ran out on a conversation that didn't include me—" The look I cut her is enough to silence the lies she's about to give me. She knows I know. I caught them. To keep pretending is an insult to both of us. "I'm not trying to hurt her." Her voice is smaller as she admits defeat and drops her gaze to her lap.

"What did you *think* sleeping with her father behind her back would do?" Anger slowly starts to rise in my chest. "How could you be so reckless? If the roles were reversed, and she was sleeping with *your* dad, how would you feel?" I lean forward, willing her to look at me. "And even if by some miracle you were fine with it, you *know* Asha's past. You know she doesn't trust easily. You had to know this would torch your friendship—"

"I know, okay!" She shoots up from her spot beside me and gives me her back. "It's not what you think. I would never set out to hurt her; neither would Warrick." Her shoulders slump with a finality that has the smallest piece of me feeling sorry for her. I've only looked at her as the instigator in this affair, the one who betrayed her best friend. But I haven't considered her feelings.

"So what... You just accidentally fell into bed with him? Week after week, lie after lie? You chose this, Syd. Every single time, you chose him over her."

"I knew him before I knew her." The confession comes out broken. Slowly, she turns to face me, and her tear-filled eyes finally meet mine. "He wasn't her father when I met him. He was just...Warrick. And when Asha and I became friends, when I realized who he was..." Her face crumples. "It was already too late." She raises her hands. "I didn't know there'd be a choice to make."

The words knock something loose in my chest. She met him first. Fell for him before she even knew Asha existed. Part of me, the part that isn't Asha's husband, can see the tragedy in that. How impossible that position must have been when she realized. But the other part, the bigger part, remembers my wife's face. Asha doesn't even know about them yet. And when she finds out, this won't be some romantic twist that makes it okay. It'll just be one more layer of betrayal. It will be a best friend who kept this secret and chose him over her, over and over again.

"You have to realize there's no scenario where this ends well for you."

"Are you saying you're going to tell her?" Her eyes search mine. "The other day in Warrick's office, that wasn't a lie. There's nothing left to tell."

"You really expect me to believe that?" I lean forward, elbows on my knees. "I *saw* you. The night of the watch party, I saw you follow him into the house."

"Making sure he was okay doesn't mean we're..." She stops and rolls her lips. "It doesn't mean we're romantically involved."

"It means you still care." I stand, needing to move. "And if you still care, then it's not over."

Her hands fly up in frustration. "What do you want me to do? Corner her the second she gets back and unload everything?"

I drag both hands through my hair and grip the back of my neck. The last thing I want is to pile this on top of everything else—the pregnancy, her mom's diagnosis. She's already drowning. "Tell me what to do, Trigger, and I'll do it." Her voice cracks. "How do I make this right?"

She's asking, but the question isn't rhetorical. I can hear it—she's been asking herself the same thing, over and over, with no answer.

Damn it.

I pace to the window. "I don't know, Syd. But I don't think sleeping with her cousin is the way to start."

The words are out before I can stop them. I'm not trying to be cruel, but I can't help it. I'm angry. I'm hurt. I feel trapped in an impossible situation where every answer is wrong, where someone gets destroyed no matter what.

"I don't plan on hurting Hollis," she says, joining me beside the window. "I really like him. But I know what you're thinking—"

"No, Syd." I turn on her, hands planted on my hips. "I don't think you do."

"You think I'm using Hollis to make Warrick jealous."

My eyebrows shoot up. "Actually, I *wasn't* thinking that. But now that you've said it..." I tilt my head, study her face. "Are you?"

"No." She blinks rapidly, fighting tears. "He's kind and genuine. I don't think I've ever met someone so...good." She wraps her arms tighter around herself. "We're just friends. I know he wants more, but I've been honest with him. I told him I'm not in a place for anything beyond that."

The tension in my shoulders eases, just slightly. At least she hasn't lobbed another grenade into Asha's life. But the one she already threw? That's a nuke. And I'm holding the detonator.

"Maybe nothing's happening between you and Warrick *now.*" I step closer. "But that doesn't erase what did happen. You can't ask me to keep that from my wife." I see her pull in a shaky breath and watch fear flash across her face. "I won't lie to her, Syd. But I'm not the one who's going to tell her." Her eyes go wide. "*You* are."

She presses her lips together, crosses her arms, not in defiance, but like she's physically holding herself together. I don't have to ask what she's thinking. It's written all over her face. She doesn't want to lose her best friend. Not after she just lost the man she clearly loves.

TRIGGER

CHAPTER 43

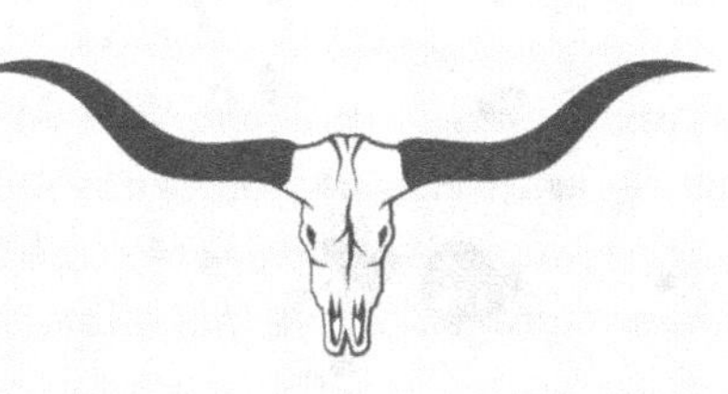

ONE WEEK LATER

I'm on horseback, but really, I'm not here. I'm still sitting on those station steps with Warrick.

Yesterday, I'd parked outside the police station, hands gripping the steering wheel like it was the only solid thing left in my world. I was ready to make it official, to turn her absence into paperwork and send out search parties. I was tired of feeling helpless. There was literally nothing else I could do to bring her back, so that was my solution. But Warrick was there on the steps before I'd even killed the engine, waiting for me.

I remember asking how he knew where to find me. *'I've walked in your shoes,'* he said, as if that explained everything. And maybe it did.

The week Maya got her diagnosis, she disappeared too, vanished the same way Asha has now. No note, no warning, just gone. Two weeks, Warrick told me, sitting on those station steps. She was gone for two weeks, the longest two weeks of his life. And he'd had a daughter to take care of then, who needed her father to hold it together even as his world crumbled around him.

I try to imagine the weight of it, and I can't. I don't have anyone else depending on me. Just this emptiness where she should be.

My horse, Knickers, shifts beneath me, adjusting to the terrain, and I shift with him.

We sat there, on those station steps, for what felt like hours. Maybe it was. Maybe it was only twenty minutes. Time has lost all meaning. Hours feel like days. Days stretch into small eternities without her.

I'd asked where Maya had been during that time. It was possible Asha was destined to run to the same places, but Warrick couldn't say for certain. He suspected she drove, mostly. *Maya loved road trips. They cleared her mind, helped her think.* He said it so simply, like it was just a fact about his wife, not a confession that he'd let her go without demanding answers. He told me that when she returned, they never talked much about where she had been. It didn't matter. What mattered was the time she had left.

'That's another reason I know she'll come back.' He'd looked at me when he said it, really looked at me, and something in his expression had shifted. *'She's her mother's daughter. Stubborn as hell. She'll come back if for no other reason than to tell you how to feel and how to go on without her.'*

The thought of being *without her*. It had stolen the air from my lungs. Still does.

'Is that why Maya reached out to Daruka Arora?' I'd asked. *'She didn't want you to be alone.'*

He'd nodded. She always believed she knew what was best. *'It's why I couldn't trust her letters.'*

He'd gone still at that. I remember that stillness.

'I'm surprised you kept them at all,' I confessed.

'I considered that,' he'd said, his voice careful. *'Opening them and resealing them, that is. But I couldn't. I didn't want confirmations. Didn't want to be angry. I just wanted to find peace.'*

Peace. As if such a thing exists when the person you love has already written your ending.

It had seemed strange to me then. Warrick, of all people, hadn't demanded answers about her whereabouts. Hadn't needed explanations. Hadn't torn open those letters to know what she thought their daughter deserved to hear.

But sitting here now, facing the same fate, swaying with Knickers' steady movement forward even though I have nowhere to go...I understand. If she came back tomorrow, I don't think I'd demand answers either. I think I'd just be grateful. Grateful she was back. Grateful that I was still worth coming back to.

The reins go slack in my hands, and all I can do is trust that Knickers knows the way home. And hope that wherever Asha is, she's finding her own way back to me, back to us.

The thought lands heavily in my chest. *Us.* Not just me and her anymore. There's a third heartbeat now, barely formed, barely real, but real enough that she ran, not from the new life itself but the math of it. The possibility that this child might one day feel their own time running out. I know this terrifies her—I know this because it terrifies me too.

Sprinkles hit the back of my neck, and Knickers doesn't wait for direction. He turns off the muddy trail and carries us under the canopy where the leaves catch most of the rain.

Warrick never told Asha about the diagnosis that could be in her future. Instead, he bartered with his wife and sent his daughter away when he thought she was getting too close to the truth. He let Asha grow up believing her mother had died of something sudden, something that couldn't be passed down like a family heirloom you never wanted. I've contemplated that choice countless times over the past week. When I think about Asha, all I see is that honesty is the only right answer because people deserve to know what they are carrying.

But when I think about my unborn child, my answer wavers. It's not so black and white anymore. All I see are timelines, a future on borrowed time. Do I want them counting down to some invisible deadline? Seeing every birthday cake, every Christmas morning, every scraped knee, and first day of school through the lens of *how many of these do I have left?*

The rain hits the leaves a little harder now, and I can't be sure which way we're going, but without Asha at home, I have nowhere to be, and right now getting lost feels like the only place where I can begin to be found. So, I let Knickers lead the way.

Warrick didn't want fear to be Asha's inheritance. He wanted her to live, not just survive. And there's a difference. A life lived in dread of its ending isn't really lived at all. And survival isn't the same as living.

I can't help but feel like, in his own misguided way, that's what he was trying to accomplish with his secrets. Days that weren't overshadowed by diagnoses and statistics. He gave her the peace of not knowing. The freedom to believe that life was something coming *from* her—her choices, her dreams, her own two hands building something—and not something happening to her, some predetermined script she had no say in writing.

I think about our child. The one Asha is carrying right now, wherever she is. If they have the gene, and, years from now, they start showing symptoms, would I want them to have known all along? To have spent their childhood, their teenage years, their twenties under that shadow? Or would I want them to have what Asha had, at least for a while?

Knickers suddenly stops and blows a sharp burst of air through his nose. The sound snaps me out of my thoughts, and I scan the trees for an animal. My spine straightens, and every one of my senses goes on alert when I spot a shadowy figure, about fifty feet ahead, moving through the clearing. I click my tongue to signal Knickers to keep walking, my eyes keenly tuned on the figure.

The closer we get to the edge of the trees, the faster my heart beats. I can't trust my eyes or this desperate thing in my chest that's been summoning her in every dark-haired woman I pass. But this shadow...it's definitely female, dressed in white, and hell if she doesn't move like her. I'd know that hourglass shape on that slender frame anywhere. I'm either seeing her, or I've finally lost my mind.

We move through the short span of woods, branches catching at my shoulders, dampening my already wet clothes more, and then we're in the clearing, and I see it. There's no more question of if. She's there—really there—standing with her back to me beside a patch of trees. Her white dress clings to her, soaked through and nearly transparent from the rain. I don't call her name as I approach. I'm too scared to say it out loud, too worried that speaking might break this spell, because that has to be what this is. There's no way I took a ride to clear my head, wound up lost, and stumbled upon my missing wife.

With each step closer, I grow more confident she hears me, Knickers' breathing, the creak of the saddle, the pound of his hooves against the sodden grass, but still, she doesn't move. She just stands there in that rain-soaked dress like a ghost I've conjured from grief.

I'm still several feet away when I swing down from Knickers, my hands fumbling through the motion of tying him to the nearest tree. I move toward her slowly, afraid that if I rush, she'll vanish. Afraid she's not real at all.

It's not until I'm right beside her, close enough to see the delicate olive veins beneath her skin, the rise and fall of her chest, that I finally speak.

"Asha." Her name comes out like a whisper as I send up a silent prayer that this moment isn't just my mind. That the edges of my vision won't start to fade, signaling the cruel end of a dream.

She blinks, and water droplets fall from her lashes. She's real.

Slowly, so slowly that I feel every second of it, she turns to me. And God, her face. Sadness doesn't even begin to cover what I see there. It's devastation. The kind that lives in your bones and changes who you are.

"I'm sorry." Her words crack down the middle, and then tears come, sliding down her cheeks to mix with the rain.

"Don't be sorry." The words tumble out as I close the distance between us, pulling her into my arms for the first time in seven days, four hours, and a lifetime of minutes I counted in the dark. I don't let go. I can't. I won't.

Her body fits against mine exactly the way I remember, and the relief of it nearly breaks me. But she's trembling. The tremors that travel through her and into me are violent and uncontrollable, like everything is crashing down in this moment. The weight of the secret, the week we spent apart, the news of our baby. All of it is colliding into these seconds, and she's not strong enough to hold it anymore. I feel her heartbeat against my chest, too hard as her sobs come in gasps she can't contain. My hand finds the back of her head, and my fingers tangle in her wet hair before I press my lips to her temple and breathe her in, holding her through it, because there's no other way.

I pull back just enough to shrug off the lightweight coat I'd grabbed on my way out the door. My hands are shaking as I drape it over her shoulders. She's soaked through and freezing.

And that's when my eyes drift past her. That's when I see it, and my blood runs cold.

Fresh dirt. Dark and wet and piled beside a headstone I can't quite read from this angle. The earth looks freshly turned, as if someone had been digging...like she'd been digging.

Fear claws its way up my throat, sharp and choking.

"I'm so sorry," she mumbles against my chest, the words vibrating through my ribs.

My blood turns to ice. "Asha." I pull back, gripping her shoulders, needing to see her face. "What did you do?"

Her eyes, the same ones that have haunted me for a week, are red-rimmed and lost.

"Why are you here? Why are we standing beside a grave? Asha, tell me." My voice comes out harder than I mean it to. "Tell me why I'm standing beside a grave. And not just any grave, one with freshly dug dirt."

It's been one week. Seven days she's been gone. I never found the truck when I drove through town. She didn't stay with friends. She could have easily driven to Illinois in that time. Could have walked into some clinic where nobody knew her name. Where they wouldn't ask questions. Where she could make it all go away and come back here to bury the truth beside her mother.

The thought finishes itself in my mind, and I can't breathe. Can't think. Can't do anything but feel the ground dropping out from under me.

She shakes her head, and the tears come faster and harder.

"No." The word rips out of me, raw and broken, as I drop to my knees beside the grave. My vision blurs as I look at the ground and shove my hands into the dirt. "Tell me this isn't our baby." My voice shatters into pieces.

"Tell me you didn't—" I can't even say it, can't force the words through my lips because they hurt too fucking much. "Tell me you didn't get rid of our baby."

"*What?*" The word falls from her mouth like she's been struck. She drops beside me, her knees hitting the wet earth, and her hands circle my arm.

She trembles as rain mists between us, her eyes wide with the same fear that grips me. But she doesn't retreat. "Why would you think that?"

"You disappeared," I choke out, the words jagged. "You were *gone*. And now you're here, standing beside a grave with fresh dirt, and you're saying you're sorry..." I can't finish. Can't say it out loud again. My hand gestures helplessly at the fresh dirt. "I thought I'd lost everything."

She makes a sound that's a half sob, half gasp, and then her hands are moving. She takes my hand in both of hers and presses my palm flat against her stomach.

"Our baby is still right here."

Her voice cracks on the words, but they land like a lifeline. I freeze as my hand rests against the cold, wet fabric of her dress. But beneath the rain-soaked material and the chill, there's warmth. Life. Still growing. Still real. Still *ours.*

The relief doesn't just wash over me; it devastates me. My hand spreads wider across her stomach, fingers splaying as if I can cover more of her, I can protect more of them. Like I can hold this moment and never let it slip away again. The warmth beneath my palm feels like the only real thing in the world. Like everything else, the rain, the grave, the week of hell, is just noise, and this is the truth. This steady, impossible warmth.

"Right here," she says again, and she's crying harder now, her hands pressing mine tighter against her. "I would never... I could never."

I love her. God, I love her so much it's breaking me apart and putting me back together all at once. Every piece of me that shattered this past week is reforming around this single point of warmth beneath my hand. The relief crashes over me so hard it steals what's left of my breath, and I pull her against me.

"I'm sorry," she whispers. "I'm so sorry I ever made you doubt...that you thought for one second I could ever do that to you—to us."

It's not her fault. It's fear. That's what fear does: it doesn't ask questions, doesn't wait for answers. It just takes your worst nightmare and convinces you it's already true.

I put a small amount of space between us, just enough so I can see her face. My hand trembles as I push the wet hair back from her eyes. "Don't be sorry. We've been through hell this past week. Unimaginable hell. But Asha, I need to know..." I pause, needing a second to breathe before continuing. "I need to know what else you could possibly bury beside your mother's grave."

"I should probably start at the beginning, but first I need you to hear something." Her bottom lip quivers before she bites it to find her strength. "I know there's no way you could have known what I accused you of that day in my father's office, but in the moment, I couldn't see past getting out of that room. I just needed to be alone." She exhales, like she's releasing the weight of her choice. "I didn't run this time—or at least, I didn't try to." My eyes search hers curiously. "I never left Bardstown. I stayed at the B&B in town and parked the truck around back, under the carport, where no one would see it. The owners know me. They floated my stay until I could pay, and I told them I would pay double for their discretion."

Her voice draws off, and she pulls in a shaking breath, her fingers still circled around my arm like if she lets go, I'll disappear too.

"I'll admit..." She swallows hard, and I see the truth in her eyes before she says it. "I thought about what you're suggesting. The idea crossed my mind, but I wouldn't make that decision without you. I *couldn't*."

Relief and agony hit me at the same time, and I don't know if I want to pull her closer or fall apart completely.

Her hand releases my arm and finds the side of my face, cold and trembling against my cheek. She gently pulls my face toward hers until we're eye to eye, close enough that I can count the flecks of gold in her irises, see my own broken reflection there.

"I was utterly broken," she whispers. "The past few days, I wasn't me. It felt like an out-of-body experience, like I was watching myself from somewhere else, somewhere far away. I was overtaken with shock at first. Then denial. And when those finally ebbed, fear and anger..." Her hand slides up my arm and rests on my cheek. "They crippled me. I couldn't move. Couldn't think." Fresh tears well in her eyes, and I see every ounce of pain she's been carrying. I recognize it, because I've been carrying it too. "But it wasn't fair to let you worry like that. I thought I'd be gone for one night. Just one, and I would come home, but then I couldn't leave the room. I didn't plan to stay gone so long. I was so selfish—"

"Don't." I catch her wrist, holding her hand against my face. "Don't apologize." I hear the strain in my voice as I try to hold myself together. "You're right. I was angry—furious, even—but my hurt and pain are nothing compared to what you've had to endure. You're the one who got the diagnosis. All I got was the grief." I force myself to hold her gaze, to let her see every raw edge of what I'm feeling. "You're the one who might be dying. I'm just the one who has to learn how to love someone I can't save."

The rain still mists around us, turning the world into a gray blur, but all I can see is her. All I can feel is her hand against my face and the way we're both kneeling in the mud beside this grave, holding onto each other like we're drowning. And maybe we are.

She shakes her head slowly, and water forms streams down her face. "Aren't we all dying?" My eyes narrow on hers. "Every day, we all grow older. We all grow one day closer to our end." Her eyes slide over to the freshly dug dirt. "My days are no more numbered than yours—or at least that's how I've decided it will be."

"What's beneath that dirt?"

"A letter." She's quiet for long moments, her eyes fixed on that patch of earth like she's saying goodbye to something I can't see. "My father was right not to trust that my mother would keep up her end of the deal." Her voice is barely above a whisper. "The last letter she left me contained the results of testing she ran behind my father's back. She admitted she hated doing it, but she hated even more that she wouldn't live to know if I would have the same fate."

My chest tightens. The answers are right there, beneath the dirt. The answers I'm not sure I want anymore.

Her eyes come back to mine, and they're clearer now. "I don't want to know." The words are absolute. "I don't want to know how many days I may or may not have left. I've always known every breath is a gift. I've known that since I lost my mom, but I don't want to count mine." Her hand tightens against my face. "I want to live in the moment, not in fear."

The rain runs between her fingers, down my jaw.

"Trigger, I love you. I can't imagine living this life without you." Her voice cracks but doesn't break. "But I've made my choice. I understand if you need to leave. I'm not saying that because I want you to..." She swallows hard, and I see it's costing her everything to continue. "I'm saying it because I understand the impossible position it puts you in to stay with me."

My mouth parts to argue, but her cold finger covers my lips.

"I know you're going to argue. It's who you are. You'll tell me this doesn't change anything, but it does. We both know that." Her thumb brushes across my bottom lip. "It will be a cloud for the rest of my life, a question in the recesses of my mind, no matter how hard I try. I know it will bleed in. I know grief is circular, and it's not a question of if my fear will return and cripple me, but when." A shudder runs through her, and I feel it echo in my own body. "This is my fate." Her eyes search mine. "It doesn't have to be yours."

I reach up and gently pull her hand away from my mouth, but I don't let go. I weave my fingers through hers, holding on like she's the only solid thing in a world that won't stop spinning.

"I knew you were nervous the night we said our vows," I say quietly, "but I didn't realize you didn't hear them." Rain streams down my face, mixing with something else I won't name. "When I said 'in sickness and health,' it wasn't conditional."

"But our marriage was."

Her words sting because she's right. Our marriage was conditional, a solution to a problem, but she's also wrong, and she has to know that.

"Not for me, it wasn't." My voice is raw. "And you know that." I shift closer, still kneeling in the mud until there's barely any space between us. "Maybe you don't want to hear it because you're scared. Scared that someone could love you so much they'd choose this journey with you rather than without. But I'm not scared of that."

Her breath hitches.

"I don't regret one second. Not one. And the only thing that scares me is thinking you won't let me stay." I bring our joined hands to my chest, pressing them against my heart so she can feel how hard it's beating. "Don't push me away, sweetheart."

The words catch in my throat, and suddenly, everything I've been holding back for months—years, even comes pouring out.

"I feel like I'm always chasing you. Like I never actually have you."

She flinches like I've struck her, and immediately, her other hand comes up to grip my arm. "You've always had me." Her voice breaks. "I've just done a terrible job of showing you."

Rain drips down her pretty face, mixing with fresh tears. "I know I'm hard to love, Trigger Hale. But you are too."

"How so?" My eyes narrow as I wipe away a tear. "I don't recall running from you."

"No." She lets out a sound that's half laugh, half sob. "No, you don't run. You never run. That's just it. I can't compete with the way you love me. The way you've always loved me."

"Compete?" I repeat the word I don't understand. This isn't a competition.

"With the version of me you've built up in your head since we were kids. The girl you've been in love with your whole life." She pulls in a shaky breath, and I can see the effort it takes her to keep going. "You love me like I'm something precious. Something worth protecting. Worth saving. And I'm terrified..." Her voice trails off before she finds her strength again. "I'm terrified that when you finally see me clearly, when you see all the broken, scared, selfish parts I can't seem to fix, you'll realize I'm not her. I'm not the girl you've been waiting for."

"Asha—"

"What if I'm not enough?" she whispers. "What if loving me becomes a burden instead of a choice?"

For a long moment, I just stare at her, at this woman kneeling in the mud with mascara running down her cheeks, her white dress clinging to her frame, and fear written all over her face. And I realize she actually believes what she's saying. She actually thinks there's a version of her in my head that's better than the real thing.

"You want to know what I see when I look at you?" I ask quietly. She hesitates then nods. "I see someone who feels everything so deeply it scares her, so she runs." I tighten my grip on her hands. "And yeah, I see someone who's hard to love. Not because you're broken or selfish, but because loving you means understanding that sometimes you need to run. And I have to let you. I have to trust you'll come back."

Her lips part, but no sound comes out.

"You think I've built you up in my head? That I'm in love with some perfect version of you?" I let out a breath. "Asha, I know exactly who you are. I know you pick fights when you're scared and shut down when you should open up. I know you'd rather burn the whole world down than admit you're hurting."

A tear slides down her cheek, and I catch it with my thumb.

"And I love you anyway. Not despite those things, just...anyway. That's not a competition, sweetheart. It's just love."

"But what if I keep running?" Her voice softens with uncertainty. "What if I can't stop?"

"Then I'll keep coming after you." I pull her closer until our foreheads touch. "Every single time, until I *have your heart again.*"

"I love you," she breathes. "God, I've never loved anything or anyone the way that I love you, and it terrifies me."

"Then let it terrify us together."

I watch the last of her resistance crumble, and then she's closing the distance between us. Our lips meet, and the world stops. It's desperate and salty with rain and tears, and nothing about it is gentle. It's a week of hell collapsing into this single point of contact. It's need and fear and grief and relief, all of it pouring out of us in a way words never could. Her hands fist in my wet shirt, pulling me closer, like she's trying to crawl inside my chest and make a home there. And I let her. God, I let her.

I kiss her like I'm trying to breathe life back into both of us. Like she's the only thing tethering me to this earth. Like if I let go for even a second, I'll lose her again, and I can't. Tears sting my eyes, and when I feel her chest shake against mine, I know she's crying too. We're a sobbing mess, holding on like we're the only two people left in the world who understand what it means to almost lose everything.

When she gasps against my mouth, I pull her impossibly closer, not ready to let her go. Our foreheads press together, lips still touching, breathing each other's air because separating even an inch feels like too much.

"Don't leave me again," I whisper against her mouth, the words more plea than demand.

"Never," she promises and kisses me again to seal it.

When we finally break apart, both of us breathless, she whispers, "Take me home."

The ride home is quiet. She leans into me, her head against my shoulder, and I hold the reins with one hand while the other stays wrapped around her waist.

Knickers knows the way, and I let him take it. My mind drifts back to Warrick on those station steps, telling me about the two weeks Maya disappeared. The longest two weeks of his life, he'd said. Now I understand why he never demanded answers when she came back. Love isn't about holding so tight that nothing can escape. It's about holding steady enough that someone feels safe to return.

Asha's hand covers mine where it rests against her stomach, our baby, and I finally understand what Warrick was really telling me that day. He wasn't just sharing his story; he was showing me that some questions don't need answers. That sometimes the bravest thing you can do is live anyway. Love anyway. Hope anyway.

Somewhere in the woods behind us, a letter is buried. Test results. Answers. The kind of certainty that steals your ability to live in the present because you're too busy calculating the future.

Asha chose not to know. And sitting here with her in my arms, feeling the rise and fall of her breathing, I realize she didn't choose ignorance. She chose freedom. Because knowing wouldn't really change anything. It wouldn't change our decision to keep our baby. It wouldn't add days to her life, and it wouldn't subtract them either. It would just color every single one she has left with the shadow of an ending she can't control anyway.

The barn comes into view, and I feel her relax against me completely.

I don't know what tomorrow looks like. Don't know if she'll wake up scared and try to run again. Don't know if our baby will carry the gene that stole its grandmother. Don't know if I'll have five years with Asha or fifty. But I know this: I'll love her through all of it. The running and the staying, the fear and the hope. The unknowns that will keep us up at night and the moments of peace we steal in between. I don't love Asha because it's easy, but because not loving her would be impossible. Some people are written into our DNA in a way that has nothing to do with genetics and everything to do with choice. Asha is my choice. Every day. No matter what.

As we dismount Knickers, and I catch her in my arms one more time, I realize something Warrick already knew: You can't save someone from their fate. You can only love them through it. So that's what I'll do. I'll love her through every terrified moment and every brave one. Through the circular grief that will come in waves. Through the questions that have no answers and the future we can't predict.

I'll love her. And we'll live. And whatever time we get, that will be enough.

Because it has to be.

THE END

ASHA

EPILOGUE

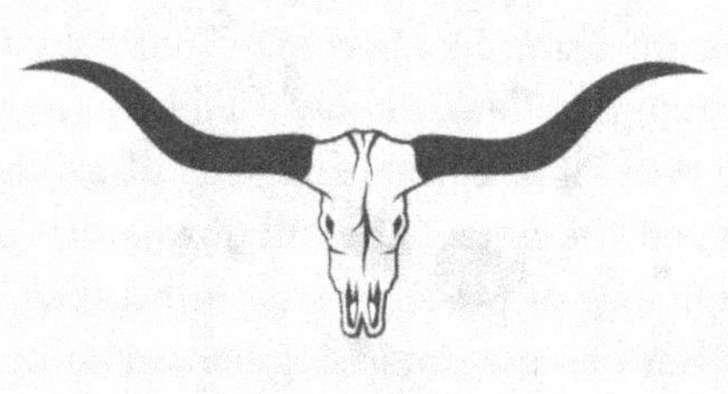

The kitchen smells like cinnamon and red wine. It's a warmth that settles into your bones and makes you forget there's a world beyond these walls. I lean against the counter, glass in hand, watching London's daughter, Grace, toddle between chair legs. Laney tries and fails to coax her back.

Across the room, my father holds Avi against his shoulder, one large hand cradling my son's tiny head. Son. I still can't believe I'm a mom. He was definitely an unexpected surprise, but one I couldn't imagine living without.

"She's got London's stubbornness," Laney says, exasperated but smiling.

"And your tendency to ignore sound advice," London adds, earning him a playful swat.

Trigger catches my eye from where he stands near the sink with Rohan. He doesn't smile, not exactly, but something shifts in his expression—a quiet recognition that still makes my chest tighten. He's always been able to unravel me with one look. Those dark eyes penetrated through my armor. Everyone else sees a puzzle—a guarded girl with trust issues and a complicated past. But Trigger solved that puzzle before I ever said "I do." He pieced together who I am underneath all the protection. He saw the parts of me I thought were too damaged or difficult to love and married me anyway.

"You're too quiet," Dar says, appearing at my elbow with the kind of knowing look only aunts can manage. "It's your birthday. You're supposed to be the loudest one here."

Rohan laughs. "When has Asha ever been loud?"

"Fair point," Dar concedes, refilling my glass without asking. "But still. What's happening in that head of yours?"

Everything. Nothing. How do you explain that your life has become unrecognizable in the best possible way? That the man you agreed to marry out of desperation, a deal with an enemy to save land you couldn't afford to lose, has somehow become the person who saved *you* instead? That you're someone's mother now, that you created this perfect little human who's currently drooling on your father's shoulder?

"Just thinking," I say, taking a sip. The wine is good. My father has exquisite taste in wine. Among other things, I'm still learning about him. Ever since he came clean about my mother's sickness, I feel like we're getting to know each other on a deeper level. He was my best friend and my whole world for so long. Then I started seeing cracks in his façade and realized I was only seeing the man he allowed me to see. Now, he lets me in.

"Dangerous," Trigger says, moving closer. His hand finds the small of my back in a casual, easy way, like he's always belonged there.

Grace shrieks with delight, having discovered a wooden spoon on the floor. The sound cuts through the conversation, and Avi startles against my father's shoulder. I watch his hand come up instinctively to cradle his head, and his lips move with words too quiet to hear. Around me, the kitchen fills with laughter and life. Laney is reaching for Grace, Rohan is refilling wine glasses, and Dar is gesturing wildly as she tells some story. Family, old and new, weaving around each other like they've always belonged in the same room. This is what I never let myself imagine. Life. Noise. People who stayed.

A year ago, I believed the worst about my father. I carried that belief like a stone in my pocket, heavy and cold. Then came his secret. The truth threatened to change everything and rewrite my entire story. The way I saw it, I had two choices: chase it down, demand answers, and let it consume me. Or let it go.

I chose the moment. Chose *this*. The warmth, the laughter, the spoon-wielding toddler. The baby sleeping on his grandfather's shoulder. The husband whose love I was too blind to see for far too long.

"Here," my father says, crossing to me. "He wants his mama."

I set down my glass and take Avi. The weight of him in my arms is still something I can't believe is real. Three months old, and already changing everything I thought my life would be.

"You okay, sweetheart?" Trigger's voice is low, meant just for me. His hand moves from my back to rest gently on Avi's head.

I turn to him and really look at him. He's the man who loved me even when I couldn't understand it. The man who gave me this child, this life, this chance at something I didn't know I was allowed to want.

"Yeah," I say, and mean it. "I really am."

Because each day is a gift. Each moment in this kitchen is a gift. I'm surrounded by family who traveled across oceans, and friends who've become family. My husband started as an enemy and ended as everything. It's all a gift. I've spent too much of my life looking back, cataloging losses, and bracing for the next blow. Not anymore.

"Happy birthday, Asha," my father says, raising his glass. The others follow suit.

I can't raise mine because Avi's in my arms, but I nod, blinking back the sudden sting in my eyes. "Thank you," I manage. "For being here. For all of it."

Trigger's arm comes around both of us, and I lean into him, let myself be held. Let myself be happy without waiting for it to crumble.

Grace throws the spoon.

Laney groans.

Dar laughs so hard her bangles jangle.

And I—I live through it, every perfect, chaotic second.

"Okay, now that the toast is out of the way. Let's eat," Dar says, carrying a dish from the stove to the table in the other room. My father offers to take it, but she swats him away. "I have it. Let me serve you. Please."

This isn't the first time Dar and my father met. They met months ago when Dar and Rohan came over with the first bull delivery. To say the meeting was tense would be an understatement. My father had a lot of things to work through, and to this day, I'm certain I still don't know the half of it. What I do know is he's trying to put past grievances aside. He's trying to look ahead, not behind, and I know a lot of that has to do with me. If I can push through and choose not to be defined by what might be, he can choose the same path. Our pasts don't have to define us.

"Well, if you decide to surprise me next year for my birthday, I'll be able to host all of you at my own kitchen table," I say, taking a seat at the long dining table in my father's dining room. "Now that Dad isn't blocking roads, shutting off power, and throwing out our permits, we can build a house." I smile.

"I never threw out permits," he objects, his lips pulling to one corner.

I roll my eyes. "Sorry, *threatened to bury them under mysterious zoning violations* is a better choice of words."

Trigger coughs into his wine glass. It sounds suspiciously like a laugh.

"Or was it the sudden need for environmental impact studies?" I add sweetly. "On land that's been farmed for a hundred years?"

My father's jaw tightens, but there's amusement in his eyes. "Well," he clears his throat, easily swatting off my comment like it's a fly. "Before you start tossing money at an architect, maybe you should open my gift." He passes an envelope down the table.

I take the envelope and hold it in my hands curiously, measuring his words against the piece of paper in front of me. Then I give Avi to Trigger beside me. When I tear open the envelope, I find a deed. At the bottom, his signature is sprawled across the page. I swallow, my throat thick with emotion as tears well in my eyes. "You're giving me Mom's house?" I say, my voice small, still unbelieving that what I'm holding is real.

The table goes quiet. Even Grace stops fussing.

My father shifts in his seat, but there's no uncertainty in his expression. He looks... decided. Like this has been the plan all along. "Your mom always wanted you to have this. I may have been her husband, but you were her daughter. This land belongs to you."

I look up at him, my vision blurring. "But what about the horses and—"

He raises his hand, stopping me. "We can discuss all that, but we both know our home in Louisville can sustain the business. Don't worry about me. You're starting your family. It's only right you do it here, in the same place you always dreamed you would."

The breath leaves my lungs. *The same place you always dreamed you would.* He remembered.

My fingers trace the edge of the deed, and I can barely see it through the tears. This was his plan all along. That's why he was being difficult. "I don't... I don't know what to say."

"You don't have to say anything," my father says quietly.

"Thank you," I whisper. "Thank you."

Dar stays quiet across the table, but I can see her blinking rapidly, her jaw tight with emotion. Trigger's hand is on my back now, steady and warm, and I can hear Avi's quickened breaths on his chest as he settles against him. A house. A home. The place where my mother lived, where she held me, where she must have stood at the windows and imagined my future. And now I get to build that future with Trigger and Avi, and whatever comes next.

Laney's crying now, and London hands her a napkin, shaking his head fondly at both of us.

"That's... that's quite the gift," Rohan says, breaking the heavy silence, his voice careful.

"Quite the gift indeed," Dar says, her bangles clinking as she clasps her hands together. "But I do have something special I'd like to give you as well."

I laugh, wiping at my eyes. "I don't think I need any more property."

"Well, that's good since I don't have any to give away." Dar smiles. "My gift is for you, but it's also for Trigger." She looks around the table, her expression softening. "In fact, I'd say it's probably for everyone at this table, since I can see these are the people who mean the world to you."

Almost everyone, I think to myself. Sydney's not here.

"Asha," Dar continues, leaning forward slightly. "I'd like to throw you a traditional Indian wedding."

I blink. "What?"

"A proper wedding," she says, her eyes bright with excitement. "Mehendi ceremony, where we are going to adorn your hands and feet with henna in beautiful designs. Sangeet, a night of music and dancing where both families perform. The haldi ceremony, where we cover you in turmeric paste for blessings and good luck. A baraat procession with Trigger arriving on horseback, maybe, with all his people dancing in the streets. Followed by tying of the mangalsutra, which is a sacred thread and applying of Sindhoor. And the Pheras around the sacred fire where you make your vows. Days of celebration, Asha. Vibrant colors, traditional clothing, so much food you won't believe it. Music, joy, rituals that have been passed down for generations." She pauses, and her voice grows softer, more tender.

"In our culture, a wedding isn't just about binding two individuals together. It's about bringing families together. Creating bonds that last generations." Her eyes glisten. "I believe your mother would have given you this, Asha. It's why she taught you how to cook Indian meals for your father." She glances down the table at my dad. "And I think it's another reason she wanted me and your father to meet. So you could get to know your family and our culture. I'm certain she would have planned every detail, made sure you knew every tradition, every meaning behind every ritual. And I—" Her voice catches. "I can't replace her. I would never try, but I can honor her and do for you what I believe she would've done."

Dar's gaze shifts to my father again, who's gone very still at the head of the table.

"I also want to give this to my brother," she says quietly. "I want this for you, for us just as much."

My father holds her gaze, his eyes softening almost imperceptibly before he looks down at his glass, and I'm certain it's to collect whatever feelings her confessions have stirred. He's trying, he really is, but my father is nothing if not stoic.

"Listen, I know love doesn't need a ceremony to be real," Dar says with a smile. "But sometimes a ceremony makes real things feel sacred. And after everything you two have been through? You deserve days of nothing but celebration. Joy, family, and honoring what you've built together and giving everyone who loves you a chance to witness it properly."

The table is quiet as I weigh her offer. Dar's right, my mother would have loved this. I know she would have spent months planning to make my big day special. She's been gone so long that sometimes I forget what I lost, what was taken from me. But Dar knows, and she's offering to stand in that gap, not as a replacement but as a bridge to what was. Plus, I do think it would go a long way in bringing her and my father closer.

"Dar," I finally manage, my voice breaking. "That's—"

"Too much?" she asks gently.

"No." I shake my head. "It's perfect."

There's a beat of silence, and then Dar's face lights up as I've just handed her the world. She actually squeals and claps her hands together. "You're saying yes? You're really saying yes?"

"I—" I look at Trigger, who's watching me with that steady gaze that says he's with me, whatever I decide. "Yeah. Yes. Let's do it."

"Oh my god, okay, okay." Dar is already pulling out her phone, her fingers flying. "We'll do it at my home. In Spain. The estate has beautiful gardens, and we can set up the mandap there. You've seen the grounds; you know how stunning they are. And now we'll fill it with color and music and celebration," she immediately goes into wedding planner mode.

"Spain?" I repeat.

"Spain," she confirms, beaming. "The villa has plenty of room for guests, and there are hotels nearby for overflow. We can make a whole week of it. End of summer, I'm thinking September. That gives us six months to plan everything."

She's scrolling furiously now, muttering to herself. "We need to find you a lehenga, red of course, it's traditional, but we can modernize it if you want. And Trigger needs a Sherwani. I know the perfect boutique in Barcelona. We'll need a pandit to perform the ceremony, a caterer, musicians, and a mehendi artist. And we can't forget we'll need to book travel for everyone, coordinate with Trigger's family." Her face flashes up from her phone. "Do you have a big family, Trigger?"

"Not particularly," he says, the corner of his mouth lifting.

"Good, that makes it easier. Still, we'll want them involved. We'll need to coordinate flights and accommodations." Her hand squeezes Rohan's arm beside her. "You'll handle the logistics?"

"Already on it," Rohan says, grinning at me.

Laney leans across the table toward me, her eyes wide. "Asha, a wedding in Spain? This is incredible. Can I help plan?"

"Please," Dar says before I can answer. "I'll need all the help I can get. We'll need to schedule a trip out there soon, you, me, and Laney. We'll meet with vendors and do dress fittings in Barcelona."

I look around the table. My father is watching Dar with something akin to wonder. Laney is already pulling out her own phone to take notes. Rohan is shaking his head fondly at his mother's excitement. And

Trigger, his eyes on me like I'm the only person in the room as he holds our son. Spain. End of summer. A wedding with everyone I love.

"Okay," I say, and I can't stop smiling. "End of summer in Spain it is."

Dar squeals again, and the table erupts in laughter and excited chatter about flights, dates, and what to pack. But as the noise swells around me, my eyes drift to London. He's listening to Laney rattle off ideas, but there's something in his expression, something careful that makes my chest tighten.

"London," I say quietly, and he looks up. "Have you heard anything from Fisher? Do you think Sydney will come?"

He pulls in a deep breath that matches the weight of my question.

I haven't seen Sydney since the day I ran out of my father's house after learning what really caused my mother's death. No one has heard from her or seen her since. Trigger said she was around the week I disappeared, and then she was gone. I know she's not dead. Her brother Fisher has told us as much, but that's it. We don't know where she went or why. She cut off all communication.

London's jaw works for a moment. "Asha," he says finally, his voice soft. "You know I wish I could say yes, but I don't want to lie to you."

I look between Laney and London, something nagging at me. "Are you guys sure nothing happened while I was gone?"

At the head of the table, my father pushes his chair out abruptly, the legs scraping against the floor and garnering everyone's attention. "I'm going to grab another bottle of wine," he says through tight lips when he notices he's caught everyone's attention.

The tension settles over the table like a blanket. London meets my eyes, his expression careful. "Sometimes people don't stay gone to hurt you. Sometimes they stay gone because they think they're doing the opposite."

I consider his words. Out of anyone at this table, he would know. He's been the guy who cut out his friends and family, leaving no trace. London had a damn good reason, but what I can't put together is what Sydney could possibly be protecting any of us from.

Beside me, Trigger reaches for my hand and gently squeezes. "Fisher will get word to her."

I let out a resigned breath. "I doubt she'll come." I brush my fingers over Avi's feet. She knew I was pregnant before she left, which means she has to know I'm a mom now, and still nothing. No congratulations, no well wishes, nothing. I release a heavy sigh. "I have to at least try; if I don't, then I'm the one closing the door." I swallow hard. "It just sucks, is all."

"It does," Laney says softly.

Dar's bangles clink as she reaches across the table, her expression sympathetic but not pitying. "The invitation will be there," she says simply. "That's all you can do."

My father returns with two bottles of wine, setting them on the table with more force than necessary.

"So," Rohan says, his voice deliberately lighter. "September in Spain. Mother, you think you can pull off a full traditional wedding in six months?"

"Six months?" Dar scoffs, already back in planning mode. "I could do it in three if I had to. But six gives us time to do it right."

"September twenty-first," Trigger says suddenly, and everyone turns to look at him. He's looking at me, Avi still cradled against his chest. "That's when we should do it. The equinox. Equal day and night. Balance."

My throat tightens. "You've been thinking about this."

"Maybe," he says, and there's the smallest hint of a smile.

"September twenty-first," I repeat, testing the words. "That's perfect."

"Perfect," Dar agrees, already typing into her phone. "I'm putting it in the calendar right now. September twenty-first. Spain. Your wedding."

Laney raises her glass. "To September."

"To family," London adds.

"To new beginnings," my father chimes in, and this time, when we all raise our glasses, it feels like a promise.

I look around the table at the people who've stayed, who've fought to be here, who've chosen to build something new from broken pieces. And I think about Sydney, wherever she is, and I hope that somehow she'll find her way back. But if she doesn't, I can't let that stop me from moving forward.

September twenty-first. A wedding in Spain. A week filled with celebration of everything we've survived and everything we're becoming. I lean into Trigger, feeling Avi's warmth between us, and for the first time in a long time, I let myself look ahead without fear.

The future is waiting, and it's beautiful.

ALSO BY L.A. FERRO

Rival Hearts

Don't Take The Girl

Trope list: Cowboy, Boy Next Door, Small Town, Friends to Lovers, Slow Burn, Rival Ranches.

Summer Nights

DIG: A Second Chance Romance

Trope list: Sports Romance, College Romance, Dark Secrets, Emotional Scars, Second Chance, Redemption.

Fade Into You

Trope list: Arranged Marriage, Sports Romance, Small Town, Single Dad, Mistaken Identity, Unrequited Love.

SALT

Trope list: Age Gap, Best Friend's Daughter, Protector, Angsty, Secret Romance, Forbidden, Sports Romance.

~

Copper Falls

<u>Rewriting Grey: Romantic Thriller</u>

Trope List: Reclusive Author, Siblings Ex, Forced Proximity, Secret Identity, Small Town.

Scoring Grey: A Hockey Romance

Trope list: Golden Retriever MC, Boy Obsessed, He Falls First, Secret Past, Reunited Lovers.

~

Shades of Dark

The Delicate Vows Duet - A Billionaire Romance

Trope list: Billionaire Romance, Off-limits, Age-gap, Secret Virgin, Different Worlds, He Falls First.

Wicked Beautiful Lies: A Taboo Romance

Trope list: Taboo/forbidden, Mistaken Identity, Enemies to Lovers, Dark Secrets.

Sweet Venom: A Why Choose Romance

Trope List: Taboo, Enemies to Lovers, Friends to Lovers, Dark Secrets, Different Worlds, Unrequited Love.

ACKNOWLEDGMENTS

To my Beta Team: Mindy, Lakshmi, Brittany, and Thorunn—I realize I sound like a broken record, but some truths bear repeating: this team is nothing short of extraordinary. Every bit of refinement and sparkle in my manuscript exists because of your sharp eyes and thoughtful feedback.

Mindy, my vibe checker—your genuine excitement for this story meant the world to me. I loved the endless tags you left for me throughout the manuscript. We're kindred spirits when it comes to suspense and mystery, and you have an instinct for whether a scene lands emotionally.

Lakshmi, our resident vampire and the heartbeat of this entire process. You're the perfect sounding board when I'm wrestling with character arcs and need someone to help me untangle my thoughts. As my sensitivity reader, your insight was absolutely invaluable in ensuring I brought Asha's character to life authentically and respectfully. You kept this project alive and made it infinitely better.

Brittany, my eagle-eyed detail guardian. You spot the discrepancies that would haunt me after publication: contradicting facts, timeline discrepencies, the small errors that would unravel reader experience. You keep my nightmares at bay.

Thorunn, your sharp eye catches what others miss. The care and attention you bring to every detail made this a better book, and I'm so grateful for it.

I'm genuinely grateful for all of you. Never leave me! You each bring something irreplaceable to the table and I am eternally grateful.

To my ARC Team: What you do for me truly matters. Every launch, I'm reminded of how fortunate I am to have people like you in my corner. Your honest feedback lights a fire in me and makes me a stronger advocate for my own work. From the bottom of my heart, thank you.

ABOUT THE AUTHOR

Hi, I'm LA.

For as long as I can remember I've been putting myself to sleep with made-up stories. As it turns out insomnia has its perks. Romance novels completely hijacked my brain with their unapologetically dramatic characters and swoon-worthy endings, and now I'm that person who writes the addictive love stories I wished I could find on every bookshelf. I hope you enjoyed this story as much as I loved writing it.